The Gypsy Man

THE GYPSY MAN

RONALD FLORENCE

Villard Books New York 1985

Library of Congress Cataloging in Publication Data
Florence, Ronald.
The gypsy man.
I. Title.
PS3556.L5853G9   1985   813'.54   84-40484
ISBN 0-394-53751-3

Manufactured in the United States of America
9 8 7 6 5 4 3 2 1
First Edition

BOOK DESIGN BY LILLY LANGOTSKY

FOR MY FATHER, HAROLD FLORENCE

I am black but comely,
  O ye daughters of Jerusalem,
Like the tents of Kedar,
  like the curtains of Solomon.
Do not gaze at me because I am swarthy,
  because the sun has scorched me.

Song of Solomon, I:5–7

N'avlom ke tumende
  o maro te mangel.
Avlom ke tumende
  kam man pativ te den.

I did not come to you to
  to beg for bread.
I came to you
  to demand respect.

PROLOGUE

Amsterdam, 1966

For seven years the concierge hadn't been inside the room on the third floor. Only two or three times had she even caught a glimpse through a partially opened doorway before the professor had politely, but firmly, shut the door. The professor was a very private person. She had said as much when she first took the room, made it clear that she would clean the room herself, take care of all of her own needs. And that suited the concierge: who needed more rugs to air or furniture to dust or floors to sweep? Still, seven years was a long time to go without so much as a peek inside a room. Strange things could happen in seven years.

A year before, when the professor had taken her first holiday, the concierge tried to take a quick look. She had gotten as close as the landing, waiting outside the door until the mailman came and left in the courtyard below and she was certain there would be no more interruptions for the day. She was ready to put the key in the lock, wondering what secrets she would find inside, when she remembered an injunction that had been drilled into her from childhood: Ladies and gentlemen do not look where they have not been invited.

And she didn't.

Another year had passed, and nothing had changed. The professor's life seemed always the same. She left the house every weekday morning at eight thirty, walking along the canal to a fine stone and timber house on the Keizersgracht. The bronze plaque next to the door of the house read INSTITUUT INTERNATIONAAL VOOR SOCIALE ANTHROPOLOGIE. For a long time the concierge thought the professor worked there, until she went over once with one of the envelopes that came for the professor at the beginning of each month from some ministry in Bonn. This one had come after a long holiday weekend, and the concierge brought it over to the institute with the excuse that the professor might have been waiting for it.

"Mej. Lanzer is not an employee of the institute," the porter assured the concierge. But he admitted that she did come every day and he promised to

3

give the envelope to her. The concierge took a few moments to register the fact that the porter didn't call her "Professor." The envelopes from the ministry, her only mail, also weren't addressed to "Professor." It was a title she had given herself.

What else did she know about the woman? She was German. It was something they had never talked about, but no secret. The woman spoke some Dutch, enough to avoid those ugly incidents when a German would ask street directions in German and be given a deliberately wrong answer by a Dutchman with bitter memories of the war. Hardly a problem for the professor, thought the concierge. She never talked to anyone. She left every morning as if she were going to work, seemed to spend the entire day at the institute, came home promptly at half past five, sometimes a few minutes later if she had stopped at the grocer or the bakery, and always went straight up to her room. She cooked her dinners on a hotplate in the room, and for the rest of the evening she would be there alone, playing music on her Victrola. Always the same music, and always quietly. Unless you put your ear to the ceiling of the room underneath, you couldn't even hear it. No one had ever complained about her.

No, the professor wasn't like those Provos or the foreign students. Take them for tenants and it meant loud music and parties, hashish smoking, orgies, men and women who weren't married staying together in the rooms, moving out without paying the rent. The professor was an exemplary tenant. Never bothered anyone and always paid her rent on time.

But seven years without anyone seeing her room?

The concierge lived a quiet life herself. An occasional movie or a concert in the park by the Rijksmuseum, dinner once in a while with a friend at an Indonesian restaurant. Not much else. But she couldn't imagine a life as sterile as the professor's. The woman saw no one, went nowhere, never dressed in anything except the same dowdy old skirts and cardigan sweaters and sturdy lace-up shoes.

It was too bad, thought the concierge. The professor wasn't a homely woman. She had a nice figure, not too fat, good legs, breasts that didn't sag yet. With a different haircut and a little lip rouge, some nice clothes and a walk that didn't make her seem so downtrodden, if she just held her head up so people could see her face, the professor could have a real life instead of being a lonely recluse. It was hard to understand why she chose to live that way.

The concierge didn't need any special key for the room. All the rooms in the house had locks that would open with keys you could get at any ironmonger's, because of what might happen if the fire fighters had to break in. She knocked twice on the door, as though that would somehow make it all right to go in, and made up an excuse of what she would say if there was an answer. Then she went in.

The darkness of the room surprised her. She had always thought of it as a bright room. She looked over and saw that the drapes were pulled on the window under the gables, and remembered that whenever she had looked up at the window from the pavement, the drapes had been closed, not wide open the way most Dutch people would keep them. The lights inside were usually dim, and there had been times when she thought she had seen the flicker of candles. The concierge smiled at the thought of the professor eating alone by candlelight.

The room was neat, spotless really. There were no new rings on the round oak table. All the furniture seemed just as it had been when the professor moved in. But something about the room troubled the concierge. It didn't seem a proper Dutch room—too impersonal, stark even. There were no coverlets on the sofa, no doilies on the tables, no antimacassars on the chairs. No embroidered pillows, no tourist ashtrays or souvenir vases. Even the *kabinet*, a nice reproduction piece with glass doors and a cupboard underneath, was empty. None of the bric-a-brac you would expect: not a single brass cup or seashell or branch of coral or polished stone or miniature basket or carved ivory piece. It was as though the professor had moved out. Or never really moved in.

The concierge started toward the armoire, to make sure someone was really living there, then saw that there were books in the bookcase, enough to fill the shelves almost. She looked down the shelves for the books she expected to see, a work by Couperus or Vondel perhaps, or one of the American best sellers, but there wasn't a single title she recognized. No novels, no magazines, nothing anyone would read for pleasure. There wasn't even a Bible.

One whole shelf was filled with matched volumes in green bindings. The titles were in French: *Études tsiganes.* It meant nothing to the concierge, who couldn't read French. She reached for a book to look for pictures or other hints of what it was about, but hesitated, afraid that if somehow the door were suddenly to swing open, she would be caught with a book in her hand.

The shelf below had another set of matched volumes, these in maroon bindings. *Journal of the Gypsy Lore Society.* The concierge could understand a few of the words, but not enough to parse the meaning. There were more books next to the matched volumes, mostly in German. The word *Zigeuner* was in almost every title, and that was enough to tell the concierge what *tsigane* and *gypsy* meant. The books were all about Romany, gypsies. Why? she wondered. She couldn't imagine that there could be so much to write about gypsies, or why the professor would be interested. She picked up a book and thumbed it quickly for pictures, but it was only text in German. From the few words she read, she could see that the book was about Indo-European languages, whatever they were. She put it back exactly where it had been on the shelf.

A Victrola was next to the bookcase, on what had been a nice little tea table. It was an ancient machine that could play only the old 78 rpm records, and the records on the back of the table looked ancient, many of them without jackets. She read through the labels. *"Zigeuner Lieder."* *"Chansons des gitanes."* "Airs for Gypsy Violins." "Flamenco Guitar of Manitas de la Plata." This, she told herself, was the music she had heard played so softly at night. Gypsy music.

On top of the bookcase there were photographs in cheap store-bought frames. The largest was of a troop of street entertainers, dressed like Russian peasants in baggy pants and tall boots. A bear was in the midst of the troop, a muzzle on its snout and a chain with a ring through its nose. A boy was passing a tambourine through the crowd.

Relatives? wondered the concierge. In any Dutch house there would be photographs of relatives on every table and shelf. But these people couldn't be relatives of the professor's. Even in the fuzzy black-and-white photograph, the people had dark, swarthy complexions. They were gypsies.

Another photograph was a color snapshot of a horse-drawn caravan, elaborately carved and painted in what had probably been bright colors, now faded with age into washed-out pastels. There was also a black-and-white photograph of men standing around a grindstone, with long knives in their hands. The men were filthy, wearing ragged clothes, but they smiled for the camera, as if they were proud of the gaps in their teeth and oblivious to the squalor around them. The last photograph was of a woman's skirt, spread on the ground with a circle of women around it. The skirt was a wild swirl of colors, and all the women had similar skirts, with bulky petticoats underneath and bandannas on their heads. It was bizarre, thought the concierge, but all of the people looked like gypsies.

She opened the armoire. The sturdy skirts were hung inside, two brown and one gray, all three threadbare in spots, but cared for, hung so they wouldn't crease. The two coats were there too, and on one of the shelves were the cardigan sweaters and the blouses. On the bottom shelf were the sturdy lace-up shoes. They were the only clothes the concierge had ever seen the professor wear. How could the woman travel without her clothes?

Next to the skirts were empty hangers, and from the way the skirts and coats were pushed together on one side of the armoire, it seemed that there had been other clothes on those hangers. Special clothes for some private life? wondered the concierge. Ball gowns? Bathing costumes? Cocktail dresses? She found it impossible to picture the professor wearing anything except the dreary skirts and sweaters.

She closed the armoire and walked over to the chest of drawers. There was another photograph on top, of a gypsy fortune teller in a tent of bright fabrics. The concierge started to open the top drawer when she heard the bell ring from the courtyard gate.

She shut the drawer. Ladies and gentlemen do not look where they have not been invited! How could anyone have known she was there?

It must have been a mistake, she told herself. The wrong bell. The professor never had visitors. Not one that the concierge could remember. No special letters or telegrams, no deliveries, no bill collectors. No one ever came to see her.

As she left the room, she looked back to make sure that she had disturbed nothing. She was still amazed that the room was so sterile, with no life in it except for the records and books and those few photographs. She went down to her own apartment on the ground floor to look out through the Judas window in the courtyard gate.

The man in the courtyard had his back to her. His thick wavy hair was barbered only around the ears. His suit was too tight for his broad shoulders and didn't taper enough for his waist. Like his hair, it was shiny black. He seemed nervous, or perhaps impatient, tapping one foot on the ground as he waited.

When the concierge came out into the courtyard, the man turned. He looked straight at her without blinking. From that moment she couldn't look away.

She had never seen eyes like his. They were set deep, the color so dark that they seemed black against his coppery skin. The irises were tiny, and the man's gaze didn't waver. Her breasts tensed and stiffened, and her cheeks flushed. She felt a shiver inside, excitement more than fear. If she were any younger, she thought, a man like that would be irresistible. Her reactions embarrassed her.

"Does Eva Ritter live here?" the man asked.

Usually the concierge recoiled when she heard a man speaking German, remembering the war and the officers who had been quartered in the house. One, a lieutenant, had come back fifteen years later with his wife and children, ringing the bell and not even apologizing, not even saying hello, just telling the concierge that he wanted to show his family where he had lived during the war. She had slammed the door in the lieutenant's face. But this man was not a German. His voice was too gentle, the inflection too soft. And he didn't look like any German she had ever seen. He didn't look like anyone she had ever seen.

"Eva Ritter?"

The man looked at her, as if he didn't believe her puzzlement. "I mean Wanda Lanzer," he said. "Does the woman Wanda Lanzer live here?"

"She's on holiday," the concierge answered. She didn't mean to say more, but the man's gaze was more compelling than a lift of the eyebrows or another question. She felt like a tittering schoolgirl, covering her embarrassment with chatter. "She went somewhere in the South of France. She took the train to Paris, and from there another train, I think."

The man didn't react, except for a hint of crow's-feet at the corners of his eyes, the beginning of a smile that didn't come. The concierge couldn't look away and couldn't stop talking.

"The professor doesn't seem the kind of person to go to the South of France for a holiday, does she? She's so quiet and to herself. And with what you read in the magazines about those places—bathing without costumes, those parties, the drugs! It's hard to believe she would go there. But that's where she said she was going. It's where she went last year too."

"Is the place she went called Saintes-Maries-de-la-Mer?" the man asked.

"Saintes-Maries? I don't know. She never really said. Is that in the South of France?"

The man didn't answer. He reached into his jacket pocket and pulled out a photograph, a snapshot that was so worn and creased that the paper was all but destroyed. "Is this the professor?"

The photograph was a head-and-shoulders pose. The woman in the photograph was only about thirty years old, and she wore a scarf in her hair and a becoming low-cut blouse. A gold chain with charms dangled invitingly into the cleavage of her breasts. Her expression was gay and teasing, almost erotic. Across the corner of the photograph was a signature in a flowing script. Loli Tschai. It seemed like a nonsense name.

"She was much younger there," said the concierge. "Her hair is gray now, and she doesn't dress like that." She thought of the photographs up in the room, the women with bandannas in their hair. She wondered about the empty hangers and shelves in the armoire.

The man had stopped tapping his foot. His lips hinted a smile that made the concierge even more self-conscious, made her wonder if he was perhaps smiling at her. She reached toward her hair with her fingers, then caught herself and fought her rising blush.

"Is she a friend of yours?" the concierge asked.

"Friend? No. Thank you for your help."

The man left without a good-bye. The concierge watched him walk through the courtyard gate and down the cobbles of the canal. The gaze of his eyes wouldn't go away, and she kept thinking about the effect those eyes had on her. Her thoughts—if only I were a younger woman!—seemed almost wicked.

And then she thought again of that barren, mysterious room upstairs, and wondered: Why would a man like that look for the professor?

PART
I

Provence, 1966

The landscape was like a familiar painting: sunflowers, cube-shaped houses with orange roofs, villages with narrow, twisted streets, workmen in blue blouses playing *boules*, old men sipping *pastis* in sleepy cafés. And everywhere, trees: olive trees, lonely cypresses, rows of plane trees alternately glimmering and shadowed in the harsh chiaroscuro of the sun. The colors—the ochre of the cliffs, the silvery green of the trees, the muddy brown of the river—were like thick oils on canvas, framed by the windows and windshield of the car. What would that hillside and sky bring on the block at Sotheby's? Jill Ashton asked herself. She smiled at the silliness of it, enjoying the fact that she could be silly.

For what seemed like the first time in three years, Jill Ashton had no schedule to meet: no meetings to rush to, no calls to return, no lunch dates, no crowded calendar to shuffle. She had come to France to negotiate for a collection on behalf of the Museum of Modern Art, but she had come two days early, a spur-of-the-moment holiday. It was a holiday that she needed desperately. There was nothing wrong, at least nothing she could put her finger on, just an inchoate feeling that she needed a little time away, a recharge of the batteries. Provence seemed the perfect spot.

She hadn't gone far across the Rhône on the road from Arles when the gentle hills gave way to the vast flatland of the Camargue, that desolate, exotic plain that spreads south and west from Arles toward the sea. The change in the landscape was sudden and dramatic. As far as she could see ahead of her, there was only sand and salt marsh, tufted with tall spiky grasses, interrupted here and there by the shape of a farmhouse on the shimmering horizon. The only trees were gnarled and stunted, doubled over from the mistrals; the only settlements for long stretches were scattered *cabanes* around tiny churches. Puffy clouds floated across the sun, making the light alternately gloomy and brilliant. The desolate landscape was a surprise, and it made her feel very alone, not the impersonal loneliness of life in the city, but a feeling of being solitary and unnoticed amidst such desolation. She found herself driving fast, rolling up the windows so the sleek black car felt like a safe cocoon.

The desolate landscape was a surprise, the second of her trip. Jean-Claude Bernard had been the first.

When she had gotten off the *caravelle* at Marignane Airport, outside Marseilles, an attractive man was waiting at the gate. His hair was straight and blond, his eyes crystalline blue, his linen suit impeccable. As she walked through the gate, she heard the man ask an airline clerk if J. Ashton, Esq., had gotten off the plane yet.

"I'm Jill Ashton," she said. Her accent sounded American even to her. "Who are you?"

"J. Ashton, Esquire?" The man's English had a singsong, Maurice Chevalier accent that made her smile. "Jean-Claude Bernard, *avocat*. You're disappointed?"

"Not at all. I didn't expect to be met. I'm not even due here for two more days. And I thought Monsieur Bernard would be . . ."

"You expected a frock coat with dandruff on the shoulders? A long white mustache with tobacco stains? Gestures like this?" He pointed with his index finger, an extravagant oratorical gesture. "Perhaps long speeches in Latin?"

Jill laughed. It was exactly what she had expected.

"You've seen too many Daumier prints," he said. "But then perhaps I've spent too much time with the wrong American lawyers. I was waiting for a tall man in a floppy suit with big shoes and a shirt collar with buttons like this." He rolled the points of his collar. His shirt was soft, silk and linen. His fingers were delicate and manicured. He was extremely handsome. "I was watching for a cravat with stripes and on the finger a big ring with the seal of a university."

Jill laughed again. The description fit every man she worked with. "Are you disappointed?" she said.

"*Au contraire* . . ." Jean-Claude took her hand. "I think I'm going to like these negotiations."

The terminal was chaotic, crowds clamoring for their baggage. Jill missed whatever gesture had summoned the porter for her luggage, but she caught Jean-Claude's authority as he threaded through the crowds, the gestures and carriage that in one culture were the earmarks of privilege, and in another might be mistaken for arrogance. His car was parked in front of the terminal. The cars parked in front of his car and behind it had been ticketed; his had not.

As they got into the lush seats, a gendarme in the street touched his kepi and said, "Maître Bernard."

"You're either rich or corrupt," Jill said.

"A little of each."

"Puts me at a disadvantage."

"I suspect you have some advantages of your own," he said. "I'm astonished by my good fortune."

"Let's see how you feel after we finish negotiating."

Jean-Claude's smile was dazzling. His eyes were pale, almost translucent; his skin was suntanned. She guessed him to be in his late thirties, although something about the easy polish of his style suggested an older man. His clothes, like the car, were expensive and carefully chosen, but worn with nonchalance. She couldn't help contrasting him with the young associates at the firms in New York, suddenly flush after the lean years of law school, running out to buy themselves flashy red Italian sports cars, convinced that every woman who saw them would turn round-heeled. Next to Jean-Claude Bernard, they were silly little boys.

"Where are we going?" she asked.

"There's a lovely restaurant at Carry-le-Rouet. The view of the sea is splendid. Perhaps you would enjoy lunch?"

She debated the invitation. The reasons were easy. Pro: He was a very appealing man, charming, attractive, and with a self-confidence that made small talk pleasant; the restaurant would undoubtedly be superb; the view of the sea, the air, and the fishing boats, the drive along the corniches, the suggestive banter—it was what she had come to Provence for. Con: She wasn't fully prepared yet, still had notes to go over; she couldn't afford to be caught off guard. His gesture of meeting the plane, of finding out, probably by phone, that she would arrive two days early, followed by his easy banter, the suggestive hints—it all seemed too flawless, too close to a script for some hopelessly romantic movie. She smiled as she thought of Grace Kelly and Cary Grant picnicking on a corniche.

"My accent is amusing?" he said.

"Your accent, Monsieur Bernard, is charming. I'd be a fool to turn down lunch." She wondered if she was making a mistake.

He returned her smile. Anywhere except France, she thought, Jean-Claude would have seemed too polished, too suave, the whole style too deliberate and affected. She found herself expecting to discover something wrong. There was always something wrong with men like that. They were empty-headed, or hung up on their mothers, or gay, or so absorbed by their own good looks that they couldn't listen or talk. Which would it be? she wondered.

The restaurant was tiny and exquisite, tables on a terrace with a view over a colorful fishing harbor. The captain and the waiters greeted Jean-Claude by name; the cook came out, hugged Jean-Claude, bowed deeply when Jill was introduced, and barked orders to the waiter. Then plates of *coquillages* and bottles of wine began appearing, one after another.

Jean-Claude tucked his napkin into the collar of his shirt and ate and drank with an enthusiasm that Jill had rarely seen in a man. Before long she found herself plunging in with the same sybaritic gusto, picking through the *langoustine* with her fingers, savoring the bread dipped into the spicy *rouille* sauces, sipping glass after glass of the white wine, and wondering why it all seemed too perfect. She couldn't remember when she had felt so relaxed with a man. Was the whole lunch a ploy to get her off her guard?

Jean-Claude explained that he was actually busy for the next two days, engagements that he would gladly break off in an instant except that the magistrates of the Court of Appeals at Avignon would not approve. He did think that he might be able to free up one night, if she would have dinner.

"Which night?" she asked.

"When I was a young man and someone asked me whether I wanted lobster or oysters, I invariably said 'Both.' It's my way. When I like something I cannot get enough of it."

"Even something you've never tried before?"

"There are some things one can be sure of in advance. Like caviar. Or champagne."

Lunch took the whole afternoon. She told him about her first years out of law school, working for Legal Aid, scraping by on a paltry salary, trying to convince herself that she was "doing good," and noticing at every court appearance that no one ever read a motion or a brief, that criminal law was nothing but revolving doors. Whether her clients ended up in jail or not didn't seem to matter. Either way, they would invariably be out on the streets within months, and arrested again soon after. It was as though the police were waiting for them. Or that they couldn't bear the unfamiliarity of not being under arrest.

Jean-Claude listened as though she were the only person in the world. He never once glanced at his watch, never took his eyes off her. It was a skill few men had. They would take her out, ask a question, then talk about themselves. Most of them, she knew, were afraid of her.

Men had always pursued Jill Ashton. She had the kind of wholesome, distracting beauty that few could resist: a thick mane of chameleon-like hair that changed suddenly from deep brown indoors to sparkling auburn in the sunlight; high, sculptured cheekbones; a wide, sensuous mouth; eyes the color and size of walnuts. She seemed taller than she was, long-necked and coltish, and she dressed and acted with a zaniness that convinced many men that she was out of their league, that hers was a world of sophisticated pleasures that they could only envy.

She knew that some men were frightened, and that others were put off by her relentlessly aggressive attitude toward her work and career. Sometimes, in the office, she had heard the nicknames, like Iceberg and Eskimo Pie. For years she had brushed them off as jealous taunts, stabs by colleagues she had bested, sexist put-downs by men who couldn't tolerate a successful woman. Yet each time the words hurt, made her feel aloof and lonely, made her question the career that she had put everything into. She could tell herself it was the price she had to pay, but the loneliness still hurt.

With Jean-Claude it seemed different. He listened, apparently fascinated, as she described how she had gone from Legal Aid to a stint with the United States Attorney's office in New York, and the sheer luck that had gotten her involved in a two-year investigation of art theft as part of a joint U.S.–French prosecution team. She had spent almost a year in France, having a good time and learning French court procedures so well that when one case came to trial in Paris, she was admitted to the civil bar and allowed to join the prosecution effort. And as a bonus, she got a reputation for being the best lawyer on art anywhere.

When the case concluded and she reluctantly came back to New York, she was invited to lunch by Sidney Millman, the managing partner of Millman, Lord & Perry, a midtown firm with the reputation of being liberal and classy. He took her to La Grenouille, told her that since she was even more attractive than he had heard, he assumed she was even a better lawyer than her reputation indicated. Then he offered her a partnership within two years, an office overlooking Fifth Avenue, and a salary that came out, in round numbers, to slightly under triple what she made at the United States Attorney's office. "Your clients will be the Museum of Modern Art and anyone else you can hustle up," he said. "Think about it. If you want, go home and sleep on it. Then give me a call."

When lunch was over she said, "I've thought about it."

"And?" said Millman.

"When do I start?"

That had been three years ago. And Millman kept his promises. She became a partner within a year, the youngest partner at the firm and the first woman partner. And Millman's assessment of her talents had proved right. She worked hard, and the business rolled in. At parties, at museum openings, wherever she went she found clients. Some were small and intersting, little galleries that the firm would take on with reduced billings in the hope that they would someday grow into real clients. But she also landed the Metropolitan Museum, half a dozen big museums outside New York, and Christie's. Most of them had in-house counsel, but turned to her when there were big stakes. She was the Wonder Woman of Millman, Lord & Perry.

"It sounds like I should be afraid," said Jean-Claude. "I think after I take you to your hotel I had better go back to my study and reread the codes."

The drive toward Arles took them around the edge of the Étang de Berre, with its spectacular vistas from the mountains over the water to the ramparts of St. Mitre.

"Tell me," he said, "what does a beautiful lady lawyer do after those long days in the office in Manhattan? What do you go home to?"

Like his compliments at the airport, the question was direct. No fishing. Her answer was an enigmatic smile that he had to swivel to see.

He flashed back a wry smile of his own. "Don't tell me you sleep alone. I'm truly sorry for the men who cannot concentrate all day long because they dream of spending their evenings with you."

Jill couldn't resist a smile.

The hotel was exactly what she wanted: small, with whitewashed walls, timbered ceilings, and red-tile floors. A porter carried her bags, and Jean-Claude joked with the manager, an elegant gray-haired woman.

"You should have written that you were a friend of Maître Bernard's," the woman said to Jill. She glanced at her books and added, "It's no problem, really. Things can always be arranged. We just shift a room or two— one goes here and one goes there. I'm certain you'll be very comfortable."

There was a travel poster in the lobby, a photograph of a religious procession at the edge of the sea. Black-garbed cowboys on white horses, with long staffs that looked like tridents, guarded the procession.

"You have plans for the next two days?" asked Jean-Claude. "I wish I could show you a little of Provence, but alas! I'm afraid I couldn't persuade the Court of Appeals that there's a lady from New York so lovely that they should allow me a special postponement."

Jill smiled at the compliment. "I thought I would poke around," she said. "Probably rent a car and drive to a few of those three-star *vaut le voyage* sights."

"Use my car. And let me know which museums or galleries you'd like to see so I can arrange for you to be given a private tour. Most of them are closed tomorrow, which makes it perfect."

It was exactly what she most enjoyed, a private tour that let you look without being rushed or crowded. But then the first rule of negotiating was never to accept favors from the other side. And she had already said much too much at lunch.

"What's there?" she asked, pointing to the poster.

"Saintes-Maries-de-la-Mer? The gypsy festival. It's mostly for the tourists. There's some kind of procession, and the gypsies play music and sell junk and tell fortunes and pick pockets."

"Sounds like fun."

"I think it would be unwise for a woman alone. Even for an intrepid lady lawyer."

Jean-Claude didn't realize it, but that remark made up her mind to go.

Although it felt as though she had crossed half a desert, she had gone only twenty kilometers into the Camargue when she saw a camp by the side of the road. Caravans were drawn up in a circle, like the wagons in an old Western movie. One was a rebuilt bus, another a flatbed truck with a tin and cardboard house on top. There were ordinary house trailers and horse-drawn caravans and cars so ancient they might have been in a museum.

She slowed for some children who were playing in the sand at the side of the road. The children ran toward the car, waving their hands and shouting. Afraid they would run in front of the car, she slammed on the brakes, screeching to a halt and raising a cloud of dust. The children encircled the car.

There were twenty or thirty of them, all holding their hands out and shouting. Their faces and arms and legs were smeared with dirt, and most of them were half naked, barefoot, wearing a shirt or a pair of ragged shorts, rarely both. She couldn't understand what they were saying, couldn't even tell what language it was. She was afraid to roll down the windows.

Beyond the children, outside one of the caravans, she saw men and women, standing in groups, paying little attention. A few of the men glanced at her. Like the children, they were dark-haired, with swarthy skin. Most of the men wore suit jackets and bandannas around their necks. The women stood in a group apart from the men, wearing colorful skirts that reached down to the ground. After cursory glances toward the car, they turned away, uninterested, reluctant to be involved.

The children began to pull at the door handles and the trunk lid. One girl pressed her face to the window on Jill's side, distorting her nose, her eyes only inches from Jill's. Jill thought of inching the car forward, but there were children standing in front of the bumper. She wondered what she could give them. Money? She had a wad of francs, but no change. And to give them anything she would have to roll down the window.

She looked both ways on the road, but there were no other cars, only the low flat landscape, punctuated with tufty spikes of marsh grass as far as she could see. In the distance she could just make out a silhouette, looking one moment like a ship stranded on the sands, an instant later like a giant windmill. She squinted, concentrating on the shimmering image, hoping it was coming closer, trying to persuade herself that it was a car.

She was angry at her own helplessness. She thought of Jean-Claude Bernard, how the crowds in the airport had parted as he walked through. She tried honking the horn. The children answered with honking noises of their own. They stared at her without blinking or lowering their gaze. Their hands were outstretched, their gestures relentless, without the retreating mannerisms that she associated with beggars. She could understand nothing of what they were shouting. There was one word that they repeated over and over—it sounded like *"gaje."* She remembered Jean-Claude's warning and got angry at herself for being pigheaded.

She watched the distant horizon, hoping the mirage would reappear. Why am I afraid? she asked herself. They're only children. They're probably interested in the car, in Jean-Claude's shiny black Maserati. And with adults just a few yards away, what could they do anyway? But the men and women around the caravans paid no attention at all. It was as if they no longer saw her.

Just children, she told herself. But she couldn't understand a word they were saying, could only read their gestures. They were a pack, and they seemed desperate. The demands of the outstretched hands were persistent, the hunger in the eyes palpable. They looked right at her, without blinking. She felt vulnerable to the big, dark eyes.

A girl outside Jill's window shouted and pointed up the road. In the rearview mirror Jill saw a swirl of dust.

More children pointed. Women from the camp walked toward the car, waving at the children. Whatever it was took forever to come down the road.

The children began running toward the camp. It must be gendarmes, Jill thought. Why else would the children be so frightened? She watched the moving dust, waiting to make out the sleek outline of a police Citroën.

But after a long wait, when the dust finally cleared, it was only an ancient, battered 2cv truck, lumbering down the road with a quirky, bouncy rhythm. The driver was a heavyset man, wearing a dark suit jacket that had been rubbed shiny and threadbare. He had a beret on his balding head. His thin mustache was comical. He pulled up next to Jill.

"Never stop for this filth!" he shouted in a hoarse voice. "Those men want only one thing from a woman."

Before she could say anything, he turned toward the camp, shouting at the children: "Pigs! Go back to your sty and your whoring mothers! Go suckle on those fat, naked teats!"

Jill was ashamed that she had been so frightened.

It took her many kilometers to relax. She kept picturing the children. She had stopped enjoying the light and the salty air.

On the road ahead of her, the mirage came back. What had seemed first a windmill, and then a beached ship, now looked like a church, perched at the edge of the earth. As she drove on, she passed more camps, with caravans, and tents made of carpets and colorful fabrics. At the outskirts of the town she passed shanties with yards full of refuse—broken cars, iceboxes, mattresses, chairs, beds—like miniature flea markets. By then the outline of the church was clear and she could understand the earlier mirages: the great ribs of the Romanesque vault were like the frames of a great ship; the truncated tower was like a windmill. Together they became a fortress church, perched between the desolation of the Camargue and the sea. She remembered a phrase from a guidebook: ". . . a citadel of faith against the terrors of the unknown."

The town of Saintes-Maries was seedy, a broken-down fishing village without a trace of charm, the few native houses and boats lost in the expanse of cheap hotels, tacky cafés, parking lots filled with tourist buses. Everything was for sale—parking places, baskets, statues, jewelry, clothing, guitars, fiddles—half the items advertised with signs proclaiming *genuine* this or *echt* that. A sign painted on the side of a hotel advertised flamenco dancing; the sign was in German, English, Spanish, and French. She wished she hadn't come.

Only in the streets did the town seem alive. The dusky, animated faces of gypsies were everywhere. Women with babies in bundles of rags begged at every corner and doorway, changing the language of their mumbled words to fit the passing crowd. Men hawked knives, tinware, woodcarvings, baskets, testing the crowd before they made their pitch, flicking glances at the tourists the way a snake tests the air with its tongue. Whole families, clans perhaps, milled in tight clusters, the bright bandannas of the men and the scarves of the women gaudy, the gold bracelets and necklaces glittering against swarthy skin and black hair.

The cafés were all alike, cheap metal umbrellas and tourist menus posted under German and English and French flags. On almost every table she saw the paraphernalia of tourism: cameras, flight bags, guidebooks. She heard two women at one table haggling over the menu in English. At another table there was a discussion of souvenir shops. Everyone was safe in their conversations, insulated by an invisible barrier from the gypsies in the streets.

She sat down at a table and ordered a *pastis*. When it arrived she flicked in drops of water, watching the thick liqueur cloud up. She sipped it, and didn't like the heavy anise taste. She wished that she had stayed in Arles, perhaps taken up Jean-Claude's offer for a tour of one of the museums or the galleries. She got ready to pay and leave, to salvage the rest of what seemed a lost day.

Then she saw the man.

He was alone, at a table on the edge of the pavement. He had been watching the crowds in the street when his gaze swung over the café and caught hers. She tried to look away and couldn't.

His eyes were dark and deep, with small irises and brilliant whites. Smile lines creased his skin, but she couldn't picture him smiling. Something in those eyes was ineffably sad.

The man wasn't really handsome. He was ungroomed, rugged, a man who had spent a lot of time outdoors. His face was broad, his hair black and wavy, his nose and forehead and lips strong. Every feature stood out, sculpted. The man's suit was cheap, the shoulders overpadded, the lapels too wide, the fabric shiny. His white shirt was buttoned at the neck, without a tie. It was something she had seen on men who were down on their luck in New York, the kind of men she had avoided as she would avoid a beggar.

Yet she couldn't take her eyes off this man, couldn't control her reactions. Her cheeks burned; she was aware of her own heartbeat and a warm and wet feeling inside. What was it? she asked herself.

A waiter stepped between them, bringing a cup of coffee to the man, waiting to be paid. He hadn't waited when he brought her the *pastis*, and she imagined the contrasting images as the waiter saw them. She was in fine clothes—tailored slacks, a silk shirt, a feathery blazer. Rich and easy, with an expensive car parked in front of the café. The man was impossible to place. He wasn't a tourist. Other than that she couldn't be sure.

The man took a Gauloises out of a crumpled pack on the table. When he saw her eyes follow his hands, he held out the pack. He was only two tables away.

It had been years since she had smoked. Strong cigarettes like Gauloises used to leave her feeling heady, a strange, floating high, almost the way she felt already. She hesitated, then shook her head no. She regretted her response immediately.

A family of German tourists came into the café, cameras dangling, children complaining. The man at the table looked up at the woman in the family. He studied her face methodically, as if he were making an identification.

Jill had no idea how long she watched the man, whether it was minutes or hours. Suddenly, for no reason that she could understand, she was afraid that the moment would slip away. She pushed the *pastis* aside and walked over to the man's table.

"Can I change my mind about that cigarette?" she said.

He held out the pack. Up close, his eyes were deeper and darker than she expected, the whites glowing, the gaze magnetic. His skin was creased, the color a delicate copper, like burnished metal in the sunlight.

"They're old," he said.

Her mind blanked as she took the cigarette. The banter with Jean-Claude had been so easy. Conversation had always been easy. But now she felt confused, empty-headed, struggling for words. The questions that formed in her mind—Are you here for the festival? Where are you from? What should I see?—weren't the questions she wanted to ask. Yet she couldn't make herself say: Who are you? Why do I feel so strange when I look at you?

He offered a match. The stale Gauloises made her head float. Now the questions were impossible.

"The festival is interesting?" he asked. He didn't take his eyes off her as he spoke, hardly seemed to blink. His voice was gentle, his French rough.

"I don't know yet. I just got here."

"Why did you come?"

She started to answer, started to explain that she had a day or two free before she had to negotiate an art estate and then get back to her office in New York. Then she realized that the very currency of her daily life—"a day or two free . . . get back to her office in New York"—had no meaning at all. Who cared?

"I saw a poster in my hotel," she said. "The horses and the procession looked interesting. What about you?"

"It would take a long time to explain. You wouldn't be interested."

"Try me."

"No." The word was firm, but gentle. He smiled as he said it, and his smile brought back her unexpected reactions to him, the flush in her face, a tumble in her insides. She had to force herself not to reach up and touch her burning cheeks.

"Have you gone to the church?" he asked.

"Not yet. Should I?"

"It's why they all come, to see the black Sara."

"They?"

"The gypsies. There aren't always so many gypsies here. Usually there are only a few. The others come at the festival, to see the statue."

"Is that why the tourists come too?"

"I think the tourists come to see the gypsies."

"Which are you?" she asked. "Tourist or gypsy?"

He smiled again, with his eyes wrinkled and lips parted. It was his only answer to the question.

"Do you know why the statue of Sara is so important to the gypsies?" he asked.

Jill tried to remember the guidebook stories about the name of the town, the tales of Marie Jacobe, the sister of the Virgin, and Marie Salome, the mother of James and John. She couldn't remember anything about the statue.

"The books say that no one knows. Whenever people who write books don't know something, they say that no one knows. But the gypsies have a story. They say that when the Maries came to this shore it was very stormy. There were great crashing waves that would swamp their boat. On the shore a gypsy girl named Sara saw them, saw that they couldn't land. So she threw her skirt on the water to make a raft, and floated out and helped them come ashore. And from that day she's been special to the gypsies."

"I like that story," said Jill.

"So do I. But I don't think it's true. A good gypsy girl wouldn't go off with strangers like that."

Jill laughed, began to feel almost in control of herself.

"Do you like gypsies?" the man asked.

She remembered the morning, the children from the camp around her car. She could remember shying away from gypsy fortune tellers. It was all she could think of.

He smiled at her hesitation. "You're not a Romany *rye?*"

"What's that?"

"A lover of gypsies."

She laughed, not sure whether it was from embarrassment or confusion. "I don't think so."

"You have a nice laugh," he said. "Your cigarette is finished. Do you want another?"

"No, thanks. They make me feel light-headed." She wanted to say more, but couldn't. She looked away, tried to clear the muddle from her head. And then before she realized it, the silence had gone on too long. The moment was finished.

"I should go see that statue," she said.

"Remember the story of Sara," he said.

"I will. Are you going to the church?"

He shook his head no. When he smiled, his lips were moist. She realized that he was the most sensuously appealing man she had ever seen, and she understood what had happened—the burning in her cheeks, the thumping of her heart, the strange sensations inside her. Yet it all still amazed her.

She left too much money for the *pastis* and didn't look back as she walked toward the church.

Each time Wanda Lanzer left her hotel she carried her small traveling bag with her. She would search out a place to change, putting her street clothes into the bag when she put on the long skirt and loose blouse. Then she would have to find a place to leave the bag. The first day, when a café keeper looked at her skirt and blouse and said that she couldn't leave the bag there, she hid the bag in the bushes behind the café.

It was awkward, but worth the bother. When she wore the skirt and blouse, she felt like a different person. Her skirt was of the Kalderash, a swirling print fabric made by hand somewhere in Hungary. Her blouse was loose and open, and the thin gold chain around her neck dangled between her breasts, the cool metal caressing her skin with every step. The movements of the fabric and the chain, the gentle puffs of air under the clothes, made her feel alive and free, as if she were young and in love. She could feel the music of every street corner, the lilting *lassús* and fiery czardas. She felt as though she could dance to that music without ever stopping.

She tried to avoid the tourists, giving a wide berth to the souvenir shops and the parking lots where the tours assembled. Instead she walked around the edges of the milling crowds in the streets, watching, listening for the familiar words, feeling the music, smelling the charcoal fires, the roasting meats, the ripe human smells of close, nomadic living.

She walked toward a café on the corner. It had been a whole year, but she remembered exactly where the German had played. She remembered his name, too, and the painted sign that said he was a star of radio and television. She had never heard him on the radio, wasn't interested in the music he would play for those audiences, the segues of popular tunes "in the gypsy style" that were arranged to entertain diners in tacky cafés. What she wanted to hear was the real music, the ancient melodies that he could have learned only from his father, and that his father could have learned only from his own father before him. She remembered how his violin had soared as he played the czardas of the Hungarian *pusztas*, those haunting, half-wild melodies that seemed to reach into the very mysteries of the steppes. She could feel her hips sway to the *lassú*. Her soul was alive in anticipation.

The sign on the easel at the café was exactly as she remembered, the name Laszlo in the same red script characters. At the doorway the café owner looked sharply at her, then seemed to recognize that despite the clothes she was not a gypsy. He pointed to a table in the back.

"When does Laszlo play?" she asked. The simple question strained her French.

"Ten minutes, half an hour. Whenever he feels like it."

She ordered a beer but didn't touch it while she waited.

It was closer to an hour. When Laszlo came in, he was wearing the same leather vest and puffy-sleeved red shirt she remembered. He was tipsy, weary more than drunk, exhausted by the endless demands of the festival audiences. He started to play the usual medley, slipping easily from one tune to another, the transitions almost imperceptible. His eyes followed his audience, establishing contact, telling each listener that the music was only for him or her.

When his eyes caught hers, he winked. A moment later the violin segued from the Broadway tune he had been playing to the melody she remembered, that wondrous unnamed czardas that only this man seemed to know anymore. His violin was suddenly alive, the notes soaring, the tone calling out from some distant steppe. She felt the music as much as heard it, sensed it entering her body, the syncopated rhythms resonating with her nerves and muscles, speaking to her soul. After a half dozen phrases she closed her eyes and let herself drift to that other world.

He slid gracefully into the *lassú*, slow and tantalizing, like a breeze in leaves, or lovemaking, or the meander of a river. She thought of each before the music segued to the closing czardas, more fiery than the opening, the tempo accelerating into what seemed an impossible whirl, faster and faster, on the edge of control. How could it go on? she wondered. How could anyone bear it? Her skin tingled; her mind was transformed, transported, yielding to her soul. She felt herself on the edge of ecstasy, as if all sensation except the music were gone.

Then, without warning, it ended. When she opened her eyes, there was a scattering of applause in the café. Most of the customers preferred the Broadway tunes.

Laszlo bowed, stepped off the tiny stage, and walked toward her table. She motioned to a chair.

"No," he said. "But thank you for coming and listening. It's good that someone likes the real music. I just wanted to tell you that a man was here looking for you. He came last year, too, after the festival. He had a photograph of you."

"A photograph?" It was all she could say before the nausea rose into her throat. A weight crushed her chest. Then a spasm of coughing doubled her over.

"Are you all right?" Laszlo asked. He pushed the beer toward her.

She waved it away and tried to stand up. Her legs wouldn't hold and she collapsed back into the chair. Her breath came in hoarse gasps.

Her mind raced. There wasn't time to make sure, wasn't even time to think. When she could finally stand she bolted for the door of the café, almost tripping on her long skirt.

The church swarmed with gypsies. Families and clans were bunched together, intimate in their enthusiasm. The long skirts of the women were painted a thousand shades; their arms and necks glistened with gold; their heads were a kaleidoscope of colored scarves. A few carried candles, mumbling quiet prayers, oblivious to the pressing crowds. Most seemed to celebrate the festival, gesturing, laughing, their sole piety the act of the pilgrimage itself.

The men stood apart from the women and the children, some in tight knots, others alone. A few had guitars and violins, or the tools and products of their trades—baskets, leather, woodcarvings. Jill's eyes roved over the faces, seeking out men with skin of copper and dark wavy hair. Her gaze stopped on a man standing outside the crowd, as much an observer as she was. His shoulders were broad, his suit shiny black. His hair curled over his collar in the back. And his head was powerful, like that of the man at the café. She waited for him to turn.

It had taken her a long time to walk toward the church, pausing every few steps, watching the gypsy faces on every side. She thought of terrible jokes about how all blacks and all Chinese look alike, and realized that she had never really looked at a gypsy before. She had seen gypsies—in New York, in Yugoslavia, on the roads in Ireland—but she had always avoided looking at their faces. It was an instinctive fear, like her reaction to the children that morning.

The man finally turned. His shirt was brightly colored, not white. He wore a leather vest under his suit. Teeth were missing from his grin. She looked away, at the church.

When was she last in a church? Was it a wedding? A funeral? It had been a long time. Then she remembered. It wasn't a church. It was a synagogue. She remembered the crowds of people she couldn't recognize. It was the same incessant laughter and chatter, as if the sheer fact of coming were enough.

There had been an argument before. Her mother wanted the funeral in the Unitarian chapel.

"He was never in there in his whole life," Jill's grandmother had said. "He was born a Jew, we were married as Jews, he died a Jew, I'll say goodbye to him as a Jew."

"My God!" her mother had said. "How ridiculous!"

"No Hebrew," her mother had said to the rabbi. "No mumbo-jumbo."

The rabbi was quiet, a patient man. "I think your father would have wanted it. In his own way he was a pious man."

"My father would have wanted it?" Her mother's voice bleated sarcasm. "It hardly matters much now what he wants, does it?" She had turned to Jill, as if for confirmation.

Stripped to its barest, the ceremony had been meaningless, satisfying no one. Her mother had felt it too, but her reaction was different. She was embarrassed to be seen in the mourners' box, embarrassed at the black ribbon they pinned on her dress, embarrassed at the ceremony of slashing the ribbon. She took the ribbon off as soon as she could.

"At least they didn't slash up this suit," she said. "This whole nonsense is idiotic. How many of the people here do you think were his friends anyway? They're my friends. And to subject them to this."

And then the wake, and her grandmother, haggard with grief, her gray skin aged ten years in that one morning, wandering into the room of celebrators, looking more asleep than awake, more astonished than outraged by the merriment around her.

"Jill, sweet, could you find your mother for me? Tell her I won't bother her anymore, that I don't want to spoil things for her and her friends. I just have one question for her."

Her mother was in the midst of the party then, her response to the relayed request a slack grin that played to her audience. "Now what?"

The grandmother apologized again. "I'm sorry to bother you. I know you're with your friends. But I couldn't sleep. It's maybe silly, a silly old woman's question, but tell me, please, was Granddad buried with his teeth? You know, he was never . . ."

"His teeth? I'm in the middle of trying to get food on the table and trying to put something together for my friends who were nice enough to come here, and you want to know whether he was buried with his teeth?" She looked around, making sure of her audience before she came through with the clencher.

"Where he's going it isn't going to matter one hell of a lot, is it?"

Jill's grandmother walked away without a word, trying to hold her head up. She didn't cry, didn't even react to the daughter she had created. That instant, Jill knew the old woman was dead too. Jill never saw her again after that day.

Late that night, alone, with a snifter of Armagnac and the melancholy duet from *Così fan tutte*, Jill had cried for hours—not from anger or regret, but from the terrible fear that she had seen herself in her mother, that she too could fall prey to that relentless, excruciating self-doubt that had left her mother an emotional cripple. As she replayed the long day in her mind, remembered the moments when cruel words had taken the place of honest feelings, she wondered if it could all happen to her, if she too could become dependent on those symbols and images—wearing the right Perry Ellis suit or driving the right car or having the right house and the right friends and the right job and saying the right clever phrase—no matter how much it hurt someone else.

The church at Saintes-Maries was like the hull of a ship, the massive stone of the walls like blackened oak ribs, uninterrupted by transepts, side chapels, statues, or ornaments. Outside the apse, a long line of gypsies, disorderly and anxious, pushed their way inside, like the creatures of the earth embarking on Noah's ark, distinguished from one another only by the swirls of color and the incomprehensible babble of language. They seemed so intimate in their closeness, the way they pressed against one another, that Jill wondered if there was room for her.

It wasn't until she was at the door that she realized it wasn't really a line, only a shifting mass of people. Up close, the shuffling feet and mumbled prayers blended with the half-oriental melodies of violins and guitars into an incessant cacophony, the words incomprehensible, the tone a relentless keening. Jill had gone to watch, but the crowd was like quicksand, drawing her in, closing behind her. She was jostled forward, squeezed into an intimacy of scents and textures and sounds and colors until she was too disoriented to resist.

Deep inside the crypt, she knew from the guidebooks, was the statue of Sara, a blackened relic that the church had been reluctant to accept, but that the gypsies had made their own. This was the goal of the crowd, and as they pressed into the church, she could feel the rising fervor, the bodies on all sides of her pressing closer until she could no longer see individuals, only a wild clash of colors and scents and fabrics. She envied them the single-mindedness of their pilgrimage. There had been a time, years before, when she had felt the pull of a cause. She had worked with a sense of purpose at the Legal Aid Society, and since then she had tried, not always successfully, to convince herself that the nostalgia she felt for those days was misplaced, that in fact the sense of purpose and belonging had all been a myth.

She realized with a jolt that she was part of the crowd. Breasts and thighs and bellies and soft naked arms pressed against her, strange bodies merging with her own in a startling intimacy. The smells of incense and burning candles and excited people blended into an overpowering ripeness. The shuffling feet and mumbled prayers and incomprehensible singing became an unbearable keen, like the wailing of women at an Arab funeral.

She shut her eyes, trying to screen out the claustrophobic swirls of color, but there was no escape from the textures and odors and the press of bodies. It was as if her own flesh were part of theirs, separated only by the accident of clothing.

She tried to think of the café, tried to remember the face of the man and the way she had felt when he looked at her. She thought of the story he had told her, about the gypsy girl spreading her skirt on the waters. The story had seemed so charming then, making her embarrassed at her reaction to the gypsy children around her car during the morning. Now she thought of the children again, and felt the same claustrophobia. She twisted and turned, trying to carve out a space for herself, fighting to free herself from the bodies that pressed on all sides. A woman next to her pulled back, her dark eyes flashing inches from Jill's own.

"*Gaje!*" the woman shouted. She pointed at Jill with an outstretched finger.

The cry was taken up by other women, and a circle opened around Jill, only inches of room on every side, just enough for her to be aware of the fingers and tongues and eyes that lashed out at her.

The air was heavy with candle grease and incense. They had come halfway down the stairs into the crypt, and in front of her the only light was the glow of candle stubs burning amidst the piled offerings of clothing. She could hear fervent prayers, imprecations addressed to the statue. Behind her she could see wisps of sunlight from the church windows cutting the dense, smoky air. She could hardly breathe.

"*Gaje!*" The same word, in half a dozen intonations, was all she could pick out of the flurries of language. Something in the tone told her that the fears were mutual. But there were hundreds of them; she was alone.

She pushed toward the doorway, feeling and watching hands and bodies recoil from her, as though she were a pariah. She was angry with herself for panicking, but desperate for air and light, desperate to be away from the press of bodies.

"*Gaje!*" It was the last word she heard as she burst through a small door, just off the stairs. The sunlight was shrill; the cigarette smoke in the air wasn't the relief she expected. She saw tourists massed outside, buying souvenirs from the stands, lining up for their buses. She turned away, looking for the sea, for the space of the sea, for sea air to fill her lungs.

That's when she saw him again.

It was the man from the café. His features were bolder than she remembered, accented in the harshness of the light. He was not as tall as she expected, and slimmer. The aura of strength came from the muscles of his neck and arms rather than from his size.

He was studying the crowds outside the church when his eyes caught hers. The crowds—the sounds, the colors, the smells, the textures, the feel of pressing flesh—were suddenly gone. She forced herself to speak, a way of pinching herself.

"You're waiting for someone?" she said.

He stepped back, turning his eyes from the church, smiling. "Yes."

"Back at the café, were you waiting for someone there?"

"Yes."

"Did you find him?"

"Her." He answered as a reflex, and seemed caught by his answer. "Not yet."

"Who is she?"

"Nobody. A ghost, maybe. Do you believe in ghosts?"

"Not really."

"You're Christian?"

"No."

"What then?"

She hadn't thought about that question for years. The answer at home had been Unitarian, but it was really only something to write on the blanks of application forms. No one objected when she announced that she was an agnostic or, later, an atheist. It was something they never talked about. A question to avoid.

"Nothing, really. What about you?"

"I'm a gypsy."

The answer didn't surprise her. "You're really a gypsy."

"I was."

"Was? I thought it was something you either were or weren't. It isn't like saying you're a baker or a cobbler, is it?"

"No. Are you a baker or a cobbler?"

She laughed. "A lawyer."

"Yes? A lady lawyer?" It was as exotic to him as being a gypsy was to her.

She held out her hand. "I don't even know your name."

"Do you need to know my name?"

"I want to."

"Ral."

"Raoul?" She liked that name. Very French.

"No, just Ral. It's a Romany name."

"Jill," she said.

"Jeel?" He pronounced it to rhyme with *teal*, and his chocolatey voice gave her goosebumps. It amazed her as much as that first moment at the café.

It took him a moment to realize that she wanted to shake hands. His hand was large, rough on the outside, the palm surprisingly tender. His grip was hesitant, as if he were afraid of hurting her.

"A lady lawyer." He said it as though the thought were astonishing. "Who are your people?"

Her people? The question confused her. "American?" she said.

"American? I think that there are too many Americans for that to be your people. It would be like me saying that my people are European. I'm not European. I'm a gypsy."

She shrugged. "You're right. I wish I had an answer. People ask what I do, and I say I'm a lawyer." She thought of the rest. People asking where she went to school, what clubs she belonged to, where she played tennis, where she shopped. None of it seemed real. "I guess it sounds ridiculous, doesn't it?"

"A lady lawyer from America. I know what you do and where you're from, but not who you are."

She grinned. "And I know you're a gypsy, or at least were a gypsy, but I don't know what you do or where you're from."

He smiled, acknowledging the neat irony.

The moment of mutual understanding seemed unbearably fragile. She looked out at the gray sea. The rocky beach was dotted with jetsam, papers and bottles and tin cans from the crowds. A half mile down the shore, on a graveled beach, the *gardiens*, French cowboys on stocky white horses, were practicing for their role in the festival. The men wore flat black hats and carried long staffs, like on the poster in her hotel. The horses pawed at the ground, oblivious to the crowds.

The hurly-burly of the streets seemed far away. The smells and colors and sounds of the festival, the ripeness of the crowds, the swirls of the skirts and bandannas, the incessant hum of prayers and songs and violins and guitars—all faded. The world suddenly stood still. Timelessness had happened to her before, at a ballet, even in front of a painting. But never with a person.

Ral broke the spell. "You ask where I'm from? Did you see the signs on the roads, '*Interdits aux nomades*'—forbidden to gypsies and travelers? Those signs are there for me. My home is wherever I am."

"What do you do?"

"I wander. When I work, it's for a week, or maybe a month. Until I know it's time to go on."

"How do you know it's time to go on?"

"The same way I know it's time to eat. Or to sleep."

"And then you just go? It sounds wonderful."

"It was, once. But that was a long time ago."

When he paused, she hung on his words, watching him look out at the gray sea.

"Now it's not so easy to wander. Everywhere you go you have to have papers. There are always questions to answer."

"How long will you be here?" she asked.

"Until it's time to go on. You?"

Until you leave, she thought, but didn't say. The thought shocked her. She saw Ral's eyes dart toward the crowds, pausing on a woman in a long skirt who was half walking, half running along the street. Despite the skirt and a scarf in her hair, something about the woman's run didn't look gypsy.

"It's late," said Ral, turning back to Jill. "You probably have far to go."

She glanced at her watch. It was five o'clock. The afternoon had disappeared, the hours uncounted.

"I don't really have any plans," she said.

His gaze darted again to the woman in the long skirt.

"I guess it's time to say good-bye," Jill said.

"Good-bye, Jill." The chocolatey tone sent a ripple through her insides.

"Good-bye, Ral."

Again she walked away without looking back. This time it took a noisy busload of tourists, pouring out of the church, complaining about the trash on the beach and the distance to their next destination, to break the trance. When Jill turned around, Ral was on the street, walking steadily, methodically studying the crowds.

She tried to think, tried to explain her incredible reactions to the man. Then she went back to Jean-Claude's car and drove fast so she wouldn't think.

There was no place to run, and Wanda Lanzer knew it. There were no trains, and the scheduled service from the bus station was sporadic. She couldn't go to the depot to wait, couldn't chance standing around hoping for a bus.

The town was filled with coaches, but they were for the tourists, day-trippers from Marseilles who came to gawk at the gypsies and buy trinkets. She thought she might find a taxi that would drive her as far as Marseilles, but she wasn't sure she had enough money. And the only way to get a taxi was to stand on the street. That she couldn't do.

She thought of the highway. If someone came along and offered her a ride, fine. If not, she could walk. She wasn't too old yet. Not young anymore, but she felt strong enough. The air would be good. In an hour or two her feet would be tough enough to go barefoot, to feel the road. Thousands had done it. They had walked those same roads for centuries. She had always told herself that she wanted to go wherever her spirit and the fates took her. This was her chance.

She wondered if she could return for her bag and her traveling clothes. She stopped walking, hung in a moment of indecision. Then suddenly she felt the nausea again, and she couldn't breathe. She clutched at her throat, wracked with coughing. She thought she would suffocate. What if a doctor came? Would she be safe at a clinic?

She began to run again, still coughing. It couldn't be true, she told herself. That Laszlo could have confused her with someone else. She could tell that he had been drinking. He could have been confused about whomever he had seen. Why trust a drunken musician? And what was there to fear? Look around, she told herself, look at the bodies that are free in the skirts, the breasts untethered, the joy and ease and freedom of these people. You can't be afraid, she told herself. You're home. Your soul is home. This is where you belong.

Her legs slowed, her breathing relaxed, the cough ceased. After a few more steps she found herself walking with the sway that came so easily and felt so sensual in the long loose skirt. She had sandals on her feet, and she could feel the powdery dust of the road under her soles and between her toes. The humid air and the running had made her sweat, and now the sweat felt cool, almost chilled.

It will be all right, she told herself. It's nothing, nothing at all. You can't let yourself get so tired. Too much excitement, too much music, too much anticipation.

She looked around, taking her bearings again, trying to remember where the road led. There was a camp farther out that road, and a marsh where the gypsies picked reeds for baskets. It was still only late afternoon. She could walk along the road, watch for the camp, perhaps even come upon some of the young girls as they picked the reeds. And it would feel good to be out on the road, in the open air, free, just wandering . . .

But then her throat caught fire again, a cough of pure fear. The only place she was safe, she knew, was in the hotel, with the shades pulled. She could read, listen to the music through the windows. Alone and private. Another day, tomorrow perhaps, late in the afternoon, after the tourists left, she could wander the road and watch the children pick reeds.

When Jill got back to her room there was a splendid nosegay of flowers on the table, with a note from Jean-Claude, written in a minuscule copper-plate script. He was terribly sorry, he wrote, but he wouldn't be free for dinner. Nothing he could say would persuade the court. He added that of course the car was hers for another day if she wanted it, until they met for dinner the next night, and, if she would enjoy it, a party with some local artists from Arles and Les Baux.

She was surprised to discover that she wasn't disappointed. She tried to picture Jean-Claude. She could remember that his eyes were pale crystal-blue and that his features were even and classically handsome. But she couldn't picture his face, couldn't see any face except Ral's.

She ate dinner alone and spent the evening walking through the book-stores of Arles, buying every book she could find about gypsies.

In the morning, without admitting to herself what she was doing, she got into Jean-Claude's car and headed toward the Camargue, driving fast on the now familiar road. She caught herself speeding up when she reached the gypsy campsite, and noticed that she had locked the doors of the car. But it wasn't necessary. There were no children playing in the sand, and no adults watching. Except for a few ancient cars and decrepit caravans, the campsite seemed deserted.

The books had been useless. Three were nothing but photographs with insipid captions, posed like the *National Geographic* stories she remembered from dentists' office, but with grainy black-and-white photographs. The prose, whether in English or in French, was like the photographs, rehearsed and unreal. Not a word of it seemed to be about living people.

She drove straight to the cathedral and walked around to the side door that opened from the crypt stairs. There was a crowd of gypsy faces outside, but overnight everything had changed. The gypsies were dressed up now; skirts were clean and bright, children wore shoes, men wore jackets over their bright shirts and vests. They were waiting for the procession of the statue to the sea.

Yet even in the formality of the Easter Parade clothes, there was a closeness and intimacy. The gypsies pressed together, unafraid, set apart by their swarthy skin and dark eyes and hair, and most of all, by the insularity of language, that strange Romany tongue that only they seemed to comprehend.

Jill remembered her grandmother speaking Yiddish with her friends, secure in the intimacy of her private language. Whenever Jill's mother had heard a phrase of that Yiddish, she would shift to her most arch, sarcastic tone: "You've been in this country for fifty years. Isn't that long enough to start speaking English?" And when her grandmother would defend herself, explaining that she only spoke Yiddish with her friends, asking what harm was in that, Jill's mother would answer: "I won't hear that Yiddish nonsense in my house. What will Jill think? What will her friends think?"

What did she think? Jill tried to remember. The Yiddish had sounded like the make-believe languages she and her friends spoke when they needed to keep secrets, a way of identifying, of deciding who was in the club. She remembered her embarrassment at her mother's cruel, relentless sarcasm. And the way those bitter phrases had worn into her own consciousness, so that when she heard the sounds of Yiddish, she instinctively thought, "You've been in this country for fifty years. Isn't that long enough to start speaking English?"

She remembered her grandmother trying to explain how there were some things that just came out different in Yiddish, that even when she knew the English words, they didn't mean the same thing to her. She felt at home in Yiddish, she said. Jill had listened, trying to understand, but she couldn't get past the automatic responses that had been drilled into her.

She skirted the edges of the crowd, watching for men who were alone, waiting until they turned so she could see their faces. Most of the men wore black suits; many even had white shirts without ties. She watched for an hour as the crowd milled, waiting for the procession to begin. Ral wasn't there.

She walked back to the café.

"*Pastis?*" asked one of the waiters, recognizing her.

She was tempted to ask the waiter if he had seen Ral. How would she ask? she wondered. How could she describe Ral? "Medium height, dark hair, dark eyes, swarthy complexion, wearing a black suit jacket, white shirt, no tie." The flat language sounded like a police identification. It wasn't the man she couldn't get out of her eyes and mind.

Her mind wandered. She kept imagining his face, recalling those eyes that had been so sad and gentle and penetrating. There was no denying her own reactions, the intensity and sheer physicality of her response. She had never before felt so vulnerable to anyone.

Perhaps he had moved on. Maybe he found whomever he was looking for. Her. A woman. Or maybe a ghost, he had said. If another man had told Jill Ashton that he was looking for a woman, or perhaps a ghost, she would have laughed in his face. But the comment had seemed natural from Ral.

She wandered toward the beach, where the crowds had gathered. They seemed disordered, except for the clear division between the gypsies and the tourists. There were no signs, but the crowds spontaneously forked, the gypsies going one way, the tourists the other, until there was a no-man's-land of unoccupied beach between the groups. She headed for that strip, not sure why, thinking mostly that it would keep her from being one more tourist, from being an observer on the edge, looking in.

The procession had already started, and like the crowd of gypsies, it was disorderly. Priests carried the statue, followed by an enormous mob, pushing, shoving, reaching to touch the cassocks of the priests or the pallet on which the statue was borne. The *gardiens* were waiting on the gravel of the beach, strange cowboys in uniforms of black, flourishing their tridents, their expressions stern as their white horses impatiently pawed the beach, shaking their manes, flicking their tails. She watched one stallion rear, the *gardien* helpless against the power of the horse. The powerful white flanks heaved, the nostrils flared, the cheeks were hollow. Sweat on the horse's white flanks glistened in the sunlight. The stallion's mind was on something other than the procession.

Loud music droned. The monotonous intoned prayers of the priests rose only occasionally above the ground of the violins and guitars. It was impossible for anyone to make out a word of the songs or prayers, but none of the words mattered. It was the mystery of the sounds that counted, the tension and excitement that the droning built. Yards away, across the sand and gravel, she could see faces intent on the procession, eyes reaching, hands stretched out, feet stamping and dancing to the music. Ecstasy was the word that came to her mind.

And then, suddenly, the unexplainable sensations came back, the fire in her cheeks, the warm wetness deep inside. She spun around even before she heard her name.

"Jill." The chocolatey voice sent a chill through her.

"Ral. You're here."

"And you've come back."

"I hoped—" She was glad that her words were drowned out by a roar from the crowd. The gypsies pushed forward, swallowing the procession the way an amoeba surrounds a morsel.

"Can you see?" Ral asked.

"Not really." The prayers and shouts and singing and guitars and violins and chants folded into an indecipherable cacophony. She had to read his lips and shout to be heard.

"Come with me." He took her hand, leading her around the perimeter of the crowd to the edge of the sea. She noticed again how gentle his grip was, and she was sorry when they cleared the edges of the crowd and he let her hand go. She stayed close to him, acutely aware of the moments when her breasts pressed against his arm, feeling her nipples stiffen each time.

When they reached the water's edge, she leaned on his arm to take off her shoes. His grip was strong on her forearm, and his fingers lingered for a moment. When she looked up, he gently pulled his hand away.

The gravel of the beach was rough, and the water was cold. Foam from the tiny waves caressed her toes. They walked to a jetty, just beyond the edge of the crowd, and he helped her climb up onto the weathered stones. To their right were the gypsies, surrounding the procession of priests and *gardiens*. Behind the crowd, the tourists held back, watching and snapping photographs from a safe distance. Before them, the Mediterranean was gray and soft, broken only by the swirling patterns of ripples from the zephyrs of wind. When she looked at the sea, the sounds and frenzy of the crowd seemed far away, the ragged motions and chaotic noise smoothed by the distance.

"Are they all gypsies?" she asked.

"They think they are."

"What do you mean?"

"It's hard to be a gypsy now."

"Why is it hard now?"

Ral shrugged, turning to watch the procession.

"Do you really go somewhere whenever you feel like going?" she asked. "Just up and leave?"

"It was like that once. When I was a boy, we lived in a *vardo,* a painted caravan. The horses would follow on leads. Sometimes in the morning my father would get up and look at the clouds and say that he saw *bahtalo drom* in the east—it means 'good road'—and we would just start walking east. We didn't need a map or papers, or a cahier. We went from our winter camp, near the lakes in Hungary, all the way to the sea, in Dalmatia, and sometimes as far as Germany or Italy. We followed little *patrin* by the road, messages that only another gypsy could understand."

With his finger he drew symbols in the sand. "This ⊙ meant that there were kind people who would always share a meal. And this /// meant that there were beets or other vegetables that could be taken. There were other signs that meant that it was a good place for horses, or that the water was very clean. I used to remember all of the *patrin*, but it's no use now. That's all gone."

"What happened?"

"What happened?" There was a trace of anger in his voice. She could sense him pulling back, catching himself. He pointed out at the crowd. "Look, they're taking the statue into the sea."

The black statue was carried high on the shoulders of the priests as they marched into the waves. The sea of gypsies waved and fluttered, like reeds in the breeze, as they shouted and reached out, trying to touch the statue.

"Will she float on a raft made from her skirt?" Jill asked.

"You remember?" Ral's smile lasted only an instant. "They've even forgotten the old stories. They want cars now, not *vardos*. No one is proud to be Rom anymore."

"Are you, Ral?"

His gaze was harsh for a moment, as though the question were too intimate. Then his features eased and his eyes smiled. Jill wondered if she was in love with this man. Strange and impossible and romantically insane as it was, nothing else seemed to explain how she felt.

Pride? The word sounded strange to his ears now. And yet pride had always been so important. There had been a time when pride and Rom meant the same thing. He could remember his father teaching him that, could still picture old Sandor flicking his thick mustache with his fingertips, hooking his thumbs into his belt, and puffing out his barrel chest so that hair showed through the open shirt. "We're Rom!" he would shout. "Romany people. Not stupid *gaji*."

Ral was five when he first learned it, maybe only four. They were living out of a *vardo* then, on the open country of the Burgenland, surrounded by the shifting numbers of their *kumpania*.

He could picture Sandor outside with the horses, brushing their flanks and talking to them in Romany.

"It's the only language a horse understands," Sandor said.

A motorcar pulled up, black and long. An aristocrat got out, dressed in city clothes, black and white, with a thin necktie and soft leather boots. With him there was a small boy, no older than Ral, but dressed in embroidered shorts and a jacket cut like a soldier's tunic. The boy wore a cap and long woolen socks and leather shoes, and he stared alternately at the horses and at Ral, who was playing barefoot in the dirt with a stick. The boy brought a toy sword out of the car with him.

Sandor greeted the aristocrat in the ingratiating, supplicating German be used with city people.

"I see I'm going to have trouble today," he said. "I can tell by the way you look at them that you're a man who knows horses. A fool doesn't know how to look at the muscles of the haunches or the flare of the nostrils. Most city men don't know to study the shading of the coat or the centers of the teeth. But I see how you look. And I know that a man who can recognize Arabian blood in a horse won't be satisfied with anything else."

Ral remembered the way the aristocrat smiled. *Gaji* always thought that gypsies knew all about horses.

The horse they were watching was Ral's favorite, a spirited white pony with a bushy forelock. The pony pranced around the makeshift corral, nipping at the cool morning air, swishing its high tail at imaginary flies. The aristocrat followed the pony on foot, pointing in turn at the pony's haunches, tail, nostrils, and teeth, while Sandor kept up his banter.

"You want to see the dam, right?" said Sandor.

He led the aristocrat to another corral, pointing out a white horse that Ral didn't remember. This one too was a spirited prancer, its tail held so high it seemed to dance. The aristocrat was pleased. He asked questions, liked the answers, then went back to look at the pony, asking to see the hooves and take another look at the teeth.

Then they began negotiating.

This was what Ral liked most, when his father turned into a thousand different people. Sandor was the consummate player, taking his cues from the other players, writing the script as he went along.

"It's foolish for us to bargain," he said. "You know what that horse is. Arabian is Arabian. Everyone knows what they're worth. You wouldn't try to take advantage of a poor gypsy."

Numbers were exchanged. Sandor's face registered shock. He pretended insult, walking away, letting the aristocrat chase after him. There were more numbers, and counteroffers. Sandor pretended to have to calculate. His hands went into the air in exasperation. He walked away in a huff.

Again the aristocrat chased after him, and again Sandor pretended to calculate. Then he disappeared behind the caravan and brought out the brightly painted pony cart, standing back like an artist at the unveiling of his masterpiece. The little boy let go of his father's legs and ran over to the cart, climbing onto the seat, beaming, begging his father. There were more numbers, more gestures of exasperation. Finally the aristocrat brought out his billfold and peeled off a roll of bills.

The little boy stayed in the seat while the pony was hooked up to the cart. He kept looking over at Ral. When the motorcar finally started down the road, driving very slowly, he waved his sword in the air, shouted "Gypsy!" at Ral, and drove off smiling.

Ral could feel the tears streaming down his cheeks. The white pony had been his favorite. At night, or when he played alone, he had dreamed that he would someday be able to drive the cart with the pony. If the little boy was old enough, so was he. He could even talk to the pony in Romany.

Sandor saw the tears and slapped Ral hard across the face. His ring cut into Ral's cheek.

"You're Rom," he said. "Rom means man. A Rom doesn't cry like a woman."

"The pony . . ." Ral fought to control his sobs. "The pony was so beautiful. And so spirited. And the cart was so pretty. I—"

Sandor's laugh shook the air. "You hear what he said? 'Spirited. Pretty.' You want to know why the horse dances?"

Ral gulped. He couldn't force out an answer.

From the leather bag where he kept his horse medicines and herbs, Sandor brought out a jar filled with wet moss. Up close, Ral could see something writhing in the moss.

Sandor opened the jar and pulled out a greenish, slimy elver, digging his fingernails into the slippery skin to hold it. "One of those in the back end and a dead horse would dance." He did a silly little dance of his own, imitating the horse.

"The man who bought that horse was *gajo*. A fool. You cry about a horse like that and you're like the *gaji*. Foolish and weak. Come!

"You want to see the dam, right?" He imitated the supplicating German he had used with the aristocrat. He dragged Ral to the other corral, picked up a slosh bucket, and poured it on the mare's back. The horse jolted as the white color washed down its flanks, showing a dull gray coat underneath.

"A nag," said Sandor. "Also with an eel in the backside. And pitch in the centers of the teeth so she looks younger."

"What about the cart?" Ral was still fighting his tears.

"Plaster and paint. One good rain and it's gone. Even a good bump and the stuff falls off." Sandor laughed again. "You're old enough to understand, Ral. The *gaji* are there and we're here. And that's that. You should be proud. You're Rom!"

For a moment Ral was proud, almost proud enough to forget the sight of the little boy driving the cart and pony and the taunting tone of that shouted epithet "Gypsy!" For the first time he knew the feeling of triumph, the gloating sense of victory that was part of Romany pride. He could picture the moment when the pony stopped prancing, when the colors washed off, when the decoration of the cart fell to pieces. What would the little boy do then? Bang the ground with his toy sword?

And yet with the newfound pride there was already the twinge that he couldn't identify yet, the reminder that he was, always would be, different; that no matter what he did, he could never trade places with the little boy, never know the simple joy of buying the cart and horse. The world of the *gajo* would always remain distant and mysterious, there. And the taunts of "Gypsy!" would never stop.

But at least for that moment there had been pride.

Now, how could you think of pride?

Below them, the statue touched the sea, and the crowd shouted, a thousand cries, each separate. That's gypsy life now, Ral thought, each separate, trusting no one anymore. How could you trust now?

He watched the rapt attention on Jill's face. She was shy. And modest. He had noticed it the first moment he had seen her, in the café. She didn't wear the short skirts to show herself. She didn't need to. She was beautiful, like a fawn, her skin suntanned but still pale. He couldn't remember a more beautiful woman. And yet she seemed so distant, not because she was *gaje*, but because he couldn't force himself to think of another day, of seeing her again. There wouldn't be another day. This was the last day. The last festival.

"What will they do now?" she asked.

"The gypsies will sell the last of their baskets and jewelry to the tourists and they'll move on."

"Where?"

Her interest was real, and he couldn't understand it. No *gaje* was interested in gypsies, except for the Romany *rye*. All his life he had known *rye*, women mostly, *gaje* who couldn't give up the dream of somehow sharing the gypsy life. Some of them went so far as to dress like gypsies, or follow *kumpania* and clans around the countryside. Others were shy, watching from a distance, taking pictures, writing notes, but always with that dream in their eye, as if the gypsies had a secret that they would somehow learn. This woman was no *rye*. Yet she had come back.

"Some will go back to the city. They live in the city and drive cars and maybe work as dustmen and each year they come here and pretend they're gypsies again."

She turned toward him, tucking her legs under herself. "Have you ever lived in the city?" she asked.

The cities tumbled through his mind, cities he had wandered, like Paris and Frankfurt and Ljubljana and Zagreb. And Vienna. He could remember the glittering Vienna of fiacres and fancy cars, and the gray Vienna of the soldiers in the jeeps.

"Many cities," he said. "When I was a boy, my mother took me every day to Vienna. We lived just outside the city and we would walk into the Leopoldstrasse, where the people were shopping. There was one corner that was ours, where I would stand huddled in her skirts. I remember that she told me never to smile, that the *gaji* didn't want to see happy gypsies. They wanted a sad gypsy face."

"What were you doing?" Jill asked.

"Begging."

She laughed.

"Why is that so funny?" he asked.

"I just remembered that every time I've ever seen a gypsy begging they had sad faces, even the children. I thought they were hungry or cold. It never occurred to me that they were acting."

Ral laughed back. "She taught me to make big eyes, to always look up at the *gaji*. When a gentleman or lady walked by, with the right kind of clothes, she would say, very loud, 'Don't bother the nice gentleman!' or 'Leave the lady alone!' And under her breath she would tell me, '*Mong, chavo, mong.*' It means 'Beg, boy, beg.' "

Jill laughed again. He enjoyed her laugh, and the memory of his mother.

But he could also remember the same street corner years later, when he was desperate and hungry and alone, his stomach talking to him because it had been more than two days since he had even been able to snatch a roll from a bakery. And then the rich *gaji* from the opera and the theaters, the gentlemen and ladies who had given so freely to the gypsy woman with her wide-eyed child, turned away from the hungry, solitary young man, cursing under their breaths that such an urchin was allowed to traipse the streets. Real desperation, he had learned then, was threatening to the *gaji*. It was the helplessness of a begging gypsy that they responded to. And it was as helpless children that they wanted to keep the gypsies. Pride was something they could not allow a gypsy.

"Gypsy!" It was the *gajo's* word. And they said it the way you would say "rat" or "scum." The word might change—*Zigeuner, tsigane, cigana, zingali,* gypsy, *gitane*—but the tone never changed. He remembered the station platform, the motley line, the shiny boots splattered with mud, the riding crop pointing. "Jews to the left. *Zigeuner* to the right." It was always the same tone.

And earlier, when they passed out the armbands and triangles: "The feeble-minded will wear an armband with the word *Blöde*, idiot. Criminals will wear green triangles, Jehovah's Witnesses purple, gypsies and other shiftless elements wear black." How many times had he heard the speech, always in that same tone?

The crowd below was still bunched, pressing toward the black statue.

Ral remembered Weimar. They had bunched up in front of the table where the American sergeant sat with his typewriter and his stacks of cigarette packs and Hershey bars. He could still picture the sergeant's wide, open face, the big belly, the bored smile.

It was the interpreter who asked the questions. He never looked up; his voice was a dull monotone, featureless. A month before, he had probably worked for the Germans, barking orders to those who hadn't yet learned the phrases of German you needed to survive in camp. The interpreter was a man who knew the art of survival, the skill of anonymity, of eyes that were never seen, a voice that couldn't be remembered.

"Name . . . age . . . ?"

Ral answered, "Twenty." It was only a guess, but close. When he was a child, they had told him he was born in the year they had sold the three stallions. Those were the only dates they had kept.

"Nationality?"

The question meant nothing. He didn't answer.

"Nationality?" It was shouted this time. "Where are you from?"

"Is this where I report someone?" he asked. "There's a person I want to report."

"This is where you answer questions. Where are you from?"

"What does it matter? I'm here. I'm from wherever I am."

The interpreter looked up, angry at the obstreperous response. His eyes were like a ferret's, tiny and sunken. He stared at Ral's coppery skin and dark eyes, the thick black hair that was clean after the shampoo with American soap. He spat out a single word: *"Zigeuner!"*

He had to translate for the American sergeant: "Gypsy."

"Gypsy?" The sergeant's tone was the same as the interpreter's, as if they were reciting alternate names of a species of vermin. For all the clothes and food and medicine and soap and cigarettes and candy they passed out, the Americans were no different from the Germans.

"It's no use," said the interpreter. *"Zigeuner* will never give you an honest answer. The lying is in their blood."

The sergeant nodded.

Ral remembered how he had reached into the deep pocket of the American fatigues to pull out the photograph. It was almost new then, hardly wrinkled. He had already memorized every line, every shade of gray. "This is the person I want to report," he said.

The interpreter was already typing papers. The sergeant reached for the photograph. His eyes went down to the open blouse, the gold chain dangling between the breasts.

"Nice," he said, winking. "Don't blame you for looking. Wouldn't mind seeing something with a little flesh on it myself." He held his hands in front of his chest, as if he were squeezing huge breasts, then winked again. "Mostly skin and bones around here now, ain't it?"

That was twenty years ago. The photograph was almost gone now, a sheet of wrinkles. For twenty years he had carried it through half of Europe, showed it to thousands of people, waiting for someone who recognized her, waiting for the moment when he found her. Even now, sitting on the beach with a beautiful woman, he was thinking about the photograph, about what he would do, what he had to do.

The afternoon slid away. They had been together on that stretch of beach for hours, mostly quiet, watching the festival build to its crescendo of excitement and fade as the priests carried the statue from the sea back to the church. It was late when the fervor of the crowds finally ebbed, the tourists went back to the streets and the souvenir shops, the gypsies slowly dispersed to their campsites and the vast parking areas filled with *vardos*, vans, buses, cars, tents, trucks, and vehicles that fit no ordinary description. Ral and Jill were alone with the gray, featureless sea.

"Still waiting for her?" Jill asked.

Ral shook the question away.

"Who is she?"

Again Ral shook away the question.

"Should I be worried?"

"Why should a beautiful woman like you worry?"

"Because you sit with me and think about another woman." Jill grinned, enjoying the play. Ral caught on, and laughed. His laugh was light and easy, not at all what the brooding eyes might have promised.

"She's nothing," he said.

"Nothing? For two days she's all you've thought about. Even when you talk to me, telling me lovely stories, there are times when you don't see me. When you watch the festival, you don't see the statue or the priests. You only see the faces in the crowd. You've looked at every face. And you keep searching. Why is she so important?"

"Why do you ask me so many questions? Why do I matter to you?"

"Because you're . . ." She hesitated, and as she refined the words in her mind, they became too clever and too vague. She rejected them for a cliché.

"Ral. You're a very special man."

"Special? I think *different* is the word you mean. I'm different to you because I'm a gypsy. And you're different to me. I've known *gaje* women, but none as beautiful as you."

"But you tell all of them that they're beautiful?"

"Of course. Except that I never meant it before."

"It's funny," she said after a long pause. "I feel strangely close to you, and yet I hardly know you. The only thing I really know is that you're looking for someone."

"Maybe we're not so different. You're looking for something too."

"Am I?" Her answer was instinctive, almost defensive. She knew he was right. She was looking for something, not sure even what it was.

"Why else would you have come back here?"

"I came back because I wanted to see you again." She answered quickly, without hesitating.

"To see me?" He looked away, started to laugh, then stopped abruptly. "I'm glad you came back."

"So am I. What about tomorrow, Ral? Where will you be tomorrow?"

"Are you going to come looking for me again?"

"Maybe."

"I don't know."

"You must know. Will you be here still? On the road? Will you go toward Paris? Toward Spain? You must have an idea."

"Tomorrow?" His voice was hesitant. "How can I know about tomorrow? We spend our whole lives waiting for tomorrows. But we never really know what will happen."

"You mean I might never see you again." It wasn't a question.

"*Stanki nashti tshi arakenpe manushen shai.*" The Romany words came out in a different voice, very soft and gentle. "It means 'Mountains do not meet, but people do.' "

"That sounds like good-bye."

She saw him looking out at the deserted beach. Without the festival crowds, it seemed tawdry, a sea of jetsam and trash.

"It's late," he said. "The festival is over. The people are all going. Can it still be interesting for you?"

She wondered that herself. How many more times would his gaze and voice evoke those strange sensations deep inside her? How long would she remember those eyes? Was she being a silly schoolgirl, half fascinated, half infatuated, as intrigued by the exotic mystery of gypsy life—so different from her own—as she was enthralled by his eyes?

And then she wondered if those questions weren't themselves a kind of defense mechanism, a way of dismissing everything. She silently cursed herself for refining her feelings into words, regretting the strange shyness that kept her so far from him. She had only held his fingers for a few moments, had only felt her body against his in accidental touches. And now it seemed all over.

"You really have no idea where you're going, where you'll be after today?"

"No."

"What was it your father used to say, when he woke up in the morning and decided where to go?"

"*Bahtalo drom.* Good road."

"Can I say '*Bahtalo drom*' to you? Is that the right thing to say?"

He grinned, shook her hand formally. "Good luck, Jill."

She leaned toward him. Her lips brushed his. There was a smile in his eyes.

Then he was gone.

Wanda Lanzer stayed in the hotel room all day, with the windows open behind drawn drapes. The streets had been quiet after the tourists had given up the souvenir shops to watch the procession from the church. She had been able to hear a guitarist who played in a café across the street. He wasn't a real musician, not like the violinist Laszlo, but the music was soothing. She had napped in the hottest part of the afternoon.

When she woke up, she could tell from the street noise that the festival was over. Cars and trucks and buses were tied up in a massive traffic jam, accompanied by choruses of shouting—the outraged shrieks of German, English, Spanish, and French tourists, and the controlled, almost choreographed cries of the Romany, cries that were as much a style of greeting as protests about the traffic. Without looking, she could identify the dialects and accents of the different Romany, the broad tones of the Eastern gypsies, the precise language of the Manush, the half-Romany pidgin of some of the Spanish gypsies. Listening closely, she could even make out tribes. She went to the window to test herself, and picked out the skirts and *diclos* and bandannas that went with the voices.

For most of the afternoon she was content to listen and watch, until the sun dropped low enough to shine straight into the window. The sun was hot by then, and she longed for the open air, for the cool afternoon breeze that would blow across the Camargue. She wanted to walk the road, out to the encampments. With most of the tourists gone, the gypsies would go back to their ordinary lives, picking reeds, weaving baskets, singing, dancing, and when they felt like it, just packing and moving on. She longed to see the girls picking reeds, and the men standing around their grindstones, or around an open fire, smoking their pipes, talking, perhaps singing with a guitar or fiddle. It wouldn't be music like Laszlo could play, but it would be real, a reminder of the old life that she could never see anymore in Amsterdam, where the only gypsies were the scrapmen with their wrecking yards on the outskirts of the city, and the rag ladies of the flea market. Those "gypsies" probably sent their children to Dutch schools.

She remembered what Laszlo had said to her, but it seemed distant now, a memory that had already faded. Even if it was true—how could it be?—no one would look for her after the festival. She was safe. She could feel it in the warm breeze that was starting to blow off the marshes. How much longer could she wait to feel that breeze lifting her skirt and rustling her blouse? How much longer could she wait to feel the dirt of the road in her toes and the freedom of her body in the loose clothing?

She thought of taking a camera or the little tape recorder, but it seemed absurd to have equipment if she was going to wear the full skirt and the open blouse. So instead she tied a *diclo* around her hair and put on the meager gold chain and bracelet. At the last minute she took the camera. It was small and would give her a chance to replace the tired pictures in her flat. Then she set off through the lobby for the road that led out of town, anxious to get out to the dirt road where she could take off her shoes and feel the dust and the breeze. It would only take an hour or two to walk to the encampment, and once there she could watch the girls picking reeds by the harsh light of the sunset and dusk, and then listen for the plaintive voices from the fires and the stoves of the *vardos*.

She would be home then, she thought.

The party was in a sculptor's studio, a rebuilt farmhouse with immense panes of glass recessed into the ancient stone walls. Jill had never heard of the sculptor before, and the few works of his on display—big welded iron constructions—seemed naive and gaudy. But it was clear that the sculptor, who stood by his latest rusty creation inviting compliments, was doing very well in the strange market of modern art.

The studio was crowded, and every one of the fifty or so people there was either attractive or cloaked in the stylish eccentricities that can substitute for good looks. One woman wore a halter top that revealed more than it concealed of her enormous bust; her white pants had to have been sprayed onto her. When Jean-Claude caught Jill staring, he whispered in her ear: "Don't be harsh in your judgments. Women without your beauty have to try much harder."

For all the flashiness of clothes and flesh, it wasn't at all like an American cocktail party. Instead of the constant mingling and milling, people broke into groups, foursomes and threesomes, to engage in intense discussions. Much of the talk was loud, sounding more like a debate than the friendly chatter of a party. There was liquor and wine, but hardly anyone drank. Instead, all energies were put into pronouncements—on the tackiness of the American art market, the follies of Vietnam, the frauds of the space program—that were served up like canapés.

Jean-Claude seemed amused by the party. He was warm and friendly to everyone, kissing every woman, greeting every man, introducing Jill with a sly, suggestive smile. Jill was aware that these artists and art hangers-on were the kind of people she would instinctively gravitate to in New York, and that their clichéd pronouncements were arguments she would have pounced on. But as Jean-Claude recognized early, she was preoccupied, her mind elsewhere.

"Your day was tiring?" he asked.

"A little."

"I'm surprised that you went back to the festival a second time. For most, a single day is enough for a lifetime."

"I loved the color and the music. And those faces. I never realized how interesting the gypsies were."

"Do you think it's real gypsies you see there? It may be more like those Dutch villages where everyone comes out in wooden shoes and traditional clothing. I always wonder whether the tour buses ever arrive early, while the villagers are putting on their costumes."

Jill felt anger erupting, but she fought it. Instead of arguing, she forced an empty smile.

"We can leave early if you're tired," Jean-Claude said.

"I'm fine, really. Just a little overdosed on sound and color."

"Come outside. The night air will relax you."

They were on the way outside when Jean-Claude turned to greet a man just arriving. The man wore a business suit that seemed out of place at the party. They chatted for a moment in rapid Provençal French that Jill couldn't follow. Jean-Claude seemed absorbed.

"What's so interesting?" Jill asked during a lull.

Jean-Claude introduced the man. His name was Émile Leclerc. "You must get him to invite you to his gallery. No one knows more about Provençal primitives."

Jill smiled, extending her hand. "Can I ask what the fascinating secret is? I can't really follow Provençal when you speak that quickly."

"Secret? How rude of me!" Leclerc took Jill's fingers and kissed them, exaggerating the gesture. "My apologies. I was only explaining to Jean-

Claude why I've come so late. There's been a murder. In Saintes-Maries. An old gypsy woman was butchered by the roadside."

Jill's mind reacted immediately, like a reporter's. Stock, formal questions were already on her lips when her insides caught up with her. There was no reason to connect anything, but the thought that Ral was looking for a woman hung in her mind. She shuddered.

"What's wrong?" said Jean-Claude. Then he seemed to grasp an answer to his own quesion.

"What time did it happen?" he asked Leclerc.

"They don't know for sure. It appears to have been early evening, perhaps seven o'clock."

"Long after you left," Jean-Claude said to Jill. His voice was tender. His hand grazed her arm. "I detest carping like an old I-told-you-so, but the gypsies really can be very unsavory. I'm glad you weren't driving late in the evening." His voice faded, as though he were puzzled by the utter blankness of Jill's face.

"Do the police know who did it?" Jill asked.

"It shouldn't take them long," said Leclerc. "They'll go to the usual informers. I frankly don't see why they bother. It would be better to let the gypsies settle it themselves, like Sicilians."

Jill bristled, feeling her mind limber up. "What makes you so sure a gypsy murdered the woman?"

Leclerc's grin was condescending. "Because, my dear, killing is something that gypsies seem to do very well."

Jill glanced at Jean-Claude, looking for his reaction. He seemed curious, perhaps amused that she was finally engaged in the party. He didn't seem outraged. She was.

"I don't believe that!" Jill said. Her tone was defiant enough to draw heads.

"What a passionate lady friend you've found!" said Leclerc.

"I'd be careful if I were you," Jean-Claude said to Leclerc. "Many talented counselors have learned to be wary of Mademoiselle Jill Ashton of Millman, Lord and Perry. I suspect that when she's aroused, as she appears to be, you'd be well advised to steer clear."

"A lady *avocat?*" said Leclerc. "Is defending the gypsies your specialty?"

"No more than stereotypes and slurs are yours."

"Well, you've found yourself quite a tigress, Jean-Claude. I hope she's as fiery when it matters."

"Right now matters," said Jill. She was surprised by her own vehemence. Usually she had the self-control to let comments like Leclerc's pass without notice. "I'd like to hear why you're so sure that a gypsy murdered the woman. How are you even sure there was a murderer?"

Leclerc's eyes twinkled. "My dear! There are some things that one learns, living in Provence. The gypsies are capable of marvelous acting, like the starving-child routine or the cases Jean-Claude could describe, such as the young men who manage to fall down whole flights of stairs in department stores, incurring paralyzing injuries which cannot be verified by medical science, but which suffice as the pretext for filing civil actions for fabulous sums. Miraculously, the young men are usually able to walk out of the courtroom as soon as a settlement has been reached. Have you ever seen a gypsy with a useless dog? Or with a horse that no longer has value for trade? Have you ever seen gypsy women fight?"

Jean-Claude reached toward Jill's shoulder, as if to steer her away. She shook off his fingers. "And what makes you so certain that the woman was murdered?" she asked.

Leclerc seemed reluctant to argue. He looked around the room for an escape. Twenty people had gathered around them, glancing back and forth as if the shifts of their eyes were enough to place bets on Jill or Leclerc.

"The corpse had multiple subdermal contusions of the head and shoulders, caused by heavy blows. There were finger marks on the throat, deep enough that they could only have been made by a man with large, powerful hands. The woman's clothing was ripped; her breasts were exposed. It's not clear whether she was raped. We shall have to wait for the laboratory report. But even without evidence of penetration, do you really think that the contusions and strangulation could have been self-inflicted? Or do you think it was an accident, that the woman fell down?"

He paused, but before Jill or Jean-Claude could respond, Leclerc went on. "I know that it's fashionable in America to dismiss all police as 'pigs.' I suspect that the French police are considered especially brutal, 'fascist pigs' no doubt, and that by American standards our justice system is thought to be little more than a revival of the Inquisition. But may I assure you that we do know how to examine a corpse, and that if we lack the facilities of the fabled FBI laboratory, we nonetheless are able, in our quaint provincial manner, to determine the cause of death of a woman who was bludgeoned and strangled by a man with strong hands."

"I wonder if a little fresh air wouldn't do us all some good," said Jean-Claude.

Jill glared at him, then spun back to Leclerc. "Did you see the woman? Or is this report of contusions and strangulation a bit of press sensationalism?"

"I don't think the press has had an opportunity for their sensationalism yet," said Leclerc. "We have laws in France to restrict trial by the press."

"Then how are you so well informed? Hearsay and gossip? Or have the police already begun building their case with the public? It appears"—she glanced around at the crowd who had come to listen in on the argument— "that stories of gypsy violence have a ready audience around here."

"Actually, mademoiselle, I'm sorry that Jean-Claude didn't finish our introduction. Provençal primitives are my *violon d'Ingres*, but I regrettably must earn my keep as a surgeon, specializing in orthopedics and trauma. In that capacity I am frequently called to consult on forensic matters. The reason I was late to this lovely party is that I was summoned to Saintes-Maries from my surgery, even before I had an opportunity to dress for the party, to examine the body in situ. So, you see, what I have told you is hardly hearsay or police invention. And I'm afraid that if I continue to answer your persistent questions, I may violate our rather strict laws for the protection of the accused, which I'm sure you wouldn't want me to do." He bowed slightly, spun on his heel, and headed across the room.

Jill reluctantly followed Jean-Claude's lead to an outside terrace.

"I made quite a fool of myself, didn't I?" she said.

"Let's say you were a bit more aggressive than one would have expected. If the discussion had been one of the more typically volatile topics—Vietnam or Israel or the usual French condescension toward the American art market—I wouldn't have been surprised. But I had no idea that you were so involved with the gypsies. I thought you went to Saintes-Maries out of idle curiosity, as a lark."

"I did. Until I got there I'd never talked to a gypsy in my life. Except maybe to say 'Go away!' to panhandlers and begging women."

"And are you always such a defender of the downtrodden?" The irony was in his words, not in his voice or his eyes.

"I guess I'm just a little overwrought."

"Perhaps we should leave. You'll need to rest up for our negotiations tomorrow. I don't think I could face a tigress like that."

"You're not afraid of American lawyers, are you?"

"You're not the first American attorney with whom I've dealt. Only the loveliest."

"Are you telling me all the others were men?"

"In fact, they were. But you're still extraordinarily lovely, Jill."

"And you're marvelously adept with compliments."

Jean-Claude's eyes turned even bluer.

The good-byes took a long time. Jean-Claude avoided Leclerc, but he had introduced Jill to almost everyone at the party, and so they made a full circuit before they left. Jill overheard comments about her conversation with Leclerc.

When they were finally at the door, Jill stopped. "If the police haven't arrested anyone, why would he be afraid of jeopardizing the accused?" She hadn't meant to ask the question out loud.

Jean-Claude's shrug was halfway between exasperation and fascination. He watched Jill pick her way through the crowd toward Leclerc, who had shed his jacket and tie and seemed to be enjoying himself, laughing boisterously with a voluptuous Italian sculptress named Goietta.

"What did you mean when you said that saying more might violate the rights of the accused?" Jill asked him.

"Mademoiselle Ashton!" Leclerc glanced at Jean-Claude before he answered, searching no doubt for a wink or other signal that he should or could ignore the interruption. Jean-Claude backed off.

"I tried to explain that I was there in a quasi-official capacity," said Leclerc, "which means that I'm really not at liberty to disclose anything more than what I said."

"In other words, you're only free to make racist slurs about the gypsies."

Leclerc's face reddened and he stretched his neck as though he were working out a tic. "In fact, mademoiselle, a man has been arrested. A gypsy. The police found him standing over the woman's body. He made no effort to escape and to my knowledge hasn't denied the crime, though I suspect that a denial would do him little good. I would be most surprised if the gypsy didn't sign a formal confession before forty-eight hours are up. If he can read and write, that is."

"I'd imagine that your colleagues could get a confession out of the president of the republic in forty-eight hours," said Jill.

Before Leclerc could answer, Jean-Claude stepped between them. "I think we should go, Jill."

Outside, in the car, he said, "Leclerc is really not a bad chap. If you found his remarks about the gypsies offensive, I can only say that his opinions are exactly those of almost everyone who has lived in Provence. We're close to the gypsies here. They are a peculiar lot."

"I didn't mean to embarrass you, Jean-Claude. I'm sorry."

"Not at all. I enjoyed your combativeness. And if I'm not wrong, that last stab at Leclerc was intentional, a bait to get him to say more than he intended. It was obviously well done."

She smiled. "I had the feeling he was hiding something. After his little speech about protecting the rights of the accused, I just had to jump on him."

"And you did it exceedingly well. But why this sudden interest in a tawdry murder? Is it only because you happened to be in Saintes-Maries?"

She shook her head. "I don't know, Jean-Claude. Maybe it's just whim. Somehow, being all day in a town, so close to so many people that you could hear them breathing, and then to have that Leclerc pour out that racist drivel about how gypsies are always violent and always killing one another. I just didn't need to hear that . . ."

She didn't realize how self-righteous she sounded until she saw Jean-Claude's smile. "Do I sound ridiculous?" she asked.

"No. But I'm surprised by your passion. Two days ago you seemed so cool and restrained. Leclerc may disagree, but I prefer the passion. Although I may have to retreat and lick my wounds after our negotiations tomorrow. Can I persuade you to spend the afternoon with me, after we settle the estate? We could go for a drive, for a sail, whatever you would like."

"Even if I come out on top of the negotiations?"

"Especially then."

· · ·

In the morning a newspaper came with her croissants and coffee, a wretched Marseilles rag that was mostly sensational headlines. Even on holiday, she couldn't stay away from the news. "The *Times* for breakfast," she remembered someone saying. "Sometimes with coffee."

The story was tiny, buried inside, swallowed up by voluminous reports on an American space shot and some scandal about the sewers in Marseilles. Only someone looking for the story, or perhaps studying the newspaper from boredom, could have spotted it. The dateline was Marseilles, not Saintes-Maries, and the language was closer to a police release than a reporter's prose. All it told her was that there really had been a murder, and that a suspect had been arrested.

She promised herself that she wouldn't bring it up, but almost before she said hello to Jean-Claude in the lobby, she asked: "Where do they take a suspect?"

"Suspect?" He seemed genuinely puzzled.

"A murder suspect. Where would the police take a murder suspect?"

"Jill! You're still worrying about the murder in Saintes-Maries? You have a spider on your ceiling."

She laughed. Jean-Claude's accent was still utterly charming, and the occasional odd phrase in English was delightful. " 'Spider on your ceiling'? What does that mean?" she asked.

"It means you have an obsession."

" 'A bee in your bonnet' in English."

"Exactly. You have a bee in your bonnet." He laughed at the phrase and touched her hair. "Up here."

She smiled, but she didn't like the way he made light of her question. "I'm serious, Jean-Claude. Where would they take a suspect?"

"I'm not sure I look forward to having you as an adversary. You're tenacious. Like a bulldog."

"You're not the first one to tell me that. What happens to the suspect after the forty-eight hours of interrogation?"

"You really want to know, don't you? All right. To begin, he is not a suspect. That's Anglo-Saxon namby-pamby, a delicacy of American and English law. In France, if the police still hold the man after forty-eight hours, he is the accused, which means he is eligible to be dragged away to a subterranean dungeon and tortured until he confesses to every unsolved crime on the police books. Usually rubber truncheons on the soles of the feet suffice. In extreme cases the police have been known to use lit matches under the fingernails or thumbscrews to the genitalia. Once the confession is signed, the man is generally burned at the stake."

Jill half smiled. Jean-Claude had just made sure that she would be her testiest during the negotiations for the Motte Collection.

· · ·

Under the terms of Motte's will, all of the works still in his possession at his death went to the Museum of Modern Art. The MOMA already had three paintings of his, and the bequest was considered a coup: it meant the collection had been grabbed from under the noses of four other museums, in France, the Netherlands, and the United States, that had besieged first Motte, then the estate, with offers. Jill had already seen a copy of the will, knew it was a secure document, and hadn't even plunged into the fray. Now she had come to Marseilles with the expectation of negotiating funds from the estate to cover shipping and insurance as well. She had been able to obtain the same concessions from other collections, usually by intervening when the wills were being drafted. The museum had come to expect that kind of hard, successful bargaining from her, and she had almost always delivered.

She assumed that it would be easy to get the same concessions from Jean-Claude. From that first moment at the airport, she had suspected that he was all show, a flashy, easy-talking charmer with little substance. The compliments and flirtation, the lovely lunch at Carry-le-Rouet, the offer of the car, the invitation to the party, even the promise of an afternoon sail— all seemed like the classic ploys of an unprepared lawyer, the kind of man who substitutes charm for homework.

She was wrong, and she knew it as soon as she walked into Jean-Claude's office.

The office wasn't at all what she expected. He worked with only a single secretary, and his private office was a tasteful but exceedingly modest book-lined cell. There was no expansive view, no conference table, no bar in a cabinet, no chairs arranged around a glass coffee table stacked up with art books. The room looked like a working office, a place where you wrote briefs rather than impressed clients.

She sat across the desk from him. When she presented her proposal, Jean-Claude listened carefully, asking her to repeat several terms and nodding to indicate that he understood. Then he put on a pair of wire-rimmed half-glasses that she hadn't seen before and read aloud from the will and from a series of notations in the civil code and the bilateral U.S.–French tax agreements.

"Even for you, I cannot change those agreements," he said.

She suggested that if the museum had to pay the entire cost of shipping and insurance, without some subsidy from the estate, they might not be interested in the bequest. "Everyone wants their stuff in the MOMA. But not everyone is a Picasso. The museum has to be selective about committing its limited funds."

The evenness of Jean-Claude's smile got to her. He didn't rise to her bait, didn't argue or counterpropose, didn't try to throw her off with another of those compliments that she had begun to find so cloying. He didn't try one of the varieties of sexual innuendo she had so often heard from male opponents who thought themselves clever, sexy, or charming. He just said that it was quite impossible for the estate to pay what she was asking, that the laws, the terms of the estate, and custom forbid it. He gestured at a stack of books on his desk, some open, others closed, with slips of paper as bookmarks.

She had seen the same gesture hundreds of times. But usually it came from lawyers who hadn't done their research and who gestured at a wall of books as if to say that "anyone who read the case law would know . . ." Jean-Claude had done his homework; his argument was rigorous. Still, she wouldn't let it go easily.

"I don't want to slug it out for every last sou," she said. "If the estate will pay half the shipping and insurance, I'll get the museum to pick up the other half. That seems fair to both sides. And Motte's kids—or whoever is administering the estate—can feel that they've done their duty by seeing that the collection made it to the Museum of Modern Art."

"But Jill, I'm administering the estate. Motte and I were close friends, I represented him when he sold works, I drafted his will, and at his insistence, his final testament has named me as his executor."

"That should make things easier."

Jean-Claude shook his head. It was a gentle gesture, a nod more than a denial, a way of saying he was dead serious about the estate.

"We agree?" she asked. "Time to shake hands and go for that sail you promised?"

"The boat is waiting."

"And the estate will pick up half of the shipping and insurance?"

"The laws and the will are quite clear, Jill. My sole authority is to execute the estate in accord with the terms of the will."

"If I remember my French estates law, especially the stuff they've added to get around those wretched clauses from the Napoleonic Code, the executor has considerable authority to carry out the spirit of the will. Which means you could authorize a subsidy to support the bequest."

"And if I did not?"

"Then I'm not sure the museum would be willing to accept the paintings."

Jean-Claude's smile was kind, not cruel. "And you would have come here for nothing?"

She thought of the ploys she could try. It was always a subtle decision whether to make a stab for the best possible deal on the spot, or to wait it out. The essential skill was to read an opponent, to estimate his position and his personality, to anticipate his moves, and then to present the options so that he would be persuaded that the final settlement was fair to both sides. It was a strange skill, negotiating, one that demanded judgment, insight, quick thinking, and especially the ability to see the matter from the other side. And she was good at it. The skills that had made her good in the courtroom, the ability to read and understand an opponent and a judge,

also made her a sensitive negotiator. And she had the most essential attrib-
ute of all: she liked to win. Or to put it more precisely, she hated to lose.

But suddenly she found herself unable to pitch in with any real enthusiasm. She knew all the options she had, from waiting him out to taking a
good stab at one-upping him on the codes, or tiring him out with endless
arguments, or even the low blows of charm, a technique at which she
thought herself just about as good as he was. It wasn't that she was bored,
or that she didn't like Jean-Claude. In fact, a little wordplay with him
would have been fun. He seemed to have a quick mind and a good dose of
slightly sanctimonious seriousness. He would have been a delightful opponent.

But *it*—the Motte Collection, the museum, the shipping costs—just
didn't matter. A week before, the thought of not coming back with a deal
that would bring praise from her colleagues would have been impossible.
She would have found a way to win what she wanted. She would have
waited it out, marched off in mock disgust, said she was going shopping,
made herself hard to find, tried any of a thousand different strategies, and
by smarts and hard work and sheer persistence and pigheadedness and dili-
gence, by just wanting to win more than her opponent, she would have
gotten what she wanted. That was the way she had made her career. But
now it just didn't matter. And she didn't understand why.

Jean-Claude waited before he gently asked, "Shall we go sailing? The
papers are already drawn up."

The negotiations had taken less than an hour.

Jean-Claude's office was in a building that reminded Jill of the Inns of
Court in London. It lacked the ivy and the quaintness of the maze of halls
and arched passages, but there was both the democratic quality of offices
established by something other than the ability to pay a high rent and the
camaraderie of a college campus. Bulletin boards displayed calendars of
the different courts. It reminded her of the days when she used to hustle
back and forth between the Legal Aid offices and the courts downtown.

But the notices also reminded her of exactly why she had been so dis-
tracted during their negotiations. She stopped to stare at the calendar of
the High Court of Assizes, listing upcoming criminal trials.

"What's so interesting?" Jean-Claude asked.

She turned to him. "Where are suspects held before trial?"

It took Jean-Claude a moment to register the question. When he did, his
smile was sly. "The gypsy would be in the Maison d'Arrêt, at least until
they finish the interrogation. After arraignment he'll probably be sent to
Les Baumettes. Especially if he's unrepresented and has no permanent address."

"How soon will he brought to trial?"

Jean-Claude's eyelids drooped in mock exasperation.

Jill said, "It's just that I find it hard to believe that a gypsy would commit a murder like that. I read up on the gypsies last night. They apparently consider the outsider fair game, but they have strong moral and ethical codes among themselves. They don't murder each other and they don't go around raping women. From what I read, it doesn't make sense for a gypsy man to have murdered some old gypsy woman."

Jean-Claude grinned broadly. "You're marvelous when you become animated. I'm thankful that you showed mercy for me on the estate matter."

It wasn't true, of course. And she had seen him do that before, avoid real conversation with flattery. It was one manner of his that she really didn't like.

"I'm serious, Jean-Claude. I was serious last night with that friend of yours, and I'm serious now. I don't even know why, but for some reason this whole thing gets to me."

"That I can see. And I'd venture that you won't enjoy a sail until your questions are answered."

She nodded. "I'm afraid that's true."

Jean-Claude looked around, then led her back along a narrow corridor to a pay phone. "Give me a minute," he said.

It took him a little more than a minute to step out of the phone booth, grinning.

"I just spoke with the assistant *commissaire* of police. He's amused that a lady lawyer from the States is interested in what he considers a trifling case, but he's willing to listen to your questions. I tried to get him to do it as a favor for an old schoolmate. When that didn't work I told him that I was quite sure he would enjoy a visit with you. Like the rest of us, he's a Frenchman, which means he's susceptible."

"Really? He'll talk?"

Jean-Claude nodded.

She squeezed Jean-Claude's arm. "Thanks."

"It's the only way we could enjoy that sail," he said.

The police offices were musty, antiseptic in smell, lit by dusty beams from high clerestory windows. In the front office there were rows of desks, with clerks on stools writing in ledgers. Officers in dress uniforms, red kepis and white belts, stood guard outside the *commissaire*'s office.

Jean-Claude and the *commissaire* greeted each other like schoolmates. The *commissaire* seemed older than Jean-Claude, with thinning hair, a paunch, and a trace of the Russian commissar in his flat-featured face and baggy suit. He feigned interest in the fact that Jill was a lawyer, but as Jean-Claude had predicted, the Frenchman came through in his roving gaze and a wink.

"The man is still under interrogation," he explained. "Hence there's little I can tell you. Jean-Claude says that you were yourself in Saintes-Maries yesterday."

"What's the man's name?" Jill asked.

"Even that cannot be revealed until the interrogation is over." He looked down at his desk, thumbed through some papers, then pushed a button on an intercom. A moment later an attractive woman came in with a file, which he quickly scanned.

"In fact, mademoiselle, we have already suspended all questioning of the accused. From the reports, there was no cooperation. None at all. His only response to every question was to insist that he wanted to be tried, a wish that will most certainly be honored. Fortunately the man is not a local gypsy. Our own are generally well-behaved. A little hanky-panky with the tourists perhaps, but no violence. This man is not from around here."

"Then there's no harm in telling us his name."

The *commissaire* glanced at Jean-Claude. "She's clever, your lady lawyer." He winked at Jill, as though she hadn't heard his remark to Jean-Claude.

"I suppose not. He gave his name as—" He glanced down at the file to make sure. "Ral Bendit."

Jill felt her legs crumpling. A lump rose in her throat. Strangely, she wasn't really surprised.

"Are you all right?" said Jean-Claude. "You look flushed."

"I'm all right. It's just that . . . I think I met the man."

"Mademoiselle!" The *commissaire* offered her a glass and a bottle of mineral water.

She pushed it away. "The man I met was named Ral," she said. "It's not a common name."

"Common name?" said the *commissaire*. "How are we to say, mademoiselle? Like everything else about them, the Romany names are strange. What sounds unusual to us may be common for them. How long did you talk to the man you met?"

"A few minutes." It was probably closer to hours, she thought.

"And this was in Saintes-Maries, yesterday?"

"I saw him yesterday, and the day before."

She caught the reaction on Jean-Claude's face: genuine surprise.

"What did he say to you?"

"Almost nothing, actually. He was waiting for someone."

"The man you talked to said that?"

She was sorry she had said it. She nodded yes.

The *commissaire* said something to Jean-Claude in rapid dialect.

"Ask her," said Jean-Claude. "I assure you, she's a woman of her own mind."

"Mademoiselle—" The *commissaire* twirled a pencil in his fingers as he spoke. "The evidence against the man is strong. He was found at the scene of the crime, he hasn't denied the crime, he's offered no alibi that would in any way exonerate him. Only his refusal to cooperate is troubling. It would be helpful to us if you would consent to identify him. That is, if he is indeed the man who spoke to you in Saintes-Maries."

"You can refuse, Jill," said Jean-Claude. "I'm sure Monsieur would understand."

"Of course," said the *commissaire*. "The man is obviously depraved. An instance of psychosexual mania, I would say. If the prospect of seeing him again repulses you, there are other grounds on which we can proceed. Even without your identification, the case won't be difficult to build. We have a photograph of the woman which we found in his pocket. It was worn, quite old, but clearly identifiable as the dead woman."

"Could we see it?" said Jill.

The *commissaire* shrugged. "I don't see why not." The photograph was in a glassine envelope. He shook it out onto his blotter without touching it.

"Also a gypsy?" said Jean-Claude.

"Possibly. It would appear so from the clothes on the body, and the clothing in the photograph. We haven't been able to establish an identity yet. There were no papers found on the dead woman. And as you know, the papers one finds on a gypsy are as often as not false. These gypsies place little credence in the conventions of civilized society."

"There's a name on the photograph," said Jill. "Loli Tschai. It sounds like a gypsy name."

"With these people, mademoiselle, everything 'sounds like' or 'looks like.' Nothing is ever what it seems. Nothing they say can be taken at face value. Which is why an identification would be useful to us. I assure you that we will arrange matters so that the man cannot see you. We have facilities that are designed to avoid embarrassment to witnesses."

"Where is he?" said Jill.

The Maison d'Arrêt was a gloomy, grime-streaked building, tucked behind the police offices. A chipped, pretentious inscription about liberty and the rights of man was chiseled into the stone arch over the doorway.

In the corridor outside the interrogation cells, the *commissaire* explained that the peepholes in the doors were designed for observation by outsiders. The man in the cell would not be able to see her at all. And, he added, in a case such as this, where the accused has no permanent address or means of support, there is of course no possibility of his being released on bail.

They turned off the corridor into an anteroom, with heavy steel cell doors on either side. There were no bars or windows on the doors, only a sliding port near the bottom and a shuttered porthole at eye level. A guard stood by the porthole on one door.

"You have my personal assurances, mademoiselle," said the *commissaire*. "The man will not be able to see you."

Jean-Claude squeezed her hand, the guard slid the shutter open, and Jill put her eye to the peephole.

Her reaction was immediate, stronger than it had been before: a burning flush in her cheeks, goosebumps on her arms, the flutter inside. She shivered.

"It's all right," said Jean-Claude. "He can't see you."

Perhaps, she thought. But inside the stark cell, Ral's eyes were fixed on her, staring with the intense gaze she remembered. The light inside the cell was a sickly fluorescent green, but his skin and hair still glowed, and his eyes burned with the smoldering sadness she remembered from the café. He didn't blink, didn't waver his gaze. They could assure all they wanted; he was looking at her.

She stayed at the peephole for what seemed a long time, then stepped back slowly.

"Is that the man who spoke to you in Saintes-Maries?" asked the *commissaire*.

"Yes."

Jean-Claude put his own eye to the peephole. He looked for only an instant before he pulled away. "I see what you mean," he said to the *commissaire*. "The eyes do have the look of mania."

"If you would sign an affidavit," said the *commissaire*.

"When will he be tried?" she asked.

"Quickly, mademoiselle. In this instance, his own wishes and ours are identical."

Jill was afraid her legs would collapse on the way out.

They watched Ral constantly. He couldn't see through the sliding port on the door of the cell, but he could hear footsteps and indistinct conversation whenever they changed guards. When he was certain someone was there he would stare at the door. He could remember other times when he had been watched like a wild animal. What kind of person would watch from behind a mirror? he wondered. What kind of man was afraid for someone to see his eyes?

The food was filthy, the bed hard. When the lights were dimmed at night he could see bugs scurry out of cracks in the wall, and he could hear scratching sounds that he knew were rats. He thought about how to kill a rat. It wasn't like in the woods, where you could make a drop or a sling or a slip trap. And catching a rat wasn't like catching a rabbit or a hedgehog. A rat was unclean. Not fit to eat no matter how hungry you were. And he had nothing to catch it with anyway. They had taken away his belt and his shoelaces. Do they think I would kill myself? he wondered.

The real oppression of the cell was that he had no privacy. He couldn't eat or wash or use the toilet hole without someone watching. And he knew why they were watching. Long before, he had seen what happened when they took away the last shred of dignity, the privacy of a person's body. It was enough to break anyone, to make proud men beg and strong women whimper. How could a man resist after he had been stripped naked in front of women and children and strangers? Until Ral had seen it, he didn't believe that even *gaji* would do that to a man.

The interrogation had gone on for hours. He told them nothing.

"Why won't you cooperate with us?" the first interrogator asked.

"I have nothing to say to you."

"Where are you from?"

"Here."

"Here? You have no residence papers for France. There are no records of you living here."

"Then I'm not from here."

"Why did you come to France?"

"For the festival."

"Why did you go to the festival?"

"To see the statue of Sara."

"Who is the woman whose picture we found in your pocket?"

He glared when they asked that question. How could they ask who she was? "Why do you ask me so many questions?"

"To determine the facts of the case."

"When the time comes, I'll tell what needs to be told."

"Did you kill her?"

"In a trial I'll tell about her."

The interrogator shouted: "Your continued silence is placing you in peril!"

"I'm a gypsy," said Ral. "What does it matter what I say?"

"Your race is of no importance. The law is blind to race."

"Yes? Then why are all the accused in this place black or Arab or gypsy?"

"Because those are the elements who commit crimes against society."

Ral laughed. The interrogator watched him for a few minutes more, then left.

The second interrogator came an hour later.

"What do you have to tell us about the crime?" he said.

"What crime?"

"The murder of the woman whose body you were found standing over."

"About that I have nothing to tell you now."

"What do you expect to gain from this silence? We have all the evidence we need. A confession of culpability would be in your favor. To make a clean breast of it would help you."

Ral exploded. "Help me? Help me what? What do you understand? When did *gaji* ever help a gypsy . . . ?" He broke off. What good did it do to tell this *gajo* with his shirt and tie and jacket, a man who never went outside, who sat all day in an office with shades on the windows, who never even pulled the curtains so he could see the sea and the beaches and the trees. What good did it do to tell a man who never wanted to breathe the air or feel the water of a brook or smell the trees and flowers. How could such a man ever understand what it was to be a gypsy? How could a man who spent his life inside know what freedom was?

So he said nothing, and that man too left. Each interrogator tried two more times. Each time he told them nothing. After a day of that they didn't come back.

And so he was left alone, with only the eyes of the guards at the peephole watching him. Almost alone enough to think. He remembered the day at Saintes-Maries, the hours watching the procession, Jill sitting by his side. She was beautiful, like a bird in a cage. So hesitant and shy. And yet she had come back. And he could tell from her voice and her eyes that she was a woman who wanted to feel the wind in her hair and the sun on her skin. She had looked at Ral with eyes that saw a person, not the glances that saw thievery and filth and whatever else it was that *gaji* saw when they looked at a gypsy.

It startled him to realize that he was thinking about a woman. For more than twenty years he had thought about only one woman. At last it was a different woman, and very different thoughts.

He wondered if he would ever see her again.

Jean-Claude was gentle and consoling on the way to the waterfront. He seemed to perceive the depth of Jill's reaction to the sight of the man in the cell, and he found ways to tell her, over and over again, that she had nothing to fear, that the man would not be released, that he would certainly be convicted. The town of Saintes-Maries, Jean-Claude explained, was dependent on tourism. The last thing they would ever want was a reputation for violence among the gypsies at the festival. They would make certain that the man stayed in detention, and then in prison, for a long time. It was even possible that he would be sent to the guillotine.

Jill watched Jean-Claude as he spoke. The crystal-blue eyes were sincere. His voice was gentle. He really cared. She nodded and smiled, and all along she thought of Ral, at the café, outside the church, overlooking the beach. Hints of the sensations she had felt with him came back to her, and she found herself alternately shivering and sweating in the car seat. She thought of Ral in the cell, under those sick fluorescent lights, and that frightening, smoldering gaze.

She had expected that Jean-Claude would own a sleek speedboat, but he led her to a mahogany sloop, about eleven meters long, with teak decks. It wasn't new, but it was beautifully maintained, the bright topsides flawless, as if they had been hand rubbed with a dozen coats of varnish.

"Who takes care of it?" she asked. "It must cost a fortune."

"I do. It's my therapy. When I feel like I have spent too long with books and papers, or when I'm angry because I've made a mistake, I come down here with sandpaper and varnish. An hour later I feel wonderful. Somehow I lose my anger in the wood. I like the smell of sawdust and varnish."

"It's incredibly beautiful, Jean-Claude. I'm almost afraid to get on."

"Don't be silly. *Maudelayne*'s a tough old girl. She's taken me to the Greek islands and back, raced to Corsica and Sardinia more times than I can remember, and never betrayed me. Which is more than I can say about most women."

"*Maudelayne?*" Jill asked. "An old fling or your mother?"

"Chaucer. I studied English literature once, read about the boatman in Chaucer, and liked the name."

"Chaucer! No wonder I was out of my league in those negotiations."

It was a balmy day, a little too warm and humid in Marseilles, but perfect on the water, with just an occasional mist of spray on the decks as the boat knifed through the swells on the reach out to Château d'If and back. Jean-Claude was absorbed at the helm. He talked about racing the boat and sailing through the Greek islands, letting Jill lie on the deck, soaking up the sun and the air. It amazed her that he was able to handle the boat by himself. When she watched him hoisting a sail, he asked if she wanted to help, and he showed her how to tail a line as it came off a winch, and later, how to grind in the big genoa jib when they were hard on the wind. But he was independent, sailing in silence much of the afternoon. It was as though he understood that she too needed the silence and the sun.

The gentle movements of the boat over the swells made her sleepy, and the balmy air was too warm for thinking. She watched his eyes take in her long body in the bikini. He was lean too, with nearly flawless suntanned skin. Beautiful people, she thought. Magazine people. Not the kind of people who think about murders. Not the sort of people who are supposed to be infatuated by the eyes and hair and voice of a gypsy man.

It was late afternoon when they tied the boat up stern-to at the yacht basin. He had sailed right into the basin, dropping first the jib, then the main, furling them neatly before he finally turned on the engine to back up to the quay.

"I bore everyone with the boat," he said, "but without it I would be intolerable. The sea and the wind can humble a man."

"I loved it," she said. "I came here to get away from everyone and everything. The boat was perfect."

They stopped at the Café New York, on the quay, for a drink, sitting and watching the parade of fishermen and yachts and tourists from the ferries coming in. The drinks were followed by plates of *coquillages*—mussels, clams, tiny shrimp, periwinkles, oysters—then by plates of raw octopus and conch sprinkled with lime juice. Before long, the waiters were bringing a full-fledged, sumptuous bouillabaisse dinner.

It was hard not to enjoy watching Jean-Claude eat. He showed her how to pick the meat out of the tiny periwinkles with a toothpick. When she started to use a fork on an oyster, he laughed, then demonstrated how to swallow it like wine, to savor the texture as well as the taste. He taught her how to stir the *rouille* into the bouillabaisse broth to make the soup fiery. There was a natural eroticism in the way he ate, enjoying the food and wine without affectation about the label or the bouquet. Yet there was no trace of the rude peasant in his manners. He was simply a man without self-consciousness, for whom food and drink were genuine pleasures. It made her realize that the elegant clothes and fancy car that she had thought affectations were actually there to enjoy, not to impress. He seemed to know and like who he was, to be comfortable about where he was and what he did, about the whole package of choices that made up a life. She envied his easy hedonism.

"You seem much more relaxed now," he said. "A sail and a dinner can do that. Would you like coffee here, or perhaps at the villa? The sky there should be alive with stars tonight."

She glanced up at the sky. The sunset was red and orange from a pale haze of pollution. She hadn't really heard a word he said. Her mind was a world away. She had been aware of something troubling her all afternoon, a thought that was just below the level of consciousness.

"How will he ever get a fair trial?" she asked. The question came out very suddenly.

It took Jean-Claude a moment to focus. Then his face lengthened and his blue eyes drooped. "You're still troubled about that man?" His hand reached out, stroking hers. "You must believe me, Jill. You needn't worry. You will never see him again."

She didn't pull her hand away. "Jean-Claude, I'm not worried about myself. I'm worried about him. I'm worried about whether he'll get a fair trial. I don't think he's the kind of man who could have murdered a woman." She described their meetings, at the café and the church and the sea. All the facts went into her descriptions, along with some of Ral's words. She said nothing about her reactions, or the irresistible pull that had drawn her back to see Ral again.

"He sounds like an interesting man. A genuine vagabond, the sort of man that our hippies of today would like to imitate."

"Exactly. And I don't think he could have killed anyone."

"Jill, you're a clever lawyer. And a very intelligent woman. But I think you're being utterly naive. You see a *gitane* in a café, talk with him for a few minutes outside the church during the festival, and on that basis you decide that he's not the kind of man who could murder—despite the fact that he was found at the side of the murdered woman, with a photograph of her in his pocket. Surely you realize that the *gitanes* are never what they seem."

He stroked her fingers again. She started to answer, then stopped, pulling her hand away.

"None of that matters, Jean-Claude. And it doesn't really matter whether he murdered the woman or not. I want to know how he is ever going to get a fair trial. Who's going to defend him? He has no home, no money, no idea how to find his way through a criminal defense. His French is no better than mine. How can he ever get a fair trial?"

She felt her voice breaking. That hadn't happened before. She was acutely aware of how much the argument mattered, and noticed that Jean-Claude had caught the break in her voice.

"A fair trial? Fair isn't a notion that we use in our criminal proceedings. Our sole concern is the Truth. Once the court finds the Truth, it can be assured that the guilty will be convicted and that the innocent will go free."

"Jean-Claude—"

He waved away the interruption with his palm. "I'm quite sincere, Jill. I want you to understand that there is a method in what you perhaps perceive as the madness of our procedures—including the forty-eight hours of detention that you seem to think so vicious. The police need to be able to question the accused before his colleagues and accomplices cover up the relevant evidence. Once the evidence is gone, there is no chance at the Truth. That, you see, is the real difference. Your courts want a verdict, a decision. They let the two lawyers duel on the field of justice: the verdict goes to the winner. In our trials, we have no such verdict. We seek only the Truth. If the Truth shows that the police were right to charge the accused, he is condemned. If the Truth shows that they were wrong to charge the accused, he is set free."

"You actually believe that—the search for the Truth, with a capital T?"

"Remember, Jill, this is France. Frenchmen like to think they invented liberty and the rights of man."

She threw her head back, running her fingers through her hair, shaking the mane. When she looked at Jean-Claude again, she questioned with her eyes, not at all sure what to make of the man. Was he playing with her?

"I've seen what happens to defendants in his situation in the States," she said. "Unless he's represented—and I mean really represented, not just by some flunky who comes in and answers the appearances in court—the defendant doesn't stand a chance. I spent a couple of years at Legal Aid watching the prosecutors and courts make mincemeat of defendants."

"Were they innocent?"

"Some were."

"How did you know that? How did you know the Truth about what happened?"

"I—" She stopped. "Intuition. The same intuition that tells me that man didn't kill the woman."

Jean-Claude nodded, sipping his wine.

"What will happen to him, Jean-Claude?"

"I, we, don't really know much about him. He was found at the scene of the crime. It appears that it was a rather brutal murder, one which required the strength of a man. He had a photograph of the murdered woman in his pocket. And earlier in the day he was in Saintes-Maries and told you, a total stranger, that he was looking for someone. Did he say then that it was a woman he was looking for?"

She hesitated. "Yes."

"Did he say why he was looking for her?"

Jill remembered her astonishing jealousy when Ral had mentioned the woman. "No. We hardly talked. He told me he was a gypsy. And that he was looking for a woman. Actually, he wouldn't have told me about her except that I saw him scrutinizing the crowds."

"If he really was searching for her, for the woman, it would appear to be a very simple case. It wouldn't surprise me if the police were able to complete their investigation quickly."

"Will he be tried soon?"

"Not unless he requests an expedited trial. And that would obviously not be in his interest. Your American procedure calls for a speedy trial, lest an innocent man be held too long in jeopardy. It is a precept of our system that the trial must not be hasty, that there must be enough time to find the Truth—for all the facts and witnesses to surface."

Jill had started to relax, lulled by the wine. Jean-Claude's words shook her awake.

"Surface? You say it as though they'll just bob up. There won't be any facts or witnesses for his side unless he has someone to find them. The police will go to their usual informers, and then get some experts like that Leclerc. How is Ral supposed to answer all of that?"

"The usual 'answer' of the accused would be a confession and a plea for the mercy of the court."

"In other words, they interrogate him until he confesses. It really is 'Guilty until proved innocent,' isn't it?"

"Not really. An individual isn't brought to trial unless the police case is so compelling that there's strong reason to believe in the guilt of the accused. And even then, the court conducts a full inquiry."

"You can describe it any way you want, Jean-Claude. It comes out the same. A poor gypsy like Ral doesn't stand a chance. They might as well take him to the guillotine now and save their time and energy."

They had been at the table for hours. Bottle after bottle of wine appeared and disappeared. Finally a cart of desserts appeared. Jean-Claude took both fruit and pastries, and Jill found herself angry that he could be so sanguine while they talked about the possibility of a man—Ral—going to the guillotine.

"Do you still have the same passionate interest in criminal cases in New York?" Jean-Claude asked.

"I haven't handled a criminal case for a long time. Over four years, if you count the time I spent with the task force on art thefts. We spent most of our time looking at museums and museum procedures. The crime was embezzling, not armed robbery. And even when I did do criminal cases, I met the defendants after they were already arrested.

It's different when you meet a defendant before the crime is supposed to have happened."

"And the accused in New York wouldn't be a gypsy with dark romantic eyes and a flashing smile."

She took a moment to answer. She knew that what Jean-Claude said was true, but she couldn't sort it out yet, couldn't separate her feelings for Ral from the argumentative position she had taken.

"Now it's 'dark romantic eyes and a flashing smile'? At the Maison d'Arrêt you described his appearance as manic! Even a gypsy deserves a decent defense. Where is he supposed to find a lawyer?"

"The man is accused of murder, possibly rape as well, and you're worried about his fate, about whether he can find an *avocat* to represent him. You're an extraordinary woman, Jill. A woman of unending surprise. I like that."

"I'm dead serious, Jean-Claude."

"I know you are. That's what delights me." He was slightly tipsy, his speech still precise and musical, but slower, the lilting accent not as controlled. "Who will defend him? you ask. Who would want such a brief? There's scant chance for more than a plea for mitigation of sentence—the usual dreary, routine plea for mercy that is so trite and so practiced that no one hears the words of the *avocat*. Who would want to make such a plea? In France an *avocat* takes a case for money or glory. And this case offers neither."

Jill saw that Jean-Claude was watching her expression carefully, as if he expected helplessness.

"Isn't there something like a public defender or legal aid?" she asked.

"Legal aid? You mean lovely women lawyers like you who take on lost causes? We have only the *avocat d'office*, usually an inexperienced younger man, or a hapless older man who didn't find his way in the system. In any case, it is a last resort. Such a defense hardly matters. You forget, Jill, that we don't have an adversarial system. We trust the wisdom of the court to protect the innocent."

She didn't want to, but she exploded.

"That's just not true, Jean-Claude! You say it isn't adversarial in your courts, but it is. We have a shootout, one side versus the other, but at least they have equal weapons. Here it's the court versus the accused. The court has the police and the medical examiners and the prosecutor and society all on their side. The accused is alone. I think the model isn't even the Inquisition. It's throwing the gladiator in with the lions. I guess that's why the Romans built so many amphitheaters around here. They found a ready audience for cruel spectacles."

"You haven't mentioned bullfights, Jill. We have them, too."

"It doesn't surprise me." Her own anger did surprise her.

"It really matters to you," he said. "And if I ask you why, you'll tell me you don't know, or you'll say 'Intuition.' Shall we say 'A woman's fancy is her prerogative'?"

She started to jump at the statement, but he cut her off with a tip of his wineglass. His eyes twinkled in the light reflected from the pale wine.

"You're a glorious woman, Jill. If it would please you, I shall take the brief."

She stared at him, unsure of his words. "You would take the brief? Defend him?"

"It's a terrible brief, and I'll undoubtedly provide some great laughs for my colleagues at the bar, but . . ."

Jill poured herself a glass of wine. "Why?" she asked. Then, before Jean-Claude could answer, she put her arms around his neck and kissed him on the lips. She heard laughter and his name from a table across the café.

The whitewashed walls of Jean-Claude's villa were luminescent in the moonlight. The quarry tile floors were cool. The rooms were huge, separated by archways, furnished with dark provincial antiques and fine carpets. The paintings on the walls were good, if not quite museum-quality, post-impressionists. The view from the terrace extended down over olive groves to the river valley below.

"You live well," Jill said. She was thinking of Ral and the sickly green fluorescent light in his cell.

"Yes, I do." Jean-Claude looked down from the terrace, over the hills. "Everyone feels at home on some spot of the earth, one place that has a special, private beauty. I'm fortunate enough to live on the one spot I think is the most perfect."

It wasn't easy for Jill to understand the simplicity of Jean-Claude's attitude. He seemed neither proud nor ashamed of his wealth, treating it not as a measure of his self-worth or emotional security, but as a privilege that he accepted and enjoyed, the way one would enjoy a beautiful sky or the breeze on an afternoon's sail. He was so different from the men she knew in New York, for whom what you could do with money was less important than the sheer achievement of making it and the prestige of having it.

"Why did you agree to take that case?" she asked.

"For you."

The answer made her angry. It seemed hollow, trite. "Because you bested me in those negotiations this morning? Feeling guilty, is that it?" She was tempted to say that she had been preoccupied, that few had ever gotten so much so easily from her.

"Not at all," he answered. His eyes stayed on the valley below. "Before this, before the villa and the Maserati and all the rest, I was a poor boy in Marseilles. My father owned a shop down by the harbor. He sold fittings for boats to the fishermen. I couldn't wait to leave. I wanted to go to Paris, to get away from the sleepy city that was always, in my mind, number two. And so I set off, like Marius."

"Marius?"

"He's the hero of a movie, really of three movies, about a family in Marseilles. I think your movie *Fanny* is the same story, but with songs—about a young man who must choose between his love for a girl and his longing to go away. He says '*Partir . . . n'importe où, mais très loin. Partir.*' And everyone from Marseilles understands. It's a dream that won't go away, to see the world, to escape.

"Well, I did escape, not to go to sea, but to Paris, and the university, and I thought I would stay in Paris, or travel the world. But I came back, because nowhere else felt like home. When I came back, as an *avocat*, I knew only the waterfront, where I had grown up. So I defended thugs and common criminals, robbers, murderers. I knew the city, knew life, knew the whole world down there. And it made me a good lawyer. I could understand what men were saying when they tried to explain what they had done and why. I did well with some clients, and my name was in the newspapers, and soon I had clients who could afford to pay me, and before long I no longer had to defend thugs and robbers. My hands were clean. That gypsy is not an appealing man, at least not to me. But you were right before: someone has to defend him, if not for his sake, then for the sake of the law. And so, I guess I will take the brief because a man like that reminds me that Marseilles is my home."

Jill looked at Jean-Claude as though she had never really seen him before. "I'm sure Ral will be happy to hear that you've agreed to take his brief."

"Will he?"

"What do you mean?"

"It wouldn't surprise me if the gypsy was hostile. He may refuse to be represented."

The idea had never occurred to her. Why would anyone refuse the services of a good lawyer? "What will you do?"

"If he refuses to have me represent him? What can I do?"

"I mean on the case. How will you handle it?"

"Jill—there's nothing I can do until the charges are clear and we know at least the extent of the evidence that the police have. When they finish their preliminary investigation, I'll go talk to him, if he'll talk to me. The *commissaire* said he was totally recalcitrant, which doesn't surprise me. Gypsies are strong-headed people."

"What if he refuses to talk to you?"

"If he refuses counsel, there is little anyone can do for the *malheureux*."

"I think he'd talk to me," she said.

Jean-Claude's grin seemed patronizing. "Jill, aren't you taking this too far? I doubt that the *commissaire* will indulge your interest, even if he was rather taken with your charms. It's a police matter now, and a grave one at that."

"But if I were assisting you on the case . . . ?"

"Assisting me?"

"I'm a pretty good criminal lawyer, Jean-Claude. And a damn good researcher. In a week I could do a lot of research."

"A week? I thought you had only a day or two."

"I did. But I'm almost embarrassed to go home with that lousy agreement on the Motte estate. Millman will probably scream like crazy, but I left things pretty orderly, and with a good long call every day I could keep the lid on. The whole case is fascinating to me. It would give me a chance to brush up on French procedures. And if I did the footwork and research, it would save you time on the case."

"It would indeed. And how will we spend the time I'll save?"

"That, Jean-Claude, is subject to negotiation."

The evening was like a movie. The moonlight on the tile floors, the shimmering iridescence of the olive leaves in the groves below the villa, the silhouette of the hills framed by the arches of the terrace—it could have been a movie set, but Jean-Claude was so unassuming, so relaxed with those props, that Jill found herself swept along. It was as easy as listening to a ballad.

There were no awkward lulls in the conversation, no wasted efforts at synchronizing signals. After coffee they walked around the terrace, looking at the hills, saying nothing. Tall shuttered French doors led from the terrace into a high-ceilinged bedroom with whitewashed walls and exposed hewed beams. The room was another set for the same movie.

Jean-Claude made love with effortless gusto, the way he sailed the boat and drank wine. He blanketed her with tiny kisses, discovering corners of her body—her knees, her wrists, her ankles, the insides of her elbows—that had always been strangely private, virginal even. He was like a musician rediscovering a long-lost Stradivarius, evoking tingling resonances, playing each passage over and over for the sheer pleasure. She was enraptured.

And yet she felt a strange detachment, an awareness of his every move, as if she were watching a play, appreciating the polish and style of a great performance without being engaged. Every move was tender and gentle, but she appreciated it all from a distance, as if from the audience.

Let go! she told herself. Feel! She waited for her body to respond, for the hints of those rhythms she couldn't control. She kissed the soft skin of his neck, but her responses felt stiff and mechanical. She wondered if he could sense her distance and awkwardness.

She tried letting her fingers play on his shoulders and back, marveling at the silkiness of his skin, the smooth modulation of his muscles. Her fingertips just grazed his skin and she watched his eyes, trying to see beyond the crystal blue. He smiled and nuzzled her. She had to concentrate to keep herself in a haze of tenuous arousal, avoiding his eyes, pulling back into herself until she was no longer aware of the sounds or movements of his body.

She shut her eyes, digging her fingers into his back, fighting the independent will of her body. She felt her hips rising to meet him, her arms and legs enveloping him. For a moment her mind went blank. She stopped thinking, stopped watching herself from outside. She forgot where she was, who she was, everything. Her body finally had a life of its own, rhythms that moved without her will, responses that came from within. How long would it last? she wondered.

Then, suddenly, everything was clear. She saw dark, steady eyes, unblinking as they looked into her own. She felt thick hair against her face, coppery skin against her body. The eyes and the skin and the hair and the strong arms enveloped her, sweeping away every other sound and sight and smell and sensation, and her body opened, yielding with a shudder that surged from deep inside her, from a core that she had never really known before. She let herself ride with it, savoring the release, closing out the world until she was alone with those eyes and the hair and the feel of that coppery skin, until all she could hear was her own breathing and the pounding of her heart.

When she opened her eyes, she had no idea how long she had been lying there. Her skin was wet with sweat, suddenly cold. She felt tender hands tuck a sheet around her. Lips brushed against her cheek. She glimpsed Jean-Claude's gentle smile. Then, mercifully, she fell asleep.

When the forty-eight hours allowed for preliminary interrogation expired, Ral was summoned before a magistrate. The magistrate sat on an elevated dais. Ral was brought in in chains, with two police guards. A clerk sat at a small table, writing down everything that was said. There were no lawyers there.

"Your name?" asked the magistrate.

How many times did they have to ask? It was easier to answer than to fight them.

"Age?"

He wanted to say "I was born the year that we sold the three stallions." What good did it do? A *gajo* would never understand.

"Permanent address?"

Ral said nothing.

"Where do you live?"

Ral looked around the room.

"Please answer the question."

"Now, I live here."

"You have no permanent address? Are you a gypsy?" The tone was familiar.

"Yes."

"Les Baumettes," said the magistrate.

The arraignment was over.

Les Baumettes resembled a fortress more than a prison. Behind the tall outer wall, there were three long buildings, one each for men, women, and minors. The only windows in the buildings were high clerestory slits, and they, like the walls of the buildings, were so covered with industrial grime that little sunlight was admitted to the cells. Between the buildings there were runs for dogs. The dogs were trained to attack first, then bark.

At the visitor's gate the guards had been told that Jill was coming.

"Are you a friend of the *commissaire* or of Maître Bernard?" one guard asked. From his glance, it was clear what he meant by "friend."

A matron searched her behind a screen, first looking through her bag, then eyeing her, as if to ask why a woman like Jill had come to see a prisoner in Les Baumettes.

"With clothes like that, there isn't much you could hide," said the matron. "It isn't good for the inmates, you know. Gives them impulses that they can't do anything about."

Jill looked down at her clothes—slacks, a shirt, the blazer that she wore almost as a uniform.

She was shown to a waiting room, behind a glass screen. The green-hued fluorescent lights made her skin look sickly, and she was reluctant to sit down on the broken and soiled plastic chairs. She had brought a spiral-bound notebook, the same kind she usually carried to depositions, and which years before she had taken to trials and preliminary hearings. She always took her own notes, so that afterward she would have not only the original transcript, but personal observations on how the subject had responded to questions. Reading over her notes, noting reactions that weren't even hinted at in the transcripts, told her how to plan future strategies.

Ral was brought into the adjoining room by two guards. He was wearing a prison tunic and his hair had been cut short. It took him a moment to see her through the wired glass. By then the reactions she anticipated had already come back, tempered this time by familiarity, but still strong and strange and incomprehensible. She wondered if her face was flushed, whether he could see her goosebumps.

Ral smiled when he recognized her. "So, you've found something interesting for today?"

His voice was distorted by the nasal buzz of the hygiaphone, the electronic intercom that connected the two sides of the glass partition.

"Very interesting," she said. She had a whole list of questions that she had prepared, but found herself instead wanting to ask the same questions that had flooded her mind when she first saw him. Who are you? Why do I react this way to you? And then she thought of the night before, in bed.

The questions wouldn't come out. Instead she spoke formally, explaining that Jean-Claude Bernard, a highly respected *avocat*, had agreed to take Ral's brief, and that she was going to assist Maître Bernard with the case.

"Why does he do this?" Ral asked. "What is it to him?"

"He's a famous *avocat*, Ral. You're very fortunate that he's taking the brief."

"Am I?" He looked at the bored guards standing behind him. When he turned back to Jill, his eyes were soft.

"This is no business for you, Jill. Or for the famous *avocat*."

"Ral! You've been charged with murder. There might be other charges. The police will have a strong case against you."

"I'll be tried. That's my right. They must give me a trial."

"Ral, a trial means nothing here. By the time they bring you to trial they'll have so much evidence against you that there won't be anything at all you can do. Maître Bernard knows the law, he knows the courts. He can plead your case for you. And I'm going to make sure he has all the evidence he needs. That's why I'm here." When she saw Ral's eyes on her fingers, she hesitantly pulled them back from the wired glass.

"Jill, you shouldn't come here. There's nothing I can tell you. Maybe someday . . ."

She waited for him to go on, but he said no more.

"Ral, we need to know everything that happened."

"Why?"

"To help you."

"Help me? This *avocat* knows nothing of me. Why would he help me?"

"I asked him to. He's a friend." She could feel Ral's eyes intensely.

"Yes? A friend? And why do you get your friend to help me?"

"Because I . . ." She searched for a word. "Because I care." *Care* wasn't exactly the word she wanted. It was too neutral, too impersonal.

"Care? About a stranger?"

"You're not a stranger."

"No."

It took her a moment to realize that his abrupt answer wasn't a question. She wasn't sure what to say, but the silence made her talk, made her ramble on with a long, gangly speech that sounded insipid even to her own ears. She heard herself telling him that she believed in the rights of the accused, that every man deserved a fair trial, that she didn't like to see someone—anyone—railroaded by the police and the courts. She believed every word of it. But it wasn't what she really wanted to say.

"All because I'm a gypsy?"

"Because I met you. And liked you. Call it fate."

"Fate?" There was a tinge of disgust in his voice. "I have nothing to tell you," he said.

"Ral—I need to know what you were doing at the scene of . . . where that woman was found." She looked around, as if to make sure they were alone. "I need to know whether you knew her and what happened between you. I need to know . . . you, Ral."

He didn't answer.

"You have to help us, Ral. We need to know who you are, why you were in Saintes-Maries, whom you were looking for, everything. If you won't tell me what we need to know, we can't help you."

"I don't want any help," he said.

When he saw the hurt in her eyes, he added, "This is no business for you, Jill. There's nothing you can do."

A bell rang. One of the guards pointed at the clock.

"I'll be back tomorrow," she said. Her fingers were spread out on the wired glass, as if she could touch him.

On the second visit Jill was more forceful.

"Ral, the police commissioner said that you won't admit or deny the murder. Why? Why won't you deny it? I don't believe that you could have killed that woman. You're too gentle. Why won't you tell them that you didn't kill her? Why won't you just say no? Or even yes?"

Ral's laugh was loud enough to be heard through the glass, to overpower the wretched acoustics of the hygiaphone.

"No or yes. That's the way a *gajo* thinks. For the *gajo* it's always one or the other. When a *gajo* goes to the fortune teller and she sees something in the future, or calls up something from the past that she couldn't have known, the *gajo* always asks, 'Is it a trick? Or does she really have powers?' Always one or the other. If a *gajo* hears that a gypsy has made a curse on someone and that person has then become ill, the *gajo* asks, 'Did the curse really do it?' Always yes or no. Did I murder the woman or not. For me the world is not this yes or no."

"I'm trying to understand that. I want to know how you think, how you see the world. But for the court it is yes or no. Guilty or not. That's what they decide."

"Jill—it's always easy for the *gajo* to decide, especially when it's the fate of a gypsy that they are deciding."

"Ral, don't!" She caught her anger, fought it down. "You were in Saintes-Maries, looking for someone. A woman. You were found near the body. You won't deny the murder. Unless you say something, they have all they need right there. Tell me, what's so wonderful about the guillotine? Is it really worth this pigheaded silence of yours?"

"I've made you angry, Jill? I'm sorry. But there's nothing I can tell you. When the time comes I'll say what I must say. Everyone can hear it then. But not now."

"Ral, I'm on your side. I care. The Maître is willing to argue your case. But without something to go on there's nothing we can do. We need to know your version of what happened. We need to know about you."

"What is there to know? What more is there to say? I'm a gypsy. *Zigeuner, gitane,* gypsy—it means the same thing everywhere. It always has. What do they care? The court hears that and their decision is made."

"My God! You won't trust anyone, will you?"

"Why should I? I've trusted *gaji* before . . ."

"What happens to you matters to me."

"I believe that," he said.

She waited, but he would say no more.

She came each day at the same time. The visiting hour was two o'clock. She was there by one thirty. The same guards were always at the gate; the same matron looked her over, usually with some comment that couldn't be answered. And she was shown each day to the same visiting room, with the same sickly green fluorescent light and the same two guards who checked her purse, looking her up and down as if they could see through her clothes. Ral always wore the prison tunic and sat in the same chair, behind the panel of wired glass. The hygiaphone demodulated their voices until it sounded as though they were speaking over a transatlantic cable.

On the third day Ral came into the room smiling.

"Today we talk about you," he said.

"There's no time to talk about me, Ral."

"Time?" He shrugged, his eyes taking in the walls. "Time a man always has. Money, freedom, love, food—maybe not, but there's always time."

"I have to go back to New York soon, Ral. I have to get something down for Maître Bernard before I leave. If you won't tell me anything, he has nothing to build a case on."

"New York? What's it like for you in New York?"

"Ral, please. They only allow me forty-five minutes per day here. We can't spend that time talking about New York."

"How can I talk to you if I don't know you? I don't even know who your people are. I know you're from New York, but I think that's like someone saying they're from Hungary. It's too big a place to be from. There must be a place where you're home, where your people live."

"Where my people live?" She laughed.

"What's so funny, Jill?" He seemed hurt.

"It's not really funny, Ral. It's just that your question is so real. In New York people ask me 'Where do you play tennis?' or 'What movies have you seen?' And then you ask where my people live."

"Well?"

"I don't have people, Ral."

"Everyone has people. That's who you are."

She shrugged.

"Where do you live?"

"On the West Side." To someone in New York it meant something, a different set of signals from saying the East Side or the Village or the Westchester and Connecticut suburbs where so many of her colleagues lived. But it was where she lived, not home. She remembered when she first came to New York and faced the constant question of where she was from. She usually ended up saying "Stanford Law School," which seemed enough for most people. In fact, there was no place that was home. There were places where she slept and ate and worked and traveled. None was home.

"What do you do in New York? What's your life like each day?"

"Ral! We can't talk about my life in New York. This"—her eyes took in the room, the Formica counter and wired glass and green-hued fluorescent lights—"is too important. What happens to you is too important."

"I care about you too, Jill. That's why I want to know about you. About your home, your people."

She knew he wouldn't yield. But what could she answer? What could she say about herself? "Millman, Lord and Perry, litigation department. Youngest partner in the history of the firm. First woman partner." Who cared? Who cared about the lists of fancy clients or the sensational deals she had pulled off since she switched from "doing good" to making money?

She couldn't answer the questions he asked, couldn't tell him what he wanted to hear, about her people, her tribe, where they were from. She hardly knew. She tried to remember her grandfather's stories, the fragments he had told before her mother had cut him off. His stories had always been a bone of contention in the household. When he would start, Jill's mother would overreact, as if any mention of the Old World were taboo.

"Have you ever heard of a town called Bialystok?" she said. "Somewhere in Russia."

"There's a Bialystok in Poland," Ral said.

"Could be. I think it was Russia when my grandfather left. I guess that's where we're from."

"You've been there?"

"No. I don't really know anything about it. My grandfather used to tell stories about Bialystok." She remembered her mother's reaction: "Do we really have to hear more about the glorious old country? If it was so great, why did you come here?"

"Do you remember the stories?"

"Only bits and pieces. I think once when my grandfather was a little boy, the czar came to visit the town in a carriage. They had to line up and wave flags and throw flowers on the road. And he told how when he was a certain age, I guess around twelve or thirteen, his father gave him a little money and told him that there was no place for him there, that he should go. So he left, went to London, and then to New York."

"He sounds like a gypsy," said Ral.

Jill laughed. "No. A Jew." She had never said it before, not that she could remember. It just came out.

"A Jew? I knew a Jew once. He was the only *gajo* I ever really trusted."

"Where is he now?"

Ral shrugged. "Yitzak? Who knows? The last time I saw him was in Trieste. That was a long time ago."

"Do you ever hear from him? Write letters?"

"Gypsies don't write letters. Tell me more of your grandfather's stories. Tell me about your grandfather and Bialystok."

"The only story I remember is that when my mother was a little girl, my grandfather decided to take the whole family back to Europe. They sailed over and spent a week or two in London and Paris. Then, when it was time to go to Bialystok to see my grandfather's family, my mother put up a real row. 'What do you expect me to do, go kiss some old creep with lice in his beard? Is that what I'm supposed to tell people when they ask what we did in Europe?' She put up such a stink that they never even went to Bialystok."

Ral listened with intense concentration. Jill realized that she had never told anyone else about that. It had been an undisturbed memory.

"Actually," she went on, "it wasn't my grandfather who told that story. It was my mother. She really liked that story. Whenever he would try to tell stories about Bialystok, she would tell that story."

"She wouldn't see her own grandfather? And then was proud of it?"

"I don't think she thought of it that way. He was just a picture, an old man with a beard."

"You're close to your mother? You see her often?"

"Not really."

"Your father then?"

"My father's a hard man to get close to. He's very quiet. Around my mother the only choices are keeping silent or screaming louder than she does. I scream back. My father crawls into a shell. What about your mother?" she asked. "Were you close to her?"

"Of course. We were together everyday when we begged. She taught me to recognize the truly rich *gaji* and those who would never give a *groschen* to a poor gypsy. She taught me to tell from the way they walked and the clothes they wore and the cast of their eyes and their smiles. You had to be able to tell, because if you begged from the wrong person, they would call the police and you would end up—" He grinned as he looked around himself.

"This isn't your first time in jail?"

"No. I was many times in jail. But usually not like this. And I didn't have beautiful women to come to visit me. In Vienna they didn't have enough jails, so they would put us with the thieves and murderers. The other prisoners would bang their cups on the bars and complain that they didn't want to be in a cell with a gypsy. So after a day they would let us go."

Jill's laugh was interrupted by the buzzer. She had time for one more quick question: "Tell me, Ral, which kind of *gaje* am I? From everything you learned from your mother."

"You?" He half raised himself from his chair, as if he could see more of her than the head and shoulders that showed through the wired glass. "You seem more like the fancy people in big open cars who drove by and didn't even see the gypsies that they splashed with mud. I mean no insult, Jill, but it is because of this that I still don't understand why you come back again and again to see me."

"Maybe I don't understand either. I just know that I'll be here tomorrow."

There were four more tomorrows. Each day Ral told her more stories of his youth, of their adventures on the roads and in the cities. His stories all stopped when he was still only a boy. During the fifth visit Jill began to press him.

"Ral, what happened after all of that? What happened during the war?"

He looked at her as though the question were either insane or impertinent.

"Why won't you trust me, Ral? Because I'm a *gaje*? Are you that pigheaded?"

He wouldn't answer. After the sixth visit she still had written nothing in her notebook.

There was no single moment when Jill realized that her relationship with Jean-Claude had changed. There was never a discussion, never an acknowledgment to punctuate the change. But although he called and took her to lunch and sometimes to dinner, and invited her to parties and a gallery opening and out on the boat again, the relationship had become flat and mechanical. Jean-Claude seemed to accept that Ral's case was truly a spider on Jill's ceiling, an obsession that had to run its course. He never questioned when she said that she couldn't make dinner because she would be in the library, or couldn't make lunch because of visiting hours at Les Baumettes. He remained polite and solicitous to a fault, his compliments still generous, his smile still guileless, his accent still charming. When she looked at him and listened to that wonderful singsong voice, she couldn't help thinking of the fairy-tale figure of Prince Charming.

But the romance was gone. Whenever they were close enough for intimacy to threaten, Jill would remember the night they had made love, and the memory of what had happened left her terrified. She would back away, sometimes with an excuse, sometimes with just a gesture. And somehow Jean-Claude seemed to understand. He never asked for an explanation.

The extra week that Sidney Millman had been so gracious about was fast disappearing. Before she spoke to Millman, she had thought of trying to take the week as pro bono legal work instead of personal days. But she had only to imagine Millman's reaction to discard the idea. To plunge into the criminal case of a gypsy being held for a murder in a small town in southern France was so outrageous and exotic, so distant from the daily tribulations of Millman, Lord & Perry, that she ran the risk of having her sanity questioned even for asking. A request for an unscheduled week of holiday, even after three years at the firm, was enough to make some of the partners question what they would call her "commitment." But she had known she could get away with it, if only because the firm needed a woman around, especially someone who worked the hours she did and turned over enough volume to pay her way and then some.

It was Friday, and she had only one more visit scheduled with Ral, when Jean-Claude told her that the police had succeeded in tracking down the name and domicile of the murdered woman.

"Well?"

"It's not good news, Jill. At least not for our gypsy. The woman was a pensioner, living in Amsterdam. She lived alone, spent her days in a library. This holiday trip to Saintes-Maries was only the second time in seven years that she had left Amsterdam."

Jill wasn't sure how to react. "Is that all they found out? Maybe there's something we don't know?"

"Did something he told you suggest that?"

"Not really."

"What has he told you?"

"Very little."

"Very little?" repeated Jean-Claude. "Such as?"

She walked across the terrace, looking out at the hills and the olive groves.

"All he's told me are stories about his life twenty-five years ago. Whenever I try to turn the conversation to what happened in Saintes-Maries, he refuses to talk anymore. It's always the same answer: 'When the time comes, I'll tell what must be told.' Sometimes I feel like I'm getting to know him, but then he'll say that again, or he says, 'Jill, this is no business for you.' And then I realize that I'm not getting through to him at all."

"I'm not surprised. I never expected that he would be an easy client."

"What do you do when your own client refuses to talk to you?" she asked.

"I've had clients who weren't honest with me. Sometimes they were afraid if they told me the truth I would no longer represent them."

"You mean they were guilty and wouldn't admit it?"

"Not always. Guilt is something the court decides. We were talking about truth. There have been times when a truth that I thought I needed to know went too deep, asked too much. The relationship of the client and *avocat* is unequal, humiliating to the client. The client is expected to bare all, to put his affairs or even his fate in the hands of the *avocat*. And all that the *avocat* ever must reveal is the amount of his bill."

Jill thought of how much she had told Ral. And how little he had told her. The relationship was strangely inverted, and it made her question her own skills, the skills of which she had always been so sure.

"We need his story, Jean-Claude."

"I'm not sure his story will matter in the end."

"What do you mean?"

"I just found out today that the police in Amsterdam spoke with the concierge of the building where the woman lived. She told them that a day after the woman left for her holiday, a man came to the building, looking for the woman. The concierge described him as having dark hair and mysterious eyes. 'Like a gypsy,' she said. Those are her own words. She also said that he showed her an old photograph of the woman. From her description, it sounds like the photograph the police found on Ral. The Dutch police are going to have the woman examine photographs. If she identifies Ral, it will make for a strong case of premeditation."

"Coincidence doesn't make a motive."

"Jill, it won't help anyone for you to be unrealistic. He was found standing over that woman's body. He had a picture of her in his pocket. And it appears that he was recently in Amsterdam looking for the woman. The public minister doesn't need a great deal more evidence to build a case."

"If it's all that clear-cut. I suspect there's a lot more here than a simple question of guilt or innocence."

"For the court it must always be a simple matter."

"What if there's something we just don't know?"

"Jill, you're too good a lawyer to put your faith in the great unknown. When the deck has been dealt as it is, with the winning cards all in the hand of the public minister, I don't think we can be at all optimistic. After this revelation, I'm not even certain about our chances for a plea of mercy or mitigation of sentence."

"What if I confront Ral tomorrow and he decides to explain it all to me?"

"Unfortunately it may be quite a while before either of us can confront him. In French law the identification of the victim changes the charges against the accused. It is no longer 'possible homicide' or 'suspicion of homicide.' Ral will be charged with 'premeditated homicide.' And when he's arraigned before a new magistrate, his visiting hours will be rescheduled to once per week."

"Once a week?"

"The *juge d'instruction* will examine him twice a week. The discovery of the truth is a long, slow process."

"And his own lawyer gets once a week? How can you build a case for him if you can only see him once a week?"

"You've seen him five—or is it six?—times and he's told you nothing. I've been assured, off the record, as you say, that he's also told the examining magistrate nothing. In view of this intractable silence, what would be the point of more frequent sessions? Wouldn't it only prove frustrating for all concerned?"

"The point, Jean-Claude, is that I don't think Ral killed that woman. Call it intuition if you want, even call it a woman's intuition. But something tells me that he didn't do it. And something also tells me that everyone, including you, has already decided that he's going to the guillotine, or if he's lucky, to prison for the rest of his life."

Jean-Claude watched Jill's face. "I'm sorry, Jill. I know how much this matters to you. But I'd do you and especially Ral a disservice if I weren't candid. At this point I can only say that I'm not optimistic. He refuses to cooperate with anyone. He won't deny the crime. He's given us nothing to go on. And he's a gypsy, being tried in a French court that from long experience is wary of gypsies and what they consider gypsy antics."

"He could still be innocent."

"Indeed he could. And it's my duty, as an *avocat*, to proceed as though he were. But I remember an expression I heard once from an American lawyer. He said: 'Never go up against Mother or Baseball or Apple Pie.' When he explained what it meant, I agreed fully. It's difficult for a court to rule against the sacred. And that, even more than Ral's silence, is our problem now. We're in the unfortunate position of being up against an innocent old lady who happens to be dead."

PART

II

Prague, 1945

The woman had never been there before, but Prague seemed familiar, like a German city. There was a comfort in the gray stone of the big buildings, the mustard-colored stucco of the blocks of flats, the worn cobbles of the streets, even the frilly architectural details of the nineteenth-century buildings that all seemed to house insurance companies. And unlike the cities in Germany, Prague had suffered almost no bombing damage. There was no debris, no rubble in the streets. The only signs of fighting were pockmarks in some of the buildings, souvenirs of small-arms fire from the desperate street fighting at the end. Except for the horse-drawn wagons which outnumbered motorcars in the streets, and the ragged clothing of people who waited in food lines, the war seemed far away.

She had to ask directions three times. Each time she noticed how people hesitated when they heard her German. Everyone in Prague knew German, but Czech had become an identity badge; anyone who didn't speak Czech was suspect. So she would smile and apologize when she asked directions in German, and with her lowered eyes and her stooped posture, and her heavy coat and sturdy shoes, she seemed so unthreatening that people would finally help, directing her along the tangled streets until she came to Kubélikova, a quiet residential street in the Fourth District. The street was lined with stucco apartment houses, four stories each. Number 29 was a pale mustard color, the paint chipped and peeling. Drapes were pulled over most of the windows.

The dim stairway reeked of cooked cabbage. At the third-floor landing she paused to smooth her hair. She wondered how she looked. Her woolen coat was shabby, too warm for the unusually mild fall day. Her shoes were good leather, with serviceable soles, but matronly for a woman in her early thirties, more service-issue than stylish. The clothes made her feel like a crone of sixty. She had argued when they gave her the coat and shoes, and she argued again when they told her what to wear, suggesting the dowdy scarf and skirt and blouse. But they had been insistent, saying that in a time of misunderstandings it was important to dress appropriately.

She knocked.

"*Ja?*" The man's voice was high-pitched.

"I have an appointment," she said.

"From . . . . ?"

"Neue Deutschland." New Germany. She felt uncomfortable with what sounded so much like a password.

The man who opened the door was thin and ascetic looking. He wore a vest, a collarless shirt, heavy woolen trousers with braces, and half-glasses that slid down his nose. He had thinning hair and a pinched and meager face. He looked her up and down before he opened the door wide enough to let her in.

"Sit down," he said. "I'll make tea."

The room was compact: a daybed, a small table with two chairs, another table with a hotplate and a breadbox. A curtain ran down the center. She had heard of that before, the crowded wartime living conditions that meant two families in a single, shared room.

The man saw her trying to peek through the slit in the overlapped curtains.

"My laboratory," he said. "Come, there's no secret."

Behind the curtain there was a drafting table with a T-square and a row of steel pens, a camera and lights on a stand, a hand-operated printing press, and a small table with trays and chemicals. The window had a heavy black curtain fastened over the sides with battens and tacks.

He let her finish looking before he served the tea in glasses on saucers. "There's no sugar. I'm sorry."

"This is fine." She sat stiffly on a straight-backed chair.

"So. Tell me what you need."

"Papers."

"Papers? Of course!" The man allowed himself a pinched smile. "It's the age of papers, isn't it, Fräulein? Everyone needs papers. Peace, war, republic, protectorate, German occupation, American occupation, Russian occupation—everything changes, but one thing is always the same: papers. First the Germans need papers to flee from the Czechs. Then it was the Jews, fleeing the Germans. Then the maquis, fleeing the Slovaks and the Germans. And now the Germans again, fleeing the Russians. Ironic, isn't it? The pursued are forever becoming the pursuers. And through it all, my business never changes."

"Really?" She wasn't sure what to say.

"Oh, yes. The papers change, but the business is the same. I've made German passports, Italian transit documents, British passports, American visas, once even currency. Can you believe it? With that little laboratory and camera and a lot of patience I made banknotes. Almost any document can be made if you have enough time and patience. It's a good business, you know. A good skill. Any Nazi with a gun could kill people. But in my little laboratory I can *make* people. How many others can say that?"

She squirmed as he spoke, aware of the power he held and the way he was using it, uncomfortable with the relationship of dependence that had already been forged between them.

"I need ordinary Austrian or German papers," she said. "Just a new name. They said you could help me. I have money."

"Of course. A new name. With a new name everything else is forgotten. Records, questions, affiliations . . ." He drew out the last word, baiting or taunting. Or so it seemed to her.

"You don't understand," she said. "It's not that at all. I've done nothing to be ashamed of. I'm not one of those . . . those snivelers who say, 'Well, I was only following orders. Everyone did the same.' I didn't follow orders. I defied them. I helped people, protected them. I saved them."

"Where will you go with a new name?"

She didn't answer. They told her not to say anything that wasn't necessary. Idle words led to more misunderstandings.

"Nowhere? Of course. So you want papers to protect you from those who gave the orders? You're afraid of the Germans, here?"

She put down the tea glass and pulled her coat around herself. The man was supposed to help her. She had gotten his name from Neue Deutschland, a loose organization of former officials, some of them members of the Nazi party—all people who had been in positions that could be misunderstood in the postwar world. The SS had their own organization, ODESSA, but Neue Deutschland was nothing like that. It was just a network of information, advice, and assistance for people who were suddenly vulnerable. The organization was there to fight backlash, the overreaction that would surely come against the one-time conquerors who were now the conquered. She had been skeptical at first, but when she saw the newspaper reports of what the Russians were doing in the East and the Americans in the West, the trials and roundups of former officials, the de-Nazification as they called it, she knew she needed help. And his was the only name they gave her.

"You see the newspapers," she said. "There are misunderstandings. People who weren't there don't know, won't believe what really happened. Identities are confused. Blame is assigned where it doesn't belong."

"Misunderstandings?" He let the word hang as he stared at her face. "Take off the scarf," he said. "Let me see your face." He reached out, tracing her jawline with his fingers, gently stroking her cheek before his fingers traced down her neck. "The coat, too. And stand up. Turn around, let me see you."

Suddenly she had a new fear. Was this the price? They had never mentioned anything like this. And with this horrid, ascetic little man, with his bony, ink-stained fingers . . .

"They said it was all arranged," she said. "There must be some misunderstanding."

"Pull the blouse tight against you. I can't see anything when the blouse is so loose." She hesitated, and he pulled the blouse himself, his fingers grazing her breasts before they slid down to her waist.

"Misunderstanding?" he said. "That's the word, isn't it? Everything is a misunderstanding. Nothing is as it is. You're only about thirty, aren't you? And not a bad-looking woman if you didn't wear those terrible clothes. The figure is nice, too."

She reached for the coat again, twisting away from him.

"Where are you going, Fräulein? There's nothing to fear anymore. No, you'll be a new person. No past except what we make up. No records. No affiliations. The Americans have an expression for it, you know. Clean slate, they call it. Wiped clean. A fresh start."

He picked up a notebook and mumbled to himself while he jotted notes. "Hair, brown . . . eyes, dark . . . height . . . weight . . ."

She sighed, not yet able to smile. Anonymity would be hers. Eva Ritter would be no more. Along with the sigh there was a twinge of regret that she couldn't control. She would lose her past, but she would also lose status, authority, respect, friends. Everything she had done would be gone. Seen that way, anonymity was a huge price to pay. After all, she reminded herself, she had done nothing wrong. She had helped people, protected them, saved them. If only people would understand.

"What kind of name do you want?" the man asked.

Saxony, Occupied Germany, 1945

To Ral, every soldier was a border guard. Yet there were no real borders. The neatly demarcated lines, the rows of marker stones, the fences and plowed strips, were gone now, leveled when the tanks had driven through. The only border was people. You left the khaki uniforms of the Americans, the guards with bright white helmets and belts and leggings and the new cars with real chrome trim, and you were in the Russian zone of crude woolen uniforms, dark green with red stars, and identical heavy trucks that were the only transportation for supplies and people.

Somewhere politicians were drawing lines on maps, and orders were being given to transform those lines into rows of barbed wire and plowed no-man's-lands, with gates on the roads and towers for machine guns and officers with machine pistols to check papers. But for now, to cross from Germany into Czechoslovakia meant only to walk through the devastation of a stretch of woods in Saxony, past the debris of war, a burned-out truck, a tank that had run out of fuel, another that had been abandoned to the scavengers. They were all that the war had left.

Ral saw a rifle in the leaves, thrown down when some soldier decided that his own war was over. He sighted along the barrel. As he expected, it had been spiked, smashed hard enough against a rock or a tree to bend the barrel out of true. It didn't matter. There wouldn't be any bullets anyway, and there were easier ways to catch a rabbit.

He knew he wouldn't starve on the road. There was nothing to compare with what the Americans offered in the DP camp at Weimar, the steam tables and cauldrons and cooks who didn't care how much you took as long as you wore clean clothes, didn't scratch, and kept the line moving. But on the road he wouldn't have to wait in a line, and he wouldn't have the fat sergeant and the ferret-eyed interpreter asking him questions. He could move where he wanted and ask his own questions. It was always easy to find food. He knew how to hustle bread in the villages, and hot meals or fresh fruit at the farmhouses. He knew how to catch rabbits in the woods and how to pick berries in the forest. And on the road he was that much closer to finding her.

Everywhere the roads were overflowing with DPs, crisscrossing Europe like the ragged bands of the crusades, except that the crusaders had a goal; these refugees didn't know where they were going. Most of them fled west, pouring out of Czechoslovakia, Poland, Estonia, Latvia, Lithuania, and the Ukraine toward Germany. Some were lucky enough to hitch a ride on a truck or a horsecart. Most walked, in bands, families, pairs, or alone, dragging what they could with them, afraid of others on the road as much as they were afraid of the soldiers they saw. It was hard to know which soldiers might be friends and which might shoot first, hard to know which papers mattered and which didn't, hard to know what to expect if you didn't have the right papers. And most of the refugees didn't know how to read a road, didn't know that a road only has food for so many. That was part of the reason Ral had gone east after he fled the DP camp. It was against the tides. He also thought that she would be in the East. She was a *gaje*, and *gaji* would always go home.

From the road signs, some in Czech as well as German, he knew he was near the frontier. It had been twenty days since he fled the DP camp, and for those twenty days the soldiers he had seen had been mostly American. He had stayed off the roads, wandering through the woods and small farms, knowing that if he were spotted on the road there might be questions, demands for the papers he didn't have. He decided to wait for nightfall, when the soldiers would be drinking whiskey or vodka to keep warm, and the woods would be his.

There was a last farm, mostly chewed up by tanks, with fields that hadn't been tilled or weeded in months. Beets, it looked like from a distance. He watched for a long time, making sure no one was camped in the remains of the farmhouse, before he scurried into the field and began digging with his hands. He remembered a lesson from long ago—dig all you will need first; never be caught with pockets full until you're ready to run. His fingers were still weak and soft, but it felt good to be digging in real earth. And the beets were ripe.

He heard a rustle behind him and froze, his hands deep in the soil and fresh-dug beets all around him on the ground. A rabbit? he wondered. Or better yet, a hedgehog? He tried to remember how long had it been since he had tasted roasted hedgehog. Could he really remember the taste, or was it only a dream, the endless camp dream of a full belly? He looked around, watching the brush for telltale flutters. He saw nothing. Then he heard another movement in the brush, too loud to be a rabbit. He stood, ready to run, and saw someone digging with a stick at the other end of the field.

"Go ahead!" the other man shouted. "There's plenty for two."

Ral hid his beets in the brush as the other man walked toward him. He was a big man, with a husky frame, a round face, a halo of curly gray hair, a straggle of beard. You could tell that he had been stout once, but now his jowls hung flabbily. The scraps of clothing he wore made him look like a giant rag doll. His jacket had only one sleeve, and the sweater underneath was more holes than sweater. His shoes didn't match, and one was held on with twine wrapped around the foot. On his back he had a sack, bulging with rags and scraps of clothing.

"Go ahead," said the rag man, holding out a bunch of beets. "A little water, a pinch of the greens for flavor, and it's fit for a *Feinschmecker*."

He glanced around, saw the beets that Ral had hidden in the brush. "Not your first time on the road either," he said. "Where from?"

Ral hesitated. Years of wariness, honed by the lessons of survival. But whoever this man was, he wasn't authority. There was no reason not to answer. "Buchenwald," Ral said.

"Americans, no? They have good food, I hear."

"I like the road better. You?"

"Bergen-Belsen, in the British zone. That good I can cook a beet." The rag man laughed at his own joke, and Ral laughed too, not because he understood, but because the robust laughter was so inviting. He hadn't laughed, really laughed, for a long time.

"So—" said the man. "*Zu?*" Where to?

Ral shrugged. "Noplace."

The man shook his head. "A man who's going noplace has time; you're in a hurry." Ral had heard enough Yiddish in the camps to be able to understand the proverb.

"Maybe. You—where are you going?"

"Prague."

"Why Prague?"

"Prague's a real city. In a real city there's information."

"And after Prague. After you get information?"

"Vienna. Then Trieste. They tell me there are boats from Trieste." The bearded man's eyes took on a faraway cast. "Boats to Palestine. I'm finished with this."

His name was Yitzak. He had lost all of his family—brothers, sister, aunts, uncles—everyone. They had been arrested separately, reunited at Theresienstadt, then separated again as one after another had been taken away. The others had all been killed in various camps. Yitzak wasn't sure how he managed to survive. "I'm a mistake," he said. "With all their lists and records, even the Germans make mistakes."

They searched out a protected clearing in the woods, built a fire, and cooked the beets in a tin from Yitzak's sack.

"You," said Yitzak. "You have anyone?"

Ral felt himself drawn to talk. How long had it been since he had trusted anyone enough to talk? He wanted to hear the words himself, hear the whole story. He pulled out the photograph.

Yitzak studied the picture, looking up at Ral's face. "Your people?" His voice was skeptical.

"I'm going to find her."

"Why?"

"Because of what she did . . . "

Yitzak cut him off with upheld palms. His eyes were shut tight, his head shaking slowly. "Don't tell me," he said. "There's nothing you can tell me that I haven't seen. Believe me. Nothing."

". . . what she did—" Ral started to explain again.

"No! I don't want to hear."

"Not hear? What will you do? Forget? You think you can forget what they did?"

"Forget?" The animation of Yitzak's face turned him into a madman, his eyes popping, his bushy eyebrows dancing. "Can a man forget the blackness of night?"

"And you want no revenge?"

"There's only one revenge. Look at you! You're handsome, young, strong. You could find a beautiful wife, fill the world with laughing children. Make a new home. Life! That's the only revenge."

"For me there is no home."

"Until you find this woman? You want to waste your youth instead of making a life? You'll wander the world looking for her. For what?"

"I'm a gypsy. We're condemned to wander."

Yitzak's laugh boomed. Then he turned to address some invisible accomplice, the straight man for his routines. "You hear? He's a gypsy, condemned to wander. I know gypsies. They were people of the sun, the gypsies I knew. They got up with the sun and they went to sleep with the sun. They wandered for freedom, for joy, for the light. Not for revenge. How will you even find this woman?"

"I'll find her."

"And then? What'll you do if you find her?"

"I'll do what I have to do."

Yitzak grinned and nodded. "What, all of twenty years old? You talk already like an old man. Maybe we've lived through too much already. If we survived, there must be something wrong with us. Look at me, an old man already, and I dream of a new life in Palestine, maybe a new wife. You think these tired loins can father a new brood? Make a woman happy still? And then you, hardly a man, hardly old enough for a family, and you talk already of revenge. Where will you look even? The Americans and the British, they have researchers and investigators, tribunals. Thousands of witnesses they can talk to. They can go wherever they want, search anywhere. And what do they get? A few of the monsters, maybe. Big fish in a dry pond, people who can't run. Those they'll try in Nuremberg, so everyone can see. But the others? The ones you and I saw every day?" He shrugged. "They'll forget them. Everyone will forget them. And in time, even those pigs will forget what they did. No one will find them. With all their researchers and investigators and tribunals, even the Americans and the British won't find them. And if they can't find them, what can you do? What can an illiterate gypsy do?"

"I'm not illiterate. I can read."

"And I'm the pope. You read and write?" Yitzak turned again to his invisible accomplice. "He calls himself a gypsy and he can read. *Di eygene zun makht bletter vays, un dem tsigayner shvarts.* The same sun that bleaches paper white makes a gypsy black. Where did you learn to read and write? Why?"

Ral started to answer. Then Yitzak threw up his hands in mock exasperation and laughed. "Eh, the world has turned over. A gypsy reads. An old Jewish peddler dreams of farming in Palestine. What's the difference? Black is white now anyway, no?" He looked up at the sky. "And now, I think, it's dark enough for us to go."

The sky had turned to twilight, dark enough for the woods to hide everything. They walked together, warily threading from one grove of trees to the next, listening for the slightest sound, watching for a movement in the trees or on the road.

But there was nothing to fear. The stone markers and barbed wire that had once marked the border were gone; the plowed strips were overgrown with weeds. There was no way even to know they had crossed until they had gone many kilometers beyond the old frontier and worked their way back toward the road. The road signs were all in Czech, with the German obliterated.

The first village was only a kilometer farther down the road, and already quiet, with the smell of woodsmoke wafting up from the chimneys and the flicker of candles in the windows. The houses were all modest, except for a big house, a castle really, on top of the hill that dominated the village. Ral pointed to the looming house.

"The Nazi lived there," said Yitzak. "Always the biggest house for the Nazi. If this village were in the West, the Americans would find the man who lived there and make him mayor of the village. They figure he already knows how to run the town, already has the experience. The Russians, they find the man who lived there and they shoot him."

Ral was hesitant, afraid of the empty house. A broken window was like a broken mirror, and an open door could lead only to trouble. He preferred the woods. But it was cold, and he couldn't risk being found without papers so close to the road. He followed Yitzak up the hill.

"Look," said Yitzak, pointing to the empty electric light bulb sockets. "The Russians were here. The Russian soldiers unscrew the bulbs and take them home. They think the bulbs will light up if they screw them into the sides of their dirt houses. Eh, who knows? If a gypsy can read, maybe the bulbs will light."

They slept on the floor, without a fire that would attract attention.

The sky wasn't fully lit when they woke up to a volley of rifle fire. Ral wanted to run for the woods, but Yitzak pointed out that the only way they could reach the woods safely was by going back toward Germany. It made more sense to wander toward the village, pausing at farmhouses on the outskirts where they might be able to trade a few hours' work for some bread or even a hot meal.

Every door was shut to them, and when they saw troops on the roads, they had no choice but to walk through the village itself. There, in the central square, in a courtyard behind the pretty little pastel church, a Russian truck was parked with the tailgate open. Troops in dark green uniforms stood behind the truck with their rifles pointed at the wall of the courtyard, where men were lined up, their faces turned toward the wall. An officer in a Russian coat walked down the row of men, shouting questions in German.

"Sudetens," said Yitzak. "They didn't run in time. If they answer in German, they'll be shot."

Ral wanted to watch, but Yitzak pointed out the soldiers roaming the streets, examining the papers of every person they met. Every third or fourth person they would push toward the truck, where other soldiers guarded them in a loose circle.

"Come," he said. "This is no place for a gypsy and a Jew."

. . .

A gypsy and a Jew. The memory slammed back.

Four years, and nothing had changed. It was Yugoslavia then, Croatia. Ral was all of fourteen, alone on the road, wandering, searching. He didn't need a photograph to wander then. Who needed a photograph of his own mother and sister?

It was the second year of the war, but he never saw a newspaper, never heard a radio. And you couldn't tell from the rumors in the family camp what was true and what wasn't. France, England, Norway, Denmark— they were all too far away to mean anything, places he had heard of but never seen. And the stories were all the same anyway. Wherever the Germans went, they won. They hadn't gone to Yugoslavia yet, so it was safe. And it was where he was sure Geza and Keje had gone, back to the gentle hills of Dalmatia. Geza had always said that the sun there was so warm you could sleep without a fire at night. And that when you woke, a branch of ripe figs would be over your head, ready to be picked for breakfast.

It had been easy to escape from the family camp at Lackenbach. He spoke German well, could read signs, and from the start he had been her favorite, allowed to come and go when others couldn't. The camp wasn't run by the SS, but by the Criminal Police, and the police were friendly to her favorites. She had been the one to separate out the non-gypsy women, even wives, and the *Kripos* had gotten those women for reclassification, which usually meant music and the offices at the end of the barracks. As long as she provided those women, a favorite of hers was a favorite of the *Kripos'*. And the wires of the camp weren't even electrified.

He spoke to no one on the roads, following the *patrin*, the patterns of tiny marks and signs that gypsies left on their circuits from Yugoslavia to Hungary and back again. There were signs telling which house was good for a meal, which ones would greet wanderers with a whip or a gun, where the water was good, where the fields were easy to steal from. And with every step south he was farther from the Germans, from the fighting, from the camps with their questions and lines and tents where the clean and the unclean had to sleep together, where the fleas shared the beds and the rats shared the food, and where she asked the questions that separated and sorted the gypsies, putting tribes and people together. Hungarians, Kalderash, Sinte, Lovari, Yenisch, Manush—she knew them all, knew them better than anyone. The gypsies, happy to hear Romany, talked to her, told all they knew of their families and tribes. And she wrote it down in her charts, filling in blanks, making trees of the names.

The woods of Croatia were peaceful and bountiful that spring, the trees bursting with buds, the streams full of fish, the brush swarming with rabbits. By following the *patrin* he found bread, hot meals, sometimes a clan that would take him in by their fire and offer him slivovitz. He asked everywhere, but no one knew of Geza and Keje, his mother and sister. Everyone pointed south. "That's where those names would be from," they said. And so he walked south, enjoying the sun by day, sleeping without a fire in the warm nights, picking ripe figs for his breakfast.

And then on a still morning he heard airplanes overhead. Within a day the armies were everywhere—tanks, trucks, wagons, guns, troops, horses—all moving as fast as the wheels would carry them. The tanks and trucks and guns didn't shock him, but he had never before seen war horses, horses pulling cannons at a gallop. And some of them were good horses, the kind of horses his father would have traded. Maybe even his father's horses, he thought.

Behind the troops came the SS in their black uniforms and tall boots, and groveling in the footsteps of the SS were the Ustashi, Croatian Fascists, their own uniforms and salutes and goosestepping modeled after the SS.

Ral retreated into the woods, staying as far from the roads as he could. It meant that he would no longer have the *patrin* to guide him, to show him the way to food and shelter, but he was afraid that if he ventured close he could be caught in the fighting. Yet no matter how far he retreated into the woods, he could always hear the rumble of trucks and the volleys of small arms and artillery. To make sure he was traveling south, he had to walk by the sun. And against the brush and thick woods, he made slow progress.

On the fifth day of the fighting, in the midst of those thick woods, where he thought he was far away from the trucks and troops, he came to a clearing, a tiny valley cleft into the hills. A German half-track had pushed its way through the brush to block the open end of the valley, and at the open tailgate of the half-track the SS officers had set up a little table, almost like in the camps, with stacks of papers and men writing everything down as the officers shouted.

A long line of men was being led into the clearing, guarded by Wehrmacht soldiers. The SS officers interrogated each man as he passed, then waved him on to the center of the cleared area, where he was given a shovel. As the men dug, the SS and the Ustashi on the sidelines shouted at them. Ral wasn't really sure of what they shouted then, didn't know the meaning of the words. "Partisans! Hostages! Fifty for every German soldier wounded, one hundred for every German soldier killed." Where else would they find those numbers except among the gypsies and the Jews?

It took a long time before the trench was dug. The ground was hard and rocky, and the gypsies especially wouldn't dig until they were prodded with guns. Every time the soldiers turned their eyes away, the gypsies would stop, or fill in what they had dug. But finally the SS men said that the trench was big enough, and they pulled back the men and ordered them to undress.

The Ustashi on the sidelines began shouting as the men took off their clothes. "Jew dogs!" they shouted. "Gypsy scum!" To them, it was like saying brown rats and gray.

The Jews were led to the trench first. Most of them had untrimmed beards and sidelocks, and they walked with one hand covering their heads and the other over their private parts, their eyes avoiding one another. They seemed more embarrassed and confused than afraid. One Ustashi spat on an old Jew as he walked by. The Jew, his head rocking in prayer, didn't wipe the spittle off, refusing even to acknowledge his tormentor. His dignity made the Ustashi so angry that the uniformed man slammed the butt of his rifle into the Jew's shoulder, knocking him to the ground. Then he kicked the old man until he got up again. But the old Jew never shouted back, never yielded up the gestures of fear and struggle that would signal ultimate surrender.

At the edge of the trench the Jews knelt. Ral could see them saying good-bye to one another. Some looked up, as if to say good-bye to the heavens. And then, from behind them, at a distance of eight or ten meters, the rifles of the soldiers barked, and as the reports of the rifles echoed off the walls of the valley, the kneeling figures toppled into the trench. Some of the German soldiers turned away after they fired. One threw up. The Ustashi stared, their faces twisted with excitement, the fervor of their shouts restrained only by the glaring silence of the Germans who had done the shooting.

When the last of the kneeling figures had toppled into the trench, another row of Jews was marched up, and after them still another. Each came in perfect silence, their lips moving in prayers that no one could hear. They took their places at the edge of the trench and said their good-byes and waited for the shots to ring out, never surrendering their dignity even as they knew exactly what would happen. Ral watched, mesmerized, not believing it was real people he was seeing. How could it be real bullets? How could people march to their deaths like that? They didn't even shout at their killers.

Finally it was the turn of the gypsies. There were only enough of them to make one row at the trench, but it took two or three soldiers to get each gypsy to the edge. They fought like cornered animals, lashing out with their feet and hands, biting, kicking up the dirt. One got away, running toward the woods, almost in Ral's direction. The guards started after him, but an SS officer signaled them away, letting the gypsy run until he was almost to the woods before he raised his pistol, steadying it with two hands as he aimed. The bullet hit the gypsy in the neck, and he was still alive, kicking and flailing like a decapitated chicken, as the guards threw him into the trench.

The rest of the gypsies were driven to the edge of the trench with clubs and whips and rifle butts. And when they could fight no more, when soldiers and Ustashi had beaten them into a rough line, forcing each man to kneel, the gypsies began cursing. These were curses Ral had never heard before, cries that hung in the air like the shrieks of dying animals: "May your children die in agony in your arms! May your women be barren! May your own sons turn on you . . . !"

Finally the rifles began to fire again. It wasn't a single volley this time.

Instead, they clubbed and whipped the gypsies into the trench and shot them there. And with each shot, as the echoes reverberated off the walls of the valley, Ral felt a stinging pain in his own lips. When he reached up, he felt blood from where he had bitten his lip.

After the first shots, the gypsies began to fight again, and the Ustashi and the soldiers began a melee of clubbing, beating the gypsies to death instead of shooting them. The Ustashi shrieked as they kicked and clubbed the gypsies.

It seemed like hours before the valley was quiet. An SS officer ordered a group of soldiers to fill in the trench with dirt. One soldier pointed into the trench with his shovel, and the officer walked to the edge and fired half a dozen shots from his pistol into the trench. Then the soldiers threw in the last shovels of dirt. The Ustashi were already picking through the clothing that had been left behind.

Ral waited until the Germans and the Ustashi had marched away behind the half-track before he walked down to the mounded trench. He stood there, unable to cry, not really believing what he had seen. He kicked the ground, trying to convince himself that it was all real. Little did he know then that what he had seen was to be common. And that later the Ustashi would grandly embellish the mechanical killing that the Germans had ordered, using whips to make their victims dance, or playing games with their clubs and pistols. And while the Germans were interested only in male hostages, exactly fifty for every German soldier wounded by a partisan, exactly one hundred for every German soldier killed by a partisan, counting carefully to make sure the numbers were right, examining and re-examining papers to make certain that it was only gypsies and Jews who were taken to fill the quotas of hostages, the Ustashi were not so picky or precise. They rounded up the hostages the Germans demanded, enough to meet the methodical counts, but they also rounded up women, especially gypsy women. And what they did with those women made even the Germans shudder.

Ral heard another volley of shots from the courtyard, the reports echoing off the walls of the church. Four years, he thought, and nothing had changed.

He tried to turn back, to the village and the wall. But Yitzak tugged at his arm. "Come along, gypsy," he said. "It's many miles to Prague."

Ral looked over and saw the old Jew wipe tears off his face with the back of his hand.

"This world," said Yitzak. "Sometimes it's enough to make a man curse God for giving him eyes and ears."

Le Bourget, France, 1966

The flights from Marseilles all went to Le Bourget, which meant a taxi or bus ride across Paris to Orly. There was a time when Jill would have looked forward to the detour, and the chance to spend a day shopping or browsing through the galleries and museums. But she felt listless at Le Bourget, hesitant rather than in a rush to get to the taxi stands. For a few minutes she stared around the terminal, watching business travelers sipping coffee or drinking at the bars as they waited for their flights. All of them seemed so busy, in such a hurry to go wherever it was that they were headed. She remembered when she too had scheduled her life in double time, needing the rush that she got from hurrying to one meeting after another, depending upon the absolute crunch of time to forestall the feelings of loneliness that threatened when she was idle. Where were they all going? she wondered. The electronic timetables listed flights all over Europe—London, Frankfurt, Milan, Rome, Madrid, Copenhagen, Stockholm, Prague, Vienna, Athens, Hamburg, Amsterdam.

Amsterdam!

She went up to the ticket counter. Curiosity, she told herself.

"The flight leaves in twenty-five minutes," said the blond KLM ticket clerk. She pushed buttons on the console in front of her. "And we have first-class space available. You're traveling alone?"

"Alone," said Jill. She handed over her passport and American Express card. Minutes later she was at the telegraph office, sending a wire to Sidney Millman in New York. Forty minutes after that she was airborne, on her way to Amsterdam.

The only police at Schiphol Airport were the Royal Customs Service, in fancy powder-blue uniforms with fringed epaulets and pistols on braided lanyards. Everything she knew about the Amsterdam police or Interpol was from mystery stories. But she did know a Dutch law firm, with whom she had dealt on the negotiations for an exhibit loan from the Metropolitan Museum to the Rijksmuseum. Over "elevenses" of coffee and *pofferties* at the Amstel Hotel, after an invitation to dinner that she was deliberately slow to decline, she got the name of a man in the Central Office for Criminal Prosecution who was sure to know about any investigations done on behalf of the Marseilles police.

From there, the going was slow. Everyone seemed reluctant to answer questions on the telephone, and explaining who she was and why she needed information was tricky. It took most of the afternoon before she wheedled her way into the prosecutor's office.

"Mademoiselle!" The man seemed surprised at her appearance. She instinctively answered in French, but from her accent he knew she was American.

"Exactly who are you?" he asked in English. "And on what authority do you wish to know the address of this woman?"

"I met her. Just a day before . . . before she died. We were both in Saintes-Maries, and she suggested that I come visit her here, in Amsterdam. She was a nice woman. I came to pay my respects."

"There is no one to whom you can pay your respects, mademoiselle. As far as we have been able to determine, Mej. Lanzer died intestate. She leaves no survivors that we know of. Her possessions have been left in the care of the concierge of her building. There was no question of a hearing on disposition. There's nothing of value. We'll just send a report to the West German government. She was receiving a pension, you know."

"I should go see the concierge," said Jill. "What's her address?"

"It's the same building. The same address as Mej. Lanzer."

"Which is?"

The man's eyebrows went up. "She didn't give you her address?"

Jill answered with a trace of a whimper in her voice, "We were planning to meet again the next day. And, then . . ." She found it was easy to lie, and disliked herself for doing it.

The concierge was a nice-looking woman, with a square face, cropped blond hair, a trace too much makeup on her eyes. She met Jill at the gate to the courtyard, then led her into her own apartment and found her a seat amidst the clutter of bric-a-brac.

"You were a friend of Mej. Lanzer?" the concierge asked.

"Not really. Our paths crossed in Saintes-Maries."

"That's the South of France?"

"Yes. We met just two weeks ago."

"It was her holiday," said the concierge. "She went there last year too. I don't know why. It doesn't surprise me that something terrible happened. After what you read about places like that."

"Were you a good friend of hers?" Jill asked.

"Good friend? Heavens, no. She really didn't have friends. Lived all alone, never went out. I couldn't understand why. She was a nice-looking woman. Not young, of course, but nice features, not too fat. I couldn't imagine living a life like that."

"No," said Jill.

"And then to go off for a holiday to the South of France. I mean, I've never been there. But I do read the papers and the magazines. I've seen the pictures of those parties. And the stories! It doesn't seem the place for the professor."

"Professor?"

"She called herself Professor Lanzer. She said that she did her studies in Germany, a long time ago. It's funny, how she always pretended she wasn't really German. Anyone could recognize her accent. And at that institute where she went every day, they didn't call her 'Professor.' They said she was an amateur scholar, whatever that is. They're coming for her books. That's all she really had, you know, books. Shelves of books. And not one that you'd want to read. They're all about gypsies. Books and records. All gypsy music. She'd listen to them every night."

"Did she ever say she was a Romany *rye*?"

"Romany *rye*? What's that?"

Jill could remember how strange the term had sounded to her when Ral asked if she was a *rye*. "Lover of the gypsies," he had called it. She could remember her confusion and embarrassment at the word *lover*.

"Could I see her things?" she asked.

"There isn't much to see. Just the records and books. And some old photographs. I gave her clothes away already. Good wool clothes, but worn to nothing. I didn't even know what to do with the books until I thought of the institute. They're coming later this week to get them."

"Can I see what there is?"

The concierge acted as though the question were somehow prurient. "You say you met her?"

"We were at a festival together. A gypsy festival."

"Is that why she went there, to the South of France? To see a bunch of gypsies?"

Jill nodded.

"And that's why you went too, to see gypsies? A pretty girl like you hanging around with those—"

Jill's grin cut off her answer.

"I guess you can see the books and records. The police said they don't care about it. Can you imagine having no one to leave anything to? Not even a friend."

The books were still on the shelves. Photographs in frames and a stack of records were piled on the top shelf.

Jill started to pick her way through the titles, then remembered that she had a notebook in her handbag, one of the spiral-bound pads that were still empty after the week of interviews with Ral. The dates at the tops of the pages reminded her of their talks, and she found herself drifting, picturing him in the cell, and then on the beach at Saintes-Maries. The image in her

mind was already slightly dreamy and hazy. She wasn't sure she could remember exactly what he looked like.

She began by taking an inventory of the books, laboriously copying the
German titles that she couldn't read. In one book she saw a bookseller's
stamp. It took a moment to decipher the pale penciled notation—a price,
and a listing of volumes, noting that two were missing. The books had been
bought as sets, not subscribed over the years.

Both sets of journals seemed folksy rather than academic, a mix of amateur anthropology, folklore, and travelog, without the footnote and biblio-
graphic apparatus of formal scholarship. Some of the volumes were well
thumbed, but she couldn't discern a pattern from the pages or sections that
had been most opened. One was about language patterns in Hungary; another about skirt fabrics in Romania; still another about the professions of
gypsies from the Yugoslavian coast.

She listed the records, too, and again there was no obvious pattern. All
were in some way gypsy music, but they ranged from Spanish to Russian,
touching almost every culture between. Guitar, violin, orchestral—the
only thing they had in common was that they were ancient 78 rpm records,
with faded, worn cardboard jackets.

Jill looked at the photographs one at a time, wondering where and why
they had been bought or taken. The photographic paper was old and
faded, and she guessed that none of the photographs was newer than ten or
fifteen years old. She tried to slip them out of the frames, to look for dates
or perhaps even processing locations on the back, but the photographs had
been in the cheap frames so long that they were fused to the backings.

Who were these strange people? Could any of them be relatives of Ral's?
The only faces that were even vaguely like his were in a photograph of
women gathered around a skirt that had been spread on the ground. The
women were sewing, and had paused to look up and smile for the camera.
It was a snapshot, slightly overexposed, and with the sun behind the pho-
tographer so that everyone was squinting. But even so, no one in the photograph really looked like Ral. They all seemed darker-skinned, with more
pronounced cheekbones and heavy brows. Their smiles were all hollow, as
if they were posing for a tourist's camera.

Jill stepped back from the bookcase, looking around the room. She had
once stayed two nights in an Amsterdam canal house, as a student traveling for the summer. Her room wasn't very different from this. The same
sturdy furniture, the same effort at cleanliness and hominess—curtains on
the windows, doilies on the tables, antimacassars on the chairs and sofa.
One table had been moved, and the floor around the footprints was faded
from the sun. The table had probably been in exactly the same place for
years.

"Do you want to take something?" asked the concierge from the doorway. "I've no use for any of it."

"No. Not really. I was just curious. How long did she live here?"

"Seven years. Paid her rent on time every month, kept the place clean herself. I was never in the apartment until I had to let the police in."

"Really?"

"Of course, really. I don't go where I've not been invited."

"She was that private?"

"Never had a visitor. Except for that man who came after she left for France. The man with the old photograph. I couldn't understand that one. Sure didn't seem like the kind of man who'd be looking for a woman like the professor."

Jill felt herself blushing, and was struck to see that the concierge too was red, and fighting a smile.

"I'll tell you," the concierge said. She turned her head toward the landing, as if looking for an eavesdropper. "That man—I can still remember him. I took one look at him and I got a shiver inside."

"Was he frightening?"

"No. It wasn't that at all. The police asked the same thing, but I couldn't really explain it to them. I don't think I could explain it to any man. But just between us, seeing that man reminded me of the first time I ever saw that Clark Gable in a movie. It just made me turn to jelly. Some men can do that, you know. It's their eyes. A woman looks at eyes like those and there's nothing she can do."

At Schiphol the next morning Jill was paged. Sidney Millman wanted her to call the office immediately.

On the way to the phones, she wondered what she would tell him, how she would answer his questions about why she was taking so long to get back to the office. She tried to picture the reactions of Millman and the other partners if she were to try to explain why she was in Amsterdam. Paris and shopping they would understand, but poking around Amsterdam, investigating the murder charges against a gypsy? She could imagine Millman's words: "What kind of crazy, cockamamie nonsense . . . ?"

But she reminded herself that the firm needed a woman lawyer on the roster, and she was good, conscientious and effective, and hardworking. They would probably secretly enjoy her adventures. Millman might gently reprimand her, suggesting that there were limits that a member of the firm had to observe. Privately, she suspected, he would brag about her at his club, where she could never go.

Maybe she was their gypsy, she thought.

Vienna, 1946

Everywhere you had to show papers. For a residence permit, a ration card, a train ticket. Sometimes, in the Russian zone, you needed papers just to cross the street. And each time Wanda Lanzer trembled as the officials scrutinized her documents, imagining that they would catch some error she was too ignorant to have recognized. Before she got to the head of a queue, she would go over the answers she had memorized, repeating to herself the addresses and dates, the maiden name of her mother, the names of the schools she had attended and the dates of her matriculation and graduation from each. Most of all, she repeated the name, Wanda Lanzer. It had been a careful choice, the right number of syllables and the accents in the right place. The bony, ascetic little man in Prague said it was important, that it was much easier to learn a new name if it had the right number of syllables. Now, she had practiced the new name so often that she would respond instantly if an official called out her name. She was ready. And yet each time she had to show the papers she trembled.

So far, there had never been a question, never so much as a hesitation by an official. For all they cared, Wanda Lanzer was another refugee being repatriated to Austria, another random victim of the war. And as the new identity began to function, as the few pieces of paper she had gotten from the man in Prague enabled her to get more pieces of paper that in turn begot still more, she realized that she was actually becoming Wanda Lanzer. Eva Ritter was nothing but a memory.

She left Prague in a hurry. The Czechs had already decided to purge the country of Germans, and those who had not left on their own were being stripped of citizenship, land, and property. The train she waited for arrived empty from Vienna. There was hardly standing room on the return journey out of Prague.

Vienna was as gray as she remembered, the January skies as damp and cold, the dialect as impenetrable. Old women still cleared the snow from the tram tracks with everything from shovels to toothbrushes. Shopkeepers still refused to believe that anything they didn't have might be available somewhere else in the world. And with rubble everywhere, the economy in

99

shambles, food and fuel the subjects of street fights, the Viennese still fawned and groveled over titles and ranks. When she went to the police station for a residence permit, the woman in front of her, wearing tattered rags, was correcting her title for the clerk. Frau Hofrat Doktor, the woman insisted each time, spending precious minutes that might have been used to find food or shelter to enforce an empty title.

When it was her own turn, she was tempted for a moment to add the "Doktor" in front of her own name. In Vienna it would mean status and privilege, the difference between the proletariat and the elite. And her Doktor was earned, not an honorific or a rank that she had married. But it was Eva Ritter who had earned that Doktor, she finally reminded herself. Not Wanda Lanzer. And Eva Ritter was another casualty of the war.

What she feared most was the job interview. She had been told where to go by Neue Deutschland, but she couldn't believe that a job interview would mean the same perfunctory scrutiny that the officials at the police station or the railroad offices had given her documents. She rehearsed answers to the questions she thought they might ask, practicing her intonation until every response came out relaxed and easy. The answers were all true. Wanda Lanzer was born in Graz in 1904, did attend the Technische Hochschule, did work as an archivist in Graz and later Linz. There were records to support every detail. What there were no records of was Wanda Lanzer's death, in an automobile accident in Innsbruck in the early days of the Anschluss. That slip-up, that bit of Austrian *Schlamperei*, had left an identity to be borrowed.

The address for the interview was a gray stone building in the Fourth Bezirk, a grand late-nineteenth-century palace that had miraculously sustained only minor damage to its exterior. On the door was a tile plaque: BIBLIOTHEK DER KULTUR DES DEUTSCHES VOLKS. Library of the Culture of the German Peoples. When she asked about the name, the people at Neue Deutschland told her to be thankful that she could get a job that would help herself and Germany.

Inside the foyer the building appeared untouched by the war, untouched even by the First World War. Everywhere she turned, there were sculptured plaster moldings and ceilings, inlaid paneled walls, tile stoves in the corners of the rooms, long heavy drapes, polished furniture on parquet floors. The woman who opened the door was dressed in an ancient woolen dress and a shawl. She said something to the porter in Viennese dialect, but addressed Wanda Lanzer in formal *Hochdeutsch* that sounded like court language from the time of Franz Josef. As they walked by the main reading room, Wanda Lanzer saw that there were no readers at the tables.

She was told to wait until Dr. Stürgkh was ready for her, but when she was finally summoned into his spacious office no one else came out, and there was no work on his desk. He was a tall man, with a narrow face and a voice that modulated abruptly from speaking too softly to speaking too loudly, so that she found herself alternately leaning toward him and recoiling from his bark. For a while he rambled on about the weather and the unfortunate "conditions" in Vienna, and she expected that at any moment he would launch into sharp questions about her background: Where had she been during the war? What was her employment record in libraries? Why had she come to Vienna?

But Stürgkh asked her nothing. She tried a few questions of her own: Exactly what did the Bibliothek do? What was the range of its research? For whom was the research conducted? Stürgkh was evasive, a master of the verbal finesse that the Viennese had raised to a high art.

"We are here to preserve German culture, as a bulwark against . . . threats," he said. And then he asked what was to be the only question he would pose to her: "Do you think Vienna is still a *Weltstadt?*" A world city.

"Of course," she said.

"You will begin tomorrow," he answered.

She was to be a cataloger. The salary was pitiful, but with the job she got a permanent residence permit, a library card, and, after they helped her find a room, rent certificates. There were enough documents to quash any question about her identity.

The room they found for her was on the fifth floor of a building with an elevator. Of course, the elevator didn't work, there wasn't enough gas pressure for the stove or the water heater, and the toilet was in a freezing room off the hallway. But there was a lock on the door of the room, and curtains on the windows. It was private, a place of her own.

No one ever asked about her research credentials. They were content that she knew languages, that she could read and catalog papers, fill out the index cards with the prescribed abbreviations. Frau Lettner, the old woman who had let her in and who shared the cataloging room and tasks with her, called herself an "independent researcher." In fact, she was a drone, a clerk who read titles of documents and assigned them card numbers. She was mystified by the flood of new documents that the library had begun to receive, documents from the occupying powers and from the trials of war criminals in Nuremberg. She thought all the new material unimportant and dismissed it with the comment she used for all change in Vienna: "There's much water in the Viennese wine now."

But Wanda Lanzer, who had to catalog most of the new documents, knew they were important. And she gradually began to understand the purpose of the library. Neue Deutschland needed this material collected somewhere, and the quiet library in Vienna, an institution no one had noticed since the bushy-sideburned courtiers of Franz Josef reigned in Vienna, was a safe hideaway where they could accumulate stores of counterpropaganda ammunition for future wars.

It didn't take her long to learn to loathe Frau Lettner and her ritualized answers to every question. Any reference to the Russians ended with "Red isn't the color of Viennese wine." Comments on the French concluded with

"Civilization is not *Kultur*." In time, the conversation between them disintegrated to an exchange of code words, predictable phrases for every situation. "We must get back to our research," Frau Lettner would say. And it made Wanda Lanzer think only of the real research she had once done, the dissertation and the articles she had written for anthropological journals. What would Frau Lettner say about that? she wondered.

But of course she could say nothing to Frau Lettner. Eva Ritter had written those articles. And Eva Ritter was no more.

She remembered when she had first set off for fieldwork among the gypsies, armed with notebooks and a camera with a telephoto lens. She stayed a safe distance and photographed at fairs, caught the flamboyant gestures when they were trading horses, the men standing around their grindstones, the street troops with their bears, the women gathered around a skirt they had made. She remembered how thrilled she was at each discovery—when she first learned that performing bears are always named Martin, and when she learned to discern the unique patterns in the dress of the different clans.

And she remembered when she had first looked at her notes and developed the photographic plates, how dull they were, how the vitality and temperament of the gypsies had eluded her. The pictures looked like the postcards that were sold on corner kiosks. Her notes sounded like a travelog. She had observed, but she hadn't understood, because she didn't understand Romany, their language. So she set out to learn Romany, and discovered that no one else was interested. No professor would help her. There were no dictionaries. No grammars. The only books she could find were dry linguistic studies that examined the relationship between Romany and certain early Indian languages, including Sanskrit, proving that the gypsies were originally from India, that they were Aryans. But that wasn't her concern, then.

She persisted, made recordings of the gypsies talking and listened until she could ask simple questions. What is your name? Where are you from? Who is your father? Which clan are you? And when she asked those questions in Romany, the gypsies would open their eyes wide and smile and answer her. It wasn't that they didn't know German. They all did. But when an outsider—a *gaje*, they called her—asked them questions, their answers seemed designed to confuse rather than explain. She learned that the gypsies had no qualms about lying to an outsider, and that anyone who spoke to them in German was automatically an outsider. She also learned that they would routinely lie when they applied for papers, or when they registered births or marriages or deaths. To get the papers they needed they would falsify names, ages, relationships. And that meant that all the research she had ever read about them, and the research she had once done, was worthless.

But by speaking to them in her few broken phrases of Romany, she gradually began to understand the complex relationships that made up the families and *kumpania* and clans. She learned to distinguish the Sinte or German gypsies from the Kalderash, and among the Kalderash, she learned to distinguish the Lovari and the many other clans. She learned to recognize appearances too—the high cheekbones and oriental eyes of the Romanians and the dark skin of the Spanish gypsies. She began compiling her own classification scheme, the backbone of her research.

They were good memories, and replaying them was the only way to get through the dreary days of cataloging, the boring pronouncements of Frau Lettner. And yet each day she had to cut the memories short, had to remind herself that they were only memories, that the research all belonged to Eva Ritter. And Eva Ritter was no more.

Outside the dreary job and the forbidden memories, there was nothing. She was afraid to venture out in the city, afraid of the cafés, even the museums and the cinema. Her whole life was the Bibliothek and her little room, a dreary monotony of loneliness. It took only a few weeks before the emptiness became unbearable. She tried going out for walks in the evenings. She told herself she was just getting some fresh air, but the walks always took her in the same direction, toward the Second Bezirk, in the Russian sector, toward the Prater and the shantytowns around it. And each evening she would stop short, long before she crossed the canal. And on the way home she would feel the struggle going on inside her, caution battling against the inexorable pull of those shantytowns where she knew the gypsies would be.

Finally, on a cold, windy Sunday afternoon, she bundled up in her wool coat, with a scarf wrapped around her head, and walked all the way to the Prater. The big Ferris wheel towered over the grounds, but everything else was rubble. There was little that she recognized. No caravans, no open fires, only a few broken-down trailers and shells of cars and shacks of cardboard and tin. She heard no songs, saw no dancing, not even the color of skirts and bandannas or the flash of jewelry. From the few faces she saw and the language she overheard, there seemed to be no Sinte or even Kalderash gypsies there, only a few Yugoslavs, probably wanderers who had come to the city in the hope of finding jobs. And once they found work, they would settle down, give up the remnants of the nomadic life that still brought them to the campgrounds. They would forget the few words of Romany that they still knew, forget how to sing and dance, forget the freedom of the road.

She ventured close to the travelers, peeking through the torn tin and cardboard doors of their shacks, trying to hear their language. A man saw her and stared. He was short and stocky, with thick black hair, a mustache, dark eyes. He looked at her as though he knew her.

She tugged the scarf around her face and ran toward the tram stop. Impossible, she thought. How could the man know her? She took the first tram all the way to the Kärntnerstrasse, then another tram around the Ring before she got off and walked back to the sterile little fifth-floor room where she was Wanda Lanzer, a woman with no past.

No past. And no future. The work in the Bibliothek never changed. Frau Lettner never stopped repeating the same trite homilies. The porter repeated the same jokes as he stoked the tile stoves. The documents went on and on, recounting atrocities, the charges brought against SS men and camp guards and generals and party officials. There were thousands of pages of testimony, and Nuremberg was only the first trial. There were more trials planned, more testimony, more transcripts, as the net was cast wider and wider, bringing in more of the "criminals." How long would it go on? she wondered. When would they stop? When would her life be more than boring days and lonely nights in the little room?

One day, on her way home from the Bibliothek, she ventured by a bookshop and spotted a record in the window, a new recording of Liszt's Hungarian Rhapsodies. She knew what even most of the musicologists didn't know, that the record was mistitled. It should have been called Gypsy Rhapsodies. Even looking at the crudely printed record jacket, she could remember the soaring melodies, the rapture of those violin passages. What would I do with a record? she asked herself. Where would I even play it?

For three days she thought about the record. She would stare at the documents and the cataloging cards, and all the time her mind would wander back to the record. Finally, when she had daydreamed so much that she was falling behind in her work, she went into the bookshop and asked if they could play the record for her. She listened to the slow *lassú* and the whirling czardas, and felt herself swaying to the eerie, haunting melodies. This wasn't the phony gypsy music of the Viennese cafés, the songs played for the Russian and American soldiers by zither players looking for tips. This was the real music of the Romany, the mysterious, half-oriental melodies that had their origins in some hidden past. She bought the record.

Fourteen weeks later, fourteen weeks without a single scrap of bacon or meat in her nightly soup, fourteen weeks without a newspaper or a cup of coffee in a café, she had saved enough money from her miserable salary to buy a small Victrola, a portable machine with a fitted cover that closed up like a suitcase. She brought it home to her room, closed the drapes, lit a candle, and played the record.

And from then on, her evenings were no longer solitary and depressing. Just listening to the songs of the vast steppes of Hungary, the solitary cry of the melancholy violin, the haunting rhythms of the guitars, was enough to assuage the boredom of her numbing routine, to drive away those inchoate fears that she could never pinpoint, but that kept her forever cowering, afraid to go out, afraid to live. In her room, with the gypsy music on her Victrola, she felt safe, safe enough to stay in that gray, dreary city for nine long years.

. . .

Ral and Yitzak traded stories all the way to Prague.

"You know why the gypsies have no religion?" Yitzak would ask. "I'll tell you. Long ago the gypsies built themselves a church of stone. The Romanians, fools that they are, built one of bacon and ham. The gypsies drove a hard bargain, they traded, and the gypsies ate their new church."

Ral laughed, then told his own version. "When God gave out all the religions, the gypsies wrote theirs down on a cabbage leaf. Then a donkey came along and ate it."

They told each other tales, mostly apocryphal, of horse-trading tricks: how the hollow eyes of an old nag could be puffed up with a straw inserted through the skin, how a quiet horse could be trained to nervousness with a bucket of pebbles shaken under his nose, how a horse with the heaves could be temporarily cured with linseed oil and dry pasture, at least long enough for a farmer to buy the horse. A week in the farmer's damp stable and the horse would have the heaves again, which meant it was time for the gypsy to send a friend over to buy the horse back, cheap.

"You know the gypsies well," Ral told Yitzak. And then he tried to teach Yitzak proverbs, if only as a relief from the endless Yiddish proverbs that punctuated Yitzak's conversation. *"Yekka buliasa nashti beshes pe done grastende,"* Ral taught him, waiting patiently until Yitzak pronounced the strange words.

"What does it mean?" Yitzak asked.

"With one behind you cannot sit on two horses."

It felt like they would be friends forever.

It took them two months to reach Prague, following the roads and the gossip. Yitzak was a *Schnorrer* by profession, a peddler who scrounged the debris of the war and traded what he found. A mess kit or a uniform jacket might be traded for a part from a wrecked truck, and then the truck part traded for a meal or a night's lodging. He never even tried on the clothes he found. All that mattered was how many chunks of sausage or loaves of bread they would bring.

Ral would tinker with whatever scraps of metal they found, banging the tin to create cups, pans, canisters, and dishes that Yitzak would then peddle. At a time when shops could scarcely function because there were neither goods nor a trustworthy currency, the two of them thrived in the villages of the Bohemian countryside.

As they neared Prague, Ral could hardly contain his excitement and anticipation.

"What do you think?" teased Yitzak. "She'll be waiting by a big sign that says, 'Welcome, Gypsies'?"

Ral didn't laugh. Yitzak knew him well enough not to tease more.

They followed the winding Moldau into the city, stopping when Ral spotted an encampment of travelers by the banks of the river. The campers were wanderers, not refugees, and they had been careful to plant their camp upstream where the water was clean. Their huts were rude piles of war debris—tin sheets, crates, slabs of cardboard.

Yitzak waited on the bridge as Ral climbed down the riverbank and walked slowly toward the men who were cooking around an open fire, holding his hands in front of him so it was obvious that he wasn't concealing a weapon.

"*Rom san?*" he said. Are you Romany?

The men backed away from him, motioning to the women and children to go inside the huts. They answered Ral in German, shouting that they were troughmakers who had fled to Prague from the countryside, running away from the troops who ravaged everything in their paths. Troughmakers were usually semi-nomadic, roaming the countryside to sell the scalding troughs for butchered pigs which they carved out of poplar logs. Now they were eager not to be mistaken for gypsies. "*Nicht Zigeuner!*" they shouted over and over as they backed away.

He took out the photograph, using sign language and German to get one of the men to look at it. The man shook his head in a sharp "No." He had never seen her, never heard of her, knew nothing about her. And he didn't want to talk anymore. The men stood protectively in front of the huts until Ral climbed back up the riverbank to the bridge above.

"It'll be like that everywhere," said Yitzak. "Nobody wants to remember what happened. What good is it to remember when you can do nothing?"

Ral stared at the tiny camp, tucked in the broad sweep of the river. "And if I stop looking, what do I do?"

"Live!"

"Live? You talk of Palestine, a farm, a wife, children. Do you really believe you'll find that?"

"Of course. There are ships leaving for Palestine every day. They're building a new land."

"Is that what you're going to? Or is it just a dream, something to believe in, to search for? Everybody needs a dream. In the camp, didn't you dream of food and sun just to stay alive? If I stop searching, what is there? This?" He pointed down at the squalid camp.

"You're young. You're strong. If this world is so terrible, build a new one. Like they're doing in Palestine."

Ral shook his head. "Look at them, down there! They're not even gypsies. There are no gypsies anymore. Maybe I'm not a gypsy anymore. I don't know what I am now."

"You don't know what you are?" Yitzak laughed. "First he reads. Now he's a philosopher. You're in Prague, philosopher. Go ask the Golem."

"Golem? What are you talking about?"

They walked through the twisted, cobbled streets of the Old Town while Yitzak told Ral the story of Rabbi Löw, the great sixteenth-century scholar who built the infallible magic robot of clay. When the rabbi wrote his magic formula on a piece of parchment and put it in the mouth of the Golem, the clay figure would rise to its feet, stretch its limbs, rub its eyes, and ask, "What do you require of me, Master?" It was said that no question was too difficult for the Golem, and ever since, people had been going to the graveyard of the Old Town in Prague in the hope that the magic Golem would reappear to answer their hopes and questions.

It took Yitzak a long time to find his way. All that was left of the old Jewish cemetery was rubble, with a few haphazardly cocked stones jutting out of the debris. Yitzak picked his way through the stones until he found what he wanted, a house of marble and granite built over one of the graves. Neat piles of pebbles were stacked around the tomb, defying the chaos of the graveyard.

"You write what you want to know on a slip of paper and put it inside that little house," he said. "And then leave a pebble nearby. Who knows . . ."

Ral looked at him in horror. What Yitzak described sounded too much like the *Hokano Baró*, the great swindle that the fortune tellers lived for. How could an old Jewish peddler know about the *Hokano Baró*?

"What are you frightened of?" said Yitzak. "Go ahead. Write something. Maybe a message from a gypsy who can write is just what it takes to get the old Golem up again after all these years."

As they stood there, an ancient man wound toward them, stooped over, wheezing with every step, stopping every few feet to marshal his strength. Each time he paused he would bend over to brush off a toppled tombstone. His beard was dirty gray, his clothes a filthy caftan. He was in no hurry.

Yitzak greeted the man in Yiddish, and before long they were in earnest conversation, their eyes animated, their hands gesturing, looking one moment as if they were negotiating a price, and the next moment laughing boisterously and slapping each other on the shoulders.

"He agrees," said Yitzak to Ral. "A note from a gypsy who reads is one thing that no one has tried on the Golem."

The old man started to tell a long story, in Yiddish and German, about how he had tried to take care of the graveyard through the war. Each day he would try to right the stones that had been toppled. It was a Sisyphean task, as gangs of thugs would break into the cemetery every night and throw down the stones he had spent the day raising.

Ral took out his photograph and thrust it at the man.

"She's a German?" the old man asked.

He laughed when Ral nodded.

"What's so funny?"

"The only place to look for a German here is in the lunatic asylum. There are no Germans anymore. The big ones went to Spain, or maybe South America. The little ones are in Germany, in the American zone. Or Vienna. You want to look for a German, try Vienna."

Ral smiled. Vienna was a city he knew.

. . .

Yitzak stalled before he went to the office of the Jewish Agency for Palestine. Boats were still leaving, they told him, but the gates to Palestine were closing fast. Some boats wouldn't get in.

"You're going?" said Ral. "You could go to Vienna first."

"What am I going to do—spend my life walking around Europe with a crazy gypsy man looking for some woman who isn't even beautiful? Why can't you be like any other good-looking young man? Why can't you just find a beautiful wife, make laughing children? Why can't that be your revenge?"

He saw the impatience in Ral's eyes and knew the gypsy hadn't heard a word he said.

"Well," he said. "I guess that means an old man like me has to take care of all the young beauties. What are you waiting for—my blessing? Bad enough a gypsy who can read. All you need is the blessing of an old Jew."

"*Bahtalo drom,*" said Ral. Good road.

Ral knew he would miss the old man, but he knew too what he had to do.

Vienna! It was the only city Ral really knew, and he knew it not as a gypsy knows a city—where the safe campgrounds are and where the police are likely to raid, where the good street corners are, which scams are safe and which dangerous—but also as a *gajo* would see a city. He had been to the museums, the concerts, the theater, the opera. He had been in the shops and cafés, sometimes only to beg or sell flowers, but sometimes to sit down for tiny cups of incredibly sweet coffee and trays of delicate pastries that melted in your mouth and open sandwiches made on bread so light it felt as if it could fly. Vienna was the place—the only place—where he had looked at *gaji*, and *gaji* had looked at him, without the barriers that made it seem that they were from separate worlds. And something told him that the city on the Danube, the city that saw itself as the gateway between civilization and the savage Orient, was the place she would go.

And yet, the Vienna he came to over the crowded roads from Prague wasn't the city he remembered. In place of the glitter of his memories, there was only darkness and rubble and drab. Where he remembered the rich people in fancy clothes riding up in shiny cars and fiacres, there were now only soldiers in jeeps and trucks. The Sacher Hotel had become transit quarters for the British troops, the lobby packed with uniformed men and gear bags. And by darkness, instead of the glitter of shop windows and streetlamps, the only lights were the headlights and flashlights of the patrolling jeeps, each with four soldiers, in four different uniforms.

He walked up the Kärntnerstrasse, in the Inner City. The tower of the Stephansdom was still standing, but the rest of the street was rubble above the first floors. Where there had once been fancy shops and restaurants, there was now only darkness. And yet, without closing his eyes, he could feel the memories flooding back, as if the war and all it had done to people and cities had been no more than a dream. This was where he had learned about the *gaji*.

He fought the memories in his mind, but still he walked to the side street, the street of his initiation. His eyes followed the facades, now scarred and chipped, hidden behind piles of debris and rubble. The streetlamp was miraculously intact, the wrought-iron scrolls as he remembered them. And across the street, the restaurant was still there, the brass carriage lamp in front not as shiny perhaps, but still lit, the leaded glass windows still glowing with the colors he remembered as the only warmth on a lonely, cold night. Any minute, he thought, the big sedan with the curtained rear window would cruise by, stopping for him. He shuddered with the memory.

A jeep turned the corner, headlights blazing. He saw a movement in the shadows in front of the restaurant. Then a slim figure was crossing toward him, running awkwardly on high, spindly shoes. She came right to him, taking his arm.

"Walk with me," she said. "If they stop, say you're walking me home. Okay?" She squeezed his arm as she asked. Her voice was young and brassy.

Her heady perfume made him dizzy, and he could feel the softness of her breasts against his arm. As the jeep pulled close, slowing down, she turned her back to the lights, nuzzling against his neck. A flashlight flickered against them, one of the soldiers said something in heavily accented German, and the other soldiers all laughed. Then the jeep pulled away.

"Thanks," said the girl. "They're bad, especially the Russians. The others are okay, but those Russians. They catch a girl alone on the street and it's trouble."

On the corner of the Kärntnerstrasse there was a streetlight. Ral could finally see the girl. She was younger than he expected, with straw-colored hair and a pretty, round face hidden behind caked makeup and smeary lipstick. He remembered his sister once painting herself with lipstick and earning a beating for it.

"Hey," the girl said. "You're only a kid. Anyone ever tell you you've got real bedroom eyes?"

"No. No one ever told me that."

"Well, it's true, dark eyes. Listen, I owe you a favor. You have dollars for the room?"

She looked him over under the light, at the U.S. Army fatigue jacket and boots he still had from the DP camp. "You're not from Vienna, are you? And I guess you don't have dollars. In fact, I bet you're hungry."

"I am."

She looked at him again, scrutinizing. "You're nice, aren't you? I mean, you look nice, but you're not strange or anything, are you?"

Her name was Lisl. Her room was a tiny walk-up, part of the conversion of a floor of a once elegant building. A coal stove struggled to keep the room warm, and on the balcony, under a tarpaulin, she had a cache of black market goods—tinned food, cigarettes, Hershey bars, nylon stockings.

She took off her coat. She was slim, her legs short but thin. She let down her hair and brushed it, letting it hang in front of her as she leaned over. The way she stroked it reminded Ral of his sister, Keje, always proud of her hair, brushing it until it glistened. When he took off his coat and warmed his hands by the stove, Lisl snuggled close to him, running her fingers through his thick hair, untangling the matted curls.

"Where'd you ever get hair like that?" she asked.

"I'm a gypsy."

"Really? I never knew a gypsy." She had flinched when he said it, a tiny gesture, imperceptible to anyone who wasn't used to seeing that flinch. "I guess that's why you're so mysterious and quiet, eh? Well, even if you're a gypsy, you're nice, aren't you?"

She teased his hair away from his forehead with her fingers, then studied his eyes, smiling and making faces at him to elicit a response. Then she made him sit down on the daybed and sat on his lap, unbuttoning her sweater and slowly undoing her bra and letting it slide down until her small, pert breasts were at his fingertips.

"You shy?" she said.

He didn't answer. To a gypsy, breasts are not the erotic symbols they are to a *gajo*. And he had seen nakedness, too much nakedness, for a long time.

But still, his eyes took in her body. She was ripe and young and healthy. Her skin was soft and clean, unblemished by sores. He ran his fingers up to her shoulders, then down her slim arms, reveling in the pale softness of her skin. It had been so long, so very long, since he had known a woman. He pulled her close to him, letting his fingertips wander over her shoulders to her back.

He stopped when he felt the long, even welts.

"What are those?" he asked.

She pulled away, lifting his fingers to her shoulders, arching her back so that her breasts were thrust impudently at him. "Nothing."

He turned her, gently but firmly, until he could see the scars. They were long and thin, parallel lines across her back. "Nothing?"

She twisted away again. "It was during the war." She spoke as though the words explained everything.

"Where did it happen?"

"Why do you want to know?" She pulled back, staring at his eyes. "You aren't strange, are you?"

"No. Just tell me. Where did it happen?"

"Here. In Vienna. There was a German major who arranged the con-

certs for the troops. I'm really a singer, see. He would give us hot food,
meat, real coffee even. Except that he was strange."

"Strange? Tell me what happened."

"Why do you want to hear about it?"

"Tell me."

"There isn't anything to tell. He was just strange. He did the same thing
to all of us, all of the girls who sang to the men. And he never touched me. I
mean, he never wanted me to go to bed with him or anything. He would
just make me undress and lie down on the bed, and then he had this little
quoit, I think it's called. And he always coughed. I still remember that
cough. It only started when he took out that quoit. The first time he hit me
I thought I would die, it stung so much. After the first time it wasn't so
bad. There were these scabs, see, and they would bleed as soon as he
touched them with the quoit. I think that's what he liked, seeing the blood.
He was just strange."

She saw the shudder in Ral's face. "What else could I do? It was the time
of the Germans. I wanted to sing, and to eat. I did what I had to do."

Ral turned away.

"Hey!" she said. "Because of that you don't want me? Maybe you are
strange."

"No, I want you," he said. But he still kept his face turned, as if he could
hide the memory that was so vivid he thought he could touch it. There was
no way to tell her. It was nothing a *gaje* would ever understand.

It was 1938, just after the Anschluss, and German soldiers were everywhere, bringing order to Austria and orders to the Austrians. Even the
gypsies got their orders, including a regulation demanding that all gypsies
carry a *Karte*, an identification card that required a permanent address.
Wandering was forbidden.

Overnight, gypsy life was destroyed. How could a man with a permanent address be a horse trader or a tinker? How could a fortune teller or a
beggar have a fixed residence? Without the *Karte*, you ended up in the
family camp at Lackenbach. It was the beginning of the end.

No one seemed to feel the weight of the new regulations more than Ral's
father. On some pretext that no one could understand, a German requisi-
tion unit showed up to seize Sandor's horses for use by the troops. He suggested a price for the horses, but the soldiers didn't seem interested in
negotiating. Their utter refusal to discuss a price was like one of his own
favorite techniques. But then they brought up the trucks, and he suddenly
realized that they were not there to bargain. The soldiers had to hold him
off with rifles while the horses were loaded into the trucks. They gave him
ten German marks for each horse. He spat on the money and threw it back
at them.

"A gypsy without a horse is no gypsy!" he shouted as the trucks drove
away. "I'm Lovari, from the steppes of Hungary. I was born on a horse."

Overnight, he turned bitter and mean. Gone was the roaring laughter, the sheer joy of his proud swagger. In its place was an empty, fiery temper. And instead of the Germans, against whom he could do nothing, he blamed his wife and children for the loss of his horses and the consequent idleness that left him half a man. He began repeating stories of his youth on the steppes, not for the laughter and awe that they once evoked, but to prove his greatness and stature, telling of the times he had bested other men in feats of strength or acumen. And the more he dwelled on those stories of the past, the more bitter his present became.

They were living in a broken-down *vardo*, scraping by on what Geza and Ral could make begging in Vienna. It was a precarious existence, because begging too was forbidden by the Germans. Mostly, they survived because of the dowry that had been paid for Ral's sister, Keje, who earlier that spring, at thirteen, had been "sold" to a Hungarian Kalderash who had come west looking for a bride. He was a huge, ugly man, and Keje had resisted, saying that she could never love him. But Sandor's word was final. "You'll learn to love him," said Geza as the girl went off to Hungary. They heard occasional rumors, but gypsies don't write. They assumed she was well.

Then one afternoon Ral and Geza came back from begging in Vienna and heard Sandor shouting inside the *vardo*. When they opened the door, Keje was there, cowering in a corner, cringing before her father's shouts.

"You dishonor me!" he screamed. "You shame me among all Rom. You know what you are? A whore! You hear? A whore . . . !"

Geza cradled the cowering girl, shielding her from the rain of insults, encouraging her to talk. Keje, red-eyed, shaking with fear, described in sobs the life she had led with her husband on those fabled steppes of Hungary that were at the center of Sandor's stories. Her husband beat her constantly, even in front of the others; made her clean up after the whole family, even after the dogs. He forced her to have sex with him every day and every night, including those times of the month when she knew she should not. Then when there was blood on the sheets he would berate her for being *merime*, unclean. Once she made a *gulyas* that he thought was not right. In front of the whole *kumpania*, he spat into his plate, then made her eat it, leaving her so *merime* that she could not be in the same room with others for weeks.

"I can never love him," she sobbed. "Never."

"Love!" shouted Sandor. "You talk of love? What about honor? My honor. The man is your husband. You leave him and you are nothing but a whore. You hear? A whore!"

Geza smoothed the girl's hair, pulling her close to her own skirts. By gypsy custom, an abused bride could be taken back by her father. But to do so would mean returning the bride price, which Sandor could not do. The bride price was a matter of honor, and with his horses gone, that honor was all Sandor had.

And so he cursed and shouted, calling her a whore and a sow and a cow and a nanny goat, repeating the epithets so often that they became meaningless. His wife and son and daughter looked at him as though he were sick, and in their eyes, he saw the last traces of his authority fading. Instead of respect or fear, their gazes bordered on contempt, as though he were a ranting fool.

He drew back his hand, as if to slap the girl. She cringed, but before the hand lashed out, he suddenly stopped, halting his hand in midair. His face twisted into a grin of triumph and terror. His hands went to his belt. Suddenly his old swagger and strut were back, his tone full of the old boastful confidence.

"There is something a whore is good for," he said. "There is something a whore can do." He paused, his sense of the dramatic still intact, his eyes lighting up as they did when he negotiated for horses or told stories of his prowess on the steppes. And his voice turned calm and steady, like it was when he bargained with a *gajo*.

"A whore can teach what she knows," he said.

He paused again, watching the eyes of his audience, playing on the suspense. "That's what a whore is good for, to teach. If you dishonor me, at least you can teach what you know. Teach your brother! Teach him what he must know to be a man."

Mother and daughter looked at Sandor as though he were a madman. The idea was too impossible to comprehend, too horrifying to be anything other than a terrible joke. And yet Sandor had never been a man to joke.

"Go on!" he said, enjoying his moment of power. "That's what a whore is good for, isn't it? Go on! Show your brother all your whoring tricks. Ral! Come here!"

Ral froze. He was almost twelve, too young to have had a woman, but old enough to have heard occasional talk of his marrying—except that they could never afford what Sandor would have considered a decent bride. And he was old enough to know that what Sandor had suggested was so vile and impossible that it was beyond the comprehension of a gypsy, so unclean that it was even beyond mention in the laws of gypsy life.

Sandor watched the faces around him. He had finally gained respect and awe again.

"Go on!" he shouted. "I want to see it. I want to see my son with a whore." When no one moved, he began unbuckling his wide leather belt.

Ral started to shake. He had only been beaten five or six times with the belt, but it had been threatened so often that his reaction was automatic and uncontrollable, like a horse that has been conditioned to the whip.

"Do it!" screamed Sandor. "Do it!"

He lashed out with the belt, making the leather snap as he screamed his taunt. After a few repetitions he lost the last remnants of self-control. The taunt, perhaps no more than an effort to shock in the beginning, became his only hold on his family. His voice turned maniacal as he shouted the words again and again, snapping them and the belt like a whip, first at one, then at the other of his children.

"Do it!" he screamed. "I want to see my son with a whore. Do it!" He repeated it so many times that the impossible had become inevitable to him.

"No!" Geza said, covering her daughter's body with her own.

Sandor seemed astonished that anyone would refuse his orders. He raised the belt, as if to strike mother and daughter with the same blow. Ral, shaking, not thinking anymore, threw himself at his father. He was as tall as Sandor, but willowy and slim, his lean arms and stringy muscles no match for the powerful arms and shoulders of a man who could wrestle horses to the ground. Sandor lashed out in a sweeping backhand that left Ral sprawled on the floor of the caravan.

"Turn on me?" he shouted. "I'll teach you!"

Sandor flailed with the belt, his rage beyond control. He was like a man too angry to curse, for whom no words are terrible enough. Even blows of the belt were inadequate to his fury. And when Ral didn't resist, his father looked down at him, spat his disgust, and slumped to the floor like a drunkard.

It took Ral a long time to stand up. He could feel welts on his back and shoulders, and dried blood on his lips. He looked for Geza and Keje, saw that the pots and some of the eiderdowns were gone, and knew they wouldn't be back.

Sandor was slumped against the side of the caravan, his face red, his puffy eyes staring at nothing. He looked flabby and soft, not at all the powerful man Ral remembered. Ral watched him for a long time, then bent over to lift his father up.

Sandor stared dully at Ral before pushing him away. He reached again for the belt lying at his side. "Get out!" he shouted. "Go with your whoring sister."

That night Ral fled to Vienna, alone.

Vienna, 1946

Ral slept in Lisl's flat. In the morning he couldn't remember what had happened the night before. Lisl was sleeping next to him, curled up like a child. He smoothed the covers over her, saw the scars on her back, and crept out without waking her.

He began walking the streets of Vienna. He had no idea how to look or where, no inkling of how to be systematic. He could remember what it was like when the Germans were searching for someone, how methodical and organized they could be. The Germans always had a list, and a method, a way of doing everything. But he couldn't force himself to do anything more than wander around the Ring, past the great buildings that he dimly remembered, the Parliament, the library, the Volkstheater, the Opera, past the signs that marked off the different occupation zones outside the central city. Something had brought him to Vienna, a pull that he could still feel. A feeling just as strong told him that she would come there too. But he felt lost, as if he were in the city for the first time. He had no plan, no idea how to search for her. With every step, the gray city felt less familiar.

He wandered up and down the Inner City until dark. When he came back to Lisl's flat, she was making herself dinner out of tinned American foods. She asked him where he had gone.

He didn't answer.

"It doesn't matter," she said. "You can stay here if you want. Go ahead, eat some peaches." As he ate she ran her fingers through his hair and kissed his eyelids. "I like you, dark eyes. You're different."

He stayed in the room, but saw little of her. She went out every night and came in late with packages of clothing or food, or cartons of cigarettes which she used for money on the black market. Ral would be asleep, waking only when she crawled into the bed and ran her fingers through his hair. And then, early in the morning, he would get up, setting off to walk the streets of the city, often not coming home until she had already left.

She never again asked where he went or what he did during the day. He was gentle and calm, he sometimes brought home coal for the stove, and she seemed content just to hold his head in her lap and stroke his hair and look into his dark eyes. She wasn't the first *gaje* who had taken him in.

It took him three days to find his way to the Prater, in the Russian zone. At the edge of the park grounds, where there had once been rows of stands that sold hot delicacies, there was a single cart selling flat cakes to anyone who had the required ration coupons. Beyond, where there had once been a vast campground, he saw the broken-down cars and trailers of the gypsies.

Gypsies? None of them were real Romany. They looked at him as though he were from another world, closing their doors or curtains to him, or running, refusing to talk or look at the photograph. He could recognize their accents and clothes. The people were all from Yugoslavia, animal trainers and performers mostly, newcomers to Vienna, people who had escaped the war by hiding in the hills of Dalmatia and Albania. They knew nothing of the camps, and nothing of the city now. And they were afraid, afraid of the city, afraid of strangers, afraid they might be kicked out of their precarious camp, afraid that even looking at a photograph or talking to a stranger could mean the end of their hopes for work.

It was the same as Prague, he thought. He felt like the last gypsy.

The next day he went to Lackenbach. It wasn't far outside Vienna, but he had to hitch rides on trucks and walk the last stretch, and when he got there he hardly recognized the camp. All that was left were some scraps of barbed wire and a few posts and pilings from the false foundations of the three barracks. It was hard to believe that this was the camp that had once held four thousand gypsies.

It hadn't been so bad in the family camp, not compared to what followed. The barracks were crowded, and no one could roam on the roads or even inside the camp, but families were together and protected from the *gaji* outside, just as the Germans promised. And inside the camp the gypsies could speak to one another in Romany, keep their secrets from the *gaji* guards, even hold on to their stubborn Romany pride as they frustrated every effort to form work parties.

He laughed out loud as he thought of the men trudging off to work on the roads or to fell trees in the woods that were to be cleared. It took more effort for the *Kripos* to get the gypsies out onto the roads than it would have taken them to do the work themselves. Of course, it wasn't easy to foil the work assignments. The relentless malingering—the sick calls and the faked injuries and the convenient breakdowns of tools and the sudden disappearance of the paving materials—was as much work as the labor itself would have been. But it had to be done. Between the gypsies and the Germans the contest of will had to be fought. The Germans had to have their way, had to give orders and have them followed. And the gypsies needed the last laugh, the conviction of inner superiority that came from knowing that the roads would never be built and the trees never felled. As long as the two sides in the struggle interpreted victory so differently, both could win.

Ral walked to the old parade ground, where they had lined up for roll calls and assignment to work details, and where the orchestra had played and the young women had danced whenever visitors came to the camp. It was only mud now, but there was still a trace of asphalt paving where the stand had been erected so the *Kripos* could stay clear of the mud while they read off the orders of the day to the *Zigeunerrat*.

The King of the Gypsies. He laughed again at the thought. The *gaji* always wanted to believe in a king of the gypsies, and the Germans were no exceptions. So the gypsies had proposed Alexander Sarkozi, a fat fool with a bushy mustache, telling the Germans that he was a very important man. What they didn't tell the Germans was that to a gypsy the word *important* is a euphemism for *corpulent*. Each day the Germans would read out the orders to Sarkozi, and he would listen in great solemnity before turning to repeat the orders to the gypsies. Then, with his mustache flopping up and down and his great belly shaking, he would shout out the orders, trying to be heard over the din of the gypsies who laughed at his every word. When the laughter made it impossible for him to be heard, he would resort to his speech about his responsibilities as *Zigeunerrat*. The gypsies would laugh so hard then that the Germans would berate Sarkozi for the outrageous display of disrespect. Sarkozi was the best trick the gypsies played on the Germans.

Only one of the *gaji* knew it was all nonsense: Eva Ritter. From the moment she showed up at the camp and explained that the king of the gypsies was nonsense, there was no more *Zigeunerrat*. The camp was promptly divided by classification—Sinte in one barracks, Romany in a second, mixed breeds in the third. Alexander Sarkozi, ever eager to serve the Germans, was to be responsible for the Romany, which meant that he was the camp informer, reporting to the *Kripos*. Lumpo Schneeberger did the same for the Sinte. The next day everyone in the camp was sent out on work details. Those who reported in sick had to clean out the latrines.

Eva Ritter didn't wear a uniform, but she had an office in the camp where she did her interviews. She was the one who told the guards about all the gypsy scams to get out of work, and about which clans and families would get along and which were likely to fight with one another. And once the *Kripos* had that information, they knew how to get the gypsies to work. All they had to do was threaten to break up a family, or threaten to put a virgin daughter from a Kalderash family into the Sinte camp, and there would be total cooperation from all of the Kalderash on the work details.

Ral wandered back to where the barracks had stood. The mud was dry now, and the breeze kicked up puffs of dust around the rotted timbers of the old foundations. At the end of the barracks was where she had had her office, and he remembered when he had been called in for his first interview. She sat behind the desk, with shelves of books behind her. At the side of the desk a *Kripo* sat with a gun on his hip and a riding crop in his hands. The *Kripo* couldn't understand a word of the interview, which was in Romany, but if there was the slightest sign of rebellion, a raised voice or a threatening gesture, he would lash out with the crop.

"To whom are you related?" she asked. "Who is your father? Your mother? Brothers and sisters? Cousins? Do you know who your grandparents were, their names?"

It was the first time he had ever heard a *gaje* speak Romany, and he watched in amazement as she wrote down the answers he gave.

"What are all those books?" he asked between her questions.

"They're about gypsies."

"All of them?"

"Yes. By scholars from all over the world."

"May I read some of them?"

"Read? What do you mean?"

"May I take one to read?"

"You know how to read?" Her curiosity was laced with a thread of hostility. "How did you learn to read?"

He shifted to German to answer. The details he wouldn't tell her, just the fact that for years he had lived with women in Vienna, most of the time with a woman who treated him almost as a son. Almost. He didn't tell her that some of what they did was not as mother and son.

It had been early in the war, when he was alone in Vienna, after the fight with Sandor. Sophie was married, but she had a pied-à-terre that was supposed to be the studio where she painted. That was where he had lived. Originally he was supposed to model for her, and many times he did. But she had also bought him clothes, taken him to museums and concerts and the opera, taken him out for lunch and dinner at restaurants and cafés, showed him the world of the theater and libraries and fine stores. In the shops and cafés she acted like his mother, carefully choosing the clothes he would wear, showing him the proper way to eat, teaching him manners and careful speech and how to look at a painting and how to listen to a concert. Then, back at the little flat, she taught him to make love slowly and tenderly, taught him little tricks that would make her happy, make any woman happy, she said. And she taught him how to read.

"Who was this woman?" asked Eva Ritter.

Ral refused to tell more. Not about his intimacies with Sophie, and certainly not about how when the gypsies were being rounded up for the family camps Sophie had tried to protect him, to get him false identity papers that would keep him out of the camps. And of course he didn't tell her that it was because he had finally run away from Sophie, run away to try to be a gypsy again, that he had been picked up by the police and put into the Lackenbach camp.

Somehow he knew that whatever he withheld from Eva Ritter was the only power he would ever have against her. It wasn't just that he wanted to

protect Sophie, who had been kind and generous and asked nothing in return except to paint pictures of Ral and love him and be allowed to lavish
on him a tenderness that he had never known before. Ral also knew, even
at that first interview, that he was destined to struggle with this woman
Eva Ritter. She was not like other *gaji*. She was a woman who knew about
the gypsies, knew more about them perhaps than the gypsies themselves.

When he reached the end of the barracks he kept walking. There was
nothing in Lackenbach except bad memories.

He wandered for weeks, going out every day, roaming through the streets
without any formal pattern to his search, hoping against hope that somewhere he would spot her. "Whole commissions look for such people," Yitzak had told him. "With researchers who read every language. How will
you ever find her?"

Yitzak was right, of course. It was an impossible task. What was he
going to do, stand on a street corner and study the faces that walked by?
Try the police department and ask if she had a residence permit for Vienna? He knew what the police would say if he asked. That is, if they said
anything before they threw him out. "What do you think, *Zigeuner*, that
we're here to help you cheat someone?" And the Allied occupation troops,
the men in the jeeps, would be no different. He could hear their answers—
different languages, but the same word: Gypsy! *Zigeuner! Gitane!* Rat!
Filth! Scum! It was inevitable. If he turned to the *gaji* for help, he, the
hunter, would become the hunted again.

He wasn't hungry, he had a warm, safe place to sleep, Lisl's company if
he wanted it, and yet he was desperate. Only one thing mattered anymore,
and it mattered more than food, more than warmth, more than anything.
He was desperate. And because he was desperate, he was suddenly scared.

It was impossible to fight the memory now. It was in Vienna, when he
was desperate, that he had learned to fear the *gaji*.

Vienna, 1938

I t had been before Sophie, only the third day after he had come to Vienna, only three days after Geza and Keje had fled from Sandor's rage. Ral had fled back to the city where he and his mother had made money begging each day. He tried begging on the same corner, crouching to make himself seem small, opening his eyes big and looking up at the passersby. He mumbled about a baby sister at home who needed milk, and a sick mother who needed medicine. He held his hand half-crooked, even tried feigning a crippled arm. After two days he had gotten nothing in response except distrustful glances. Twice he was chased by the police and had to run through the back streets until he lost them. The *gaji*, he was learning, had sympathy for a gypsy child, not for a young man. His stomach growled with hunger, and there was no place he could go except back to the caravan and Sandor.

The nights were worse. He was afraid of the cold, afraid to sleep in the open, afraid of the darkness of the streets. He huddled in the light of a lamp on a side street, fascinated by the ornate ironwork. Across the street the leaded glass windows of a restaurant glowed with warm light. The faces that went in and out were lit by a huge iron carriage lamp. The people were bundled in fur and heavy lap rugs as they got into motorcars or occasionally a fiacre. He tried to approach one party, holding his eyes down and mumbling. The doorman of the restaurant, dressed in a hussar's uniform, chased him back across the street, to the shelter of his lamppost.

He waited there for hours, watching people come out of the restaurant, studying the silhouettes of diners through the leaded windows. It was late, almost closing hour, when a huge sedan drove by on his side of the street, close enough to splatter him with mud and snow from the street. Ten minutes later the car came by again, pulling up at the curb. A light glowed in the curtained rear window, and Ral saw someone peeking at him. He imagined how warm it must be inside the car.

The driver's door opened, and a man in a blue uniform and cap got out. Ral hesitated as the man came toward him, thinking about the warmth inside the car. When he began to run, he was too late. The man caught him by the arms and dragged him to the windows of the car. Ral could see someone nod in the dim interior, before the front door was opened and he was thrown inside. A screen blocked his view of the back of the car. Once they began to drive off, he was so happy for the warmth and so fascinated by the instruments and controls of the car that he forgot his fear of where they might be going.

The house they drove to was beyond the Ringstrasse, in the hills below Oberdöbling, a stone mansion with iron gates in front and tall ceilings and parquet floors inside. They parked the car on a steep hill outside, and Ral was led into a kitchen on the ground floor. The cook gave him a plate of schnitzel, fried potatoes, bread, and salad. There was milk to drink, and a plate of pastries on the counter.

"Why?" he said.

"Just eat and be thankful," answered the man who had driven the car. He and the cook laughed.

At the sight of so much food, Ral forgot his qualms about eating in a strange house, except that he used his fingers instead of the fork and knife that were offered to him. Strange utensils might be unclean, he thought.

"Looks like a gypsy, this one," said the cook. "Watch how the little animal eats with his fingers. Well, you know what they say about them . . ."

When he finished eating, they took him to a bathroom, with a steamy tub and a tray of soaps and shampoos.

"Why?" he said.

The driver smiled. "You'll find out soon enough. Clean yourself up and put that on." He pointed to a white nightshirt that hung on a hook on the back of the door.

"What about my clothes?"

"Never mind."

The nightshirt was clean and soft, and when he put it on, he was shown to a high-ceilinged bedroom, with brocaded drapes on the windows and thick oriental carpets on the floor. "You wait here," the driver said.

Ral sat on the big four-poster bed, exhausted, but too apprehensive to sleep. The room was filled with luxuries he had never seen before—ornate furniture, paintings, silk carpets. It was the first time he had ever been inside a *gajo* home.

Then he heard the door open.

The man who came in was tall, white-haired, with a closely trimmed mustache. He was old, but he stood rigidly straight, like an army officer. A heavy brocade maroon robe was draped over his shoulders. He paused at a small round table to pour a glass of wine.

"Did you like the motorcar?" he asked.

Ral smiled. He had liked it. He had never before actually ridden in a car, and only once or twice had he even seen a car as fancy as that one.

"Daimler-Benz," the man said. "The finest car in the world. That's a special phaeton model, custom-built. There isn't another anywhere just like it."

The man sat next to Ral on the edge of the bed, venturing a smile of his own. He reached out, running his fingers down Ral's cheek, then reaching back into Ral's hair.

Ral tried to pull away, but the strong fingers locked into his hair, using just enough force to hold him. "Your eyes are very good," the man said. "The hair, too. Excellent." The big hand slid down Ral's neck, pausing on his shoulder, squeezing the muscles of his shoulder and arm through the nightshirt.

Ral squirmed, trying to escape across the bed, but the man held him firmly, putting down the wineglass so he could grip Ral's other shoulder. He stared into Ral's eyes, then in an instant he was all over Ral, mumbling, drooling, slathering. Ral tried to twist free, to escape the powerful hands, but it was useless. For all his age, the man was bigger and much stronger. And before Ral could twist free, the man was on top of him, his weight pressing on Ral's chest as his hands lifted the nightshirt.

Ral felt a hand between his legs. He tried to shout, but nausea overcame him and he gagged on his own words. He closed his eyes. What was happening couldn't be true, he told himself. It was a nightmare. It was something he could never have imagined, something as impossible as what Sandor had proposed for him and Keje. As the man reached all over him, touching everywhere, squeezing and pressing him, taking his pleasure with Ral as he pleased, it took all of Ral's concentration to hold his eyes shut, to try to blind out what was happening to him, to stifle the pain and shame that welled up inside him. And there was nothing he could do.

He held his eyes shut until after the man left. The driver came into the room with his clothes, and he all but threw Ral down the stairs to the kitchen, then out into the street. Before he slammed the door, the driver threw a leather purse at Ral.

Ral vomited in the street, wretching until his whole body ached. He hurt everywhere, but he forced himself to get up and walk down the street, toward the city. He had to find some kind of moving water where he could wash himself. He was *merime*, unclean. Even if it was his own secret, it was a curse.

He didn't know the outskirts of Vienna, had no idea where to go, where to find water. On one corner he saw two policemen, and when he ran they began to chase him, until he stumbled into an alley and hid under a pile of refuse. There were signs on the street corners, but they were in German, not the *patrin* with which he was familiar. After he had walked for an hour, the streets began sloping up again, and he knew he had gone the wrong way, away from the center of the city.

It was dawn when he finally found a fountain in a tiny park. The basin of water was covered with a sheet of ice. He found a stone to break through the ice, and then splashed himself with the icy water, rubbing his skin until it was red and tender. Then he dressed again and, using the sun as his compass, started back toward the sloped streets of the outskirts. He saw signs that he remembered, and even though he couldn't read the words, he could follow the signs, until he was back on the steep hill.

It was the iron gates that he saw first, with the stone mansion behind. Then he saw the car, long and shiny in the early morning light. It was bigger than he remembered, the finish deeply polished, almost iridescent. He traced the letters of the name plate with his fingers, D-A-I-M-L-E-R B-E-N-Z, and wondered what the name meant. As he looked at the front of the car, the chrome headlights seemed like eyes, the landau brackets on the sides were ears, the grille an open mouth. It was as though the car had a face. He remembered how warm it had been inside the car.

The driver's door was open, and Ral got in. He had never driven a car, but anything mechanical had always been easy for him. Even as a boy of eight, he could hammer at a forge or bang tin on a stone.

He honked the horn, then turned to look for faces in the windows of the house. He saw curtains pulled back, and caught a glimpse of white hair and the brocade bathrobe. Then he found the brake, released it, and jumped clear.

The hill was so steep that the car rolled by itself, careening from curb to curb as it accelerated. He saw it crash into the iron fence on the curve of the road. The weight of the car tore the fence away easily as the car tipped forward and first rolled, then tumbled, down the slope. It landed upside down, the top crushed, the body mangled beyond recognition. A pool of gasoline ran out from under the car.

He heard voices shouting behind him and he ran down the street, stopping only for an instant when he spotted the purse that the driver had thrown at him the night before. Ten minutes later he was in the back streets of Oberdöbling, and safe. Then he opened the purse and found more coins than he and his mother had ever gotten in a week of begging.

He had heard that about the *gaji*, that they would pay for almost anything, for things so unclean that they were inconceivable to a gypsy. But until that night he could never have imagined what those things might be. Just as he could never imagine how much he would learn to fear the *gaji*, or how much the *gaji* could be attracted to features that had always seemed unremarkable to him. That his eyes were dark and deep, his hair black and curly, his skin coppery . . .

How little he knew of the *gaji*! How strange was their world! He threw the coins down on the street. He was Rom! He wouldn't take money from a *gajo* for that.

New York, 1966

For a day Jill was a celebrity in the office. Everyone managed to admire her midwinter tan. A few people assumed she had gone to the Cannes Film Festival. Evelyn, her secretary, winked and asked about the topless beaches. Two young associates wondered out loud how she managed to wheedle an unscheduled week out of Sidney Millman. "You think a man could ever get away with that?" one said.

Finally Sidney Millman came in, looked to see if the secretaries were out of earshot, grinned suggestively, and asked what kind of man Jean-Claude Bernard was.

"He's a good lawyer," Jill answered. "A lot better lawyer than I expected."

"Is he?"

"Why else do you think he managed to get me to agree to the museum's picking up the whole tab for insurance and shipping?"

Millman's only answer was a grin.

"How was the extra week?"

"None of it was billable, if that's what you're going to ask. Call it pure self-indulgence."

"It was a friendly question, Jill. I really just wanted to know how your week was. I guess I was hoping that a week off would leave you more relaxed."

"What's that supposed to mean?"

"Hey, easy!" His broad grin was like a dog rolling over and exposing its throat to show that it wasn't attacking. "I didn't mean more than what the words say. You're an amazing woman, Jill. You work as hard as anyone here, and you pull off deals that absolutely amaze me and just about everyone else. When you're away we miss you. But I've been worried that you're into it too much. It seems as though you're still trying to prove something to the partners. Or maybe it's to the world. I could understand it when you first started. But you've proved yourself. You're in the firm now. No one has any qualms about you or your work. No one objects to your taking a vacation once in a while. I just wanted you to know that."

Her smile made Millman wink. "Thanks," she said. "For a minute there I thought you were going to tell me I should get married, or have a kid, or take up a hobby, or exercise, or who knows what."

"None of those would be so terrible, Jill."

"You sound like my grandmother. Are you going to ask me if I met a nice eligible man in France?"

"Did you?"

"What's happening at Christie's?" she asked. "Any deals cooking?"

By midmorning, Jill had finally faced up to the mountains of papers that had been arranged so neatly on her desk. Evelyn had sorted matters by priority, which at least gave Jill a battle plan. But within an hour she realized that she had been away long enough to forget what it was like, to forget the incredible busyness of her life in New York, the breathless pace that had for so long been her way of fighting off loneliness and emptiness. As soon as word got out that she was back, phone calls began to stack up, until the pile of pink and white slips grew to match the mountains of paperwork. Evelyn hovered between her anteroom and Jill's office, waiting for work, or passing in little notes saying that so-and-so wanted to see Jill as soon as she was off the line, or reminding her that this call or that was urgent, that certain work was due that afternoon, the next day, the next week, that she had a luncheon date with so-and-so. There were tickler messages to make dates with or call or write or get a meeting together with a whole battalion of clients, opponents, and colleagues.

After the initial shock the routine came back quickly. By two o'clock she was up to speed, handling three calls at a time, dictating to Evelyn and into the machine, scribbling notes on one matter while she negotiated another on the phone, shouting at Evelyn because some paper she needed wasn't right there at her fingertips when she needed it. Later that afternoon she overheard the secretaries talking in the hallway outside her office.

"For a while there, I thought she'd changed," said one. "She seemed kind of mellow this morning."

"Wonder Woman?" said the other. "She'll never change."

A week later Jill had whittled down the stacks of work and was back to pace, whirling through the calls and the meetings and the memos and agreements. On the outside it was like the old days. But to Jill everything seemed changed. She wasn't really engaged, not the way she once had been. Nothing sparkled. She had turned out some long memos and wrapped up the loose ends on a couple of tricky negotiations that had been pending, and her work was all respectable, but it was all done on sheer brains and charm. Getting by.

Weeks went by and no one said a thing; no one seemed to notice that she really wasn't the same old Jill Ashton. And so it was a surprise when Sidney Millman came into her office, a month after she had gotten back from

France, wearing a pixie grin that suggested he had something other than another estate on his mind.

"Can we talk a minute?" he asked.

"Sure. What's up?"

He looked out in the anteroom and closed the door. "I don't know. What's up with you, Jill?"

"Still want to know if I met the right man in France? What would I do without my own surrogate grandmother here in the firm?"

"I'm serious, Jill. I get the feeling that something's troubling you."

"There's nothing wrong, Sidney."

"Sure?"

"What are you getting at?"

"You're just not on top of it, Jill. It's not that the work you're turning out isn't good enough. It is. Hell, you can turn out acceptable stuff with half of your brain working in slow motion. But something's missing. There's no spunk. No hustle."

"Is this all because I wouldn't go out for dinner with that creep who wants to consign his collection to Christie's? I thought I was here as a lawyer, not a courtesan."

"Jill, what's so demanding about a business dinner? It never used to trouble you before. Understand me: I'm not here to tell you to do this or that. What I'm saying is that if there's something wrong, if something's bothering you, just tell me."

"Would you ask the same thing if I were a man?"

"Of course I would."

"I doubt that."

"Jill, it's got nothing to do with your being a woman. I've worked with you for three years. I like you. I value you as a friend and a colleague. It troubles me to see you off your form."

"Off my form? Look, Sidney, if I'm not pulling my load, you let me know. Just tell me to work harder, and I'll do it. But don't give me this vague business about being 'off my form.' Next thing I know, you'll be asking me if I have feminine problems. What the hell! I'll save you the trouble: I'm not pregnant, I don't have my period, and I'm not suffering from premenstrual tension. Okay?"

Millman got up from his chair without responding.

When he left, Jill closed the door and looked down at the stacks of folders and call-back slips that Evelyn had tried to organize. As if you could organize a life by putting it in neat stacks.

Then she looked at the spot where Millman had been standing, remembered his gaze, the way he had looked at her, avoiding her eyes. Most men had to force themselves to look at a woman's eyes. And when they did, it was always self-consciously, trying to look sexy or concerned or caring. Like Millman. He had probably been sincere in what he said, but his gaze was forced, as if he were embarrassed by the intimacy of eye contact.

She remembered how easily Ral had looked into her eyes. For Ral, the direct look was the only look. His eyes were wide open, inviting you inside himself.

She remembered their talks, in the café and on the beach. They had said so little; the pace of the words had been so gentle and soft, like the tiny foam-flecked waves that had caressed the rocky beach. Yet those few words seemed so significant alongside the flurry of words she heard all day, the barrage of language in the folders. She spent her whole day with words, talking on the phone, reading, dictating, always moving at breakneck pace, always caught up in a maelstrom of words. Return the call; decide whether it was better to do it yourself or have Evelyn do it—each time it was an important decision. Important? It was nothing. Ral was waiting for a trial, charged with murder. Murder!

The spiral-bound notebooks were in the top drawer of her desk, where she had put them her first day back. She glanced at the dates she had written on the top of each page, and remembered the frustrating conversations on each day of her visits to the prison. Then she came to the list of journals, the German titles that she had carefully copied in Wanda Lanzer's empty room in Amsterdam, knowing they were about gypsies, but with no idea what she would do with that information.

She couldn't read a word of German, but looking at the titles she thought of Nat Hirschmann. He was still a scholar, she knew, a specialist in Modern European history. She hadn't seen him for years, but had followed his career in the newspapers, where he had been celebrated on and off as a leader of the New Left. From Berkeley, he had gone on to Harvard, then to NYU. His notoriety was as a radical and speechmaker. But he would know German, and maybe something about the gypsies.

They had dated for most of a year, while she was in law school at Stanford and he was a graduate student at Berkeley. He had gotten serious one evening, and began talking of commitment. She immediately backed away, not because she didn't like him, but because she couldn't imagine letting a commitment to anyone interfere with the career that had somehow become her destiny.

She looked up the number and dialed it herself. He picked up his own phone.

"Jill Ashton?"

"How are you, Nat?"

"Jill Ashton, my God! That's fantastic."

"I need a favor."

"Your place or mine?"

"I'm serious."

"So am I. And I know better than to discuss favors on the phone with brainy and beautiful lady lawyers. You should be careful about what you say to me on the phone anyway. I usually have at least someone from the

FBI or the New York City police listening in on my line. If they get you down on one of their lists, it could be a permanent taint."

"At least you always have an audience. If we can't talk on the phone, how about lunch?"

"Sure. When?"

It took her a moment to glance at her calendar. There was something scribbled in for lunch every day for weeks. That day she was supposed to meet with someone from the Museum of Modern Art. She could already imagine every word of the conversation as they rambled on about the next estate they wanted to get their hands on and what they thought the foibles of the owner were and how to begin the campaign to land the estate.

"Today?" she said.

"The busy lawyer can clear her calendar that fast? And for a superannuated radical? I can't wait to hear what's up."

Hirschmann showed up in a tweed sports jacket, blue jeans, and a workshirt. His beard and medium-long curly hair were clean and neat. He looked content with himself and the world. When the maitre d' insisted that he wear a tie, Hirschmann borrowed one with aplomb.

"Joining the Establishment has been good for you," he said when they sat down. "You look terrific."

"You too, except I'm not so sure about the *nouveau pauvre* costume."

"It's important, a symbol. I need the jacket so the security guards at NYU will know I'm faculty. The rest is a uniform. I ought to deduct the whole thing on my income taxes the way a painter deducts his overalls."

"You pay income taxes? Things have changed."

"Not really. You're still hiding behind quips."

She smiled. "I have the feeling you know me better than I remembered." She ordered white wine, and waited until it came before she went on.

"I need some help, Nat."

"That's kind of a first for you. You were the one person who never needed help from anyone, for anything."

"This is different. Tell me, what do you know about gypsies?"

"You got taken? That is a first."

She held out the notebook. "Do you know what these books are?"

He glanced at the list. "Folklore, it looks like. The kind of dreary stuff that methodical amateur scholars love. Where did you copy these? And why?"

"I met a gypsy, a man . . ." She described the festival in Saintes-Maries and meeting Ral, then told how she had found out about the murder, realizing as she went on that the story was coming out disjointed, a faltering narrative that didn't quite come together.

"The Gypsy Defense Fund? I thought you'd given up on causes. I can still remember what you said, about how no one really gives a damn anyway. And then the business about how you haven't really made it until you've made it in New York. I always thought that was why *we* didn't make it. Naive fool that I am, I still believed. And you didn't."

"You're right." She saw a hint of a frown on his face. "I mean about causes. I did kind of give up, or at least slide away from it all. But this matters."

"What does the list of books have to do with it?"

"They were in the woman's apartment. The woman who was found."

"I thought she was just visiting in Saintes-Maries."

"She was."

"So where was the apartment?"

"Amsterdam. I stopped off on the way back."

"You went to Amsterdam, just to check out where she lived? This really matters to you . . . ?"

"I'm not exactly sure why, but yes, it really matters."

Hirschmann leaned back, grinning. "It's about time for you, isn't it?"

"What are you talking about?"

"Even goddesses have emotions."

"That's mean."

"No, honest."

She reached out, touching his arm. "I really do need help, Nat."

"And you know I can't resist. Of all the near misses, of all the women that never quite worked out, you're still the one I'm sorriest about. I envy the guy. If I ever could have guessed, I'd have tried to pass for a gypsy. What's he like?"

"Different." Her grin was sheepish. "When I'm with him I feel strange. I've never felt like that before."

"Classic symptom, I'm told."

"How do I research the background of a gypsy?"

"Why? Your mother want a background check?"

Jill laughed. "My mother? She'd croak on the spot if she met Ral."

"What about the wedding? What'll she do there?"

"Nat! He's being held in detention, in Les Baumettes, in Marseilles. Do you know anything about criminal trials in France?"

"Not since the Dreyfus case. I've seen the CRS and the police in action against a demonstration in Paris. When they finish with a suspect, I don't imagine there's much need for a trial."

"Exactly. Without some kind of a defense, Ral hasn't got a chance. And right now his defense is zilch."

"What does he say happened?"

"He won't say."

"Did you ask him?"

"I saw him in prison seven times. Forty-five minutes each time. He was willing to talk about his youth, about things that happened twenty-five years ago. Then the story just stopped."

"You know he's German?"

"German-Austrian. He grew up in the Burgenland, outside Vienna. Every spring, when the snow began to melt, his father would say '*Bahtalo drom*'—it means 'good road'—and they would—" She stopped when she realized that she was repeating one of Ral's tales.

Hirschmann thought out loud. "Twenty-five years . . . 1941 . . . is that when his story stopped?"

Jill nodded.

"What did he do during the war?"

"He wouldn't talk about it. He wouldn't have been old enough to have been in the army anyway. Were gypsies in armies?"

"Some. But I doubt that he'd have been in the German army. That would be like a Jew in the SS. If it happened, it was because there was a mistake. And mistakes with gypsies are easy to catch."

"So where were the gypsies, if they didn't go into the army?"

"The Nazis classified them as 'shiftless elements' in the camps. Strictly speaking, they were internees, but when the Final Solution got rolling, the Nazis threw them in with the Jews. Thousands of them were killed in the gas chambers."

"Do you think Ral could have been in a camp?"

"Any gypsy would have to have been hiding or passing as a non-gypsy to be in Nazi-occupied Europe and stay out of a camp."

"Would there be records somewhere? Evidence that he was in a camp?"

"He never mentioned it?"

"He never said anything about the war. Whenever I asked him about anything after 1940 or so, he would say 'I'll tell about that when the right time comes, in my trial.' It was almost as if his life were split, a part he would talk about and a secret part."

"A lot of survivors had that reaction. There are clinical studies of Jews who refuse to talk about the camps. Some ended up dumb—total silence, the kind of thing you'd treat with shock therapy."

Jill looked away, as if to seek privacy. "That could explain his eyes. There's something in his eyes, a kind of infinite sadness, that I've never seen before."

"You're really hooked, aren't you?"

"Where would I find records?"

"You won't. The Jews have made a minor industry out of tracking down who was in camps and who wasn't. For the Jews, survival and the written record are a kind of revenge. They wrote notes, secreted them away, made lists and buried them. That's why the Eichmann trial was so important, to remind the world of what happened. But I've never heard of any gypsy records. Most gypsies don't read and write anyway. It's a matter of pride for them. They're even afraid that if they let their children learn to read and write, the children will quit the gypsy life."

"Ral can read and write."

"Really? You're sure he's a gypsy?"

"What about German records? Didn't the Nazis keep records?"

"They were methodical. They wrote down every name, coded every list, cross-checked when trains arrived, made sure the numbers matched, even invented euphemisms to annotate the list for people who supposedly died en route. But most of those lists were destroyed at the end of the war. No one wanted to be caught with a list like that. Especially in the East. When the Russians swept in, those camps just fell apart."

"What about the West? Suppose Ral was in a camp in the West."

"Unlikely. The main camps were all in the East. And trying to find documented evidence that someone was in a camp, especially a gypsy, is close to impossible. Why won't he tell you what he did during the war?"

"He's a mysterious man."

"Even while he's facing a murder trial?"

"Especially while he's facing the trial. I guess I have to find out without his help. How do I do it?"

"Jill, you're talking about a major project. It would take months, maybe years of phone calls and letters. It's not like there's some master index you can consult. If you're lucky, you can pick up a hint here or there, maybe find someone who remembers a name or a list that no one else knows about. Every so often a list surfaces that someone has been carrying around for twenty years. But it's all fragments. A few names, maybe. A list of the members of some community or family. What's he afraid of anyway? Why won't he talk?"

"Ral doesn't trust *gaji*." She smiled at Hirschmann's recognition of the word.

"It's not going to be easy to prove he was in a camp unless he tells you where and when. I'd say it's almost impossible, unless you can get some help."

"I was thinking of getting some help."

"From?"

Jill grinned. It took Hirschmann a few seconds to realize that he had been nailed.

"Why me?"

"I don't know who else to turn to."

"What do you know about the woman?" Hirschmann asked.

Jill told what she knew, describing the books, the quiet room, the fact that the woman was German and left no relatives or friends.

"How did she support herself?"

"That's the next thing I'm going to find out."

"How? You said she had no one. It sounds as though the concierge was close to useless."

"I'll find out," said Jill.

"You really know what you want," said Hirschmann. He finished his lunch, including dessert. "One last question, Jill—"

"Shoot."

"Do you think he killed the woman?"

"I don't know, Nat. I really don't. If he did, I'm sure he had a reason."

"Everyone has a reason. Most people are willing to tell what their reason was."

"But Ral's not most people. He's a gypsy."

Hirschmann's only reply was a peevish grin.

That afternoon Jill ignored the piles of work on her desk and the accumulating stack of calls to return. Instead she called the Cloisters, asking for Professor Edmund Sonntag, an art historian who specialized in medieval ivories. She had worked with him arranging a loan from a museum in Koblenz for an exhibit.

Sonntag was in his late sixties, white-haired, kindly, and so absent-minded that he left burning cigarettes all over a room as he talked or worked, forgetting each one as he lit another. Yet he could laugh at himself as a caricature of a German scholar, and once Jill had gotten used to the fact that he could use a name in one sentence and forget it two minutes later, they got on famously.

They exchanged pleasantries on the phone for a few minutes before Jill explained that she needed to talk to someone in the German consulate who could help her with a bureaucratic matter.

"Have you tried the cultural attaché? I can't remember his name, but I think you met him at the opening for the ivory exhibit. He's usually helpful."

"Schorer?"

"Yes, that's the man."

"He seemed nice, but I need someone closer to the bureaucratic nitty-gritty. I'm trying to track down a person. I'd guess that Schorer would be more useful if I were looking for a painting."

"What sort of person?"

"A woman. She was German. I think she might have been a pensioner. I thought that someone at the consulate could help me find out about her."

"Sounds intriguing. Did she leave behind a fabulous collection of art?"

Jill thought of the photographs in Wanda Lanzer's apartment. "Not really."

"It might prove difficult to find much about her. Those records are usually confidential."

"That's why I need help," said Jill.

"I see. Well, there's a man in charge of pensions and that sort of thing at the consulate. I once had some dealings with him. It turned out that I was entitled to a pension because of the years I had taught at Tübingen, and he arranged it all. I tried to turn it down, but he insisted. To this day I get a check every month from Bonn. His name is . . . actually it's slipped my mind, but I'll call you when I remember it."

"Maybe I should call you back. You might forget to call."

Sonntag laughed. "Don't be unkind to an absentminded old man. I'll find out right now. And then I'll call him and tell him to expect your call. But you have to promise to come up to the Cloisters one of these days for a picnic."

"I'd like that. We'll make a date when you call back."

Vienna, 1947

Ral had been wandering the streets for months when he saw the woman. The collar of her mouse-gray coat was turned up and pulled tight, like a turtle's shell, as she waited at the tram stop on the Prinz-Eugen-Strasse, not far from the Belvedere. He had gone there to wander among the trees, as a relief from the endless days of walking the streets.

For a moment he had to force himself to believe it could be true. After so long, was it possible? He remembered telling Yitzak that Palestine was only a dream. Was seeing her only a dream?

While he watched, she disappeared inside the tram. The car started down the hill, picking up speed quickly.

He ran after the car, losing his footing in the loose cobbles, twisting his ankle as he stumbled on the tracks. When he got up he could hardly walk, the ankle hurt so much. He was out of breath, gasping for air. His heart was pounding. The car was receding in the distance.

He stood on the tracks, trying to catch his breath, his face in his hands. Would he ever get another chance? Or was this the end of the dream?

When he looked up, the car had stopped at the bottom of the hill, blocked by workers who were moving wheelbarrows and buckets of rubble across the right-of-way. He tried to run again, stumbling headlong as he lost his footing on the twisted ankle. How long would the tram wait this time? It felt like he had never moved more slowly.

He caught a handrail of the tram just as the car started up again, pulling himself aboard and trying to find a foothold against the dense pack of late-afternoon passengers coming home from work. The people stood so close to one another that he couldn't see around or past them. He tried to edge forward, into the car. Two women with newspaper-wrapped parcels watched him move toward the part of the tram where the seats were, then glanced at each other and pushed their hips together, blocking his way.

"*Zwo schillinge!*" shouted the trainman, trying to collect his fares.

"*Entschuldigen,*" said Ral, trying to edge his way into the car. "Pardon. *Entschuldigen, bitte.*"

People looked up as he passed. He heard a coarse whisper: "*Zigeuner!*" It was followed by a flurry of whispers. The two women pulled back, opening the way for him.

Without warning, the tram stopped again. He tried to see forward, to watch the next exit in front to see if she got off, but there were too many people in the tram. He could see nothing. Before he could edge his way to a window, the tram started up again.

It stopped two more times before he made it to the front of the car. At the third stop he jumped off and studied the faces of everyone who got off. There were men with battered, bulging briefcases that he was sure carried black market goods. Everyone wore ragged clothes that they tried to tug and smooth into a semblance of dignity. They all seemed so purposeful as they walked off toward the rows of gray flats. They seemed to know exactly where they were going.

The woman in the mouse-gray coat wasn't there.

He ran back along the tram tracks to the previous stop, watching as other trams came down the line. The bells would clang when the drivers saw him on the tracks. Passengers shouted at the crazy gypsy who was slowing down their train. When he got to the station, he watched the crowd get off a tram, hoping that somehow she had changed trams and would be on this one.

She wasn't.

He looked around the neighborhood at modest apartments, half of them rubble, the others peeling, unkempt, shattered visages of what had once been a neighborhood of character. The ubiquitous debris of war made all the neighborhoods of Vienna the same now.

He looked up and down the rows of doorways. How long would it take to ring each bell? To wait outside each building as the trams came in? What if he waited at the tram stop, stayed until morning? Anyone who came home in the evening would probably ride back to a job in the morning. He could be there, waiting.

He smiled, all for himself. He didn't have to stay. He knew where to look now.

The next morning he was there early. He waited until the crowds disappeared onto the trams. By late morning he was the only one at the stop. No one who even looked like her had been there, so he walked along the tram tracks, studying the neighborhoods, making sure he was back at the Prinz-Eugen-Strasse station in the late afternoon.

For a whole week he followed the same routine, spending enough time at the stations that he got to know faces, recognizing the few people who smiled at him, and the many who turned their faces when they saw him. No one ever talked in those crowds. They were private faces, hugging their briefcases and bundles, pulling coats tight around themselves, going home to their private worlds.

The second week he began riding the tram each day, following it to the end of the line and back again, watching every passenger get on and off, waiting for her to get on.

"You can't ride to the end and back," said the trainman when he realized what Ral was doing.

"Why not? If I pay, I can ride."

The trainman turned away, not caring if he had an audience for his hoarsely mumbled *"Zigeuner!"*

After four days of riding and seeing no one who looked at all like the woman in the mouse-gray coat, Ral went back to walking the neighborhood where he thought she had gotten off that first day. He tried stopping people on the street, showing them his photograph. Most people ran away when they saw him coming. The few who stopped at his hail quickly went on their way when they realized that he didn't have the expected offering of black market merchandise.

By the fourth week he had all but given up. He would wander the streets of Vienna aimlessly during the day, and only show up at the station on the Prinz-Eugen-Strasse in the late afternoon. He really didn't expect to see her again, wasn't sure anymore that the woman in the mouse-gray coat was really Eva Ritter. But even as he lost hope, he followed his pattern, substituting habit for conviction. What else could he do?

It was exactly six weeks after he had first seen her that he saw her again. She was getting on the same tram, at the Prinz-Eugen-Strasse station. She wore the same mouse-gray coat, pulled it close around her neck. As he watched, mesmerized, he almost missed the tram.

She boarded in the front. He got on at the rear, after the tram had started up. This time he was careful. He stayed near the rear platform and stepped down at each stop, watching as the passengers got off from the front. This time, he told himself, she wouldn't slip away.

She got off at the third stop. When he started after her, the trainman shouted, "Hey, you . . . *zwo schillinge!*" and ran after Ral.

While he paid, he saw her walk quickly, almost running, toward the shadows along the sides of the streets, under the facades of the buildings. By the time he started after her, he couldn't make her out anymore in the dim evening light.

He was going to run, but thought that would frighten her. So he stayed in the shadows and walked just a little faster than she had walked, gradually closing the distance until he finally saw her again. The coat was still wrapped tightly around her neck as she slipped from one shadow to another on the dim street. He slowed his own pace to maintain the distance between them, waiting for her to turn toward a side street or even a window, just so he could see her profile again.

He remembered Yitzak's questions. So you find her? Then what? Ral wondered what he would do. What should he say?

She turned. Without thinking, he ducked into a shadow, as though it were he who was being followed. When he peeked out, she was standing outside the entrance of a four-story apartment building.

He began running, afraid she would escape again. He could sense her fear in the way she fumbled in her pocketbook for keys, all the while clutching her coat tightly around herself. He could hear his own gasping breaths and feel the wild thumping of his heartbeat. He was close enough to reach out and touch her when suddenly she turned, her face tense, her eyes terrified by his nearness.

"Who are you?" she shouted in his face. "What do you want?"

He looked closely to make sure. The woman's eyes were blue, a watery gray-blue. And the nose and forehead that had looked so familiar from a distance at the station were all wrong, much too weak and sloped. While he stood, staring, the woman turned away, opened the door, and slipped through. He heard the bolt snap shut.

He stood there for a long time, staring at the closed door. This was the one city he knew. He had searched for months and he had no clues. What about the other cities? Where would he go next? Bratislava? Budapest? Trieste? Ljubljana? Zagreb? And what if she wasn't in a city he had ever known? What if she was somewhere in Germany? Or in a city where they spoke a language he didn't know? How long could he look? Another six months? Six years? Would it be any different in another city? Would there be anyone who would even talk to him? Another kind *gaje* like Lisl, perhaps. But what about the Romany? Would they all be like the poor wanderers he had found in Prague and Vienna, people for whom the terrible past was nothing but a great blank?

It was hopeless. He knew that. And still, he knew he would go on, search until he found her. It wasn't something he could explain, not to a *gajo*, or even a Romany perhaps. But it was something he had to do.

He said good-bye to Lisl that night. The next day he took to the road.

It would be more than eight years before he came back to Vienna.

Vienna, 1955

The feeling of security came to Wanda Lanzer gradually, almost imperceptibly. There was no moment when she suddenly felt safe, but the moments of anxiety, of that inchoate feeling that something terrible was going to happen, that someone would look at one of her identification papers and say "No, that's not who you are," came less and less frequently, and with less severity. Finally, without her being aware of when it happened, they stopped. She forgot her fears.

Mostly it was time that did it, and the numbing sameness of the routines she followed. Month after month, year after year, for nine long years she went every day from her room to the Bibliothek and back again. For nine years she cataloged and filed documents and transcripts and clippings about the Nazis, filling occasional requests from Frankfurt for information from the files of the Bibliothek to defend some charge that had been brought in a civil proceeding, or to supply facts for a newspaper story that was being planted to answer another wave of anti-Nazi propaganda.

She treasured the security of her new life, but that security cost her dearly. The price was anonymity, giving up her past, her achievements, her status, and, of course, recognition. Once, she went to the Stadtsbibliothek during lunch to look at their serial collection, checking in the old handwritten file lists exactly which issues of the now defunct prewar anthropological journals they still had. A week later she went back and filled out two request slips.

It took the librarians a long time to find the obscure journals. One woman came back to confirm one of the requests, saying that it was stored in a basement and was very inconvenient to retrieve. A moment later Wanda Lanzer thought she detected a strange look from the other librarian, as if there had been something suspicious about the requests. She was ready to say that she didn't really need the journals, when the woman said, "Well, it'll be a while. You better sit and wait." Half an hour later a young man appeared with the two musty issues.

Wanda Lanzer sat down at the table and thumbed through the stale pages of the journals, glancing over her shoulder to make sure no one was watching her before she turned to the articles by Eva Ritter. She read them slowly, interrupting her concentration to look up and make sure no one was looking over her shoulder. Even after so many years, the phrases she had once labored over were still familiar to her ear. She wished she could make photocopies of the articles to take back to her room, but she was reluctant to ask. There were probably records kept of requests for photocopies, she thought. And while she would have liked to go back to the Stadtsbibliothek again to reread the articles, just to see the heading with her name—Eva Ritter's name—as author, she never did.

One morning in October 1955, Dr. Stürgkh called her to his office. Although he was at the Bibliothek every day, she rarely saw him. The sudden summons worried her.

"We have a new reader coming tomorrow," he said in that peculiar modulation of his that boomed and faded so suddenly. "A man who wishes to examine some of the Nuremberg documents. He's being sent over by the Stadtsbibliothek because our own collection is more complete than theirs. Will you be available if the man needs help?"

"Of course." She was pleased. Working with a reader seemed like a promotion.

"You know," said Stürgkh, "before the war we had a very high caliber of reader here at the Bibliothek. Scholars and well-educated patrons. But Vienna isn't what it was anymore. Don't be surprised if the man is ill-prepared, even ill-mannered. It's our obligation, unfortunately, to honor these requests for the use of the collection by the so-called public."

"Of course."

That evening she laid out some summary materials and a general index to the document collection on a table in the reading room.

She didn't see the new reader come in in the morning. At ten o'clock Frau Lettner came back from the reading room with her face twisted up as though she had smelled something horrid.

"Dr. Stürgkh is far too hospitable," she said. "I really don't know why we let readers like that into the Bibliothek. What would that sort of man want with our collection anyway? He looks like . . . like an Indian, or Lord knows what. Oh, Vienna has changed so. And all for the worse. You will help the man, won't you? I can't bear . . ."

"Of course," said Wanda Lanzer. She left the catalog room in a hurry so she wouldn't have to hear any more about the water in the Viennese wine or the difference between civilization and *Kultur*.

The man was sitting at the far table, where the light from the tall windows fell on the table. He didn't look up as she opened the heavy, swinging door, but she could see him clearly in a full quarter profile.

Her reaction was sudden and overwhelming. Her head swarmed with dizziness. Her legs turned to rubber. Waves of nausea surged into her throat. She let the door swing shut and staggered toward her desk, unsure whether her legs would carry her those few steps.

"Fräulein!" Frau Lettner caught her before she slumped to the floor, led her to a chair, then bent her head down between her knees and put a damp cloth on the back of her neck.

"What have you eaten, Fräulein Lanzer? You must be more careful. Vienna isn't what it once was, you know. They sell meat that shouldn't be sold, tins and even fresh food that's hardly fit for dogs. You rest just as you are for a few minutes. Then have some mineral water. If you still feel unwell, you must go home and rest."

Frau Lettner's words floated in a cloud. As Wanda Lanzer came back from the near faint, and the waves of dizziness subsided, she pictured the face she had seen, the sad, accusing eyes. It couldn't be, she told herself. It was impossible. But the image of that face wouldn't go away.

"You really must go home, Fräulein," said Frau Lettner. "You're not well at all. I can see it in your eyes. You must drink mineral water and nothing else until the system purges itself. If it were me, I'd have a clyster to cleanse the system. A time like this and you give Nature a helping hand."

"Yes," said Wanda Lanzer, in an emotionless monotone. She imagined how simple it would be if an enema could purge her fears.

Her legs were still wobbly when the porter and Frau Lettner helped her on with her coat.

Back in her room over the park, Wanda Lanzer pretended that she was ill, lying down on the daybed, covering her eyes with a cold compress, sipping at the mineral water that Frau Lettner had recommended. She tried to sleep, tried to force herself not to think of what she had seen. If she could only sleep, she told herself, everything would be all right.

But she wasn't ill, and she couldn't sleep.

He couldn't be alive, she told herself. It was impossible. But how could anyone else look just like him? And the man in the reading room of the Bibliothek could read; why else would he be there? How many other gypsies could read?

She took out the bottle of slivovitz that she kept in a cupboard, filled a small glass, and downed it in a gulp. Then she put on a record, hoping the familiar melodies would drive her fears away.

What was there to be afraid of? she asked herself. She had done nothing wrong. She had helped them, helped him. Anyway, he couldn't be alive. It was over, finished. The horrible, sick world of yesterday. Eva Ritter's world. And Eva Ritter was gone too, without a trace.

The music failed to soothe her. She switched to another record, a solo violin, and downed two more glasses of the slivovitz. The music soared, a melancholy *lassú* that cried out with the solitude of the Hungarian steppes. She tried to let her soul soar with the music, tried to ride the wavering cry of the violin to that oblivion of emotion. But the music was too familiar, the memories it evoked too confused. She pulled the arm off the record and buried her face in her hands.

It can't be, she told herself. Not after so many years. But the face she had seen was too real, the hair and eyes and skin too unforgettable. She couldn't bear to see him again, couldn't bear even a quick secretive glimpse at the library to make sure.

She went to the armoire and took down her traveling bag. Everything she owned fit in easily. Under her other arm she could carry the Victrola with its fitted cover. As she went down the stairs, she avoided the concierge in the hallway. The rent was paid. There was nothing that had to be said.

She waited until she was outside the railroad station before going to a telephone to call the Bibliothek.

"This is quite improper," said Frau Lettner when she heard that Wanda Lanzer would not be coming back to the Bibliothek. "Where will you go then, to a sanitarium? It's really not necessary. Your condition isn't that serious. And after so many years with us, one would think that you could give proper notice. You even have a pay envelope owing to you tomorrow. Will you not be in to pick it up?"

Wanda Lanzer needed that pay envelope. All she had were the pitiful savings she had eked out of her salary, hardly enough to live on for a few months. But she couldn't bear the thought of going back, of seeing him, of maybe being seen by him.

Under the soaring arches of the station, there was a list of departures on a board: one train went to Budapest–Belgrade–Sofia–Istanbul; another to Venice–Rome–Naples. There was an afternoon departure to Paris, another to Warsaw with a connection to Moscow. There was no place you couldn't go, it seemed; trains left for the whole world. Except that Wanda Lanzer had only Austrian personal registration appers, and no passport. Without a passport she couldn't travel outside Austria and Germany. The choices were dreary.

At the gate to the trains, where every boarding passenger would have to walk past her, a young gypsy girl, not more than sixteen years old, stood in bare feet, a bundled baby in her arms. Her whispered plea to each passenger was barely audible, even up close. *"Per le bambino . . . bitte . . . für Milch, latte . . . per le bambino . . ."*

The girl wasn't Italian; that was obvious from the scattered German words and from her clothes. It was a tradition that Wanda Lanzer recognized: gypsy girls begged money for their children in Italian, always for the bambino. She never knew why.

From the girl's jewelry and the way she wore her *diclo* tied under her hair in the back, she looked like Hungarian Kalderash, possibly a Lovari. Wanda Lanzer listened to her plea again, hoping for a few phrases of Romany so she could be sure. She had seen so few Romany since the end of the war, and heard the language so seldom. She hovered by the girl, listening, hoping the girl would talk to her baby.

Then restraint took over. She backed away, keeping a safe distance, trying not to stare too obviously as the girl approached the steady stream of
travelers. *"Per le bambino . . . bitte . . ."*

The bundle in the girl's arms was probably empty, Wanda Lanzer
knew. She knew dozens of the scams, like faking injuries to file claims, or
teaching children to walk like cripples when they went out begging, or the
empty-bundle trick. She had been appalled when she first learned about
some of the scams, especially when she finally grasped the workings of the
Hokano Baró that could systematically clean an unsuspecting *gaje* woman
out of a whole fortune, down to the last *groschen*. Amoral people, she had
thought the gypsies then, people with no scruples or values, no sense or
grasp of the social precepts that were necessary to keep a society function-
ing.

And then, by listening and watching and talking, she had gradually
learned that what the gypsies had was not a lack of morals, but a lack of
restraints. They were without the tethers that bound the rest of society.
They didn't need registration papers, passports, documents, titles. They
went where they wanted, traveled when they wanted, afraid of nothing.
They were free.

And after all that had happened, she still envied them.

Trieste, Italy, 1955

It had taken Ral eight years on the road to reach Trieste. He followed
the same circuit that he had followed every spring and summer as a child.
When spring came, they would leave the long winter camp in the
Burgenland for Bratislava, then Budapest, Pécs, Belgrade, Zagreb, Ljubljana, and finally on to Trieste before looping back to the Burgenland. He
hitchhiked and walked the same roads that he had once traveled in a caravan, sometimes even saw *patrin* that he remembered on the roadsides,
reminders that there had been a farmhouse that was always good for a
meal, or streams that were once full of fish, fields that were ripe with
crops.

But everything was different now. The streams had dried up, the fish
killed by the red and gray filth of the factories on their banks. Fields had

been plowed under to build blocks of apartment buildings on the outskirts of the cities. And even in the cities and towns that hadn't been touched by the war, where the yellow stucco buildings and cobbled streets were as they had always been, the pace of life had changed. Cars and trucks and buses made the roads perilous for a walker; it would have been impossible for a *vardo*. And there were no more gypsies on the roads. The few gypsies he found had all adapted, giving up tinkering to work in the auto body repair shops and horse trading to become dealers in wrecked cars.

"Modern times," some of the gypsies told him. "You gotta keep up."

But it wasn't just adaptation they were talking about. They might still use plaster of Paris and paint to fix up an old wreck and sell it to an unsuspecting *gajo*, but being a wrecker instead of a horse trader meant they were tied down, sedentary instead of wandering. And settled, the gypsies forgot the Romany life. They sent their children to *gajo* schools, where they learned Hungarian or Serbian or German or Italian instead of Romany, and then pressured their parents in turn into forgetting whatever Romany they had once known. Instead of welcoming a gypsy traveler, they were wary, and even the old customs of ritual cleanliness were forgotten as relics of the wandering life. With the customs went the spontaneity and ease of gypsy life, the ability to drop everything at a moment's notice and head off in pursuit of a whim.

Wherever he asked about the woman in the photograph, it was the same. Some refused to talk to him. Others were friendly, but hesitant to look at a picture, reluctant to talk about the war, about anything from the past. No one had heard of Eva Ritter. No one recognized the photograph. The war was a hiatus that had already been expunged from memories. Outside a café he heard a young Sinte man use the epithet *"Hitlari!"* in an argument. He asked the man if he knew what the word meant. The Sinte shrugged and walked away.

And so he moved on, through town after town, searching out the gypsies, asking, showing his photograph, then moving on again, stopping only long enough to work a few weeks in a body shop when he needed money, before he went back to the road.

In Trieste he wandered instinctively toward the junkyards, a vast free market within the free city. It was a permanent flea market, presided over by a wealthy Piedmontese gypsy named Gaspucci, who ruled his domain from a grand saloon trailer.

Gaspucci glanced at the photograph and shook his head.

Ral tried to tell him about Eva Ritter—who she was and what she had done.

"Look!" Gaspucci answered. "All I know about the war is that it means good business now. The Italians buy anything now. They buy. I sell. I do all right, no? Look at this!" He waved at the gaudy plastic-covered furniture in his trailer, of which he was immensely proud. The trailer and furniture made Ral think of the old *vardos* and their stacks of eiderdowns inside.

"You're sure you've never seen her?"

Gaspucci glanced again at the photograph. "*Gaje*, no? From one of the camps, you say? Ask the Jew, why don't you? He was in a camp, I think." He pointed across the flea market to a storefront shop next to a café.

"The Jew? Who's he?"

"Who's he? He's the Jew. Ask him who I am, and he'll say 'the gypsy.' It's enough for him, and it's enough for me. Go ask him if he knows the woman."

The storefront was prosperous, brimming over with merchandise—pots, clothing, boxes of stockings, radios, blankets—all piled in chaotic disorder. A heavyset man was hunched over a book at the counter, his clothes mismatched and ill-fitting. He looked up when he heard the bell ring, lowering his glasses.

"What?" he said, getting up from his stool. "You came back for my blessing? The gypsy who reads is back?" He enveloped Ral in a bearhug.

"What happened to Palestine?" said Ral.

Yitzak shrugged. "The boat left without me."

"You tried to go?"

"Sure I tried." He pushed the book aside to make room for Ral on the counter.

"With a little baksheesh here and there I got a place on a boat. For two days we had to wait on a mooring in the harbor. They gave me a bed to sleep in that was maybe as big as this counter; to scratch an itch in that bed I had to ask myself permission. All night the boat rolled until I'm black and blue everywhere, and in the morning they wake us up with whistles and a horn, so I jump up and bang my head on the bed above. After two nights I ask myself, 'Yitzak! You want every morning to wake up to a whistle? And every night have your insides roll around?' Anyway, I heard it's hot in Palestine, they have no beets, and the women are not so beautiful, not like here anyway."

Ral looked around the shop. The bag of junk Yitzak had carried on his back had been transformed into a business.

"It's good here," Yitzak went on. "The Americans bring in ships full of everything, for the occupation troops. I buy from them and sell to the Italians. Tell me, would you think the American sailors and soldiers need so many pairs of nylon stockings or so much lipstick? And what about you? No wife yet? No laughing children?"

Ral shook his head.

"In the pocket, still with the photograph of the woman?"

Ral nodded.

"You find anything about her?"

"No one remembers her. I stopped in every village on the old routes, asked every Romany I could find. It's like I'm the only one who ever saw her."

"And still you look?"

Ral shrugged. "When I find one person who remembers her. Just one . . ."

"Just one? Maybe there isn't just one. Maybe you're the only one who remembers."

"The only one? You know how many Romany—?"

Yitzak held up his hands, palms out. Ral remembered the gesture.

"Gypsy man! The mind is a wonderful machine. People tell you how smart a little boy is when he can do sums so big you can't even write them down. Or a genius like that Einstein comes up with a way to make a big enough bang to kill everyone. But you know what the real wonder of the mind is? It's not these geniuses. The real wonder is forgetting. Why do you think that café next door does so well? People go there, they have a few glasses of wine, and they forget. Or they come here and buy nylon stockings and high shoes and lipstick, and they can forget that home is maybe cardboard and tin sheets and soup with no meat in it. Even war they can forget, gypsy man. That's how wonderful the mind is."

Yitzak watched the unchanging expression on Ral's face. "Ah, with you it's no use. Come on." He flipped over a sign on the inside of the door and led Ral to the café.

"Look at them," he said, gesturing toward the young men and women at the tables of the café. "They lived through the same war as you and me. Now they laugh and flirt and marry and make babies. Look at those girls! You think it's me they're making eyes at? And you! You don't even smile back. I tell you, gypsy man, if I had a face like yours . . ."

The waiter brought a carafe of wine and a glass, gave Ral a puzzled glance, then brought another glass.

"So," said Yitzak. "Ten years you've looked for her. Where?"

Ral described the gypsies and wanderers he had met, the tinsmiths and whitewashers and makers of kitchen spoons, the musicians and bear trainers and fiddle makers, the masons and herb growers and locksmiths and boot makers, the woodcarvers and fortune tellers and downright hustlers and con men—people who sometimes didn't themselves know they were gypsies.

"Why are you so sure she'll be with gypsies?"

"Look at the photograph." The photo was so fingered that the paper had broken down in folds and creases. "You see that signature? Loli Tschai. It's a name she gave herself, supposed to be a Romany name. She's a *rye*. Gypsies are all she cares about. She can't stay away from them."

"How do you know she's alive? She could have been killed. Or arrested and tried."

"You said yourself that they only arrest the big ones. To them she would be a little fish."

"There've been many trials. The Poles, the Germans, the Russians, the French, the Americans—everyone holds trials. You can read, gypsy man. Look at the records."

"The police will show me nothing. When I ask they think it's for some gypsy scam."

"Not police records. If she's hiding, she wouldn't register with the police anyway. Court records. Documents. There are records of all those arrests and trials in books. If she was arrested, there would be a record that you could read."

"Where?"

After a few days, even Yitzak could appreciate Ral's impatience enough to send him on his way. The officials of the American Military Occupation Forces Information Office in Trieste explained that while they didn't have a copy, the records Ral needed would be available in many big city libraries, almost certainly in Vienna.

Vienna, 1955

The reading room of the Bibliothek reminded Ral of the museums that Sophie had taken him to, somber rooms without a whisper of air or a ray of the sun, where you couldn't hear a human voice or the call of a bird in the hush. Nothing could have been further from the gypsy life he had known. Even when Sophie had taught him how to look at the paintings and statues, to see the beauty in the human forms that she was forever comparing to his own body, he had always felt awkward in those rooms, always wanting to pull back the drapes, open the windows, and shout.

No one had spoken to him since he arrived in the Bibliothek. A stack of books and a typed guide to the collection had been waiting for him on the table. The spindly, pinch-faced woman who scurried in and out of the reading room, and the porter who overstoked the tile stoves in the corners of the room, came and went as if he weren't there.

It didn't surprise him. It was the third library he had been to, and at the others they had been reluctant even to let him through the door. "You can't sell flowers or cigarettes here," the porter at the National Library had told him. "No begging," they told him at the Stadtsbibliothek. Even after he had explained what he wanted to see, the responses were skeptical, raised eyebrows and shrugs that said, "You? Why would you be interested in that?"

It was exactly what Yitzak had predicted. "A gypsy who reads?" he had said. "They'll welcome you like they welcome me to a Mass. Only I'm not so stupid that I go to a Mass."

The books that had been left stacked for him on the table were as dreary as the room. Much of the material was in English and French, and he had to pick his way through the pages, looking for the few words he knew, like *gypsy*. Or her name, of course. After two days and some twenty volumes, he had spotted neither.

He finally caught the spindly, pinch-faced woman's attention when she came through the reading room.

"A name?" said Frau Lettner. "You're looking for a name? Use the index. You do know what an index is, don't you?"

As she left the reading room, he heard her mumble under her breath, "Doesn't know what an index is . . ."

The index was no help, and for another day he went through Nuremberg trial documents, the green series volumes and the red, looking for a single mention of Loli Tschai or Eva Ritter, even a single reference to a gypsy.

Then, on his fourth day at the Bibliothek, Ral spotted a name he recognized. It was in the transcript of the trial of a minor war criminal, a physician named Beiglboeck who had conducted medical experiments in the Dachau concentration camp. One of the witnesses was a man named Karl Hollenrainer, a gypsy. Ral remembered him from Buchenwald, at the end of the war. Hollenrainer had only been in Buchenwald for a couple of days when his name was called out during the morning roll call of those who were being sent away to work. No one paid much attention. Work usually meant bomb disposal. They said that after you helped disarm ten bombs you would be set free. They said. Ral had never heard of anyone who had been set free. And he had never heard of Hollenrainer again.

In the trial transcript Hollenrainer came to the stand and tried to tell his story, how when he got to Dachau he was starved of all food and water and given only seawater to drink, in his case a vile yellow seawater that made him vomit. He explained that he had been told that it was an experiment to determine how long downed Luftwaffe pilots might survive drinking seawater, and that they told him that the gypsies who were selected for the experiment should be honored to help the cause of the Reich. Within days of starting the experiment, he said, he and the other gypsies who were given seawater were raging with thirst, foaming at the mouth, fighting with one another for the right to suck the moisture out of a rag that had been used to wipe up slop from the floor. One gypsy refused to swallow more seawater, so the doctors had rammed a tube down his throat to pour it in.

The prosecutor cut Hollenrainer off in the midst of his story to begin the methodical questions that the proceeding demanded.

· · ·

Q. Now, upon arrival in Dachau you then went to the quarantine block, is that correct?

A. Yes.

Q. You stayed there for a day or two and were given a physical examination?

A. Yes.

Q. Did you also get an X-ray examination?

A. Yes.

Q. And then you were transferred to the experimental block?

A. Yes.

Q. And there you met a professor or doctor?

A. Yes.

Q. Do you think you would be able to recognize that doctor if you saw him today?

A. Yes, immediately. I would recognize him at once.

Q. Would you kindly stand up from your witness chair, take your earphones off, and proceed over to the defendants' dock and see if you can recognize the professor you met at Dachau?

[Hollenrainer left the stand.]

Q. Walk right over, please.

[Witness attempts assault on the defendant Beiglboeck.]

Ral could picture it vividly, understand those words completely. What else could a man do?

Hollenrainer was restrained by the guards and led up to the bench. He pleaded with the court: "Would the tribunal please forgive me? I am married and I have a small son. This man is a murderer. He gave me saltwater and he performed a liver puncture on me. He has ruined my whole life. I am still under medical treatment. Please do not send me to prison."

"That is no extenuation," said Presiding Justice Beals, an American. "The contempt before this court must be punished. People must understand that a court is not to be treated in that manner . . ." He sentenced Hollenrainer—the victim!—to ninety days in the Nuremberg prison for contempt.

Ral could hear the justice's voice, the tones of authority and condescension, instructing Hollenrainer as if he were a child. Ral looked down and saw the book trembling in his hands as his knuckles turned white with rage. Then the book slipped from his fingers, slamming down on the wooden floor.

Frau Lettner ran into the reading room. "What's happening here?"

"It was an accident," said Ral. "The book fell to the floor."

Frau Lettner's face was tight, her lips pursed.

"That is no extenuation," she said. "You must understand that books from the Bibliothek are not to be treated in that manner."

The same words. The same tone. For an instant Ral saw an SS officer in muddy boots. "Jews to the right, gypsies to the left." And then the badges. "Gypsies and other shiftless elements will wear the black triangle."

The wave of rage passed. Frau Lettner hadn't even seen it on his face.

"I'm sorry," he said. "Can you tell me if there are more books about gypsies in the library?"

"Gypsies? Gypsies are hardly a subject of interest to us. We're a library of German culture." She thought for a moment, avoiding Ral's eyes. "Perhaps in the clippings files. I know nothing about them. They were put together by a colleague, and she has left the Bibliothek staff."

The files were in cardboard boxes, in chronological order. Most were from German magazines and newspapers, articles about former Nazis who were in government and business positions, performing responsible jobs. There were no clippings about women.

Ral went through them anyway. The last clipping, only two weeks old, caught his eye.

MUNICH, 18 October 1955

Professor Karl Clauberg, head of the so-called experimental medical center in the Auschwitz (Oświęcim) extermination camp, returned last Thursday from Soviet captivity in a convoy of 598 war prisoners.

At Camp Friedland, the West German reception center, Dr. Clauberg told reporters of the *Süddeutsche Zeitung* that Heinrich Himmler had assigned 400 women prisoners, Jews and gypsies, to him for experiments in sterilization. Dr. Clauberg spoke of his experiments with a sense of scientific achievement, and appeared to be inordinately proud of his work. He said that he had actually succeeded in developing a new method, consisting of a simple injection, to produce the results required. The professor said that he had used his method on 150 women, and he went on to say that the new method could be applied nowadays to "special cases." Dr. Clauberg did not elaborate.

Special cases? That was always what they called it. When numbers were called out at roll call, it was for special handling. The hostages in Yugoslavia were special cases. No one ever called anything what it was.

Clauberg! Ral had never known the man's name. They had talked about him, the doctor who did the operations. But no one knew who he was. Ral stared at the wall, trying to picture the young girls who came out of the surgery, asking what had been done to them. He could hear their screams of pain, screams no *gajo* could ever understand, after they were told that they were barren. To be barren is the worst curse that can befall a gypsy woman. Until a child is born, a gypsy marriage isn't truly consummated. Now he knew the name of the man.

Was it a brother's duty to avenge? There was no law for that, no *kris* you could ask. For rape, for a beating, for abandonment, for maltreatment of any kind, the gypsy laws had an answer, a custom that the *kris* could call up. But for what that doctor had done, there was no answer. How could a gypsy even conceive of cruelty like that?

"Are you finished with this material?" asked Frau Lettner. "When you're finished the material must be replaced in the cartons exactly as you found it."

"Why do you have this?" Ral asked.

"What do you mean?"

He held out the clipping. "Why do you keep that? Why is it important to you?"

"I really have no idea. As I explained to you, the clipping files were assembled by my colleague, Fräulein Lanzer. She has left the staff now."

Ral heard only the inflection of the name, the rhythm of the two short syllables, the "-er" at the end. "What was her name?"

"Lanzer. Wanda Lanzer. Why do you ask?"

Wan'-da Lan'-zer. E'-va Rit'-ter. Could it be?

He pulled out the photograph. "Is this the woman?"

Frau Lettner recoiled from the proffered photograph. "I have no time . . ." Then the image caught her eye and she stared at it. "There is a likeness," she said. "That could be her. Why do you have her photograph?"

Ral stood up, the intense excitement vivid in his eyes. "Where is she? Where is she now?"

"I told you. She's left the library staff. She didn't tell us where she was going. She was taken ill quite suddenly."

"When?" His eyes, more than his tone, seemed to frighten Frau Lettner.

"A few days ago."

"After I came?"

The woman thought for a moment. "She left Monday. Is that when you came?"

"Where does she live?"

"I'm not sure that's any of your business. This is a research library, not an information bureau."

Ral's eyes pinned the woman as he asked again. "Where does she live?"

The last remnants of color drained from Frau Lettner's face. She looked ready to scream. "I must confer with the director," she said.

"Why does it matter if you tell me? I knew her once."

Frau Lettner watched Ral's eyes for another instant. "I guess it doesn't matter. She moved anyway, I think. Her room was in the Fourth Bezirk, Hauslabgasse 2/13. She had a view over the Alois Drosche Park."

New York, 1966

I f his name had not been Johan Klinger, Jill would have sworn that the man she met in the Fifth Avenue office of the German consulate was English. He wore a natty brown tweed suit, a tattersall shirt, and a bow tie. His mustache was clipped. He spoke with the crisp accent of a BBC announcer. And he had the friendly leer that Jill associated with randy middle-aged English gentlemen chatting up a young woman at a pub. Every time she raised a question about researching the background of Wanda Lanzer in the German pension records, Klinger would find a way to shift the discussion to a favorite restaurant in London, a favored pub in some remote corner of Sussex, or a reminiscence of his days as a Rhodes scholar at Oxford. She was growing impatient.

"How do I file an application for information from those pension records?" she asked.

"Professor Sonntag was right: you're not only inordinately charming, but persistent. Unfortunately your charm and persistence are to no avail. The pension records are private documents. They can be opened only for a government agency with a bona fide inquiry."

"Would they be open to a French prosecutor?"

"A French prosecutor? I doubt it. We have little patience for the French. Under the guise of intellectual rigor, they're little more than Latins with northern accents."

"Mr. Klinger! The woman is alleged to have been murdered. We need to know more about her in order to understand what may have happened."

"We?" Klinger's leer took a turn toward the lascivious. "My dear! I'm delighted that you and I have become a 'we' already. But I'm afraid that I don't yet share your interest in this matter. My duty is to register and certify pension claims to the Bundesrepublik. I really have no interest in a woman who was murdered at . . . where was this alleged to have occurred?"

"Saintes-Maries-de-la-Mer, near Marseilles, a little more than two months ago."

"And why are you so passionately involved in this? It would appear to be a matter for the French. Indeed, we have a consulate in Marseilles that could certainly handle any official inquiries. The police have their own mechanisms, through Interpol, for questions of identity."

"Identity isn't the problem. The woman's been identified. But all we know about her is that she lived alone and had some kind of German pension. And that doesn't explain why she was murdered."

" 'We' again. How has this case become your concern, Miss Ashton? From what Professor Sonntag told me, you're a specialist in art matters. Was the woman involved in some art scandal?"

"It's a long story. I'm not sure it's really relevant."

"Oh, but I'm sure it is. And I'm eager to hear a long involved story, especially a tale of intrigue and adventure topped by a murder in some exotic town. Perhaps we could have lunch, or a drink, and you could tell me the whole story then."

"And how soon could you get the pension records?"

"I told you, pension records are private documents. Unless there is a special ruling."

"And who makes special rulings?"

Klinger winked. His mustache suddenly seemed more Teutonic than British. "I do," he said.

It took one lunch and two meetings over drinks before Klinger agreed to file a request for the pension records of Wanda Lanzer. The second time they met for drinks, he groped for Jill's knee under the table and suggested that they really ought to meet for dinner some evening.

Graz, Austria, 1955

Graz was booming. The vast Steyr-Puch-Daimler car factories and the cellulose mills hummed through three shifts a day. Workers came and went at every hour, carrying their lunch or dinner in briefcases, the Austrian way of pretending that there were no class differences between workers and those who went to offices.

But Wanda Lanzer knew there was a difference. A worker with a skill could walk into one of those factories and get a job on the spot, no questions asked. She couldn't. Wherever she inquired—libraries, agencies, small engineering firms—there were questions: Where are you from? Why did you leave Vienna? Do you have a residence permit for Graz? Have you registered with the police? Do you have references from your last job? Some of those questions she couldn't answer.

Maybe the man she had seen was only in her imagination, she tried to tell herself. A fantasy. She really hadn't been feeling well. Maybe it was something she ate. She could just telephone the Bibliothek and tell them that it was all a mistake, that she was feeling better now and would be coming back. A few days' more rest and she would be just fine.

But the image of the man she had seen wouldn't go away, even after weeks. Going to Graz didn't help. Playing the records didn't help. Nothing helped. And she knew she wouldn't go back. Instead, she walked the streets, asking about jobs, trembling in anticipation of the questions she couldn't answer.

At one employment agency the man looked her up and down, then asked her to take her coat off and turn around for him. She remembered the horrid, ascetic man in Prague.

"There's a position open for a chambermaid in an inn," the man said.

"Chambermaid?" She felt words rushing. I am Doktor Eva Ritter. I have six languages. I have published articles in scientific journals. . . . She caught herself. Eva Ritter was dead. And Wanda Lanzer needed a job, badly.

"I'd like to think about it," she said. "I'll tell you tomorrow."

"Tomorrow there won't be a job. They'll get a peasant woman who can lift an ox. Or an illegal from Yugoslavia who'll work for next to nothing. Look, I'm doing you a favor. I know about people without papers. And it won't cost you much, really." He winked.

She hitched her coat against the shudder of revulsion and ran out.

How did the man know she didn't have papers? Could he see it from her face? Was she already walking like the frightened ones, shrinking into her coat, cowering?

Back at her cramped room near the train station, where she lived on rolls and soup and tea to conserve the dwindling funds in her little snap purse, she looked at herself in a mirror. Her clothes were still presentable, her traveling bag was almost new. The Victrola in its traveling case looked hardly used. But she wondered: How long would it be until she was like the desperate ones she saw outside the station, the new immigrants from the East who carried their possessions in cardboard suitcases tied up with twine? When would she too be trekking and begging, dragging her possessions in a twine-wrapped suitcase, scavenging the trash barrels for food and clothing, waking up on park benches or in station waiting rooms?

After twelve days in Graz her job search had already dwindled to perfunctory motions. She spent as much time wandering, watching trains come and go, dreaming that she could be on one, as she spent in the rounds of offices. Then one day, as she waited for nothing in particular, an old-fashioned *vardo* pulled up outside the station, pulled by a shaggy gray horse, and painted with abstract flowers and a sunrise on the side. There were curtains in the windows, a smokestack for the stove inside, and a sign on the back:

FORTUNES TOLD

PALMS READ

CONSULTATIONS ON LOVE AND THE FUTURE

The *vardo* stopped outside the station, a window in the side opened into a counter, and from the door in the rear a man and two boys got out to feed and water the horse, and then to pass leaflets to passersby.

Wanda Lanzer hesitated before she took a leaflet. But the boy, only eight or ten years old, was persistent, and she finally took the crudely printed flyer. The prose was semiliterate: "Madame Latavya. Love Problems, Emotional Problems Fixed. Fortunes. Palms Read. Tarot." The price of consultation was hardly enough to buy a loaf of bread, but Wanda Lanzer knew that the money meant nothing anyway. It wasn't for those few tokens that the fortune tellers plied their trade.

She watched from a distance, waiting for someone to go up to the *vardo*. It would be a woman, she knew, probably middle-aged, maybe older, a widow or a lonely married woman suffering a stuffy husband, the routine of a hausfrau, the dreary isolation of provincial Graz, a woman who dreamed of a different life, of escape, of fantasy, perhaps of a lover for whom she was already too old, or adventures that could no longer happen. "It can't hurt," the lonely woman would say to herself as she read the sign or the leaflets. "For a few schillings it might be amusing."

Wanda Lanzer watched for more than an hour, but no one in Graz seemed interested in the *vardo*. The fortune teller leaned out of the window. "Come on," she urged. "What can it harm you? A few schillings and you'll know what the future's got for you."

Wanda Lanzer started to retreat, but the eyes of the fortune teller caught her—wide, beckoning eyes that stared without blinking. "Come in," the woman said. "Let's see what the cards have to say." The woman came out through the back door of the *vardo*, her skirts rustling as she walked, her wrinkled face smiling enough to show hollow teeth. Through the open door of the *vardo*, Wanda Lanzer could see wall hangings and a garish painting of the holy family.

Up close, Madame Latavya smelled of pipe smoke. The hair that peeked out from under her *diclo* was gray and brittle. The loose front of her blouse revealed thin, sagging breasts.

Madame Latavya stared at Wanda Lanzer's hands, looking for rings perhaps, or for the soft, manicured hands of a woman of money and leisure. The glance was quick but exact, like a glance Wanda Lanzer remembered from many years before, from a fortune teller whose name she had finally forgotten.

Eva Ritter was all of twenty years old then, anxiously awaiting her marriage to a fine-looking, hardworking young man named Ernst who inexplicably bored her to tears. A week before the wedding her father gathered the two families together and made a speech.

"We're not old-fashioned," he said. "We don't talk of a dowry. But I've worked hard and led a devout life. By the grace of God I've everything a man could want—a loyal wife, a good daughter. Soon I'll have a fine son. I know Ernst will work hard and that you both will lead devout lives. And to get you started on the path of life, there will be a little nest egg." He pulled out a thick envelope filled with crisp banknotes, opening the flap so everyone could see. "For after your marriage," he said as he tucked the envelope back in his pocket.

All week the house was being readied for the big day. Fresh antimacassars went on the chairs and sofas, doilies on the tables. Table linen and plates were set for the spread of cakes and pastries. Clothes were laid out, pressed, laid out again. Eva's mother even allowed her a peek at some of the finery in her trousseau, the delicate nightshirts and fine sheets. One afternoon she tried to explain what Eva should know for her wedding night, but she faltered with embarrassment. "Ernst seems like a gentle boy," she said. "You needn't be afraid. Just close your eyes and think about something else."

As the day neared, the house became too close to bear, the preparations so intense that the house smelled like a bake shop. Eva ran out, into town, just for air. In the Hauptplaz she spotted a *vardo*, very much like the one she would see years later in Graz, with a sign advertising the madame, and young men passing out leaflets.

Bored, anxious about the wedding, she took one of the leaflets as a lark, wondering whether the fortune teller would see the same promising future that her mother and father had predicted. The old woman, with a maplike, wrinkled face and chains of gold jewelry on her arms and neck, came out and took Eva's hands, gently feeling the palms and fingertips for calluses that would tell her as much as Eva's clothes and shoes. A moment later she took Eva inside, looked straight into her eyes, and began talking in a gentle, reassuring voice. After a few sentences the steady, monotonous intonation of the voice was mesmerizing.

"I see a great yearning," she said, "a yearning that is a secret to the world. And I see unhappiness . . ."

Surprised by what seemed to her an extraordinary perception, Eva said, "What else do you see?"

"I see a choice, a choice that will decide your life." The old woman hesitated. "One choice is happiness, a great happiness; the other . . ." Again she hesitated, watching Eva's reactions.

"Yes? The other. . . ?"

The fortune teller brought out tarot cards and silently began flipping through them. Then she began to argue with the cards. "No! This can't be. You're too young." She flipped more cards, angrily shaking her head as they came up.

"You mustn't listen to me," she said, taking Eva's hands again. "I'm just a foolish old gypsy fortune teller. And you, a young, beautiful girl, starting out in life. No, go on your way; laugh, dance, sing, be merry. Ignore me, you hear?"

"What did you see?" Eva asked.

"The cards must have lied," said the old gypsy woman. "It's never happened before, but they must have lied."

"What was it?"

"No! You tell me about your life. Tell me about your dreams."

And Eva told her, told how she had hoped to go on to the university, and how her father had sternly opposed the idea, saying that a good marriage was the only future for her. She didn't mention the dowry, which she knew was a bribe to get her to marry Ernst.

"I hope you'll be very happy," said the old gypsy.

Eva took out her purse, but the old gypsy woman waved it away. "After what the cards tried to tell me, I couldn't take your money."

"But you must."

"No. I'd be cursed if I did."

Eva came back the next day. Perhaps there was something that the old woman wouldn't tell her, she thought, something she really ought to know.

The gypsy woman feigned wariness. "I don't want to throw the cards again," she said.

But Eva insisted, and when the cards began coming up as they had come up before, the old gypsy woman began flipping them angrily, arguing with the fates that she couldn't control.

"No!" she shouted. "A young girl, beautiful, full of life, setting out on life's road . . . no! This can't be!"

"What is it?" said Eva.

"Twice?" said the old gypsy, talking as much to the cards as to Eva. "Could they try to lie to me twice?" Then with a histrionic shudder she clutched both hands to her breast. "I see grief!" she cried out. "I see pain." Her fists pounded at her breasts. "I wish it weren't so. I wish I could see only happiness. But I see something terrible—a curse."

"A curse?"

With a gesture of self-rejection, the old woman pushed away her own words. "You mustn't listen to me. Go! Live your life! Forget what I say.

You're too young and too lovely for this." She took Eva's hands in her own, letting her fingers and her eyes caress the girl.

"What kind of curse?"

"We mustn't touch it," said the fortune teller. "We mustn't look deeper."

"How can it hurt?" asked Eva. "How can it hurt to look?"

"The truths of the tarot could be painful for a young girl."

"Tell me," pleaded Eva. "You must tell me."

And again the fortune teller, sighing with resignation, began flipping the cards, pausing always with one, pushing it aside, then coming to it again.

"What is it?" said Eva. "What is that card?"

"Wait! Perhaps it's something else. Perhaps the cards are wrong. It can't be that. It mustn't be that."

But no matter how she tried, shaking her head, casting the cards again, the same card came up. Finally she leaned back from her table and spoke in a breaking whisper. "Money. There is cursed money."

"Money?" Eva was genuinely surprised. She hadn't said a word about money to the fortune teller.

"I wish it weren't so. It's the worst of curses."

"Money? What money?"

"Somewhere there's idle money—in a bank or under a mattress or in a drawer or I don't know where. That money carries a curse. And as long as the curse remains . . ." She seemed visibly shaken, unable to go on.

"How can you know that?"

"I only know what the cards tell me. Look, you see that card. How many times has it come back to us? The cards don't lie."

"How can there be a curse on money?"

The old woman's eyes went up, to invisible forces too distant to see. "Some things we can never know. We can discover a curse. We can fight it. But we can never truly understand it."

"Fight it? How can you fight it?"

"There's magic against curses, my child. But first we gotta be sure. This isn't an easy business. You have to find the money. Not any money, you understand, but money that sits idle, like in a bank or a drawer somewhere. You find that money and you bring three banknotes, each of a different denomination. And they must be new, you understand? The magic won't work with old money. You wrap them up in a handkerchief, your own handerchief. And with it you bring a live chicken."

"A chicken?"

"There's no other way to be sure."

"Where would I get a chicken?"

"From the butcher."

"But I've never bought a chicken in my whole life. The cook does that."

The old gypsy turned away, sensing resistance. "We could try an egg," she said. "An egg you can get. It's not as sure, but we can try."

Eva was there early the next day, with the handkerchief and the egg. With the house in a total commotion of preparations for the wedding, it had been easy to sneak into her father's bedroom and find the envelope with the money in his top bureau drawer. She was sure she could put the bills back before he discovered that they were missing.

When Eva held out the handkerchief and the egg, the old gypsy recoiled in horror. "No!" the woman cried out. "Cursed money I don't touch."

She told Eva to hold the egg over the money, while she said mysterious-sounding incantations, waving her fingers and hands over the egg, calling on the spirits to exorcise the curse. When her incantations reached a fever-ish pitch, she suddenly snatched away the egg, exaggerating her avoidance of the money. She cracked the egg open over a saucer.

Inside the yolk was a minuscule, hideous, yellow-green skull, with the horns of a devil. Eva jumped back in horror as the old gypsy woman whirled the contents of the saucer into the stove behind her and stoked the fire with a faggot of wood until smoke billowed out of the chimney.

"Did you see it?" she cried. "The face of the curse? If I could fall to my knees and pray with you, my child, I would. But prayers aren't strong enough for this curse. That was the Devil himself."

Eva was trembling as the fortune teller put an arm around her shoulders, stroking her hair, murmuring assurances to her. "I won't abandon you, my sweet. I'm your friend. You needn't fear. We won't let the Devil take your happiness."

But what can we do?"

"There's lots we can do, my child. But first we gotta see if our medicine is strong enough to fight this Devil. He's powerful, and I'm only an old gypsy woman."

She had Eva take one bill out of the handkerchief, a crisp ten-mark note. "Tear it in two," she said. "Then you take the rest of the money, take it away from me." With a flourish of her waving fingers, and more mysterious incantations, she wrapped the two halves of the ten-mark note in the handkerchief and pinned the thin package inside Eva's camisole. "It has to stay there, over your heart. You don't touch it for the whole night, you understand? No matter what, you don't touch it. Otherwise the magic's no good. Then you come back in the morning and we'll see if our medicine is strong enough to fight the curse."

Eva left, still skeptical, a little afraid, but very much relieved. The moments she had spent with the old gypsy woman had been her only respite from the deadly hours of preparations for the wedding, the sessions of fitting her gown and stacking her trousseau, the scurrying of the cook, the talk of who was coming and what the wedding gifts might be, and the endless praise of hardworking, boring Ernst.

The next day she went to see the old gypsy woman so early that the gyp-

sies were still shaking out their eiderdowns and drinking coffee by the fire
they had built outside the *vardo*. When Eva appeared, the old woman said
something to the others and they scattered as she led Eva into the *vardo*.

"You look," she said to Eva.

"Look at what?"

"The money. You haven't touched it, have you?"

"No." Though tempted, she had resisted the urge to peek inside the
handkerchief. All night, as she slept fitfully, thinking about the wedding
and Ernst, she had felt the package against her skin.

"Go ahead. Take it out."

Eva unpinned the handkerchief and slowly unfolded it, reluctant to look
inside. What would be there? she wondered. Another skull?

There was nothing inside except the ten-mark note, intact.

"My God!" Eva shouted. "What happened?"

The old gypsy woman began dancing, moving her shoulders in strange,
jerking motions. She cried out, "We've done it, my child! We've beaten the
Devil!" She reached for Eva's hands, taking them in her own.

"The curse is gone?" said Eva.

The gypsy smiled. "The curse? Not yet. But now it's time to really fight
that Devil. You come back this afternoon with the money. All of it. You
understand? You leave even a single banknote and it won't work. There'll
be nothing we can do."

"I understand. But it's impossible. I don't know how I can come back today. They have so many plans for me. The wedding's tomorrow. It's difficult for me to come even as often as I do. I have to sneak each time."

"The wedding's tomorrow? Then you must come today, before it's too
late. Your happiness is too precious to waste."

It took scheming, arguments, and a bold-faced lie, but Eva managed to
sneak into her father's bedroom and get the envelope, and then slipped out
of a last-minute fitting on her gown to go back to the fortune teller. She
still hadn't really decided whether she believed what was happening or
not. It didn't really matter. She enjoyed her time with the old woman immensely, enjoyed the sympathy and concern, the warmth of the woman's
hands on hers, the exuberance of the dancing and shouting. And she secretly admired the easy life of the gypsies in their *vardo*. They got up when
they felt like it, cooked out in the open, shook out their eiderdowns in the
fresh air, washed in the stream nearby. Their whole life seemed so easy and
simple and spontaneous and joyous.

When she came back that afternoon, running breathlessly, the thick envelope concealed inside her blouse, she found the *vardo* neat and tidy. The
old fortune teller was wearing a *diclo* and skirt that Eva hadn't seen before. No one else was around.

Inside, the table was cleared off, the quilts were all folded and stacked,
everything was straightened out and neat. The stove was open and clean,
with no fire inside.

The old gypsy saw her looking around. "To make such strong magic," she explained, "you start with everything clean."

"I have it," said Eva, holding out the envelope of banknotes.

The old gypsy recoiled from the package, refusing to touch the money. "No! Don't even show it to me. You wrap it in something of your own, a handkerchief or a scarf. Then put it on the table. Nothing must show, you understand? If a single corner of the money shows, it won't work."

While Eva wrapped the money in a scarf, the old woman began to wave her arms, chanting strange incantations, occasionally slipping in a phrase of German so Eva could understand. "Material things are nothing . . . money is nothing . . . only happiness matters . . ."

She caught Eva's eyes after the money was wrapped and put on the table. "Look at it!" she said. "The cursed money. Without that curse, you'll be free."

"What will it feel like?" asked Eva. "What will be different?" She wasn't sure what she wanted to hear. Perhaps that the wedding would come out all right after all, that even married to the dreary, hardworking Ernst she would know something other than the confined routine of her mother's life.

"You see the birds outside, how they fly and sing as they will? That's what your life should be, young one. You should be as the birds. And without the curse you will be. Money! Who wants it? I have no money. It's enough for me to have friends like you. I go as I please, where I please, when I please. I'm free. That's what I want for you, my friend. Only that."

"Do it!" said Eva. "Let me be free too."

The old gypsy began weaving her hands over the bundle of money, her eyes holding Eva's, her voice shouting out strange-sounding words as she invoked the spirits, calling on them to take away their curse. Her incantations became louder and faster, a pulsing rhythm broken only by cries of sympathetic pain and grimaces. She injected just enough German for Eva to understand. "Take away your curse!. . . What do we care about material things? . . . Let us be free like the birds."

And then she would lapse back into the strange-sounding words, weaving her body in a dance of exorcism that became steadily wilder and more hypnotic.

Finally, when Eva thought it impossible for the cries to be louder or more histrionic, the old gypsy, her eyes on fire, whirled in a fit of pique and passion, suddenly grasped the package of money and threw it into the open stove.

"*Take it!*" she shouted. "Take your cursed money!" She rammed a poker into the stove after the money and tamped furiously. Suddenly a burst of white smoke poured out of the stove, filling the *vardo* and driving the two of them out into the fresh air, coughing and gasping.

"Did you see?" she shouted. "It worked. We beat the Devil. Our magic worked. That's what those flames are. Our magic worked." She hugged Eva to her as she shouted with joy. "You're free now, my child. Free like the birds."

"But the money?"

"You saw it! You saw the Devil take the money. The stove was empty, and suddenly flames. That was the Devil, taking the curse. You're free, my young friend. The curse is gone."

"But what will my father say? How will I ever explain it to him when he discovers that the money is gone?"

"Tell him what happened, what had to be done. It wasn't your fault. You couldn't have brought down a curse like that. You're an innocent, a child. The money was cursed."

Eva started to cry. "He would never understand. He understands nothing. All he cares about is that I marry Ernst. And now . . . oh, my God!"

The old woman hugged Eva, smoothing her hair. "Your tears are of joy, my child. And soon you'll laugh, too." While the old woman held her and soothed her, Eva saw that the rest of the gypsies were getting the *vardo* ready to leave, pulling the chocks from under the wheels, hitching up the horse, packing the brazier that had been set up outside.

"You write to me," said the old gypsy woman. "It's very important to me. You write *poste restante* and I'll find your letters and I'll know that you're free and happy, like the birds." She waved from the back of the *vardo* as it tipped and swayed down the road.

Eva walked in circles on the way home, imagining her father's anger, the tone of his voice when she told him.

"You took the money? . . . It wasn't yours to take. . . . You gave it to a gypsy? . . . She what? . . . She burned it? . . . A curse on the money? . . . You foolish girl. You know what this means? There will be no marriage, no dowry, that's what it means. Why would a hardworking boy like Ernst want a foolish girl like you?"

Eva knew she should have been upset, depressed. In fact, she gradually admitted to herself, she was elated. The money *was* a curse. The old woman had saved her from a life of dreariness.

And even years later, when she learned about the *Hokano Baró*, how a mixture of hydrochloric acid and ammonia, mixed by the stirring with the poker, could stimulate the smoke of a fire and leave the money untouched, her feelings were not anger or the embarrassment of being swindled that keeps most victims silent, but gratitude and admiration—admiration for the consummate skills of the old woman, who was as sensitive a psychologist as she had ever encountered, and gratitude for the salvation from the dreary life of a hausfrau that the marriage would have meant.

It had been the moment when she found her soul.

And more than twenty years later, as Madame Latavya's *vardo* left Graz, weaving and swaying down the road, untouched by time it seemed,

Wanda Lanzer tried to picture herself on the trail, following the *vardos* south, taking photographs and quiet notes, speaking to the gypsies in Romany, the language of those strange incantations that she now understood. She tried to imagine herself in a *diclo*, with gold jewelry on her arms and neck, her blouse open at the throat and her skirts swirling.

But as hard as she tried, she couldn't make the image focus. Instead all she saw were the hapless vagrants of the train station, perched on their twine-wrapped boxes, fighting over scraps of food that they scavenged from trash barrels as they waited for worse times.

Vienna, 1955

"**W**hat do you want?" The man at the apartment building spoke through a partially opened Judashole, as if he were hiding something.

"I'm looking for a woman named Wanda Lanzer," said Ral.

"What's she to you?"

"I knew her once."

"Well, she's not here."

"Does she live here?"

"No."

"Did she live here?"

The man hesitated. "I told you, she doesn't live here now."

"Do you know where she is?"

"I don't know anything. She left. No notice, nothing. Didn't even say good-bye. That's the way things are now. Nine years here and they don't even say good-bye. Well, I'll tell you something: it doesn't really matter to me. She was paid up, and it'll be easy to rent that room. I can't help it if people have no manners."

"May I see the room?"

The man scrutinized Ral though the Judashole before he opened the door. "You have a job in Vienna?"

"I work."

"What kind of work?"

"Auto repair. I bang fenders."

"Where?"

"Anyplace they need me."

"You ain't a gypsy, are you?"

When Ral didn't answer, the man went on.

"Reason I ask is that I once had a bunch of 'em renting a room. Real nice room too, big windows, good wood floors. They moved in, and the first thing I knew they had this tent thing up in the middle of the room. Put the furniture out in the hall and slept on eiderdowns, like the furniture wasn't good enough for them or something. And instead of using the gas rings, they were cooking on a brazier, right in the middle of those nice floors. And with all the coming and going, I never knew who was living there and who wasn't. One day it'd be one bunch and the next day there'd be another bunch. Kids running all over the place, half naked too, dogs, women with their blouses loose so the other women in the building were complaining. They'd stand right in the hallway and suckle those little ones. No shame at all. When they finally left, they owed me for three months. If you're one of them, I got no room."

Ral smiled. He'd heard it all before, every time he tried to rent a room. "Could I see the room now?"

The elevator was broken, and there were five flights of cold stairs. "Worked before the war," the man said. The room at the top was tiny and empty, furnished only with a daybed, a table and two chairs, one other chair, and a pair of gas rings on the sideboard of the kitchen sink. There was nothing on the walls, not even a faded outline where a picture might have hung.

"Heat works fine," the man said. "Hot water for the sink, too. WC's in the hall outside, one floor down."

Ral looked at the shelves over the table. Empty. Not even a scrap of paper.

"You want it?" the man asked. "You pay two months now, then prompt on the first of every month. The gas you pay separate. You can have all the visitors you want, but no loud noise and no parties. And nothing funny like tents in the rooms or braziers on the floor, you hear?"

"Did she leave anything behind?" asked Ral.

"What do you mean? The furniture all goes with the room: bed, chairs, table. Look at it. That's good wood furniture, not junk."

"Did she . . . did Wanda Lanzer leave anything of her own behind? An address, books, a place where mail could be sent to her?"

"Hey, you interested in the room or not? I told you, I don't know nothing about her. She was real quiet, kept to herself. Always paid on time, didn't make no noise, and didn't leave no mess. Only thing I found was a little rubbish in the dustbin."

"Do you have it?"

"Have what?"

"The rubbish."

"Hey, what's with you? You come up here to look at the room, or are you weird or something? I don't go picking through trash. What do I care what she throws away? Come to think of it, I don't think the room's available anymore. Only gypsies are interested in trash, and I don't need no gypsies here."

As the man hustled Ral out into the hallway, they passed a trash barrel. On the top was a record jacket, heavy cardboard with sleeves for the records. LIZST it said on the cover, in block letters. Smaller script letters underneath spelled out *Hungarian Rhapsodies.*

Ral reached out for the record jacket. He couldn't remember what it sounded like, but he knew he had heard that music before. And he remembered where, remembered it as well as anything he had ever known.

New York, 1966

"Y ou're getting slack."

It was a statement of fact, not the opening of an argument. Sidney Millman's tone wasn't combative.

"What's that supposed to mean?" Jill regretted her contentiousness as she spoke. She knew exactly what Millman meant, and knew too that pretending ignorance wouldn't make it go away. She had been working hard, putting in the usual long hours, but the work that used to challenge her— complicated consignment deals that took virtuoso negotiating and subtle fine tuning to get them accepted by all parties, even the working lunches at the museum where her reports would be followed by private tours of new acquisitions in the basement restoration rooms—none of it excited her anymore. She felt like an automaton, putting in the hours, churning out the work, but without the reward of feeling good about a job well done. And it wasn't Sidney Millman's fault.

She knew what was wrong. She was obsessed by Ral. In the midst of the most complicated work she would think about things he had said, about stories he had told, and about what Hirschmann had said, the possibility that Ral had been in a concentration camp. What troubled her most of all was her total inability to do anything about his case. Except for waiting for that pompous, lewd Klinger to find out something about Wanda Lanzer, there was nothing she could do. She had made the case her private crusade. Yet she was a passive bystander, powerless to change events, or even influence them, and that powerlessness left her feeling disconnected and out of sorts. Her sense of responsibility meant that the work in the office got done, but it was done in the most perfunctory manner, without enthusiasm or spark. Still, she found it impossible to admit her obsession, to confess her vulnerability.

"You've got no hustle," said Millman.

"Is that why I'm in the firm, to hustle? And all this time I thought I was supposed to be a lawyer."

Millman got up from the chair and went to the doorway. "Hold all calls, would you, Evelyn?" Then he shut the door and sat down again, directly across the desk from Jill.

"Don't give me that feminist crap, Jill. You know exactly what I mean. Until you came back from Europe you had something—I don't even know what to call it, but it was the difference between being one more lawyer and being good. Really good. You think I hired you because you're good looking? Or smart? Hell, brains are easy to find. And a good-looking woman is nothing but a distraction for the horny bastards in this firm. I hired you because you were different. From the first day I saw you argue in the Southern District, you had more hustle, more moxie, more sheer balls—if you'll excuse the expression—than any other lawyer in the firm. If someone threw you a matter, you didn't just get it done. You did it with a vengeance, a passion. You figured out a better way, or you got a better deal, or you turned around a losing matter and made it a winner. You just had whatever it takes, that incredible ability to convince your clients, your colleagues, even a judge, that you had it all together. Now it's as though you've lost it. And that, Jill, is what bothers me."

"I told you before—if I'm not pulling my load, let me know."

"Jill! Listen to me. I'm not talking about pulling loads or earning your keep. Hell, you could pull your load in your sleep. I'm talking about enjoying your work and being happy. This isn't like going into a factory and punching a clock and putting in your eight hours. You're either a lawyer or you aren't. You either love it, love the work, love the life, or you're going to be miserable. You used to be turned on to work. You got off on a good brief or a good deal. Now I don't think you care much."

"That's the whole choice for you, the whole question of identity? You're either a lawyer or you're not?"

"For me, yes. For someone else, maybe no. That's why I came in to talk, Jill. I have the feeling that it's changing for you."

"Your view makes life pretty simple, doesn't it? The questions that every sophomore debates with his roommates all night long boil down to a simple formula: You are what you do."

"I'm afraid that's the way the world works. Maybe it's different somewhere else. But right here it does come down to that. And I have the feeling that it isn't working right for you."

She started to answer, a quip that was meant to throw Millman off guard, but she caught herself and stopped. He was sincere, and he was right on target. "You're right," she said. "I am off-kilter. Preoccupied. But it isn't something I can talk about. It's just something I have to work out."

"It helps to talk. Have you seen anyone?"

"You mean a shrink?" Her voice was tight.

"A shrink, a rabbi, a friend. Someone you can talk to. I'll listen if it'll help."

Jill smiled warmly. Millman's sincerity was appealing.

"Is it a man?" he asked.

"What do you think?"

"Our dashing French lawyer, Monsieur Bernard?"

She hesitated. "Kind of . . ."

"That could be rough. Three thousand miles is a long way to pine."

"I know."

"Want some time off? Fridays maybe? I don't think anyone else could pull it off, but I suspect you could swing weekends in France."

"Not now. Maybe in a few months."

"Just give me some advance warning, okay? I took a lot of flak when you stayed over there an extra week. I figured it was something like this, and I thought it was a good thing for you. But not everyone here is such a dyed-in-the-wool romantic. Anything else I can do?"

She tried to think. Millman was incredibly well connected. There were few doors that wouldn't open to his name, and a phone call from him was usually better than a bribe. This time she could think of nothing.

"Thanks," she said. "I guess I just have to wait things out."

"How serious is it?" Millman asked.

When Jill grinned, he added, "I guess that smile means I'm asking too many questions?"

"Only that I have too few answers."

As soon as Millman was out the door, Jill picked up the phone to call Johan Klinger at the German consulate. Klinger tried his leaden charm on the phone, suggesting dinner or a drink, moving his invitation ahead day by day as she turned him down.

"How long is it going to take to find out about that pension?" she asked.

"How long is it going to take to get to know you, Jill?"

"It's been four weeks," she said. "I'd think that the computers could finish a search for a record like that in two minutes."

"Couldn't we discuss this someplace more comfortable than on the phone?"

"Call me when you have something from the computer. We'll meet then."

"Today, then? The computer has completed its search."

Jill felt her mouth go dry. Getting a word out was like chewing cotton candy. "Well?"

"Could we meet in the Oak Room, say at six o'clock?"

"Klinger!" Her tone was angry. "What did you find?"

"What passion! You'll be there at six?"

"Yes! I'll be there. Now, what did you find?"

"The report from Bonn says that there's no record that a Wanda Lanzer ever received a pension from the Bundesrepublik. They have no record of the woman at all."

Vienna, 1955

For days Ral stalked the building, waiting on a bench in the nearby park, cautiously approaching neighbors who came and went. "Do you have a light?" he would ask. Or, "Could you tell me the time?" And then, after a little banter about the weather, he would segue into a question about Wanda Lanzer, asking people if they knew her, knew where she shopped, who her friends were, where she worked, where she might have gone.

No one answered his questions. With typical Viennese restraint and fear of intimacy, people shied away as soon as the conversation got beyond the weather. Some turned away when they saw him coming. Word had gotten out, it seemed. Warnings had been spread about the strange gypsy man in the park.

On the fourth day, while he waited in the park, huddling in a chill rain, a police Mercedes pulled into the cul-de-sac, pausing with the engine running. Two officers got out. Ral walked toward the park. They followed. He ducked into a side street, looked over his shoulder, and saw them still following. He started to run. Behind him he heard their footsteps, keeping up. When he turned, one had a pistol out, its lanyard snapping in the wind.

They didn't ask questions until they got him to the station. Then, name and address weren't enough.

"Where's your identification card?"

"I lost it."

"What authority issued the card?"

"I don't remember."

Other police officers joined the interrogation.

"You have no identification?" asked one.

"I haven't done anything," sid Ral. "Is it a crime to ask questions?"

"We ask the questions. You answer."

The only paper they found in his pockets, aside from the photograph, was a ration card. When they checked, they found that it was bogus, forged.

"Typical *Zigeuner*," said one policeman.

After two days in a crowded cell with five vagrants and three drunkards, Ral was brought before a magistrate who read some papers in an incomprehensible mumble. Then a policeman and a man in a business suit drove him out of Vienna on the Bratislava road, toward Czechoslovakia.

They stopped at the border. The man in the business suit went into the checkpoint, then to the middle of the no-man's-land, where he argued for half an hour with a border guard from the other side.

"Can't really blame them," the man in the business suit said when he came back to the car. "Nobody wants a *Zigeuner* around."

Ral was taken back to the cell. A different set of vagrants and drunkards were his cellmates. At the end of the week he was brought up before the magistrate again, to hear another incomprehensible order.

"Do you understand?" the magistrate asked Ral.

"No."

"The order says that you must leave Vienna within twenty-four hours. If you're picked up again for vagrancy and disturbing the peace, you'll be deported from Austria."

"Deported to where?" said Ral.

"We ask the questions," said the policeman who was guarding Ral.

They gave him a map of Austria, with a circle drawn to indicate the fifty-kilometer radius from Vienna that was closed to him. Ral stared at the map, the spiderweb of roads that led out in every direction from Vienna, going to what had once been the far reaches of a mighty empire. Now, Vienna was a *Wasserkopf*, the swollen head of a dwarf nation. Where would he go?

That wasn't the question, he told himself. Where would she go?

He knew the cities of the old circuit, from the Burgenland down through Klagenfurt and Graz toward Yugoslavia. He had roamed the old roads for eight years, searching out the gypsies, asking anyone who would listen, showing his photograph to anyone who would look. The rest of Austria— Linz, Salzburg, Innsbruck—was strange and distant. Would it be any different now?

He set off without a route, wandering more than searching. Everything was changed now. After the war, when he had walked and hitchhiked the roads, it was enough to work an odd job here and there for a meal or a night's shelter. He would repair pots and pans, tinker with broken-down farm machinery, occasionally put in a few days banging fenders in an auto body shop. Everyone was poor then. Economies were just gearing up from the ravages of the war. An odd hand was sometimes welcome.

Now everyone had a job. People could buy sleek new cars and tractors; no one needed to repair an old wreck. Factories stamped out new pots and pans. All that was left for the gypsies was to collect the detritus of progress, the cast-off cars and pots. And the life as keepers of the junkyards changed the gypsies. The trading tricks that were part of the game with horses were viewed as downright larcenous with cars.

The new Europe took its toll on Ral, too. Where he had once been able to follow his whim on the road, now he had to search out jobs, sign up for weeks at a time, coming in each morning and staying to the end of the workday, sweeping out the shop if there was no real work, waiting until the end of the pay week before he got his envelope.

He hated the regimented life, fled it at the least provocation. In time the freedom of the road became as important as his search for Eva Ritter. Spending weeks or even months at a time in a body shop, repairing cars for *gaji* who would not speak to him except to reprimand him for failing to show up on time, he craved the moments of freedom when he could walk the roads, stopping whenever and wherever he wanted, picking ripe fruit from the trees or catching fish with his hands in the streams. He dreamed of the taste of bread cooked on a hot rock, or around a stick in the embers of an open fire. He craved hearing the sounds of the birds and animals, feeling the wind and the rain, smelling wet grass or budding trees or coffee cooked on an open brazier.

As the months and then years ticked away, gradually, imperceptibly, his search slowed; he took weeks to cover distances that he would have once covered in a day. And just as gradually and imperceptibly, he lost track of the real goal of his search. No one recognized his photograph. No one had seen or heard of Wanda Lanzer or Eva Ritter. What did he have to go on? he asked himself. A fleeting identification by the contemptuous *gaje* at the Vienna library? A record jacket? Maybe Yitzak was right, maybe she didn't exist anymore. Maybe he was the last gypsy who remembered.

And yet he kept on, counting the hours and days at each job, dreaming of the peace and freedom of the road, struggling to remember but gradually forgetting as the dreary rhythms of work anesthetized his mind into a deadly solitude.

Linz, Austria, 1959

Wanda Lanzer's clothes weren't torn or ragged yet, but they were heavy with dirt and grease, and they hung off her, at least two sizes too large now. The constant hunger hardly bothered her, but the filth of the clothes did. She tried brushing them, and washing them in the lavatories of the train stations. No matter what she did, they looked gray and greasy.

The purse was finally empty. She had worked on and off, sometimes for only a week or two, once for almost six months. But nothing lasted. The longest job was for a man in Linz who rented a garage to store clothing and machine parts that he smuggled into Eastern Europe. The company was called Trans-Europa Trading. She typed correspondence, translating bills and letters from Hungarian and Romanian into German. But the job had ended as they all did. One morning she woke up afraid to go to work. She argued with herself, tried to convince herself that her fears were nonsense. Nothing had happened, she had seen no one, she wasn't even sure whom she was afraid of. But she couldn't make herself get out of bed, couldn't even open the curtains in her room. And when she finally went back to work, two days later, the man didn't care about her explanation. He just fired her.

Now she was sleeping in the train station, waiting near the wurst bar for a hurried traveler to leave a half-eaten sausage or roll, or a half-full cup of tea. Her bag was gone, sold when there was no longer anything to carry in it. She still had the Victrola, but she hadn't played it in months. Where could she plug it in?

The policeman who found her asleep was being helpful. "What are you doing in the station?" he asked.

"I was traveling. I lost my money. I'm waiting for money to be sent from Vienna." She had rehearsed the answer, the way she had rehearsed her new name years before.

"May I see your identification card?"

She hadn't shown it to anyone since she left Vienna. She fretted while he looked at it.

"Is this still your address?" he asked.

"Yes."

"When do you think the money will be here?"

"Soon."

It was a good Austrian answer, vague enough to mean anything, but sufficient for the policeman. He left her alone, with her Victrola, on the bench.

"Soon?" she repeated to herself. All that would happen soon was that it would be winter, and in winter the station would be too cold for sleep. There was no place she could go, nothing she could do. Without money, she was a prisoner. Why? she kept asking herself. It wasn't true for them, for the Romany. They never seemed to need money, never seemed to lack for it. Whether it was the forests that gave them food, or friends that gave them shelter, they survived. Even in the worst years, they got on. Why couldn't she live that way?

But of course she couldn't. And so she waited, scrounging the trash for food, struggling to keep herself clean, eluding the police by dodging into the restrooms at strategic moments, fighting the anxiety that wouldn't let her sleep and the depression that wouldn't let her fully awaken.

But after days of intolerable exhaustion, she fell asleep again on a bench in the station, with the Victrola as her pillow.

The same policeman woke her.

"The money is delayed," she said.

"We'll help you get it."

"No, it'll be all right."

He insisted on taking her to the station, apologizing all the while.

"Is this your present address?" they asked her when she produced the identification card.

"I used to live there. I'm temporarily without a permanent address."

She overheard the talk between the police officers. "She's not a *Zigeunerin*, after all," said one. "Just a little down on her luck." The other nodded.

"There are agencies, you know," the policeman said. "If you go back to Vienna you could get help. Enough to tide you over."

"I don't need any help."

"Well, you can't sleep in the station. You've been warned about that now."

"Then I'll move on."

The pawnshop offered her a pittance for the Victrola. "It plays the wrong kind of records," the man said. "There are new records, long-playing records from America. No one wants the old ones."

"It has a nice case," she pleaded. "And it's in very good condition. I've taken very good care of it."

He repeated his offer.

"Couldn't you make it enough to get outside?"

"Train fare to Germany? You want enough to buy train fare to Germany? Whatever for?"

She could hardly believe Frankfurt. The New Germany looked like the photographs she had seen of America: Neon signs blazed everywhere; slab-sided buildings cut off the sunlight from the streets; picture windows were filled with cameras and clothes and radios and televisions, all at prices she couldn't imagine. As she stood on the sidewalks, she was jostled by packs of youths on motorbikes, then splashed with mud from big Mercedes sedans, their passengers invisible behind the black glass and curtains of the rear seats.

The address she had was a six-story building. The door of the office on the fifth floor had no sign. She rang the buzzer.

"*Ja?*" the answer squawked through an intercom box.

"Is this Neue Deutschland?"

"What do you want?"

"I want to speak with someone."

"About what?"

"You helped me once. I need help again."

She was shown into a small office, divided from a warren of others by partitions.

"We're not a welfare agency," said the man who came in in shirtsleeves. He was tall, with a thin nose and pomaded hair that he combed straight back. His hands were manicured and his breath smelled of strong mouthwash. She was acutely aware of the greasy grayness of her clothes and her skin.

"I know," she said. "You helped me once. Just after the war."

"Your name?"

"Wanda Lanzer."

He left the office and came back a few minutes later with a file.

"You were working at the Bibliothek der Kultur des deutsches Volks, in Vienna. You left suddenly, without an explanation. That was an excellent job you had. Many would have appreciated such a job."

"I know."

"The work there was very important for those who believe in Germany."

She nodded.

"Why did you leave that job?"

"I . . . the weather. I was bothered by the weather. It was damp. I had a bad cough from the dampness. I still have the cough, see." She coughed, and spit into her gray handkerchief.

"Frau Lanzer! Our organization has limited resources and a vast mission. Our purpose is larger than individuals. Those who are unwilling to work for our goals, we cannot help."

She was repulsed by the naked authority, so much like that of the wiry man in Prague who once held the power of granting or refusing her a new name.

"I'd like to work again," she said. "I have languages, research skills. I'm a trained anthropologist."

His smile condescended. "We have no need for trained anthropologists. We helped you once. Many from situations not unlike your own could not be helped. They had to leave the German-speaking community, go into exile, forgo the privileges which you have enjoyed. You abused our help."

"What could I do?" She fought a sob in her voice. "I had anxieties. I couldn't sleep, couldn't work. For months, years now, I haven't been able to concentrate. The anxieties are terrible."

The man had lost interest already. Glancing at another file, he answered her from residual courtesy. "What were you afraid of? Was someone bothering you?"

"Yes. No, not really. I don't know, exactly. It's not easy to explain. I just became anxious. I was afraid all the time."

"What have you done all these years, Frau . . . ?"

"I couldn't work. I tried, but I couldn't concentrate."

"If your health is actually incapacitating, you should seek medical care, perhaps disability compensation. You're probably"—he thumbed through her file distractedly—"yes, here it is. Four years. You were in service more than the minimum. If you can demonstrate that this anxiety stems from your wartime service, you would be eligible for disability compensation."

"Well, it does. It must. But how could I . . . ?"

"It's quite simple, really. You go to the Ministry of Social Services and fill out the forms. There are the usual bureaucratic delays and so on, but they can provide you with emergency funds and shelter while your application is being processed. And when it's approved, you get your pension. It's paid every month, directly into your bank account."

She brightened, wiping an errant tear off the side of her nose. "It's that simple? And I could apply under my present name?"

"What do you mean?"

"I took a new name at the end of the war. It must be in your files. It was necessary, you see, to avoid misunderstandings. I was sent to a man in Prague."

"This is not the name under which you served?"

"No. Of course not. There would have been misunderstandings."

"Well, then it's quite clear, isn't it? You must claim pension benefits under the name in which you served."

"But after so many years, there could still be misunderstandings. I've read the papers, the trials."

The man looked at her sternly. "Did you do anything of which you should be ashamed?"

"No."

"Then what have you to fear?"

"Others who did nothing were tried."

"That was under the Occupation. Things have changed. Thanks to our efforts, people are beginning to learn the truth about the war years. If you've done nothing to be ashamed of, you have nothing to fear."

"But how would I explain that I lived so long under a different name?"

"Tell the truth. That you were afraid of excesses. Everyone realizes now that there were excesses in the Occupation administration and the so-called justice meted out by the Occupation courts."

"But after so many years living under this name . . ."

The man was too busy with his files to look up.

"How could I explain what happened? If they ask questions, there's no one who would remember."

The man got up and led her to the door. "I'm sure things will work out for you," he said.

The ministry was a glass and concrete building with a bank of elevators and a huge directory of offices in the lobby. The room they sent her to had long counters, plants in buckets, and benches filled with haggard-looking men and women. Some were crippled or blind; all of them looked at least seventy years old. How could she be old enough for a pension? she wondered. Or did she already look that old and downtrodden? She had avoided mirrors for so long that she wasn't sure anymore.

At the counter they gave her a sheaf of forms, four copies of this, three of that, one each of three different cards. They pointed to another counter with pens on long chains.

She began filling out the forms—birthplace, birthdate, dates of service, areas of duty, decorations, description of injuries received, continuing medical problems, dates of hospitalization, treatments received. She filled out every blank carefully. For medical problems she wrote "nervousness," then crossed it out and wrote "chronic anxiety." Then she took the forms back to the counter.

The woman scanned them quickly. "You haven't filled in your name."

Wanda Lanzer looked down at the stack of papers.

"Well?" said the woman. "Are you going to write in your name? We can't check your records until we have your name, you know."

"I think I'll take them home with me," said Wanda Lanzer.

"Do you need help? Did someone else fill them out for you and forget to put in the name? It's no problem. If you can't write, we'll fill it in for you. Now, what's your name?"

"It's all right," said Wanda Lanzer, taking the forms. She walked quickly, almost running, out of the building.

It was almost five o'clock. Workers were pouring out of office buildings all around her, heading into bars with neon signs that advertised English and American whiskeys. Everywhere she looked there was glitter—bright signs, fancy clothes, new cars. Everyone was in a hurry. It was as though they were waving money in their hands.

She got back to the ministry just as they were shutting the counters for the day.

"Come back tomorrow," said the woman at the counter. "We open at eight thirty."

"Couldn't you take the papers now? I filled out the name."

The woman glanced through the forms. "What about your address?"

Wanda Lanzer said nothing.

"Where can we reach you?"

Wanda Lanzer shook her head.

"Where are you staying? Where do you sleep?"

"I've just come here. I have no place."

"And no money?" The woman said it as though she had heard the tale before. "Here—" She handed over a form with a notation scribbled on it, almost like a physician's prescription. "You take that across the hall and down one flight. They're there until eight in the evening. They'll find you a place to stay."

"And the pension?"

"You're in a real hurry, aren't you? You'll hear from us when the forms have been processed and reviewed. A few weeks, perhaps two. But you must stay at the same address or you won't receive notification. Do you understand?"

"Yes."

"Well, good night, Frau Ritter."

The walls of the hostel were so thin that she could hear every cough and ablution of her neighbors. The other women talked incessantly, mostly about the food, which was plentiful but thin—soups, porridge, baskets of day-old split rolls. The delivery of the mail each morning was the high moment of the day. After three weeks she had still received nothing.

She tried calling the ministry and was told to be patient.

She wrote a letter. It took two weeks for a reply: "Your application is being processed. You will be notified when the procedure is completed." And so she waited, surprised each day that it didn't seem to matter that she was once again Eva Ritter. No one paid any attention at all.

She had been at the hostel for six weeks, long enough to know that the meager menus repeated at two-week intervals, and the conversations at twenty-minute intervals, when she heard her name called at the morning mail distribution. It was a business-sized envelope, and she clutched it to her, running back to the privacy of her cubicle before she opened it.

It had been a long time since she had received mail. She even tried to remember what the last letter had been, but couldn't. She slipped a finger under the fly, tore halfway, and stopped when the return address caught her eye. It was an official envelope, but not from the Ministry of Social Services. It was from the Ministry of Justice.

YOU ARE HEREBY SUMMONED TO APPEAR AT 1300 ON 23 OCTOBER 1959 IN ROOM 562 OF THE MINISTRY OF JUSTICE BUILDING, FRANKFURT AM MAIN, FOR A PRELIMINARY INQUIRY REGARDING YOUR ACTIVITIES IN THE CRIMINAL POLICE, THE WEHRMACHT ADMINISTRATIVE OFFICE FOR YUGOSLAVIA, AND THE WVHA CAMP ADMINISTRATION, FROM 1941 TO 1945. YOU ARE ENTITLED TO BE REPRESENTED BY COUNSEL AT THIS INQUIRY. IF YOU ARE NOT REPRESENTED BY COUNSEL OF YOUR CHOICE, YOU MAY REQUEST THAT THE MINISTRY APPOINT COUNSEL TO REPRESENT YOU. FAILURE TO APPEAR FOR THIS HEARING WILL RESULT IN AN ARREST WARRANT BEING ISSUED IN YOUR NAME.

The letter fluttered in her fingers.

Why? It was a mistake. It had to be. Mistakes were made all the time, mistakes of identity, confusion. If she just explained that she was never in the Criminal Police or the Wehrmacht or the WVHA, perhaps they would understand.

She tried calling the ministry, begging the woman who answered to connect her to someone who would know about the letter. She was cut off the first time she called, put on hold the second time. Outside the telephone cabin, a woman began banging on the door. "You've had long enough, dearie. There's others of us that'd like to make a call too, you know." She waited on hold until the woman outside was banging so loudly that there was no way to hear if anyone did come on the line.

She thought of writing a letter. She could still write clear, emphatic prose. A no-nonsense tone would be right, she thought. Then she remembered the results of her last letter.

She could run. She had fled before. How much worse off was she now? Her cough was gone. She didn't have the Victrola to drag around. She wasn't hungry anymore.

But of course she couldn't run. She had no papers at all now. She would never get through any border. And the last sentence of the letter was terrifying: "Failure to appear . . . an arrest warrant . . ."

There was only one thing she could do. She borrowed a plastic raincoat to cover her wretched clothes and walked to the Ministry of Justice.

"I don't understand this letter," she explained to the receptionist.

Half an hour later she was before a neatly dressed young man in a tiny office. He was extremely polite, offering her a chair and speaking loudly and slowly, as though he thought her hard of hearing.

"You applied for a disability pension?"

"Yes."

"This inquiry is part of the review of your application. Your application states that the disability stems from your wartime service, which must be reviewed. It's routine."

"What is the part about being represented by counsel?"

"You may have a lawyer present to make sure that your side of the matter is fairly represented."

"But I have nothing to represent. I've done nothing."

"No one has accused you of anything. As I've tried to explain, it's a standard procedure."

"I don't want a standard procedure. I . . . . I'll withdraw the application for a pension."

"Very well. That's something you take up with the Ministry of Social Services."

"And then there will be no hearing?"

"No, the hearing will still be held. You must still appear."

"But if I withdraw the application, it would have no meaning. It would serve no purpose."

"The purpose is to examine your activities during the war."

New York, 1966

When Jill stopped accepting his calls, Johan Klinger began sending her gifts. First it was flowers and plants, then perfume, then a sterling silver Tiffany keychain. With each delivery there was a note suggesting that they have dinner or a drink. She called him after the first two gifts arrived, thanked him, and refused his invitations. She never acknowledged the others.

He began waiting for her outside the building, parking his Mercedes with its DPL plates at the sidewalk so he could watch the exit doors. For a week he was there every day when she came out, and only by rushing into a taxi could she shake him. She angrily accused Evelyn of telling Klinger when she was leaving, and only after Evelyn burst into tears did Jill realize that he didn't know when she was leaving, that he actually waited there from early evening until she appeared.

She had tried to get back to her old self by sheer routine, working long hours, burying herself in complex negotiations, trying to lose herself in the piles of paper and the stacks of unreturned phone calls that accumulated on her desk, expecting to get so backlogged that she had little time for worry. She still thought about Ral and Jean-Claude and the case, but it was as though the entire trial were a cancer in remission, its symptoms fading and its threat receding until what had once been an obsession became a memory. She had spoken to Jean-Claude twice, and each time he had been warm but reluctant to discuss the case because he too had nothing to report.

"Have you been seeing Ral?" she asked.

"I've tried to. He refuses to see me. And while he has no choice about seeing the *juge d'instruction*, he has adamantly refused to talk to the judge. He is the most intractable, stubborn client I have ever encountered. I don't see what anyone can do for the *malheureux*."

"There must be something," she said without conviction.

Then one day Evelyn came into her office, close to tears again.

"What is it?" Jill asked.

"That Englishman just called again. That makes four times this morning. I've given him every excuse I can think of, but he won't give up. 'Tell Jill it's of the utmost importance,' he says. It's impossible to work when he keeps pestering like that."

"I'm sorry," said Jill. "I'll talk to the creep. I promise you he won't call anymore."

Klinger came on the line immediately when Jill identified herself to his secretary.

"Mr. Klinger!" Her choice of address was deliberate.

"I have what you want," he said.

"Please don't call here anymore."

"Did you hear me, Jill? I have what you want."

"What are you talking about?"

"Shall we meet for dinner?"

"Mr. Klinger! We aren't meeting for dinner or for anything else. And I don't want you calling me or pestering my secretary or waiting outside this building to waylay me."

"Does that mean you're no longer interested in that woman?"

"You said there were no records, that the computer searches showed no trace of her."

"That was a preliminary search. I've made further inquiries."

"And?" Jill didn't believe Klinger, but a lingering doubt told her not to hang up.

"Where shall we meet, Jill? And when?"

"I told you, I'm very busy now."

"Too busy for the records of that woman's pension application and the transcript of the Ministry of Justice inquest on her wartime activities?"

Jill's throat went dry. "You're sure it's the same woman?"

"Of course I'm sure. We Germans do not go off half-cocked."

Klinger wouldn't send the papers over by messenger, insisting that only dinner would do, since Jill would need help with the German. So she met him. He wouldn't discuss the papers until they had finished dinner. Then he said the papers were at his apartment, on Eighty-second Street.

"We can have a nightcap," he said. "And you can see the papers."

The apartment looked as though it had been lifted, unchanged, from some *Penthouse* magazine decorator's manual. The sterility of the white shag rugs, leather, rosewood, and chrome was magnified by the pin-neat cleanliness. It looked as though a housekeeper had been there minutes before. Jill let Klinger pour her a cognac.

"Now, where are the papers?"

He took a long time to fish a manila envelope out of a Danish Modern rolltop desk and hand it to Jill. The papers inside were Xerox copies of documents. The cover sheet was printed in Fraktur type, which she could hardly decipher. She searched the heading and the first few pages and couldn't even find the name Wanda Lanzer.

"What is this? It doesn't even have her name on it."

"The application was filed under a different name," said Klinger.

"Loli Tschai?" asked Jill. She had pronounced the name to herself a dozen times since she read it on the photograph at the police commissioner's office in Marseilles.

"Come again?"

"Was the name she filed under 'Loli Tschai'?"

"That's a name? It sounds like nonsense. The name on the document is Ritter. Eva Ritter. That was the woman's real name. Wanda Lanzer was a pseudonym. Would you like me to read you a page or two tonight?"

"You're sure it's the same woman?"

"Absolutely."

"How do you know?"

"The computer indexes pseudonyms to deter cheating. In this case there was no effort at cheating. She applied under the name Eva Ritter, which was the name under which she did her service. The pseudonym was listed in the application and picked up by the computer. Here, we have time for a page or two tonight."

"A page or two? I'll have the whole thing translated first thing tomorrow."

"I can't permit you to take the documents away from here, Jill. I'll be glad to translate for you, and I can even arrange to be free every evening. It would be my pleasure to work on the matter with you."

Jill carefully put the papers back into the envelope and held it out to Klinger.

"Would you rather begin our translation later?"

"I take that with me," she said. "Or I never see you again. Period."

"Jill, what you propose is quite impossible. I assure you, I'll translate the

entire document for you. But it will take us some time. Come, we can begin now." He patted the seat next to him on the leather sofa.

Jill picked up her trenchcoat and headed for the door.

"Jill, I went to extraordinary lengths to obtain these documents. It's
quite illegal to use confidential personal records for other than official purposes. I do you a great favor, and your thanks is to walk out? I should have
thought you would be a little more appreciative."

She looked at the envelope, letting a dozen possibilities run through her
mind. Then she smiled, putting down the coat.

"You're right, Johan, of course. Don't you think we should get a little
more confortable first?"

She watched a grin spread across Klinger's face. Then she smiled and
spoke very slowly and deliberately:

"You know, Klinger, I really don't mind a corrupt official. I deal with
them all the time. I don't even mind a boring dinner or two with a
puffed-up old fart and his phony British accent. What I do mind is half-
assed proposals from a horny, two-bit, holier-than-thou bastard who
thinks I'd jump into bed with him to get a look at some papers. If it's so
illegal to use personal records for anything other than official purposes, I'd
really like to hear you explain to the consul just why you got those papers."

Klinger turned red. "Do you actually think I'm afraid of your threat,
Jill?"

"I don't really give a shit, Klinger. But if I were you I'd come up with a
damn good story of why you've spent every afternoon for the last two
weeks parked in front of my office in that consular Mercedes with the DPL
plates."

Klinger stood there, his mustache twitching, as she walked out with the
envelope.

She called Nat Hirschmann from a pay phone. He was breathless when he
answered.

"It's almost midnight, Jill."

"I know. Can I come over? I just got the pension records of that
woman."

"Pension records? Jill, you didn't pick a very good time to call. Could it
wait until tomorrow afternoon? I finish my office hours around three
thirty."

"How about breakfast?"

"Jill, this really isn't a great time for me to talk. I've got company here.
Call me tomorrow, okay? Or I'll call you."

Jill took another moment to catch on. She didn't call again until seven in
the morning, and picked Hirschmann up at seven thirty.

"You're really crazy, you know that?" Hirschmann said as he thumbed
through the documents. "I had some fancy explaining to do last night. And
I still don't know why I'm here."

"The creep who got those papers for me said that the woman filed for the pension under the name Eva Ritter. Wanda Lanzer is a pseudonym. What did she do that needed a change of name?"

Hirschmann sight-translated the first page, skimming as he read off a few entries. ". . . Criminal Police Detention Camp at Lackenbach, Austria . . . Wehrmacht Administrative Office for Yugoslavia . . . Detention Camp at Zemun . . . WVHA Administration . . ."

"What's that last thing, the WVHA?"

"That's the agency that ran concentration camps. You found yourself a real winner, it looks like."

"How soon can you translate it for me?"

"I might be able to get a student to do it later this week."

"I'll pay triple the going rate if he can do it today."

"*She*, Jill." He grinned. "You better be careful with your assumptions. What's the hurry anyway? What's this got to do with your gypsy?"

"I don't know yet. If we know who she was, and what she did, maybe we'll know why Ral . . ."

"Still can't say it? Still can't admit that he killed her? You've got it bad, Jill."

"I know," she said.

OFFICIAL TRANSCRIPTION
PRELIMINARY INQUIRY, MINISTRY OF JUSTICE,
GERMAN FEDERAL REPUBLIC
Frankfurt am Main, 28 May 1960
Present: Dr. Waldemar Althusser, Presiding Magistrate
Dr. Eva Ritter
Mr. Jahn Andress, representing Dr. Ritter

PRESIDING MAGISTRATE ALTHUSSER: Dr. Ritter! This is not a trial, but a preliminary inquiry, concerned with your activities from 1941 to 1945, specifically at the Criminal Police Camp at Lackenbach, Austria; the Wehrmacht Detention Camp in Zemun, Austria; and the WVHA facilities at Auschwitz-Birkenau. A transcription is being made of the testimony given here, but there are no charges of any kind against you. Do you understand?

[At the request of Mr. Andress, Dr. Ritter was given a glass of water.]

DR. RITTER: I understand.

ALTHUSSER: You were born in Passau in 1912?

RITTER: Yes. That's correct.

ALTHUSSER: You are by training a social researcher?

RITTER: Yes.

ALTHUSSER: Where did you study?

RITTER: Zurich. And Vienna.

ALTHUSSER: Why did you travel so far to study?

RITTER: My father opposed my studies. Without a certificate from him, I could not enroll in a German university. There was no such restriction in Switzerland. After several years in Zurich, I enrolled in the University of Vienna to study anthropology.

ALTHUSSER: Your studies in Vienna had nothing to do with the Interpol Central Office for Fighting the Gypsy Nuisance?

RITTER: No! Of course not.

ALTHUSSER: When did you complete your studies?

RITTER: I did fieldwork for two years, among the Romany . . .
[Mr. Andress interrupted the testimony to speak privately with Dr. Ritter.]

RITTER: 1940. I finished my studies in that year and I was awarded a Ph.D. from the university.

ALTHUSSER: And at that time you took employment?

RITTER: Yes.

ALTHUSSER: Where?

RITTER: In Germany.

ALTHUSSER: With?

RITTER: I worked alone.

ALTHUSSER: For whom did you work?

RITTER: I worked for the Ministry of Health.

ALTHUSSER: The name of the department?

RITTER: It was called . . . I forget the name . . . something like the Office of Research.

ALTHUSSER: The Racial Hygiene and Population Biology Research Unit?

RITTER: Yes.

ALTHUSSER: What were your duties?

RITTER: Research.

ALTHUSSER: Could you explain a little more, please.

RITTER: It was similar to the work I had done as a student. I worked with Romany people, gypsies. I was very qualified for this work.

ALTHUSSER: Where did you do this research?

RITTER: I traveled from city to city, in Germany and Austria.

ALTHUSSER: Do you remember which cities?

RITTER: It was mainly big cities. Munich, and of course Vienna. In Germany I worked primarily with the Sinte. In Austria it was the Kalderash, especially the Lovari.

ALTHUSSER: When were you posted to the Criminal Police Detention Camp in Lackenbach?

RITTER: It was in 1941, I think. The camp had been greatly expanded to accommodate a large influx of gypsies, three of four thousand of them in all. The nomadic gypsies were in great danger at that time, because the war cut them off from their usual livelihoods and the routes that they traditionally followed in the spring and summer. They were brought to the camp for their own protection.

ALTHUSSER: What were your duties at the camp?

RITTER: I was there as a researcher. You see, through my studies I had many languages, including Romany. There are very few non-gypsies who speak Romany.

ALTHUSSER: So you helped the rest of the camp staff give orders to the gypsies in their own language?

RITTER: Orders? No, it wasn't necessary. Most of the gypsies spoke German, too, at least enough German for them to understand the camp administrators. It's just that when they speak German they are sometimes evasive. They trust someone who speaks their own language.

ALTHUSSER: And you used that trust to further the goals of the camp?

RITTER [After conferring with Mr. Andress]: I don't understand the question. When I arrived at the camp, there were many misunderstandings there. Some of the gypsies were being mistreated. The guards were sometimes cruel, taking advantage of the childlike nature of the gypsies.

ALTHUSSER: These are your fellow officers at the camp you are speaking about, are they not?

RITTER: Fellow officers? No! I was not on the staff of the camp. I was only there as a researcher.

ALTHUSSER: According to the records of the Criminal Police, Dr. Ritter, you were an administrative officer of the Lackenbach camp. You were issued uniforms, you had an office, and you were assigned a room in the officers' barracks at the camp.

RITTER: But those were only administrative details. They said there was no other way for me to do my research.

ALTHUSSER: This research you have mentioned repeatedly—what exactly did you do?

RITTER: I studied family structures. By interviewing the gypsies I compiled genealogies, showing the interrelations of the different families and clans. Often the gypsies themselves do not have a clear sense of these relationships. To understand the gypsies it is essential to understand these family structures.

ALTHUSSER: How many other people did this work?

RITTER: No one. No one else was qualified.

ALTHUSSER: And what became of your research?

RITTER: My notes and tables? They're gone, of course. Years of research—it's all gone now. Destroyed, I suppose. Or lost. Everything was lost.

ALTHUSSER: You mean it was lost in the war?

RITTER: Yes. Of course.

ALTHUSSER: Did you ever search for the material after the war?

RITTER: No. Never.

ALTHUSSER: And in Zemun, the Wehrmacht Detention Camp in Yugoslavia, you also did research there?

RITTER: Yes. I knew Zemun, the gypsy quarter of Belgrade, from my field research as a student. When the camp was established, I was invited to go there and continue my research.

ALTHUSSER: And in Zemun, you were attached to the office of General Franz Böhme, the Plenipotentiary Commanding General in Serbia?

RITTER: No! That was only an administrative arrangement. Serbia was a war zone. There could be no civilians there. After the camp was set up, the control passed to the Croatian authorities, and they would never have allowed me to work there if I didn't have military credentials. But it was only on paper.

ALTHUSSER: And you had nothing to do with the military program in Yugoslavia?

ANDRESS [Objecting]: Could Your Honor specify what military program you are referring to?

ALTHUSSER [Reading]: "Pacification efforts directed at the civilian population . . . deportations . . . executions of hostages . . . relocation of families . . . detention of Jews and other racial groups . . ."

RITTER: No. I had nothing to do with any of that. I only did my research, tracing genealogies, helping to keep people with their own families. The camp officials, especially the Ustashi, the Croatian Nazis, had great difficulty understanding the gypsies. They were of exactly different temperaments.

ALTHUSSER: And the records from your research at Zemun?

RITTER: Gone, of course.

ALTHUSSER: And after you finished your service at Zemun?

RITTER: I was sent with a trainload of gypsies for resettlement. The gypsies were German and Austrian, Kalderash and Sinte who had been caught in Yugoslavia on their annual circuits when the hostilities broke out. They did not belong there, and it would have been unfortunate for them if they had been kept in camps there for too long. The Ustashi were very hard on the gypsies, you see. They blamed the gypsies for the partisan activity, and they victimized the gypsy girls. Once we discovered that these gypsies did not belong in Yugoslavia at all, they were sent to a safe area for resettlement. I accompanied them to continue my researches, and also to assist in interpreting for them.

ALTHUSSER: When was this?

RITTER: Late in 1942, if I recall correctly. Or possibly early 1943.

ALTHUSSER: And the new camp was?

RITTER: It was just being built, an addition to an older labor facility in Silesia.

ALTHUSSER: The name, please?

ANDRESS: You have the name in the dossier, Your Honor.

ALTHUSSER: You are perfectly aware, Counselor, that all evidence must be in direct testimony. The name of the camp facility, please, Dr. Ritter?

RITTER: Birkenau.

ALTHUSSER: And what were your duties at the Auschwitz-Birkenau camp?

RITTER: The same as at the others.

ALTHUSSER: Which was?

RITTER: Just as I explained. Research. The gypsy camp at Birkenau was very large, and separate from the rest of the camp. There were as many as twenty thousand gypsies there, from all over Europe. Not just German and Austrian gypsies, but Romany from Greece, Romania,

Italy, Norway, Denmark, Holland, France, Poland, Russia, Hungary, Bulgaria.

ALTHUSSER: Did you have any duties other than this so-called research?

RITTER: No. Except in cases of misunderstandings, or where hardships among the gypsies could be alleviated. For example, it was obvious to me that the gypsy camp needed its own hospital, and a kindergarten for the children. And for many of the men, it was important that they be allowed to keep their musical instruments and be encouraged to play. Music is very important to the gypsies, especially if they are confined without the freedom of the road.

ALTHUSSER: Dr. Ritter—according to the camp records, you were seconded from the Wehrmacht to the SS at Auschwitz-Birkenau, where you held a series of camp ranks in the WVHA, the Economic Administration Main Office in charge of the concentration and extermination camps.

RITTER: No! That's not true! That was only for administrative purposes. They ran the camp. I couldn't be there to conduct my research except under their auspices.

ALTHUSSER: Did you ever obtain a letter or other certification of this status?

RITTER: Why would I? I was allowed to pursue my research. It was all that mattered to me. And I was often able to see to it that the gypsies were not abused, that they got adequate food rations and medicine and clothing and blankets and hygiene facilities. The gypsies were my friends. They trusted me. And I did my best to . . .

ALTHUSSER: You knew nothing of the other activities of the Auschwitz-Birkenau camp?

ANDRESS: May I confer with my client?

ALTHUSSER: Of course.

RITTER [After conferring with Mr. Andress]: I knew that terrible things were happening. It was impossible to know nothing. It was a city, a whole world. There were always rumors and stories. But I could no more change what happened in the rest of the camp than I could change the war policies in Berlin, which I also knew were bad for the gypsies. What was important was that in the gypsy camp they had food and medicine and clothing. War is very difficult for the gypsies, you see. They do not have the same temperament as we.

ALTHUSSER: In 1944 you were still at the Auschwitz-Birkenau camp?

RITTER: Yes.

ALTHUSSER: Were you aware of the mass executions that were taking place there?

ANDRESS [Objecting]: Your Honor! Dr. Ritter has testified as to her own activities in the camp. Unless there is evidence of wrongdoing by Dr. Ritter, no purpose would be served by reviewing the stories of executions and other alleged atrocities.

ALTHUSSER: Will testimony of the witnesses address the subject of Dr. Ritter's activities in the camp?

ANDRESS: Yes.

ALTHUSSER: Very well.

ANDRESS: Do we adjourn for today?

ALTHUSSER: Not yet. Dr. Ritter, what did you do after the war?

RITTER: I went to Vienna.

ALTHUSSER: Under what identity?

RITTER: I had taken a new name. I was called Wanda Lanzer.

ALTHUSSER: Why did you take a new name?

RITTER: When the Russians came, I was frightened. There was no real information then. People traded in rumors. They said the Russians would shoot anyone who had been in a camp, no matter what. I was afraid of such a misunderstanding.

ALTHUSSER: But surely you were safe in Vienna. You could have resumed your real identity then.

RITTER: Yes, but when I came to Vienna I took a job. A very good job. I was afraid that if I tried to change back to my old name there would be misunderstandings. After a while I got used to the new name. I had picked it, you see, to sound like my real name.

ALTHUSSER: Why did you leave Vienna?

RITTER: My nerves were bad. I had trouble sleeping and concentrating. Sometimes it would be all right for a while, but then another wave of anxiety would come. The doctors say it is like what happens to a soldier who has been under fire too long.

ANDRESS: Chronic anxiety is the diagnosis. We are only claiming partial disability, even though the manifestations are sufficiently severe to make further gainful employment unlikely. You have the medical testimony in the dossier, I believe.

ALTHUSSER: Yes. I've read it. The witnesses will be ready to testify tomorrow?

ANDRESS: Three witnesses are ready to testify.

ALTHUSSER: All speak German?

ANDRESS: Adequately.

ALTHUSSER: Then we will adjourn until thirteen hundred hours tomorrow.

[29 May 1960]

PRESIDING MAGISTRATE ALTHUSSER: The witnesses understand that this is a preliminary inquiry, that the testimony they give is privileged, and that nothing that takes place in this inquiry is to be disclosed outside this room?

MR. ANDRESS: They do.

ALTHUSSER: And both you and Dr. Ritter wish to be present during the questioning of the witnesses?

ANDRESS: We do.

[The first witness was invited into the hearing room.]

ALTHUSSER: Your name, place of residence, and profession?

WITNESS: Dr. Émile Hoffman. I live in Strasbourg, and I am a physician, specializing in gynecology and obstetrics.

ALTHUSSER: Do you know the woman sitting at this table?

HOFFMAN: I did.

ALTHUSSER: What is her name?

HOFFMAN: Eva Ritter.

ALTHUSSER: When and where did you meet her?

HOFFMAN: During the war. We were both at Auschwitz.

ALTHUSSER: In what capacity were you at the camp?

HOFFMAN: I was incarcerated as a Social Democrat in 1940. When it was discovered that I was Jewish, I was turned over to the German authorities and sent to a series of camps. At Auschwitz-Birkenau the authorities decided to take advantage of my training as a physician, and they put me to work in the hospital of the gypsy camp, to treat the women there.

ALTHUSSER: What did Dr. Ritter do in the camp?

HOFFMAN: She was a social researcher, as far as I could tell. She interviewed the gypsies and compiled charts of their family relationships. She spoke their language, which was very useful for us. At times, when gypsy patients were hysterical, or could not describe their symptoms in German or any other language that the physicians spoke, I and the other physicians relied on her to translate for us.

ALTHUSSER: Can you tell us what other functions she performed in the camp?

HOFFMAN: Functions? It was not an official function, as far as I knew, but she served as an advocate for the gypsies. She persuaded the administration of the camp to build a kindergarten for the gypsy children, and she obtained extra rations of milk and sugar for them. She got medicine for the hospital. She was very concerned about their welfare, which is not something I would say about anyone else in the camp, including most of the physicians, and of course all of the guards and administrators.

ALTHUSSER: How long were you at Auschwitz-Birkenau?

HOFFMAN: Until May 1944. I was then transferred to another camp, at Lublin, where I was asked to perform gynecological surgery, actually sterilizations. I refused, and I was incarcerated as a regular prisoner. I was spared execution only because the Russian armies advanced faster than the camp authorities anticipated.

ALTHUSSER: Is there anything else about Dr. Ritter that you would like to add to your testimony?

HOFFMAN: Only that I never saw her do an unkind thing to a gypsy. She never even shouted at them. She was the only person in the camp who never lost patience with the gypsies. They were sometimes charming and appealing in their behavior, but they could also be truculent and dissembling, faking symptoms to get into the hospital or to get extra rations, or lying to avoid work assignments or to get special privileges. She alone never lost patience with their behavior, even when the gypsies on occasion were not properly appreciative of her efforts. She never stopped trying to better their lot.

ALTHUSSER: Thank you very much for coming to testify, Dr. Hoffman.

[The witness was excused and the second witness was invited into the hearing room.]

ALTHUSSER: Your name, place of residence, and occupation?

WITNESS: I am Professor Soren Elvstrom, of Göteborg, Sweden. I am a jurist and academician.

ALTHUSSER: Do you know this woman?

ELVSTROM: I have had the honor and privilege of meeting Dr. Ritter.

ALTHUSSER: Could you tell us when and where?

ELVSTROM: It was in 1941, at a place called Lackenbach, outside Vienna. I was there with a Swedish Red Cross inspection team. We had come from Theresienstadt, where we inspected the concentration camp. In Lackenbach we inspected a camp run by the Criminal Police, mostly for Romany. Dr. Ritter introduced us to many of the Romany detainees, and she also interpreted for us. It was our understanding that the Romany were detained in the camp because the wartime conditions made it impossible for them to follow their usual nomadic life patterns.

ALTHUSSER: Was Dr. Ritter always present when you spoke with the gypsies?

ELVSTROM: No. We spoke to them privately as well. That was a specified condition of our inspection agreement.

ALTHUSSER: Did any of the gypsies speak about her?

ELVSTROM: Yes, many. I recall that many of them told us that before she came to the camp, conditions had been very oppressive. The camp authorities had thrown together families and clans who were at odds with one another, and some of the camp guards had abused detainees, especially some of the younger gypsy women. There had been no attention paid to the special hygienic needs of the gypsies, who have categories of uncleanliness that are very important to them. I reread a copy of our report before coming here, and I noted that while we criticized conditions in the camp and the food that was served to the inmates, we singled out one member of the staff for praise, in particular for her sensitivity to and concern for the detainees. Dr. Ritter was the individual singled out.

ALTHUSSER: May we make a copy of your report?

ELVSTROM: For the purposes of this hearing, yes.

ALTHUSSER: Thank you for coming to testify, Professor Elvstrom.

[The witness was excused and the third witness was invited into the hearing room.]

ALTHUSSER: Your name, place of residence, and occupation?

WITNESS: My name is Josef Hörthy. I'm a fiddler. In Munich.

ALTHUSSER: Do you know this woman?

HÖRTHY: Loli Tschai? Of course I know her. How can you not know a person who saved your life?

ALTHUSSER: What was the name you used for her?

HÖRTHY: Loli Tschai. It's a gypsy name. It's not her real name, but it's what we called her.

ALTHUSSER: Do you know her real name?

HÖRTHY: Dr. Ritter?

ALTHUSSER: Could you explain how she saved your life?

HÖRTHY: What's to explain? Thousands were dying every day, and she saved my life.

ALTHUSSER: When and where did you meet Dr. Ritter?

HÖRTHY: In the war. I don't know exactly what year or month it was. I was at the camp for maybe a year or a year and a half when she came.

ALTHUSSER: Which camp was that?

HÖRTHY: Birkenau, the gypsy camp. Thousands of us were there, from all over. Germany, Austria, Hungary, everywhere. I never even knew there were gypsies in so many places. Until she came, it was terrible. But she spoke Romany, and she understood Romany ways. She got them to let us keep our own clothes and let families stay together. She got us musical instruments, sometimes our own, sometimes fiddles and guitars from other parts of the camp, like the Canada camp where they collected things from everyone. She got milk and food and candies for the children. And toys. Camp is very hard for children. They don't understand about war and camps. She made it easier for them.

ALTHUSSER: You said before that Dr. Ritter saved your life. Could you explain what happened?

HÖRTHY: Well, she did. It was near the end of the war. I don't know the exact date like you probably want. Everyone knew that the Russians were coming pretty soon, and we heard stories about what they would do. But before they came she got us sent out of the camp. Me and my brother. She got us released and sent back to Germany. We even got to take our fiddles with us. We went to another camp, in Germany. There wasn't much food there, but no one had much food then. And after that, the English came and we were set free. Now I'm a German citizen. My children go to school. They read and write German and do sums without their fingers. I pay taxes even. If it hadn't been for Loli Tschai, who knows what would have happened to me? So you see, I owe her my whole life because she respected us and put us on that train to save us.

ALTHUSSER: Thank you for coming to testify, Mr. Hörthy.

[The witness was excused.]

ANDRESS: With the permission of Your Honor, we would like to introduce the testimony of a witness who cannot be present to testify because of diplomatic difficulties.

ALTHUSSER: You wish to read testimony into the record?

ANDRESS: I have a sworn affidavit of oral testimony in the Croatian language from Sedja Letaja, now of Sarajevo, Yugoslavia. This is a certified translation.

[Mr. Andress read the testimony in German.]

"I know this woman Eva Ritter that we also know as Loli Tschai from early in the days of the war. Many Romany were taken by the German soldiers and the filthy Ustashi to a camp in Zemun, in the old gypsy quarter of Belgrade. The Germans were shooting gypsy men as hostages but they wouldn't shoot the women so they put us in a camp. Also the children. And in that camp the filthy Ustashi did terrible things to the women. Things for which a gypsy man would kill them or worse.

"These things could have happened to me and maybe to my children except that the woman Eva Ritter that we also know as Loli Tschai got them to let me go from the camp. She knew me, knew I was Kalderash gypsy, and she got them to let me go. If she didn't do that then the filthy Ustashi would have done their terrible things to me and I would right now be lying in some grave in the woods.

"Every night of my life I pray for Loli Tschai. I only hope that when I die I will go to some heaven and then maybe I will see her again."

ALTHUSSER: Does that conclude the presentation of evidence?

ANDRESS: We have no further evidence to present.

ALTHUSSER: Thank you, Counselor. We will recess for one hour.

[The hearing reconvened at 1700.]

ALTHUSSER: Dr. Ritter! Mr. Andress! It is the conclusion of this inquiry that there is no basis for any further investigation of Dr. Ritter's activities during the war. Indeed, I believe the ministry will join me in thanking Dr. Ritter for what she has done for Germany and for the humanity of the German people. It is unfortunate that the opprobrium which has properly been placed on the guilty few has also brought suffering and anxiety and pain to the innocent, such as Dr. Ritter.

[Dr. Ritter conferred with Mr. Andress.]

RITTER: Will I receive the pension?

ALTHUSSER: The final decision on your pension, Dr. Ritter, is not within my power. I intend to submit a summary of the evidence we have heard in this inquiry, along with my own recommendation. I will be recommending that if it is at all possible, you should receive a full disability pension. I would be very surprised indeed if that pension were not awarded. The German nation owes you a great deal for what you have done.

RITTER: Thank you, Your Honor.

Strasbourg, 1960

"**W**hat do you think, gypsy?"

It was a game the workers in the body shop played. Each morning they had a different subject—a soccer game, a sex crime, a government scandal—usually chosen from a newspaper headline, and without an excess of facts that might limit their discussion. They would rattle out their opinions until one of the big, hulking men, who wore their blue blouses like badges of proletarian membership, would turn to Ral for his opinion. The others would laugh then, knowing Ral would have been half-listening at best, that their question would awaken him from some private daydream.

This time it was a worker named Clément who asked. When Ral looked up he said: "What was it this time? Dreaming of some dark-skinned wench with her skirts up and her blouse open? How good are gypsy women anyway? Me, I never had one. Just about everything else, but never a gypsy. I don't know if I could stand the smell."

"Shut up," said Ral.

"Leave him be," said another blue-bloused worker. "Unless you want him to start telling us about your sister."

Everyone laughed, except Ral.

"It's a stupid question anyway," someone said. "How could there be 'a good Boche'? It's like saying 'a nice flic.' "

"I'm just telling you what it says in the newspaper," said Clément. "There were Nazis in the camps who were saving people. A doctor from right here, from Strasbourg, testified about it."

"Probably a Jew doctor," quipped someone.

"A Jew? Why would a Jew say there were good Nazis?"

"A Jew will do anything to get more business. That doctor probably thinks that if he says something nice about the Germans, they'll all cross the border and come to him."

The men laughed again, but Clément wasn't content. He turned back to Ral. "Well, what do you think?"

Ral looked up without saying a word.

"Always so superior," said Clément. "A lousy gypsy, and he sits there, listening with that long face and the deep eyes, like everything we say is boring. How about just once telling us what you think? You think there were any good Nazis in those camps?"

"No."

"Listen to him! No explanation. Just 'no.' What the hell do you know about it anyway, gypsy?"

Ral spun toward the man. "What do I know?" He caught himself, nipping his anger. "Why should I talk to you, *gajo?* What do you understand? You just watched it all happen anyway, didn't you?"

"You calling me a collaborator?"

"I'm calling you a stupid *gajo.* Anyone who thinks there is such a thing as a good Nazi is a fool. It doesn't matter what the Nazi says or what your *gajo* doctor in Strasbourg says. In the end a Nazi would always betray everyone, even the helpless children and the women. I know."

"He knows! Listen to him! Look, gypsy, right here in the newspaper it tells about a good Nazi in one of the camps."

Ral pushed the newspaper away. "What do I care about your stupid *gajo* newspaper?"

"And where are the smart gypsy newspapers you read?"

A blast on the whistle, an answering chorus of grumbles, and they went back to work, the cacophony of hammering, grinding, polishing, and welding filling the shop with a din of screeches, sparks, and dust. Talk was impossible as each man fell into his own private world amidst the chaos and noise.

Ral was hand-banging the side panel of a van, easy work for him because he was good with a hammer and anvil. But as he worked the panel with the heavy mallet, he couldn't focus on the ridges and swirls he usually saw in the metal, the patterns that would guide him as accurately as any gauge or template. He tried to shake the thought away, as if it were a cobweb or a sleeping bug in his eyes, but the light and the swirls and the din of the shop coalesced into a vision, a memory he thought he had driven away forever. Through the cacophony of the shop, he could hear the laughing of the Ustashi, the taunts in their voices.

He tried to pound the memory away, beating at the metal as if it were the faces of the Ustashi, as if he could destroy those leering grins. He pounded faster and faster, beating the metal to make the swirls and the faces disappear.

"Ral!"

He looked up, only half-focusing. It was Étienne, the foreman, pointing down at the panel. Ral followed the finger and saw that he had pounded through the overworked metal.

"You drunk?" asked Étienne.

"No."

"What the hell do you think you're doing?"

"Sorry."

"You do that again and you're out of here."

"Sorry," said Ral. There was no way to explain.

He went back to the panel, working carefully, trying to concentrate on the ridges in the overworked metal. But he couldn't escape the memory anymore. It would have been like telling himself not to think of hedgehog stew. All he could do was force himself back to the beginning, to Yugoslavia.

Yugoslavia, 1941

The Nazis had been in Yugoslavia for more than two months, and Ral had been working his way south with only the sun to guide him. It was only three months since he had escaped Lackenbach and begun his search for his mother and sister. Now he had to flee the roads with their familiar *patrin* for the safety of the woods, trying to stay away from the airplanes and trucks and tanks and troops. He lived off figs and berries and an occasional rabbit or fish as he worked his way through the mountains toward Belgrade.

He came to a secluded glen on a hillslope, overlooking the river below. Three donkeys were tied up, and a slim, fawnlike girl was feeding them, all the while dancing in the damp grass, playing out some secret pantomime. Ral watched quietly, afraid to disturb her as she swirled and skipped in the grass, stopping to stroke one donkey on the nose and to sing a silly song to another.

He had never seen anyone like this girl. Her hair was like copper straight out of the flames, a thousand colors in the sunlight that filtered through the trees. Her skin was honey and milk. She wore a billowy skirt that was short enough to show her slender legs and feet, and her *diclo* had slipped down to her neck, letting her hair tumble free as she danced. He watched her bend over to pick a tiny wildflower. She so reveled in the aroma of the flower that Ral couldn't resist reaching out for a similar flower in the grass near him.

As he rustled the grass, she turned. "I thought I was alone," she said. He had expected Romany, but she spoke in Serbian.

She pulled the *diclo* up to cover her hair, and smoothed her skirt, without lowering her big, soft eyes. "Who are you? Why are you here?"

"My name is Ral." As he said it, he realized that it had been a long time since he had spoken to anyone. He had been totally alone, like an animal in the woods.

To his surprise, she didn't run. A Romany girl would have been frightened of a total stranger, but she smiled and talked easily with him, letting him follow her down to a campsite.

Her name was Elena. She was with a band of fourteen people, more men than women, and all tall and handsome. The men had bold mustaches, and they wore red caps and waistcoats and black billowy trousers with white leggings. In their belts they carried daggers and fearsome double-edged swords.

One man, taller than the others, nearly a foot taller than Ral, with mustaches that reached almost to his neck, stood protectively as Ral approached. He carried a dagger and a sword in his belt, and a pistol and two cartridge belts over his shoulder.

"We're Montenegrins," he said. "If you're not a German or an Italian, you're welcome to share our fire and our food."

The man's name was Eleazar. He was Elena's father and the leader of the band. They weren't gypsies, although Eleazar spoke a few words of Romany. But the way they lived was familiar to Ral. They were modest. The men, when they had to urinate, talked about "visiting the donkeys," the kind of euphemism a Romany would use. And the women apologized if they accidentally walked with their skirts lifted in front of a man, lest they shame him. They made sure their drinking water came from farthest upstream, with washing and bathing water farther downstream. Among Ral's own people the rules had been even stricter. But he could understand these people.

Except for Elena. She wasn't at all like a Romany girl. She sat near Ral, laughed openly, smiled gaily at him, hadn't been ashamed to walk with him. No Romany girl would behave that way with a stranger. And there was nothing coy in the way she brought him figs and stew and bread. He guessed her age at fifteen or sixteen, although she had both the innocent grace of a child and the self-assurance of a woman. He couldn't help comparing her to the women he had known in Vienna, women who had dressed and groomed and trained themselves to be beautiful, buying expensive clothes and having their hair styled and their faces painted, and who for all of it could not begin to compare with the easy grace and natural beauty of this girl.

The band was traveling south. They shared their food and fire with Ral, and as darkness came they began to tell stories. Their tales weren't very different from the *swatura* Ral had heard as a child, except that the stories he had heard from his father and uncles were about successes in swindling *gaji*, or tricks that had been played when trading horses. Eleazar and the men in his band told stories of their great victories in fighting anyone who had tried to conquer the Montenegrins, the people of the Black Mountain. Each story ended with the same ritual phrases. The teller would draw his *yatagan*, the wicked curved sword, and swear upon the names of his ancestors that just as they had never surrendered to the Turk, so he would never surrender to the Italian or the German. Ral had never met warriors like these men.

After each man had told a story, Ral told a story of his own, beginning with the ritual phrase he had heard a thousand times as a boy. "This is the *paramixta* of Sandor, and as he once entertained us by telling this story, so too I will try . . ." The Montenegrins delighted in his story of foolish *gaji* being tricked by clever gypsies, and Eleazar passed around a bottle of slivovitz so each man could take a swallow of the plum brandy.

When they broke up the camp the next morning, Ral went with them.

"Why do you go south?" Eleazar asked.

Ral explained how he hoped to follow the *patrin* to find his mother and sister.

"It's not good for the gypsies here," said Eleazar. "The Ustashi have a camp for gypsy women and children, in Zemun. After the Germans shoot the men, the women and children go into the camp. You pray that your mother and sister aren't there. I would kill my own daughter, kill her with my bare hands, before I would let the Ustashi touch her."

Ral told them about Lackenbach, and the mass execution he had seen in the hills of Croatia, the Jews and gypsies lined up next to the ditch, and the desperate struggle of the gypsy men.

"It happens every day," said Eleazar. "And worse. It is said that they now have a special gas van for the women, a truck from Germany that takes them on a journey from which they never return."

"Can no one stop them?"

Eleazar touched the handle of his sword. "If it was only the Germans and the Italians, we could do something. We know the land and they do not. We could fight them as our fathers' fathers fought the Turk. But the Ustashi, those pigs of Croatian Fascists. . . ! To fight them is to fight a disease inside. That is not so easy."

Although no one really explained, Ral gradually understood that Eleazar and his band were wandering traders. Before the war they had gone from village to village, living out of caravans, buying and selling among the farms, bringing goods and news in the wagons they pulled with their donkeys. Now the wagons and caravans were gone; they lived off the woods, hiding from German patrols as they worked their way south. Almost daily, Eleazar would point to traces of the Germans—truck tracks, spent shells, discarded supplies, occasionally a glimpse of a bivouac or a convoy on the move.

After they had been traveling for a week Eleazar came back one morning from a scouting trip and gathered the clan. He described what he had seen, and when he finished, the men dug into the packs on the backs of the donkeys and brought out hidden rifles and pistols. That night they sharpened their swords and daggers, and the men preened their mustaches.

Early the next morning they took up positions on the rocks alongside a narrow mountain pass. Eleazar strung a thin wire across the road at the height of his chest, fixing the wire to the rocks on one side of the road and to a tree on the other. They waited behind the rocks, listening for the rumble of heavy vehicles.

Finally a German supply convoy appeared, three heavy trucks led by a jeep, all moving as fast as the steep, twisting road permitted. On the slopes below, Ral could see the burned wreckage of other trucks. He could hear the trucks shifting gears. The sounds of the convoy faded and it seemed that they had turned around or found another route.

Then, suddenly, the jeep and the trucks rounded an immense outcropping of stone and accelerated down the straightaway below. The windshield of the jeep was down, and the rising sun was in the eyes of the driver. An instant later, when the jeep reached the wire, the head of the man next to the driver snapped back. The driver reached for his throat and the jeep swerved, then crashed into the boulders on the roadside, toppling over and blocking the road. The trucks screeched on their brakes, but not soon enough, as they piled into one another.

Eleazar, a pistol in one hand and a sword in the other, leaped out from behind the rocks. The others followed him, and in an instant they were all over the two trucks.

The battle was over in minutes. The Germans had time to fire only a few shots before they were all dead, their bodies strewn on the road. The Montenegrins hadn't fired a single shot. They killed all the Germans with swords and daggers.

In the back of one of the trucks they found stores of flour, tinned food, hams, wine, and brandy. They unloaded the food, then burned the trucks and buried the bodies. Later that night they came back with donkeys to take some of the food.

"What happens to the rest?" asked Ral.

"It's for the villagers," said Eleazar. "They'll see the flames. They'll know what to expect. It's their food anyway."

The next morning, as they were setting up a new campsite, Ral saw one of the women using paper to start a fire.

"What's that?" he asked.

"It's just paper. From the Germans."

"Let me see it?"

"Can you read?" said Eleazar.

The papers turned out to be quartermasters' manifests and a schedule of supply convoys for the antipartisan patrols. It took Ral a long time to translate the names of villages from German to Serbian, but once they had the villages and dates straightened out, the operations of Eleazar's little partisan band were no longer haphazard.

Eleazar came to depend on Ral. They ate together, slept near each other, planned every move of the band together. And when they weren't planning or fighting, Eleazar seemed to encourage Ral to spend his time with Elena, walking in the woods with her, or watching as she danced and sang, carving out a tiny niche of peace and beauty in the midst of the war. She teased him about his glumness and reminded him of the things he had once enjoyed, like the animals of the woods, the joy of following a rabbit or a fox—not to hunt, but to watch the craftiness of the animal in escaping his pursuer, his ability to melt into the woods, his instinctive wisdom in knowing when to freeze and when to run for it.

Elena was like no other woman he had known. She seemed fearless, afraid neither of the woods nor the Germans, nor of him or any other man. Somehow, she had never learned the wiles and guile that he had seen in Vienna, and he gradually realized that he had seen too much in Vienna, learned a toughness and sophistication and cynicism that was all wrong. But because of it, because of what he sensed in himself, he was afraid to touch her, afraid it would be like plucking a wildflower for its beauty, only to see it die in your fingers.

And so they walked and talked and laughed, sharing wonder and joy in how different and how similar their lives had been. Occasionally they held hands, but otherwise they were as innocent as children, as though the reminders of war all around them kept them too close to death to think of life.

Then one afternoon Elena led Ral far away from the camp, to a secret glen at the base of a tiny waterfall. Mist from the falls had wet the grass, but Elena spread out her skirt and told Ral to sit next to her.

"I like you so much, Ral," she said as she reached up to touch his cheek and his hair. "I like your mysterious eyes and the way you sometimes smile without moving your mouth."

She leaned back and he held himself over her, brushing the coppery hair away from her face. The last woman he had kissed was Sophie, ever hungry and demanding, an animal when she was aroused. With Sophie, a kiss had always been fervid, almost painful, as she drove herself for the release she craved like a drug. But Elena looked up at Ral with gentle sloe-eyes, her lashes damp, her grin elusive as her lips parted and her tongue tickled her teeth.

"Are you afraid?" she asked.

"Maybe."

"Why? Don't you like me?"

"Of course I like you. You're wonderful."

"Then why are you afraid?"

"You hardly know me," he said.

"Yes, I do know you. I know that you're quiet and secretive, that you never let your eyes say what you're really thinking. And I know that you're the handsomest man I've ever seen, that when you look at me I feel funny inside. Isn't that enough?"

"Perhaps."

He kissed her again, his body pressing against hers, gently, as her lips parted. He could feel her rounded breasts, the nipples taut through her thin blouse. His hands roved over her body, caressing her, as they kissed again and again.

Her fingers wound through his hair and over his neck and shoulders, barely touching him, leaving electric tingles. Ral could feel the tumescence in his own flesh and hers, the arousal that had so often seemed mechanical before, and which was suddenly magical.

When he found the waist of her skirt, she reached down and brought his fingers to her lips.

"Now who's afraid?" he said.

"I'm not afraid," said Elena. She sat up, looking into the churning water at the base of the falls. "It's this war. Do you know that I cannot even be a mother now? After the Germans came I stopped bleeding each month. It's happened to some of the other women too. I know it's not right to speak of this with you, but who else can I tell?"

"What about your mother?" said Ral. "What happened to her?" No one had ever mentioned Elena's mother. When he had once asked, around the fire at night, no one had answered.

"The Germans," said Elena. She looked away.

"What did they do?"

Elena looked back at Ral, her eyes down, her expression frozen between the thoughtful anxiety of a few minutes before and a sadness Ral had never seen before in her face. "Why do you want to know?"

"I want to know everything about you."

"My mother was beautiful," she said. "She had blue eyes, like my brother."

"Brother?"

"He was only three when the Germans came. When our caravan was taken and we had to walk, he got sick. He was always a happy little boy, but he began to cough all the time. There was nothing we could do. We had no medicine, no milk, no honey for the cough. He got so weak and thin that we had to carry him or put him on a donkey. But we couldn't stop running, because of the Germans.

"One night we were hidden deep in the woods. The fire was out, because we could hear a German patrol looking for partisans. All they had to do was find the guns and they would kill all of us. For hours we could hear them searching and see the lights shining through the woods, and there was nothing we could do. There were too many of them to fight. Then the baby woke up. As young as he was, he would never cry, even when he was hungry. Somehow he knew he mustn't cry. But he began to cough, and you could see his face turning red as he tried to stop. My mother had saved a lump of sugar, in case such a thing should ever happen, and she gave it to him to suck. But then it was gone and he started to cough again. So my mother held him close to her, as if she could still suckle him, so the warmth of her breasts would maybe quiet him.

"It was a long time before the Germans finally went away. We all turned to see how the baby was. He was deep inside my mother's arms, and her face was white, like the ashes from a fire. When we spoke to her, she didn't answer. Eleazar had to peel her arms away from the baby."

Elena looked away again, at the waterfall. "My brother was dead. My mother had smothered him so his coughs wouldn't bring the Germans. His body was so tiny that Eleazar carried him away with one hand to bury him. My mother never cried. And she never spoke again. Not one word.

"Two days later the men attacked a convoy. My mother was supposed to wait in the woods, but when she saw the soldiers she ran out and tore at the face of one of the Germans with her hands. Before anyone could help her, the Germans put twenty bullets into her body from their pistols and machine guns."

"I hate them," said Ral.

Ral waited almost a week before he spoke to Eleazar. By then they were only a few days from Belgrade.

"Why do you want to marry her?" said Eleazar.

"Why? She's beautiful."

"Beauty cannot be eaten with a spoon." Ral recognized the expression. *Shik chi hal pe le royasa.* Romany fathers said it all the time, and never meant it.

"Who is to speak for you?" said Eleazar. "You think it's enough that you ask?" He didn't let on a smile, but Ral knew he was being kidded. He liked that about Eleazar, the way the man could laugh and joke even as they fought and fled the Germans.

"I will speak for myself."

"For yourself? And what do you demand as a dowry?"

Ral looked puzzled. Among the Romany, it was a bride price that was paid, the father of the groom paying on the basis of what it was thought the bride would ultimately earn telling fortunes or begging. "Whatever you offer is enough," said Ral.

"You insult me and Elena!" said Eleazar, feigning outrage. "If you truly want her and respect her, you must demand a great price."

"But how could you pay it?"

"If I cannot pay what you demand, you won't have to take her."

"But I want her."

"Then demand!" Eleazar boomed with laughter, delighting in the antinomy. "It's good for you to laugh too, Ral," he said.

Ral grinned, waiting for Eleazar to stop laughing. "I want a fine horse and three boxes of gold," he said. "And don't try any gypsy tricks on me. I know horses."

"One box of gold."

"Your daughter is worth only one box? Two at least."

"Done!" shouted Eleazar, holding a straight face as Ral laughed. He went to the donkeys and dug under the blankets that covered their packs. Ral remembered gypsy *vardos*, years back, that had concealed caches of gold under the coverings of rags. Could it be that Eleazar and his band were more than partisans? Bandits, perhaps?

Eleazar came back with a new Mauser rifle in one hand and boxes of cartridges in the other. "This," he said, holding up the rifle, "is a fine horse. And each of these is a box of gold."

"It's fair," said Ral.

"You drive a hard bargain, gypsy man," said Eleazar. "What makes you think Elena will have you?"

On the day of the wedding they were camped in the hills outside Belgrade. Although everything was scarce, somehow the women managed to prepare a wedding feast of rabbits and thrushes roasted on a spit, with wine and brandy and sweet cakes. Everyone dressed gaily, with a bright scarf or flowers or a sash. Eleazar wet his mustache and put on two cartridge belts, a pistol, two daggers, and his sword. Elena spent the morning with the women. When she finally appeared, she had flowers in her hair and her *diclo* had been tied behind her neck, so that curls tumbled around her face. Ral thought her the most beautiful girl he had ever seen.

There was little ceremony. Ral was expected to offer a token present to Eleazar, a glass of brandy and another of wine. Eleazar made a show of refusing, until the other men gestured at the rabbits roasting on the spit. Then he drank the wine and brandy, each in a single gulp. Elena walked from his side to Ral's side, reaching out for her new husband's hand. One of the women cackled: "See, they can't wait."

Then everyone fell to the banquet, eating and drinking in prodigious quantities. Someone brought out a *gusle*, a one-stringed fiddle, and began playing a haunting melody. A goatskin drum beat out the strange syncopated rhythm of the oriental tune.

The music and eating went on until Eleazar stood up. The music suddenly stopped and he began a slow erotic dance that seemed impossible for a man so large. His fingers snapped and clicked, and his body wove a story that was mysterious but unmistakable. For a long time he danced alone, without music. Then the other men joined him, and finally Ral was invited to dance as the rhythm quickened. They danced as if the war and the Germans were a million miles away. It wasn't long before some of the women began to tease Ral: "Well! What are you waiting for? Your mother would be anxious to look at the sheets."

Everyone laughed, even Elena. Ral, only a year away from all he had seen and learned in Vienna, was embarrassed. He gathered his rifle and cartridge belt, saw that Elena had a bundled eiderdown, and together they walked into the woods, up the hill behind the camp to a clearing, encircled with tall trees, but open to the sky above. Elena spread out the eiderdown. They could hear the faint strains of the music from below.

Ral kissed her lips, her cheeks, her chin, her hair. Her arms reached around him, her embrace strong. "I love you very much, Ral," she said.

"And I love you, Elena."

The music from below died away. She nestled even closer to him as he kissed her neck and her shoulders. Then he saw the distraction in her eyes.

"What is it?" he asked.

"Listen."

It took a few minutes before Ral recognized the sound of a truck. The engine was racing, as though the truck were struggling with a heavy load.

"What do you think it is?" Elena asked. "Was there anything in the papers about a convoy here?"

"No." He held her close to him as they listened. They expected the truck to get closer or to recede, but it did neither. They tried to ignore it, turning to each other, holding their arms tighter. But once they had heard it, they could think of nothing else. Ral reached for his gun.

"Don't go," said Elena. "Not now."

"I just want to see what it is." He knew the road on the other side of the hill, a steep switchback that wound up through the passes in the mountains. As he stood up, Elena stood with him.

"Don't argue," she said. "If you go, I go."

They climbed over the crest of the hill and down the slope on the other side, stumbling in the darkness, scratching their arms and faces in the rough brush. Far below them, they could still hear the truck, its engine racing, but the sound not moving. At every step they had to hold on to each other to keep from sliding down the steep slope.

Then, as they rounded a ridge in the slope, they saw the beams of the headlights of a jeep shining over a clearing next to the road. In the center of the clearing, men in prison suits were digging a pit. The truck was at the side of the clearing. It was larger than any they had seen before, with solid sides instead of canvas. Its engine was racing, but the truck stood still.

"What is it?" said Elena. The ominousness of the scene resonated in her voice.

While they watched, the truck backed to the edge of the pit. The engine was shut off, and the men in prison suits, urged on by uniformed Ustashi, opened the tailgate of the big truck. Bodies tumbled out of the back of the truck, bluish in the light of the headlights, twisted, convoluted, covered with streaks of excrement. They were packed so closely that the prisoners had to pull them free from the clumps of arms and legs.

Elena's fingers dug into Ral's arm. He heard her swallow a sob, and he shuddered, feeling waves of rage and revulsion in his gut. Then a strange calm came over him, as if the rage had been stilled by the duty to witness. His eyes gradually adjusted to the light, and he could see that most of the corpses were women, old crones who had withered to nothing, and nubile young girls, their bodies scarcely rounded. They were tumbled together in a tangle of limbs and excrement and hair.

Down in the pit, the prisoners were stacking the bodies in rows, stopping only to strip off the jewelry and clothing that a Ustashi guard gathered in a sack. Some of the clothing was gypsy, broad colorful skirts and blouses and shawls. Ral could recognize the patterns of Kalderash clans.

Ral watched one prisoner hesitate over the body of a young woman, as if he recognized her. The prisoner cradled the corpse in his arms, brushing the hair and filth away from the face. There was a shout from the Ustashi guard, but the man still held the body, the face inches from his own. Then came another shout and a burst of machine gun fire. Dust jumped up around the feet of the prisoner. He dropped the body and moved on. Ral could feel the tears on the man's face.

It took a long time to unload and stack the bodies and then to shovel a layer of soil into the pit. When the bodies were covered, the prisoners were herded into the back of the truck and locked in, and the Ustashi brought out bottles of slivovitz, putting down their automatic weapons as they drank and pawed through the jewelry and clothing that had been looted from the dead.

Ral and Elena said nothing. He could feel her fingers digging into his arm, and when he turned to her, she was white, her jaw clenched, her face suddenly old and angry, as he had never seen it before. She saw him looking at her, and her eyes went up to the graying sky. Her lips moved silently.

"No curse is terrible enough," he said.

They were close enough to see the warts and unshaved beards on the faces of the Ustashi, and they could hear them belch and fart and laugh as they traded necklaces and skirts and bracelets, gulping the slivovitz and occasionally firing a shot into the air.

"Can you go back and get Eleazar and the others?" said Ral.

"What are you going to do?"

Ral checked and saw that there was a shell in the breech of the Mauser.

"There are six of them," said Elena. "You have one rifle."

"I hate them," said Ral. "And I love you. Now go get Eleazar."

He walked out of the brush, the Mauser that Eleazar had given him in front of him. Then he turned and waved for Elena to go back.

The Ustashi didn't see him until he was within ten meters of them. Then one glanced up, saw Ral, and reached for a pistol. Ral waved the muzzle of the Mauser at the man. "Get over to the pit!" he shouted. "All of you."

"What do you want?" said one of the men. "This junk? We'll give you some. There's plenty for everybody." He belched as he offered a slivovitz bottle.

Ral wondered how quickly he could fire the rifle, how rapidly he could cock the mechanism. What if he shot one or two and the others rushed him?

"Get over there!" he shouted again, and the men all got up, walking slowly toward the pit. Even from a distance, the nauseating smells of excrement and decay wafted up through the thin layer of soil. The men walked slowly, watching Ral over their shoulders.

At the edge of the pit they turned, their faces green from nausea and fear. One man stared behind Ral, and Ral thought he heard noises from the woods behind him, brush breaking. Could it be Eleazar already? He was afraid to turn to look.

Then he saw the Ustashi smile as they watched over his shoulder.

When he turned to look, a German half-track broke out of the brush. Four men were on it. One aimed a mounted machine gun at Ral.

"Drop the gun, dog!" the machine gunner shouted in German. Ral spun back and shot at the Ustashi. Before he could get a second shot off, he had been knocked to the ground by the half-track.

He started to get up, swinging wildly at the hands that held him. Then, from behind the trees, he saw Elena step out into the clearing.

"No!" he shouted. "Run!"

But she kept coming, walking slowly, looking at no one else until she stood beside him. Everyone seemed mesmerized by the sight of the beautiful girl walking so calmly out of the woods.

"I'm your wife," she said. "I must be at your side."

The Germans took them in the half-track, making the disappointed Ustashi follow behind in the jeep. They were driven for more than an hour to a field office, inside a high barbed-wire fence. Ral could see the buildings of Belgrade in the distance, across the river.

A plainclothes security officer asked them questions from behind a desk.

"Who is the leader of your partisan band?"

Ral shrugged.

"You were carrying a German rifle, interfering in an official operation in a restricted area. You are a partisan. Who is the leader of your band?"

Ral looked at Elena. She didn't react to the questions.

"What were you doing on that road?"

"It was our marriage journey," said Ral.

The guards laughed.

"They're clever, these gypsies," said the security officer to no one in particular. "Almost like the Jews with their lies." He walked toward Ral, raising his hand as if to slap him. He watched Elena as he threatened Ral.

"No," he said, dropping the hand. "I won't soil my hands. It's better to leave the violence to the Ustashi. It comes easily to them, you know. Our policy is to shoot partisans. The Ustashi say it's a waste of bullets when clubs, fire, and quicklime are so cheap. And what they do to the women . . . !" He twisted his face in disgust, glancing at Elena. "You wouldn't want to watch, I assure you."

Ral saw the blank expression on Elena's face. Was it bravery? he wondered. Or because she didn't understand German?

"Will you cooperate with us?" said the officer. "Or shall I have the Ustashi take her outside? You say she's your bride? They'll like that."

Ral tried to lunge for the man, but the two guards behind him locked his arms tightly. When he stopped writhing, he heard footsteps at the doorway. A woman in a Wehrmacht uniform, with a skirt instead of trousers, came into the room. She had no decorations and no hat. Ral recognized her immediately.

"Who are they?" Eva Ritter demanded of the security officer. "Why wasn't I notified?"

"Partisans," said the officer. "He tried to attack a Ustashi patrol."

"Let me talk to them," said Eva Ritter.

The officer shrugged.

"Alone."

Eva Ritter stared at Elena. "Who are your people?" she asked.

"I am Montenegrin," Elena answered. "This is my husband." She smiled at Ral.

Eva Ritter turned to Ral. "You're not Montenegrin." She stared at him for a moment. "You were at Lackenbach, weren't you? What is your name?"

Ral didn't answer.

"Don't you understand? I can help you. You don't belong here. What is your name?"

Still he didn't answer.

Eva Ritter thought for a moment, still staring at him. "Your people are Lovari, horse traders from the Burgenland. You were in Vienna."

She turned to the security officer. "This man doesn't belong here," she said. "He's a Lovari Romany, an Austrian native. Pure *Zigeuner*."

"He's a partisan," said the officer. "He was captured with a German rifle, attempting to disrupt an operation."

"Operation!" shouted Ral. "Is that the word for what those filthy pigs were doing? You stinking *gajo* dog!"

A guard raised a handgun, as if to pistol-whip Ral.

Eva Ritter shouted at the officer. "Tell that guard not to touch this man! This man doesn't belong here. He's to be transferred into the detention camp pending resettlement."

The officer shrugged. "What about the girl?"

Eva Ritter turned back to Elena, asking her name in Romany.

Elena looked at Ral, then back at Eva Ritter. She said nothing.

"What is your clan? Who is your father?"

Still no answer. Elena hadn't understood a word that had been said to her.

"Do you understand German?" said Eva Ritter.

"A little."

"Serbian?"

"Of course."

"Then you're not Romany?"

"We're wanderers, from Montenegro."

"We?"

"My husband and I."

"This man"—Eva Ritter nodded at Ral—"isn't a wanderer. He's a pure Romany."

"What about the girl?" said the officer, bored now.

"The girl is mixed blood," said Eva Ritter. "A native wanderer. We're dealing only with pure Romany for the resettlement program."

They were separated in the courtyard outside the building. Ral was guarded by the German soldiers. Four Ustashi came for Elena. The leader of the Ustashi detail, a stocky man with a few days' growth of raunchy beard, grinned as he listened to the orders of the German officer.

"Bride, eh?" he said.

They led Elena only a short distance away, across the courtyard. She looked over her shoulder at Ral, until the bearded Ustashi thrust his hand up under her skirt. She screamed and tried to bite the man. Another Ustashi put his hand over her mouth.

"No wonder she fights," said the bearded man, his grin lascivious. "I think this bride is maybe a virgin. So much for the husband."

The Ustashi guffawed.

Ral broke free. He ran toward Elena and tore at the face of the bearded man, wrenching him away from Elena.

A rifle butt hit him in the stomach. As he fell back, another rifle butt came down on his shoulders. He fell face-first into the dirt, breathless, tasting the dry dust of the courtyard. Boots came down on his back, but he could lift his head just enough to see Elena.

By then, the Ustashi had her down on a bench, with her skirt up to her waist. Her legs flailed until two more men held her down. She twisted and bit the hand over her mouth. Then she cried out, a single long wail that hung in the air. "Ral . . . !"

"Elena . . . !" he shouted back. By then they were dragging him away.

He never saw her again.

New York, 1966

"I'm sorry, Jill, but that's a damn good translation. There are a few phrases where the tone is a little off, but the meaning wouldn't change. The upshot of that inquiry is that the woman was closer to a heroine than a villain."

Hirschmann seemed uncomfortable behind his desk. After he finished reading the translation and the transcript of the inquiry, he got up and came around to sit on the front of the desk, close to Jill.

"There's got to be something," she said. "A cover-up, maybe. Aren't the Germans always covering up for war criminals? Trying to shorten the statute of limitations, finding excuses not to try someone?"

"They gave her a hearing, Jill. And it seems to me that the magistrate was pretty fair. He started out trying to find chinks in her dossier and her testimony. He asked her about the Interpol office to combat the gypsy menace. He got out that she worked for some office of racial hygiene. But then you've got those witnesses. That's pretty convincing testimony."

"I doubt whether they'd be so convincing if I had a crack at them under cross-examination."

"Jill!" Hirschmann waited until she looked at him. "Why are you so sure the woman was some kind of war criminal? Because your gypsy killed her? Is that the logic: You like him, he's accused of killing her, therefore she must be a villain?"

"Do you believe that sugar-shit testimony?" Jill asked. "You really think she was some kind of saint?"

"On the basis of the transcript, I'd guess she was a hell of a lot better than most. It sounds like she had a streak of humanity in her and did the best she could do in the circumstances. Do you think you or I would have been so different if we had ended up in her situation?"

"Not everyone chooses to end up in her situation. She did."

"Jill! You're grabbing at nothing. There were thousands of guards in the camps, physicians and researchers and ordinary people who ended up with jobs no one could envy. A few tried to be heroic and ended up in the gas chambers. The rest did what anyone would do—they shut their eyes to

205

what was happening. And they've probably spent the last twenty years trying to purge their memories or their consciences. Some of them probably
deserve punishment, if the memories and consciences aren't punishment
enough. But they don't deserve to be murdered. Any more than I think this
woman deserved to be murdered."

"If she was murdered . . ."

"Right, Jill. If she was murdered. . . . I think you're looking at the
wrong end of this case. I'd try to find out what happened to him during the
war. See where their tracks crossed and what his grievance might be."

"He won't tell me."

"Did you ever ask him directly?"

"I tried. It was always the same answer. 'I'll tell about that when the
time comes, when I have a trial.' "

"Has that French lawyer had any better luck?"

"I think he's all but given up. I've talked to him twice, and both times he
said that Ral wouldn't tell him anything. If Ral wouldn't talk to me, I
don't think he would ever talk to Jean-Claude."

"Maybe, maybe not. It might turn out that he's more willing to talk to a
man. If I were you, I'd send a copy of the transcript to that lawyer and let
him ask the gypsy about the camps."

What Hirschmann said made sense, but Jill saw herself left out, watching from the outside. What if Ral did talk to Jean-Claude instead of to her?
What was left for her then?

"Where would I look to find out if Ral was in a camp?"

"I told you, Jill. That's a long, slow process. And the chances of success
are close to nil."

"Just tell me where I start, Nat."

In rapid succession she tried the Weiner Library in London, YIVO in New
York, Yad Vashem in Jerusalem, and the new Simon Wiesenthal Center in
Los Angeles. She wired directly to Wiesenthal in Vienna, to see if there was
anything in his private files. Her inquiries weren't the usual paced queries
of a scholar, but rapid-fire telexes, followed by phone calls and offers to
come on the first available flight and look through records herself. She had
thought her interest and energy would speed up the search, but in fact, in-
stitutions used to the leisured pace of scholarly inquiries were put off by her
brash demands.

Although it took two months before she heard anything, the search
proved easier than Hirschmann had predicted. The reports from the
libraries dribbled in, some with lengthy listings of their materials on gypsies in the war camps, others with terse replies to her multiple inquiries.
There were no false leads, no blind alleys, no dangling chains of fragile
connections. Everywhere she had inquired there was nothing: no trace of
Ral, no record of any gypsy with a name like that.

"Doesn't anyone care about gypsies?" she railed to Hirschmann.

"Jill, why don't you try asking the gypsy. Maybe he's changed his mind in the last months and is willing to talk now. Have you written him?"

"How can I write when I don't have anything that would help him? What am I going to say in a letter?"

In fact, she had been trying for days to write a letter, struggling to get words down in a way that wouldn't sound insipid or mechanical, trying to recall and express her feelings and at the same time invite information from Ral. She wrote draft after draft, starting, pouring words out in longhand that she could hardly read, then going back and rereading and tearing up the letter because it was too emotional, or too dryly professional, or too evasive. She found excuses not to send every version she tried. When she finally sent a letter, it wasn't because it was at last right, but because she could see that succeeding versions were getting less and less satisfactory.

"What else can I try?" she asked Hirschmann.

"There's a long shot," he explained. "It won't place him in a camp, but it might give you a lead. The U.S. Army archives in Alexandria have lists of persons who were in DP camps in the American zone. Those records would tell you if a DP was previously in a German camp."

"I'll go tomorrow," she said. "Come with me?"

He shook his head. "I could take the time off, Jill, but it means spending the night. And I don't think I'm ready for a night in a room across the hall from you."

She didn't go immediately. Excuse after excuse came up, until she finally admitted to herself that she was postponing what she knew was the final chance for a clue about Ral. She told herself that if she got a reply to her letter, an answer to her questions, she wouldn't have to go. But after a month there was no reply. Finally she took a shuttle on the spur of the moment, as if to finally get it over with.

"A gypsy?" The clerk in the huge archive building raised her bushy eyebrows. The uniform and the total lack of makeup made her seem hard.

"You have anything except that name? Where was he picked up? When? Nationality? Age? Anything?"

Jill shook her head. "He was German. Or he might have put down Austrian."

"That won't help much. I'll look, but don't hold your breath expecting anything."

From the counter where she waited, Jill could hear steel drawers opening and closing, and the riffling of cards. The woman went from one row to another, slamming drawers shut, yanking them open, then moving on. She came back to the counter carrying a yellowed four-by-six-inch index card.

"Buchenwald," she said.

"You found him?" Jill reached for the card, stopping her fingers in mid-air. "What else does it tell you?"

The clerk smiled, genuinely happy to be able to help. "The card should have prewar address, nationality, classification number, German camp ID numbers, relatives, disposition, agency referrals, and cash payments and services provided. This gypsy either wasn't talking or they weren't asking. It says 'gypsy' and 'previously incarcerated in Buchenwald concentration camp.' That's it. No disposition, no relatives, no address. Nothing. Sorry."

Buchenwald? thought Jill. Why couldn't it have said Auschwitz?

"What happened to him?" she asked. "Does it tell you that?"

The clerk turned the card over and laid it on the counter. Stamped in block letters across the bottom it said MISSING, 18 IX 45.

Amsterdam, 1965

Amsterdam was the best decision she had ever made, thought Wanda Lanzer. The Dutch were friendly and tolerant, asking few questions, never demanding information that wasn't volunteered. They made no secret of their dislike for Germans, but as long as a visitor made token efforts at Dutch—even a badly mangled *"Goeden dag!"*—the Dutch would no longer conceal their own knowledge of German. It was easy to get along.

She had fled Frankfurt the day she saw the article in *Der Spiegel*. One glance at the story, at the details about her clothes when she first came to Frankfurt and the facts that she had rehearsed with the lawyer from Neue Deutschland but never used in the inquiry, and she knew that they had given her story to the press. She had trusted them, accepting the lawyer they provided for the hearing, following the infinitely detailed orders they specified for her conduct in the inquiry. And in return, they had used her, making propaganda out of her inquiry, ignoring her own desire for anonymity. Now anyone who read that magazine knew about Eva Ritter, about that past she had tried for so long to forget.

She left even before she had time to make sure her pension was transferable. And once she crossed the border into Holland, she stopped using the name Eva Ritter. The magazine said that the inquiry had cleared her of any wrongdoing, but it was too easy for some people to remember the wrong things, to confuse the past that still haunted her. And it was easy to use the name Wanda Lanzer again. She didn't even have to practice her answers to questions about her background.

In Amsterdam she found a room close to the Central Station. After only two days the memories of train stations proved uncomfortable, and she packed up and found a new room, in a quiet old house on the Herengracht. The room was small, tucked under the gables, but it had a nice view out over the canal, the furniture was clean, and it was very private, the only room on the top floor. The concierge asked few questions and seemed pleased when Wanda Lanzer said that she would clean the room herself, that she would require nothing. Wanda Lanzer explained that she was a pensioner, and that she expected to live quite modestly.

"So young to be a pensioner," said the concierge. "You'll have a nice stay in Amsterdam, I'm sure."

Wanda Lanzer smiled. It was as long a conversation as she was to have with the concierge.

The room was only one canal over and a short walk from the Instituut Internationaal voor Sociale Anthropologie. Even before the war, the institute had been famed for its ethnographic and linguistic collections and its tape library of folk cultures. The Romany section was not one of the stronger collections, but the institute had a reputation for being hospitable.

She waited two full months before she went to the Institute, long enough, she thought, for the story in Der Spiegel to fade from memory. She had seen the story mentioned in some of the newspapers, but it was such a small article, with nothing special about it, that she thought no one would ever remember it.

"Have you any academic affiliation?" asked the young woman in the reading room after she read through Wanda Lanzer's application for a reader's card.

"I'm a private scholar."

"You've published?"

"Many years ago." She regretted the answer immediately.

"You haven't listed the citations," said the young woman.

"It was immature work."

"Do you have any academic references?"

"References? No, not really. My studies were interrupted for many years."

The woman jotted notes on the application. "Is there a householder here in Amsterdam who can vouch for you?"

"Vouch?"

"It's a formality."

"I've only just come to Amsterdam. I know no one."

"Your concierge, perhaps."

"She hardly knows me."

"It's only a formality, Mej. Lanzer."

The institute proved hospitable and comfortable. It didn't take long for Wanda Lanzer's life to fall into a pattern. She would walk to the institute each morning, arriving at the opening hour of eight thirty. She would read or listen to tapes until noon, then step out for a *broodje* and a cup of tea before she went back to the reading room until closing at five o'clock. Then she usually went straight home to her room, stopping only to buy food. The hotplate in the room was all she needed for cooking.

It turned out to be simple to transfer her pension. She sent a notarized letter to the ministry in Bonn, giving them a post office box number in Amsterdam. She would then cash the checks at a bank in the Dam Square, and take the money back to the post office to deposit it in a giro account in the name of Wanda Lanzer. There were no questions about cash deposits, and the checks proved ample for her needs. From the first four checks she set aside enough to buy some new clothes—woolen skirts, cardigan sweaters, plain blouses, sturdy shoes—all well made, anonymous clothes. Three more checks and there was enough left over to buy a luxury, a small portable record player. It didn't take long to find record shops that had the kinds of records she wanted, old recordings mostly, authentic versions of the czardas and rhapsodies of the *pusztas*.

In the evenings, in the privacy of her room, she would pull down the curtains, and sometimes light candles, and put on a record. She played the music softly, but the haunting oriental melodies were still enough to transform the plain and sparse room into a refuge, a place of solace where the fears that had haunted her for so long would disappear. In the room she could tell herself that her fears were foolish. No one had ever paid any attention to the story in *Der Spiegel* or the newspapers. There were dozens of stories every week. Hundreds of names in every issue of the magazine. Even when people read a story, they forgot it in a day or two, forgot the names and the facts, forgot even the point of a story. And most gypsies couldn't read anyway. Perhaps some of the younger ones, like the children of that fiddler Hörthy; but how many of the older gypsies could read?

She gradually learned enough Dutch to greet the concierge and to deal with shopkeepers without embarrassment. And as she gained confidence, she began to explore the city, which for her meant only one thing: searching out the gypsy encampments along the outskirts, near the junkyards. She was wary at first, walking by the caravans and shacks without stopping, glancing furtively as she listened for familiar phrases. But the gypsies were too busy to notice one more gawker, and she gradually became more confident, going almost every Sunday afternoon, mingling with tourists for whom the flea market and the gypsies were one more sight in photogenic Amsterdam.

After three weeks the staff at the institute stopped asking how her work was coming or how long she anticipated her studies would require. She had become a regular, sitting every day in the same seat, keeping her table orderly, making few demands. In time they noticed her no more than they noticed the chairs or the tables. Once, she overheard the reading room attendant describe her to some visiting scholars from England: "Oh, she's just a nice old lady who likes to come here and read."

For months the routine went on, unchanging. One day was like the next, one month like the next. Even the seasons hardly mattered as she went from the institute to her room and back again. She rarely read a newspaper, never listened to a radio or watched a television, hardly talked to anyone except for occasional greetings to the people she saw every day. Her world seemed to stand still. She wore the same clothes, ate the same food, walked the same routes, listened to the same records—insulating herself from fear by routine.

Then, one bright, sunny morning in the fall of 1964, after she had been in Amsterdam for almost five years, she was looking at her hair in the mirror, trying to decide whether she needed to have it cut again, when she noticed a change. She looked closely, and decided that what she had seen were blond highlights in the cap of dark hair. But as more "blond" hairs showed up in the mirror and on her hairbrush, she had to admit to herself that it was gray hair she was seeing.

The shock was terrible. It wasn't vanity. Except for insisting on cleanliness and neatness, she had long stopped thinking about how she looked. But she had never thought about getting old. Life for so long had been a wait—waiting until the fears would go away, waiting until she got a pension, waiting until she could venture out to see gypsies again—and there had always been a certain comfort in the waiting, a security in the faith that someday everything would be all right. But the pages of the calendar were turning too fast. *Someday* might never come.

She decided, almost overnight, that she was too old to wait. When she looked closely in the mirror again, she could see that her skin was wrinkled; there were crow's-feet around her eyes and lips. The flesh on her arms was loose, her legs were thicker, her breasts drooped. She wondered how she would look in a loose blouse now. How would gold jewelry look around her wrinkled neck? How about a *diclo* in her graying hair?

For days she avoided mirrors, preferring instead to imagine herself dressed not as Wanda Lanzer or Eva Ritter, but as Loli Tschai. That's who she really was, she knew inside. And now time was running out. She might never be herself again.

She was reluctant to buy clothes at the flea market, except that she saw tourists buying sandals and blouses and scarves, and unlike them she had an eye for the authentic, for jewelry and fabrics in the traditional patterns instead of the fake gypsy clothes that were manufactured in some factory in Hong Kong. She studied the clothing for a long time, shrugging off the teasing of the gypsies who tried to bargain with her.

"You could tell fortunes in that skirt," said one old Kalderash woman.

"You leave that blouse open in the front and men don't look the other way. You understand me?"

She bought the blouse. And a *diclo* and skirt. She had them wrapped in paper and took them home and hid them on top of the armoire.

The first time she put the clothes on, she was embarrassed. She locked the doors of her room and closed the curtains and pretended that she was studying the clothing, as though it were an ethnographic document. But she liked the way she looked in the mirror, and it soon became part of her everyday ritual. She would have a quick supper from the hotplate, then put on a record and dress in the skirt and blouse and *diclo*. Sometimes she would dance, slowly and tentatively, letting her body sway to the music from the little portable Victrola. Usually she just sat on the floor, spreading the skirt around herself, reveling in the freedom of her body inside the loose fabric. The clothes and the music were like a magic carpet, whisking her far away from the demons that still haunted her, letting her forget those inchoate fears that had followed her across Europe.

It was only a few months later, in March 1965, that there came the slightest interruption to her comfortable routine. She was on her way to the institute one morning when she saw a man she had seen almost every morning for years. Except that morning, instead of his usual *"Goeden dag!"* and a finger to the brim of his hat, he said, "It must be spring. You're smiling this morning." Then he touched his hat, added a *"Goeden dag,"* and was gone.

The man's words took a moment to register. Yes, she realized, she was smiling. It was a crisp day, the Amsterdam sky seemed more blue than gray for a change, and she felt just fine, about herself, about the world, about everything. How long had she waited for that feeling? she wondered. Should she not even go to the institute? Celebrate instead?

She thought about it all morning, hardly concentrating on the books and tapes around her, counting the minutes until noon. When the lunch break came, instead of going to a *broodje* shop for her usual sandwich and tea, she walked over to the Kalverstraat to window-shop.

She walked the whole length of the narrow street, stopping to look in the windows of dress shops and boutiques, wondering if she should buy herself something to wear, a pretty dress or a hat maybe, or a new coat for spring. It wasn't until she had passed three travel bureaus that the idea took shape in her mind: She would take a holiday.

She knew exactly where she would go. The weather in the South of France would be warm and sunny in late May. Lots of people would go for the beaches and the fragrance of the air and the festivals. There was even a poster for a film festival. She would be one more tourist enjoying the sights and the sun.

The travel agent was only vaguely familiar with the town. He suggested other towns, package tours by bus or airplane, all of them much more holiday for her money. Spain or the Canary Islands were the best bargains, he assured her. France was too expensive and not as nice.

No, insisted Wanda Lanzer, she knew exactly where she wanted to go. She wrote down the dates, giving herself a few days' leeway to arrive before the festival. The travel agent assured her that she would need no passport to cross the border by train.

As the weeks went on, her excitement mounted. She bought more clothes, another blouse, skirts, *diclos*, sandals, trying each tentatively at the flea market, always buying from someone she hadn't bought from before, then bringing the clothes home for her evenings of music, letting the magic of the loose clothing bring chills to her skin.

A week before she was scheduled to depart, she bought a small traveling case. She brought it home, put it next to the portable Victrola, and suddenly the bad memories flooded back, the moments of blackness and despair and hunger and fear and degradation. She decided that she couldn't go, that it was too risky.

But later that night, listening to the accelerating rhythm of a czardas, with her skirt spread out and her blouse open and a *diclo* tied in her hair, she forgot her qualms and fears. In a week, she told herself, she would be in Saintes-Maries-de-la-Mer. Home.

France, 1965

Ral's first fight was in Nancy, in a seedy working-class bar outside the gates of a metal fabrication plant. Two blue-bloused workers had called him a lazy gypsy. It was said in a joking way, but instead of returning an insult, or insulating himself with that distant, hooded gaze he had relied on for so long, he had swung at one of the welders. Even as he did it, he remembered something Sandor had said. *Mashkar le gajende leski shib le Romeski zor.* Surrounded by the *gaji*, the Rom's tongue is his only defense. Words were the answer, not fists. Later, as the bouncer dragged him, sore and bloody, into an alley behind the bar, Ral knew he had invited the fight, that he had gone into the bar looking to be insulted.

He had begun drinking, too, mostly cheap plum brandy, as close to the slivovitz of Yugoslavia as he could come. He drank enough to get himself raging drunk, putting his mind into a stupor that let him forget the memories. And when clear air and fresh water brought him back to sobriety and a mirror, when the headaches and the buzzing went away, he would look at himself and laugh.

"King of the Gypsies?" he would say to the image in the mirror. "King of the body shops." And then he would roar with painful, forced laughter.

He was ragged now, sleeping on park benches between the occasional luxurious nights in flophouses. He couldn't bear work anymore. He tried banging in a shop in Lyons and quit in the middle of the first day. The gleam of the metal, the sounds of the hammer, the shrieks of the grinders—they were all something else now. Each time he fled the memories they evoked, the nightmare of Yugoslavia.

From Strasbourg he wandered unfamiliar roads, not back to the Europe he knew, but wherever the roads would take him. There were no maps he could use anymore, no *patrin* to follow, no memories of orchards and streams and fields. Now the only maps were the *gajo* maps of lines and words and numbers. The only world was the *gajo* world.

He lost track as the days and months and years rolled by. In 1965, after wandering in circles that went nowhere, he found himself in Paris. He gravitated instinctively to the flea market, expecting to find gypsies. Instead, he saw teenage boys and girls, marriage age to a gypsy, hanging around together. The girls wore tight sweaters and short skirts that hid almost nothing, and they hung on the boys, necking, kissing, sharing cigarettes. While Ral watched, two of the boys walked over to a pissoir and stood in the open, in full view of the girls, to urinate. There was no privacy, no notion of cleanliness, no sense of shame. And yet from their skin, their eyes, their hair, he knew they were gypsies.

"*Rom san?*" said Ral when the boys came back. Are you Romany?

"What's with him?" one of the boys asked the other.

"He's cute," said a girl. "*Mignon. Un type.*"

"Where are you from?" asked Ral.

The boys stared at him. "We're not *pieds noirs*, if that's what you're asking," answered one. Then they turned and walked away, with the girls hanging on their shoulders.

No pride at all, thought Ral. No sense of who or why. Are there any gypsies left?

He wandered through the shanties of the flea market, houses of tin and cardboard and plywood. A few old women wore traditional clothes. Everyone else wore the cheap, tacky clothes of any poor Frenchman.

On the wall of one shack he saw a torn poster, a color photograph of the procession of the *gardiens* into the sea in Saintes-Maries-de-la-Mer. Gypsies swarmed around the powerful horses in the photograph, reaching out to touch the statue that the priests carried on their shoulders.

Ral knew about Saintes-Maries-de-la-Mer, as even a lapsed Moslem knows about Mecca. He went up to a man banging copper ornaments in front of the shack.

"When is it?" said Ral, gesturing at the poster.

The man scrutinized Ral, then the poster. He shrugged.

The streets of Saintes-Maries were empty when he arrived. Only piles of debris, the offal of the crowds, told him that there had been a festival. He asked and found that he was two days late.

Typical gypsy, he thought, laughing at himself.

He wandered the streets, past tight knots of Spanish *gitanos* and French *gitanes*, their backs turned to him and the rest of the world. It had been a long time since he had seen so many Romany, and yet he felt not at home, but an outsider.

He pondered it, argued with himself. Had he changed? Or had they? What had he become in those years of melancholy? Twenty years of searching, and he was no closer now than he had been at the start. He wasn't even sure what name he sought. Was she Eva Ritter again? Or was she still Wanda Lanzer? Or maybe another name? The Eva Ritter of twenty years before would have been near gypsies, couldn't have stayed away. But twenty years had been enough to change him, making him something other than a gypsy. It had been enough to make the world forget the gypsies and what had happened to them. Was it enough to change her too?

From outside a tawdry café he heard a solo violin, soaring through the rising scales of a czardas. The melody was strange to his ears, but he recognized the rhythm, and it evoked a tingling in his body that he couldn't control. He tried humming to himself to follow the elusive syncopations, but the music quickened in tempo and suddenly, abruptly, faded into a mesmerizingly slow *lassú*. Just listening from the street, he could picture the whirl of dancing skirts, the blur of kicking feet.

He wandered into the café. A few old men were scattered around the tables, drinking wine or *pastis*, paying no attention to the man with the fiddle, who stood at a table at the side of the room, with sheets of music spread all around him. The man wore a leather vest and a wide-sleeved red shirt. A scarf was tied around his neck and he wore heavy, black-framed glasses. Ral read a painted sign propped on an easel:

LASZLO
Star of Radio and Television

He listened while Laszlo played through the *lassú*, stopping again and again to replay a passage until he was satisfied. When Laszlo finished, he put down the fiddle and acknowledged Ral with a nod.

"You like it?"

"I remember it," said Ral.

"Yes? No one else does. All they want to hear now is flamenco or show music. Tourist music."

"*Rom san?*" asked Ral.

Laszlo laughed. He put down the fiddle and took a gulp of wine from a glass standing amidst the music. Then he laughed again.

"That's like asking 'Are you Catholic?' A man hasn't taken communion in twenty years, hasn't confessed in so long that it would take him a full month in the booth to recite his sins, and still he says, 'Yes, I'm Catholic.' *Rom san?* you ask me. I would say lapsed, if you understand my meaning."

He took another sip of wine, watching Ral's eyes for understanding. "And you? You're searching for the true gypsy, maybe? Or are you the last true gypsy?"

Someone understood. Ral felt like hugging the man. He contented himself with a grin. This man Laszlo was a brother. He would understand the grin too.

Laszlo waved to the bartender, and another glass appeared. "Go ahead, gypsy man," Laszlo said. "Drink some wine. I'll play you some real gypsy music."

He began plucking the strings of the fiddle, searching for elusive melodies. He segued into a rippling scale that turned into another haunting czardas.

Ral listened until the music was too familiar to bear. "What's that song?" he asked.

"Another czardas. Hungarian, the real music. That's what you've come for, isn't it?"

"I've heard that before."

"Of course you have. Others play it. My father played it. He even recorded it."

"On a record?"

"An old seventy-eight. You remember them? Went around real fast, like this—" Laszlo whirled his finger in a circle.

The memory flooded. Ral reached into his pocket for the photograph. "This woman, do you know her? Have you ever seen her?"

Laszlo finished a long, complicated phrase before he put the fiddle down and picked up the photograph. "This picture must be from before the war," he said. "How can you see anything with all these cracks and fingermarks?"

"Look carefully, please."

Laszlo squinted, turning the photograph to pick up the dim light from the open doorway of the café. "I've maybe seen her," he said.

"When? Where?"

"She was here, I think. Came to hear me play. Said that she had heard my father play too."

Ral hung on the words, waiting for more. "Where is she now?" he asked.

Laszlo shrugged.

"When did you see her?" Ral's voice was taut.

"Easy, gypsy man. What's she to you? She's another Romany *rye*, that one. Came here all dressed up—skirt, *diclo*, jewelry. There are dozens of them. What do you care about her? You play music and they're always around. If I want one, all I do is make eyes like yours."

"Where is she?" said Ral. He forced calm into his voice.

Laszlo shrugged again, his gesture maddeningly disengaged. "She said what they all say. Calls herself a researcher. From some institute."

"Institute?"

"It's a place where they study folk culture. That's what we are now, you know. Folk culture. They take pictures, make recordings on tape, write books about it. Once when I did a concert in Stockholm they had me come to the institute so they could ask questions with a tape recorder on. Never in your life have you heard such stupid questions as those researchers ask. *Gaji!*"

"She's in Stockholm?"

"How do I know where your Romany *rye* is, gypsy man? They have institutes all over. London, Paris, Stockholm, Amsterdam, I think. You can find Romany *rye* like that at any of them. You got stories to tell, they'll listen. A gypsy man with eyes like you got is just what they're looking for."

It took Ral a week in a Marseilles body shop to earn train fare to Paris, the closest city Laszlo had mentioned. He knew before he bought a ticket that he would be there only long enough to find the institute. And if she wasn't there, he would move on, to whatever city had an institute. And from there to another city, until he found her.

As he boarded the second-class coach in Marseilles, he remembered that it was only the second time in his life that he had ever taken a train. The first was a train of cattle cars, still smelling of decaying hay and manure as the gypsies were loaded on at the station across the river from Belgrade. They were crowded so close that no one could turn around without negotiating room from half a dozen others. The gypsies were loaded down with every possession they could drag with them—food, clothing, violins, guitars, even hammers and grindstones—as though the train were a novel mode of transportation for their annual circuits. Only their animals and knives had been taken away.

Just before they boarded, she made a speech to them on the platform. In Romany and then in German she said:

"You've been selected for resettlement. For your own safety, you're being transported to a safe area, away from the fighting, to a camp facility where families can stay together. You'll be protected from the bombing and the guns and from treatment of people like the Ustashi. You'll have medical care, shelter, food. You'll live with other gypsies and be allowed to follow gypsy ways."

For all the long days of that train ride, people who had no room to sit or lie down, who ended up standing in their own excrement and urine, fighting over scraps of salami and moldy bread and an occasional sip of water, talked of nothing except what she had said. Some said that she would get in trouble for what she said about the Ustashi. She was always getting into trouble for the way she stood up for the gypsies, said others. And as they speculated, with only a lucky few who stood near the wooden slats of the sides of the cars able even to catch glimpses of the countryside outside, the train crossed half of Europe, rolling across the *pusztas* of Hungary, the hills of Slovakia and Moravia, and into the flat, damp plains of Polish Silesia, until they finally stopped and the doors of the cars were pulled open so they could see the freshly painted station that awaited them.

The neat little sign said OSWIĘCIM, but they were soon to learn to use the German name, the only name anyone ever used. In German the station was called Auschwitz.

New York, 1966

N at Hirschmann gave Jill the first books. From the footnotes in those she found others. Before long she needed titles that she could get only at the main library on Forty-second Street, and she was stealing time in the middle of the afternoon to read. She went through memoirs, descriptions of the camps, biographies of Hitler and Himmler, the autobiography of Rudolf Höss, the commandant of Auschwitz. She skimmed quickly, watching for references to gypsies, but as Hirschmann had predicted, the comments were sparse and vague, typically: "Jews were not the only victims of the holocaust. Communists, homosexuals, the mentally ill, gypsies, and other persons who were branded as 'antisocials' were at times subjected to incarceration or internment, medical experiments, and sometimes death." In every book she read, the gypsies were bit players.

Still, she read on, through descriptions of the ovens and gas chambers and mass shootings, the ghettos that were meant to kill the weak by systematic starvation or disease, the experiments that tested medical ideas so bizarre that they could never have been contemplated had there not been a ready population to use as guinea pigs. The reading became a new compulsion, filling her hours and driving off the occasional moments of loneliness and despair.

At times she would have to stop reading in the middle of a paragraph because she found herself choked with sobs, unable to comprehend the deeds that came across in such sober prose. But she kept on, through every book she could find, looking for the faintest hints of what had happened to the gypsies, of what sadism and torture and anguish Ral could have experienced or witnessed in the camps.

The more she read, the more she felt that she was beginning to understand Ral, to comprehend the brooding silence in his eyes. At times she even thought she could understand his refusal to discuss the case. But then she tried to imagine how she would have reacted, what she would have done if she had been in his shoes. And when she realized that she would have immediately called a trusted lawyer and told him everything, it dawned on her that she didn't understand Ral at all, that their worlds were as far apart as they had been that first day in Saintes-Maries, when her breath had stopped and her insides had turned all warm and wet, and she had realized that perhaps for the first time in her life she wasn't in complete charge of herself and her emotions.

She read compulsively for almost three months, enough to become an amateur expert on the holocaust. When she had all but exhausted the sources she could find in English and French, she pressed Hirschmann for more.

"What are you looking for, Jill?"

"I want to understand Ral. I want to understand what he went through, what made him the way he is."

"And you think that if you read enough you'll understand?"

"Is there an alternative? He wouldn't tell me what happened, and he won't answer a letter. What else can I do?"

Hirschmann looked around the dim Washington Square bar, as though the place were all wrong for what he was about to say. "You're trying to answer the wrong questions."

"Am I?"

"Every time I give you a book, you come back and tell me there was no mention of the gypsies in it. You'd think he was the only person to go through the holocaust."

Jill looked away, shaking her head. "Don't you see, Nat? He was a gypsy, wandering the roads, used to that freedom. I remember asking him how he knew it was time to move on. He answered that he knew the same way he knew when he was hungry or tired. And then to be put into a camp, with that absolute structure, with no choice of when you sit or stand or eat or sleep or anything else."

"You really think that six million other inmates of those camps didn't love their freedom?"

"I don't know about them, Nat. I never met them."

"Never met one of them? Do you think people go around saying, 'What do I do? Oh, I'm a holocaust victim'? No one volunteered for concentration camps. They were chosen."

"Exactly," she said. "The Chosen People. That's the attitude in every book, always as though the Jews were the only people who counted. They wrote the books, too, didn't they? That's why they're in the books and the gypsies are left out."

"Aren't you forgetting something?"

Her eyebrows went up.

"Like it or not, you're part of the tribe."

"Because my mother's mother was a Jew? Does that make me a Jew? I'm not applying for an Israeli passport, so I don't think the legal definitions mean much. The only time I've ever been in a synagogue has been pretty much on the order of an anthropology field trip. It's usually been quite an experience. They all but lock the doors and ask everyone to make their pledge for the year. I guess that pretty much sums up the faith for me: how much you can pledge, how much your kid's bar mitzvah costs, and how much your people suffered in the holocaust. It's as though they had a monopoly on the suffering."

"Maybe it wasn't a monopoly, but they sure as hell had a plurality. You can't escape history, Jill. Until you understand that, you haven't got a prayer of understanding that gypsy."

She remembered the times Ral had asked her about her people, and her inability to answer. "The only reason I'm reading this stuff is to find out about Ral, to figure out what happened to him and what makes him tick. Something happened between him and that woman in one of those camps."

"She was in Auschwitz, Jill. The only hard evidence you have says he was in Buchenwald."

"We don't know that he wasn't in Auschwitz too."

"And if he was? Hundreds of thousands of people were in that camp, millions if you count those who never came out. How many of them killed a woman who worked there? And don't forget, Jill, that inquiry didn't exactly paint her as another Mengele."

"Mengele?" She shook her head. "I've read about so many of those monsters I can't even keep them straight."

"He was the chief physician at Auschwitz. About as bad as they come. If your gypsy was going to murder someone from Auschwitz, Mengele would have been a good choice."

"We don't know that he murdered anyone. He's accused, Nat. Not convicted."

"Am I supposed to say 'alleged murderer' every time I mention him? You know that I instinctively take the side of the accused. If the French police are on the other side, I'm for your gypsy. But don't try to explain what he did because he was in a concentration camp. There are probably people sitting on those benches in the park out there with tattoos on their arms. And if you took a good look at your Unitarian family tree, you'd find a few not-so-distant cousins who died in the camps."

"Maybe. But I never met those cousins. Ral is real. I can close my eyes and hear his voice and see his eyes and know that nothing else in my life matters as much."

Before they said good-bye, Jill asked Hirschmann if he knew of any good books about Mengele.

It was two months later when Jean-Claude's telegram came. She hadn't spoken to him for months, and when they did talk they seemed to have little to say beyond pleasantries. In her mind the trial was months away, a vague, distant date that would approach gradually. She kept imagining that she had time to spare, time to explore and investigate and contemplate and analyze and finally understand. She assumed that long before the trial approached she would have an answer to the vague mysteries, and that once she gave the answers to Jean-Claude, the outcome of the trial would be all but decided. All she needed was a little more time. And then, out of the blue, came a telegram with the upcoming date of the trial. "I do hope you're still interested," he wrote. "Of course, you'll be welcome at the villa."

She didn't answer the telegram. The date burned in her memory, but she kept procrastinating, finding extra work to keep her in the office, never mentioning to Millman that she might be leaving for France in a few days. How could she go back now? she asked herself. How could she face Jean-Claude with nothing except the slim evidence that Ral had been in one concentration camp and the woman Eva Ritter in another? And how could she ever face Ral? She hadn't gotten an answer to her first letter, and hadn't written again because she couldn't find words that didn't sound banal. She had expected that when she next saw him, their relationship would have changed, that they would be bound together by a common understanding, that she—she alone—would understand his secret, and him. But after so many months it wasn't so. She didn't understand him any more than she had the first time she met him.

She procrastinated to the very end, until there was no more time left. Two days before the trial was scheduled to begin, she came home and picked up the last book left, a collection of portraits of missing war criminals that Hirschmann had recommended when she asked about Mengele. She turned to the chapter on Mengele, the physician of Auschwitz. People remembered him. Survivor after survivor described the same image: When the trains arrived at the camp, Mengele would be waiting on the platform, dressed in immaculately pressed pants and shiny boots, a riding crop in his gloved hand as he reviewed the line of disembarking passengers. He would wave his riding crop, left or right, as he chose who was to go to which camp. Later they would discover the difference between the camps—that one was for work and the other for death. Everyone remembered that he smiled as he made the selections.

The portrait described the medical experiments that Mengele had organized, and the atrocities that were attributed to him. Jill had already read too much to be shocked or surprised. But then an almost incidental reference caught Jill's attention: a physician who had worked in the camp remembered that Mengele had a special interest in the gypsies, that he had passed out sweets to the gypsy children and extra milk to the nursing mothers in the gypsy camp, had even set up a kindergarten and a hospital for the gypsies. The physician remembered that whenever Mengele appeared in the camp, the gypsy children would come running, clinging to his legs, holding up their hands for sweets.

Jill put the book down in her lap. Her hands were trembling, her eyes blurred with tears. It was like reading about a child molester, luring his victims with sweets and soft words before he did the unspeakable to them. She tried to picture Ral as a teenager, his eyes not yet hiding the secrets that she was trying so hard to understand. What had he seen?

She was at the airport in time to catch the ten o'clock flight to Paris.

PART

III

Marseilles, 1966

The guards at Les Baumettes recognized Jill. Even after six months, an attractive lady lawyer from America who had visited a gypsy prisoner every day for a week was hard to forget.

"Back again?" asked one. "Nice of you to visit us."

"I came to see Ral."

"The gypsy?"

"I have to talk to him."

"I understand he's not much of a talker."

"I'm still assisting Maître Bernard. It's important that I talk to Ral."

The guard gestured toward the clock. "It's not visiting hours. He's on restricted hours anyway. You'd need special authorization from the *juge d'instruction.*"

"There isn't time," said Jill. "His trial starts tomorrow."

"Time? He's been there for months without a visitor. Now all of a sudden it's an emergency? Does the Maître know you're here?"

"I just got off a plane from New York. I haven't even had time to call him."

She watched the guards exchange glances. Their whole lives had been spent in Marseilles: the idea of "just getting off a plane" from New York was so exotic that they both smiled at the idea. It took her a second to realize that they were also smiling at the fact that no one, not even Jean-Claude, knew she was there.

"Really? Just off a plane?"

"I wanted to get here while you two were on duty."

"Yes?"

"I knew you'd understand."

The guards exchanged winks. What do they want? she wondered. A bribe?

"What's in the handbag?" asked one.

"Nothing." She held out the big shoulderbag. "No files, no hacksaws, no pistols, no bombs. I came to talk to him, not to spring him."

The guards laughed. One put his hand into the bag, without looking. They both had their eyes on her, staring at the unbuttoned collar of her blouse and down her long legs.

"Trial starts tomorrow?" said one. "I guess you really want to see him."

"What about the body search?" said the other. "There's no matron on duty."

Jill caught another exchange of winks.

"It's the rules," said one. Before she could react, his hands were under her jacket, fondling her breasts through the blouse, his fingertips pausing on her nipples. Then his hand slid over her rear and under her skirt, up one leg, down the other, all in deliberate, slow motion. She forced herself not to react.

"You're fine," said the guard, grinning. "Just fine."

"The regular visiting room?" said Jill.

"The search isn't over," said the other guard. "We're not experienced like matrons. It takes two of us to do a search."

She stood expressionless while the second guard repeated the frisk, stroking, fondling, letting his fingers linger. She deliberately forced herself not to show her disgust. While the hands paused and poked, she stared at the heavy wire grates on the doors and the exposed heavy masonry of the walls. Why did they derive enjoyment from that? she asked herself. It wasn't erotic. It was only a gesture of power. The guards grinned because they had the power. The whole prison was a gesture of power, built not just to keep inmates in, but to remind them of their powerlessness. In the few months in New York she had forgotten that.

The guards chuckled as they led her into the visiting room. She overheard them bragging in prison argot on the phone while they summoned Ral.

She had forgotten the visiting room too, the sickly green of the fluorescent lights, the hygiaphone with its annoying hum that turned every nuance of a voice into flatness, the odor of disinfectant and old paint and stale air, the filthy plastic seats, the cloudy wired-glass window that separated the visitors from the prisoners.

The door on the other side of the wired glass opened, and Ral came in between two guards. When he saw her, he smiled. Even in the strange green light, the whites of his eyes glowed.

"Ral—" She spoke before he sat down, forgetting the hygiaphone. With a jolt, she realized that her memories of him weren't from the prison. She had remembered his face sculpted in strong sunlight, his skin radiant against the white of his shirt. She had pictured the ill-fitting suit stretched across his shoulders. And now the reaction she had anticipated—the chills and goosebumps—didn't come. Only the intimacy of his eyes was still there to confuse her thoughts.

"After so long, it's still interesting?" he asked. His voice was distorted by the hygiaphone, without the chocolatey tones she remembered.

"More than interesting."

For a long moment neither of them said anything.

"I'm sorry I only wrote that one letter," she said.

"You wrote? They told me there was a letter, but I didn't believe them."

"You mean you never got it?"

"The guards want money for a letter. What did you write?"

"I asked about you—what you did during the war, what happened to you, where you were. That was before I found out about her. And about you. Ral, I need you to tell me everything now. If you'll explain it to me, I think we can do something in that courtroom tomorrow."

Ral leaned toward the glass. "Her? What did you find out about her?"

"That she was in those camps: Lackenbach, Zemun, Auschwitz. She was with the gypsies, doing research. Ral, tell me what happened. Tell me what happened between you."

"Where did you find out about her?" His voice was flat. The smile was gone.

"She was investigated, in Frankfurt. I got the transcript of her hearing."

"Frankfurt? Who investigated her? What did they find about her?"

"It was the West German Ministry of Justice. She told them she was in the camps doing research. There were witnesses who said that she helped the gypsies."

"Witnesses? Who were the witnesses?"

"There was a French doctor, a judge from Sweden. And a gypsy."

"Did they give their names?"

"Of course. I have the transcript in my bag. It's outside."

"Can you remember the name of the gypsy?"

"I think it was Hörthy. Something like that."

"Hörthy? A German?"

"From Munich, I think. Ral, the trial is tomorrow. Let me help you. If you don't tell me what happened, there's nothing I or the Maître can do. There's nothing anyone can do."

His eyes dropped. "No." She remembered the tone. She had asked him a question when they first met, and he had answered with that same tone, firm, almost abrupt, and absolutely unyielding.

"Tell me about New York, Jill. Were you happy to be home?"

"Ral, stop!"

"No, Jill. You must stop. This isn't for you. I know what I must do. You can't change it."

"What do you have to do—get sent to the guillotine? Ral, you matter to me. I can't let you throw away everything."

"I care about you, too, Jill. I thought of you every day. Even in here, I could remember your hair in the sunlight, and the way you walked with no shoes on the beach, so the little waves washed over your feet. I remembered how you learned to say 'Bahtalo drom' and the story of Sara."

"Ral . . ." Her fingers were spread out on the wired glass, and she watched him put his own palms up on the glass, spreading them to match hers.

"Ral! I remember all of that too. But you have to tell me what happened. What happened on the road? What happened in the war? You were in the camps with her, weren't you? I know about Buchenwald. What about the others? Tell me, Ral. Please . . ."

"Buchenwald? What do you know about Buchenwald?"

"I know you were there. At the end of the war, when the Americans came."

Ral smiled. "The Americans? I think you're the only other American I ever met. I can still remember the soldiers. They had boxes of candy bars and cigarettes. In the camps, people would kill for a cigarette, and the Americans had whole boxes of them. And cars with shiny bumpers. The military policemen wore white belts and white helmets and white leggings on their boots. Everything all clean and shiny. We lived in mud, and they had white leggings."

He watched Jill's eyes, looking to see if she was listening.

"Go on, Ral. Tell me about the camp. I'm listening."

"It's still interesting?"

"Ral, I want to know everything about you. Especially about what happened—"

"They served food from huge pots. They said to take as much as we wanted, so we piled our plates up like mountains. We were afraid they wouldn't be there the next day, that maybe the Germans would come back. But our stomachs were so small that we couldn't eat what we took. Everyone took the food anyway, and they would try to hide it, so they could have it when the Germans came back. From nothing we went to too much."

"What happened before Buchenwald, Ral?"

"Before?" He looked away, then back at her. "Jill, this isn't for you. This is something I must do alone."

"Why don't you trust me, Ral?"

"You can't help me. No one can help me."

"Ral, the trial starts tomorrow. The Maître has nothing to go on. You'll be all alone up there."

"I've always been alone. I'm a gypsy. What does it matter what the Maître or anyone else says?"

"Because they'll send you to the guillotine. Is silence worth dying for?"

He looked puzzled, until he said, "Silence is no virtue to a Rom. A Rom's words are his weapons. When I can be heard, I'll tell everything—in the courtroom, where I have a right to talk. Not here. Now we should talk of other things."

"Ral . . ."

"We should talk of you, of your life. Sometimes, especially in the afternoon when I could see just a little light through the filthy window in the cell, I remembered being with you on the beach at Saintes-Maries. I tried to imagine what you would be doing, what your life was like in New York. Now I see you, see that you're just as I remembered. And so I must know if my imaginings were right. Tell me, what did you do in New York? What is your life like there?

"Ral, please." She felt her anger rising, felt herself ready to shout.

"Time's up." Jill heard the guard behind her before she saw him. When she turned back to Ral, there were two guards on his side of the wired glass.

"No, please," she said to the guard. Then she tried to talk to Ral, calling out his name until the guard pointed to the hygiaphone and told her it had been shut off.

"We need to talk more," she said. "It's important. We've hardly started."

"That's the most talking he's done since he got here," said the guard. "He can do all the talking he wants tomorrow. They'll be all set for him at the Assizes."

She watched Ral turn in the doorway, between the guards. He was smiling, but he seemed very far away.

Jean-Claude was waiting in the lobby of Jill's hotel. His eyes brightened when he saw her, and he hurried over to kiss her on both cheeks.

"You're as beautiful as I remembered," he said. "I looked for you at the airport, but I seem to have gotten there too late."

"My flight was early." Jill had forgotten the crystal blue of Jean-Claude's eyes, the evenness of his smile, the charm of his Maurice Chevalier accent. She was fascinated. It was like meeting him all over again.

"By the time I got there you had disappeared. Do you have time for a drink? Or do you want to check in and go up to your room?"

She noticed how careful he was not to pry, not even to hint a question.

"I'd like a drink," she said. "We need to talk."

"You still have the . . . what is it?. . . bee in your bonnet?"

"I still care about what's going to happen in that trial, if that's what you mean."

They found a table outside, on the sidewalk, facing a tree-shaded square. When Jill hesitated in ordering, Jean-Claude suggested whiskey. "I like American bourbon," he said. "Jack Daniel's. I remember that you prefer Scotch."

"I went to see Ral," she said. She waited for his reaction, expecting him to be shocked.

"I know."

"How do you know? Do you have spies at Les Baumettes?"

"Not really. It seems that some guards got in trouble for letting you in, word got back to the *juge d'instruction*, and from him to the *avocat général*. He called to chide me, saying that you were obviously an enterprising lady, and that with you on my side he was no longer confident of his case. How did you persuade those guards to let you see Ral?"

She described the body search.

"One can hardly fault the guards for trying," said Jean-Claude. "They're only human."

"That search was nothing except an exercise in humiliation. They did it just to prove that they could. It made me understand how a man can break down in a prison. Or a concentration camp."

"You're reaching too far, Jill. The guards are human. Nothing more. Working in a prison is dull, a dreadful routine. So they enlivened it a little. I'm not sure I would behave any differently. I too am unable to resist your charms."

"Jean-Claude, what are you planning? For tomorrow. What is your case going to be?"

"Unless Ral told you more this afternoon than he has told me or the *juge d'instruction* in the last months, there really isn't much I can do. What can one plead except mercy?"

"You're giving up?"

"No, Jill. I'm not giving up. I'm doing all that can be done for a client who refuses to cooperate with anyone, and who seems determined to get himself condemned to Corsica. Even a plea for mitigation of sentence is difficult when the man refuses to confess or deny the murder."

Jill's voice was matter-of-fact, flat and calm. "Ral was in a concentration camp at Buchenwald. He may have been in another camp too."

"He told you that?"

"He admitted it after I confronted him with the fact. I found his name at the U.S. Army archives in Virginia. He was interviewed as a displaced person after the Buchenwald camp was liberated." She was aware as she said it of how angry she would have been if someone working with her had withheld information.

"Did he admit anything else?"

She hesitated. "Not yet."

"Yet? The trial is tomorrow."

"I know. That's why we have to talk. There's something else. I think if we put it all together we have the beginning of a defense."

She dug the English translation of Eva Ritter's Frankfurt hearing out of her handbag and handed it to Jean-Claude. While he flipped the pages, she sipped her drink.

"Well?" she said.

"It's a translation, isn't it?"

"Yes."

"I assume it says the same thing as the original version in German."

"It's supposed to be a good translation, if that's what you're asking."

"I read the original, Jill. The Dutch postal authorities traced the woman as a German national from her pension checks. Typically Dutch—they applied to the Germans for burial expenses from the pension. The Germans sent the transcript of the inquiry along. I got it from the *commissaire*. He seems to have a certain bizarre sympathy for my case, probably because of you. I was reluctant to tell you, because it seems to wrap up the *avocat général's* case."

"They were both in concentration camps. The answer must be there."

"Jill, the woman was at Auschwitz. And at camps in Austria and Yugoslavia. He was in Buchenwald, in Germany. Those camps were thousands of kilometers apart."

"Buchenwald is all we know about. He could have been in others."

"He could have been. And thousands of other people were. I'm not sure it will be in Ral's interest to have that transcript in the testimony. I don't think I could draft better character references than the witnesses in that hearing gave her."

"It has to be the answer. Something happened between them, something terrible."

"Something terrible happened between them on that road outside Saintes-Maries. That's what we have to confront."

"He's scared, Jean-Claude. He's a gypsy. He was used to living on the road, sleeping under the stars, eating by a stream. And then to be thrown into a concentration camp, behind barbed wire. . . . To go from the sun to that darkness is almost worse than death. Something happened, something that left scars. Something she did to him."

"You're ready to concede that he murdered the woman?"

"The question is why, Jean-Claude. What did she do to him?"

Jean-Claude looked away, at the quiet square, gathering his thoughts.

"Whatever happened in a camp, if anything did happen between them, was twenty-five years ago. I can't plead justifiable homicide, or even mitigation of sentence, on the basis of wrongs that might have been done to him twenty-five years ago. And even if he comes out with an incredible tale of atrocities that she did, it would be his testimony against the record of that trial in Frankfurt. The witnesses at that trial have impressive credentials: a physician and a jurist are tough to go against. She will come off a lonely old pensioner, a woman who had always cared about gypsies, who protected and aided the gypsies in the concentration camps. I can imagine the *avocat général*'s summation, about how her only mistake in life was to love the gypsies so much that she took her holiday in Saintes-Maries, where a crazed murderer waited for her."

"If only we knew what that woman did . . ." Jill said.

"Unfortunately we do know. Unless Ral can come up with some magic evidence, that Frankfurt hearing will be the official version of her past. And in any case, it hardly matters to the court. Anything he says about the camps can only become an argument for the public minister: an admission that he was hunting for her twenty years is tantamount to a confession of premeditation, which could mean the guillotine."

"Jean-Claude! I think Ral wants to tell what happened, the whole story, in the courtroom. That's why he won't tell us anything now."

"I understand that, Jill. What I'm saying is that letting him tell an involved tale of wrongs and revenge may prejudice his chances for the mercy of the court. He's not like your American demonstrators against the Indochina war who want to make their speeches in the courtroom. His crime was murder, a brutish, repulsive murder. The question is how to exact some measure of mercy from the court, and I don't think that is going to be helped by tales of the past."

Jill listened numbly, aware that Jean-Claude's logic was sound, his arguments persuasive. She buried her face in her hands. After a moment she threw her head back and shook her hair away from her face.

"I'm sorry," she said, rubbing her eyes. "Seeing Ral, seeing the pain in his eyes, that sadness that never seems to go away. . . . All he wants is to tell his story. If he can't, if he doesn't get a chance in that courtroom, it was for nothing."

"*It*, Jill? *It* was for nothing? We're talking about a woman who was strangled and bludgeoned to death. I've seen photographs of the body. It wasn't a pretty sight."

"Ral isn't stupid. If he wants that desperately to have his day in court, there must be something he has to say, a story he has to tell. Maybe he'll deny the murder. Maybe he has a perfect alibi. He just wants his day in court."

"That day in court may cost him the rest of his life."

"Maybe it's worth it to him. How can we put our logic and values on a man whose life is so different, whose logic is so different from ours? When Ral tells about his past, he talks about his people. What happens tomorrow isn't going to be a trial; it's going to be a Greek tragedy."

"I'd guess that you're right, Jill. We'll undoubtedly hear appeals to a higher law, to the law of vengeance or retribution. We'll hear about crimes that ordinary men, such as the court, cannot judge. We'll hear that we, as *gaji*, cannot comprehend the wrongs that have been visited on the gypsies. But in the end, when the words are over and done, the court will judge Ral by the only laws they know, and those are the laws of the République

Française. They will search for the simple truth of just what happened on that road in Saintes-Maries. The rest of what happens in the courtroom, the tragedy you anticipate, will be only that—a drama."

Jill heard the earnestness in Jean-Claude's voice, saw the sincerity in his eyes. She suddenly felt weary, tired from the flights, tired from the frustration of meeting with Ral, tired from trying to understand why everything mattered so much, why she felt as though she were on trial the next day instead of Ral. She knew she was too weary to say more, and that there really was no more to say, or to do, until the drama opened.

Ral had planned to stay up most of the night, going over what he would say in the courtroom. He had asked over and over, every time he met with the *juge d'instruction*, and they had assured him that in the courtroom he could tell his story, that he could say anything he wanted that was relevant to what happened.

"My whole life is part of it," Ral said.

"If the court rules it relevant, you may say it," the *juge* answered. "Why don't you tell your story now? Then there will be no question of relevance. The court will understand your explanation of events and incorporate it into their inquiry."

Ral stared at the *juge*, sitting in his big, comfortable chair, with the draped windows behind him. It was a sunny day outside—Ral had seen that when he was brought over from Les Baumettes—yet the *juge* kept the curtains closed and the lights on. The office was the same inside as it had been on gloomy, rainy days. Everything was the same—the smell of the stale air, the papers on the magistrate's desk, the chairs that Ral and the guard and the magistrate sat in. Ral knew he could never tell what he had to tell to this man.

He had never spoken to a crowd before. Sometimes, when he was camped with other gypsies, he had told *paramixta* and tales, but that was different. The others knew what you would say, could anticipate the words. That was why the stories were so important on the road, because they were predictable, a reassurance after the unpredictability of the wandering life. But now he would have to tell a story that no one knew, that no one was willing to hear. Even Yitzak wouldn't hear. They were all afraid, afraid of the past, afraid of what had happened. He had to find the words that would make people know what had happened, what it was really like.

Yet as he tried to practice the words, tried to tell the story to himself in the quiet of the cell, he couldn't concentrate. Instead of the phrases he wanted, he kept thinking of Jill, of how she had come back after so many months.

He remembered the dream that had come so many times. He would be walking a road, with trees on both sides, thick trees that turned the light into a pattern of shadows on the road. He would come to a fork that he had

never seen before and look for *patrin*, for signs carved into a nearby tree
or etched on a rock, signs that other gypsies had left to tell the next traveler
about the road. He would walk back, walk into the woods, search every
tree and every stone, but there would be no *patrin*. So he would choose a
fork and walk, and no matter how far he walked, the road would go nowhere. And then he would run back, run as fast as he could to get back to
the fork, sure now that the other road was the right road. Except that he
would never get back to the fork . . .

And then she came back.

He hadn't expected ever to see her again. She wasn't a *rye*; she had a
whole life in the *gajo* world. Why would she come back to find him? He
thought she would always be only a dream, a vision of softness and sparkling sunlight and gentle breezes in golden hair, a memory that he could
turn to when the walls were too gray, when he wanted to see sunlight and
feel the breeze so much that he felt like screaming, and kept himself from
screaming only because he knew that was what the guards would want to
hear.

Jill was the only woman he had thought about for a long time, for
twenty years really. Except for Eva Ritter. And now, when he was finally
able to think of a woman, to think about having her close to him, to think
about her eyes and her voice and her hair in the wind and the way she
walked on the gravel of the beach with her toes in the foam of the waves, it
was too late.

The Palais de Justice was an immense, slab-sided building, overbearing,
designed to impress, scaled to make individuals feel small, to display the
majesty of the law and the republic. The walls rose straight up from the
narrow Marseilles streets, broken only by high barred windows. A portico
loomed over the entrance, with tall steel-strapped doors that looked as
though it would take six men to swing each of them open. The ubiquitous
Second Empire architecture might have fooled someone into thinking this
was one more grand public building, a department store or the offices for
yet another bureaucracy, except that the inscription over those tall doors
reminded everyone that this wasn't just a courthouse. This was the Palais
de Justice—built on that grand scale as yet another reminder to anyone
who would dare to trifle with the majesty of the law.

Anyone, that is, except the unruly crowd of gypsies milling in the streets
outside the Palais. The narrow streets on the sides of the building were
clogged with caravans, battered buses, vans, huge old American cars.
Some were brightly painted, with curtained windows and colorful murals.
Others were near-wrecks, ramshackle combinations of parts held together
with bailing wire and perhaps tape and prayers, sufficient to get there, no
more. Most of the license plates were French, but there were others from
Italy, Spain, and Yugoslavia in the free-for-all of double-parking. When

there was no more room in the second row of cars they triple-parked, ignoring the shouts and threats of the police as they turned the streets into a gypsy campground.

Jill hadn't anticipated the gypsies. As she watched them swarm on the steps of the building, she thought of the dances of honeybees. She had read so much about the gypsies, thought so often of the stories Ral had told her, that from a distance the people seemed familiar. The swarthiness of the complexions was no longer exotic, the clothes no stranger than fashions she saw on the streets of New York or London. But hard as she tried, she couldn't help noticing filthy feet and rag-swaddled babies. And she couldn't help remembering how frightened she had been on the road to Saintes-Maries, when the gypsy children surrounded her car. The memory troubled her.

She wondered how the gypsies found out about the trial. Other than the standard published notices of the court calendar, there had been no publicity. Was there a secret grapevine, like jungle drums, that brought gypsies from everywhere? Any *gajo* straying into the crowd was accosted with the haughty, proud glares she remembered from Saintes-Maries—open, unblinking stares that were impossible to answer. She heard a few phrases of French, but the gypsies spoke to one another mostly in the strange sounds of Romany. The secret language, totally unintelligible to *gaji*, was a wall to outsiders.

It was impossible to go in through the main door until police officers, threatening with sticks, forced the gypsy crowd to one side. She watched the gypsies when the police approached. They didn't move, didn't avert their eyes, didn't so much as acknowledge the police officers until the sticks were raised, or the gendarmes began shouting or blowing their whistles. And even as they moved to one side of the stairs in front of the doors, the gypsies looked at the police with disdain.

Another crowd, smaller than the gypsy mob, waited in a ragged queue on the other side of the door. Their conversation was a mix of terse reviews of past trials and speculation about the upcoming calendar of the Assizes. The comments and laughter angered Jill. It was like someone talking during a concert. It took a moment for her to digest the fact that their lack of interest in Ral's trial was what really troubled her. She had anticipated passionate observers, demanding blood or freedom, perhaps demonstrations in the streets. She looked for reporters, listened for agitated discussions of Ral's innocence or guilt, but all she heard were comments about the last trial of the Assizes, a sordid and confusing bedroom murder, with testimony that had gone beyond the expected to revelations of homosexuality and mutual infidelity.

"What do we get this time?" someone asked.

"A gypsy. He strangled some old woman by the road in Saintes-Maries."

"And what's the next trial?"

. . .

The courtroom was dominated by a raised tribunal at one end, elevated under cornices and moldings of sculpted gilt. The president and the lay judges, all robed in scarlet, sat on thrones like the king and jacks of a deck of playing cards, looking down at the open area of the courtroom before them, the *prétoire* where the action of the coming drama would be staged. At the rear of the courtroom, separated by an iron grillework, was the gallery for the public. Along the sides, straddling the doorways, were policemen in parade-dress uniforms, the bright red of their kepis and the glistening white of their belts and leggings tempered by their grim expressions and stiff poses.

The *prétoire* belonged to the *avocats*, their black robes billowing in waves as they circulated, greeting one another, watching the crowd assemble, assuming their positions as the aristocrats of the courtroom. Jean-Claude had warned Jill that the courtroom might be crowded, that many of his colleagues would probably attend the trial for the amusement of watching him plead such an unpromising brief and perhaps for a glimpse of the woman who had gotten him to take the brief. She had dismissed his warning as cant, but now, from only a few feet away, behind the iron grille, she could hear the *avocats* chattering, their courtroom jargon heavy with the envy of ambitious novices toward a star who was barely their senior. One *avocat* she and Jean-Claude had seen in a Marseilles café grinned at her, then winked. Frenchmen! she thought, remembering the guards at Les Baumettes.

Above the *prétoire*, to one side, the *avocat général* posed in his pulpit. Like the judges, he was robed in scarlet, as if to show that he too was on the side of the mighty. It was no chance of architecture that his pulpit was at the level of the tribunal, so that he too could look down on the railed box for the accused.

Beneath him was the press gallery, the two young reporters looking bored at the prospects of a case that seemed to suggest few surprises. Like the court followers who stood in a cluster behind Jill, the reporters had spent weeks following the sessions of this Assize Court, watching the same president, the same lay judges, the same *avocat général*, even the same *avocats* for the defense—all performing together like a repertory company.

Jill wasn't watching when the side door of the courtroom opened. She turned when she heard a chorus of whispers in the gallery.

Ral stood for a moment in the doorway. The drabness of his clothes—he was wearing the black suit and white shirt he had worn when she saw him in Saintes-Maries—was accentuated by the colorful uniforms of the police who flanked the doorway in their fancy dress uniforms. The collar of his shirt was buttoned, and the suit that had once seemed too tight now hung off him. But in the bright light of the courtroom, his skin glowed like molten copper. The dull, greenish cast Jill remembered from the visiting room at Les Baumettes was gone. And his eyes, tired and drawn the day before, wearing the gray of months behind those bars, were bright and alert now, the whites brilliant and the pupils deep and dark.

As he was led across the room, Ral scanned the faces of the courtroom, focusing in turn on the robed figures of the tribunal and *prétoire* and the crowds in the galleries. As his eyes passed each sector of the courtroom, the chatter and whispers of the crowds gave way to an ominous muffled hum, like the roll of the drums as the convicted man is led to the gibbet.

The procession paused outside the railed box for the accused, directly across the courtroom from the pulpit of the *avocat général* and far below it. The guards turned to face Ral, and he held his hands over his head, showing the chains that led from his wrists to a heavy belt around his waist. It took the guards a full five minutes to remove the chains. The rattle of metal against metal silenced even the hum of the courtroom as everyone turned to watch the ceremony of degradation.

Jill heard voices behind her, commenting.

"Nice spirit, that one. I heard he wouldn't tell them a thing. Refused to confess."

"Probably couldn't confess. Doesn't know enough French."

"You think he'll hold up under questioning?"

"He's a gypsy. What more do you have to say?"

She wanted to silence the voices. Even more, she wanted Ral's eyes to find her. But like everyone else in that room, he was already responding to the pull of the stage.

The trial opened without ceremony.

The president of the court leaned forward from his throne on the high tribunal. Under his broad velvet beret, his eyebrows and mustache were white and trimmed, and his long face and angular nose seemed out of place in a room dominated by the round Mediterranean faces of the gallery. He spoke directly to Ral.

"You are Ral Bendit, age approximately thirty-nine, born in the Burgenland of Austria, presently stateless and without permanent address?" His tone was harsh, as though he were reading a list of diseases in a quarantine notice.

Ral nodded.

"Do you understand French?" asked the president.

Ral nodded again.

"Do you expect the court recorder to write down that the accused nodded? You must answer each question for the record of the trial."

"Yes!" said Ral. He spoke slowly and emphatically. "I understand French and I am Ral Bendit."

The president leaned forward, his expression grave. "Ral Bendit! You are charged with the willful assault and murder of the woman Wanda Lanzer, age fifty-four years, of German nationality, on May twenty-fifth of this year in the village of Saintes-Maries-de-la-Mer, Département du Bouche du Rhône. Are you represented by counsel?"

Jill saw a rustle of robes in the *prétoire*. Jean-Claude strode out into the clear area of the *prétoire*, looked back at her, then turned to face the tribunal, his robes flowing behind him. He seemed utterly relaxed, as if there were nothing extraordinary about the dramatic costume.

"We will plead for the accused," he said. "Jean-Claude Bernard, *avocat*."

"Maître Bernard!" The president said the name with obvious respect. "The accused is most fortunate."

"Monsieur le Président!" Ral's unexpected voice drew heads toward him.

He stared deliberately at Jean-Claude before he spoke. "I don't want that man to speak for me," he said. "I will speak for myself."

The president looked at Jean-Claude, then back at Ral, then down at the sheaf of papers in front of him, and around again. He seemed distressed.

Then he held up the papers.

"Now you refuse counsel?" he said to Ral. "You have refused to respond to the legitimate interrogation by the police. You have been adamantly uncooperative with the *juge d'instruction*. Now you say that you do not wish to be represented by your distinguished counsel. I assure you: this truculence ill serves your own interests. Perhaps you do not understand the severity of the charges against you or the sentence which may be imposed by this court."

"I understand," said Ral.

"Do you understand that the sentence for the crime of which you have been accused could be *travail à force perpétuel*—hard labor for life—or the guillotine?"

"I understand."

"And you still refuse to be represented by counsel?"

"I will speak for myself."

Jean-Claude turned to look at Jill. She wanted to say something, but it already seemed too late.

"May it please the court!" The *avocat général* spoke softly, slurring the words of the ritual phrase. He was older than Jean-Claude, heavyset, seemingly bored by the demands of the trial. He waited for the nod of the president before he went on.

"Is it in the interest of the court to accede to this obvious stratagem by the accused? How often have we seen it before? First there will be the charge of police brutality. Then the list of supposed violations of procedure. The accused knows he cannot carry on this folly while represented by responsible counsel. Must we allow the precious time of the court to be wasted in these futile maneuvers?"

Jean-Claude turned again to Jill, caught the puzzled look on her face, and smiled.

"Monsieur le Président!" His voice rang out in the courtroom, a spoon against a crystal goblet. "Is it not possible that the accused acts from fear or confusion, rather than obstinacy or stratagem? Perhaps he is not familiar with the procedures of the court. Might I suggest that if Your Honor were to explain the ample opportunity the accused will have to speak on his own behalf, he will not refuse counsel."

The president glanced back and forth from the *avocat général* to Jean-Claude, and then down at Ral, as if he needed visual reminders to decide the question. The other judges all watched him, and as he became aware of the eyes of the courtroom on him, he sat very straight, recasting his glances with a furrowed brow.

"The Maître's point is well taken," he said.

Was it a victory for Ral or a defeat? The trial had hardly started, the contests of the courtroom hadn't even defined themselves, and already Jill was confused, muddled, unable to think clearly. She felt disconnected, an ill-prepared spectator. She had always been able to place herself outside, to see an issue from the other side, to analyze the question from all perspectives with an objectivity that left her free to maneuver. Now, as she watched Ral, alone against the court, she knew she wasn't detached, that she was deeply, profoundly committed to him and to what he had to say. The question of guilt or innocence didn't matter. She had to know the secret he held inside.

"The accused must understand our procedures," said the president. His tone was heavily patronizing, as if he were a headmaster addressing his youngest pupil. "You will be questioned by the court. You will have ample opportunity to present your story before we hear from witnesses and experts. And at the end of the trial, after pleas have been entered by the public minister and your own *avocat*, you will again have an opportunity to address the court. Do you understand?"

"In open court?" said Ral. "I may speak out in the open court?"

"Of course in open court. We do not conduct our inquiry in camera. Our law is in the open, for all to see."

Ral smiled.

"Will you now accept Maître Bernard as your *avocat?*"

"As long as I can speak, I don't care what he does."

The president leaned over the tribunal again, addressing his words to Ral, but speaking loud enough for the whole courtroom to hear him clearly.

"I have explained to you that you will have ample opportunity to speak. But you must understand that this court seeks only the truth. We will not tolerate irrelevance. We will not allow digressions or obfuscations. We will excavate beneath structures of falsehood, mine down to the very bedrock of truth. We will waylay stratagems intended only to distract us from our duty to the republic and to the people of France. And we will not rest until we have uncovered the truth."

When he finished, the president sat back in his throne, surveying the courtroom as though the silence were an accolade for his speech. In fact, after the first few phrases, no one had listened. It had been a ritual speech, a judge's signature on the trial that was about to begin.

It was all ritual, thought Jill. Showy ceremonies. Ral deserved better.

"May it please the court . . ." Jean-Claude stood at the bar as he spoke.

The president of the court smiled. He seemed to like Jean-Claude.

"Maître Bernard!"

"Monsieur le Président! Before the *acte d'accusation* is read, the defense would introduce Mademoiselle Jill Ashton of New York, who has assisted in the preparation of our brief." Jean-Claude bowed toward Jill in a gracious wave, the kind of exaggerated gesture he had mockingly used at the airport when he had first met her. She felt like a schoolgirl who was expected to curtsy.

"The court welcomes Mademoiselle Ashton of New York," said the president. His polite smile turned into a grin, as if there were some private joke between them.

"With the permission of the court," Jean-Claude went on, "we would ask that Mademoiselle Ashton be admitted to the *prétoire* for the duration of the trial, in order that she may assist in the defense pleadings."

The president nodded.

The *avocat général* leaned forward from his pulpit. "May it please the court . . ."

How long would they go on like this? Jill wondered.

"Does Mademoiselle Ashton stand before the bar in the courts of the French Republic?" asked the *avocat général*.

"Mademoiselle is an experienced litigator in American practice," answered Jean-Claude. "She has appeared in French courts on numerous occasions, has served on a joint American-French investigative and prosecutorial task force, and is widely read in the law. We would argue that her assistance is essential in the pleading of our case."

"The rules of practice are unambiguous on this point," said the *avocat général*. "There can be no question of admitting the American woman to the *prétoire*."

"An exception is within the prerogatives of the court," said Jean-Claude. "And would be in the interest of truth."

"One would not expect the distinguished *avocat* to stoop to such a statagem," answered the *avocat général*.

Jill swiveled back and forth to follow the verbal Ping-Pong. Would the whole trial be like this? she wondered. What chance would Ral ever have amidst such theatrics?

The arguments went back and forth until the president said, "The court will rule." He waited for both men to face him.

"The court would have Mademoiselle Ashton assist the Maître from the gallery."

The *avocat général* gloated. Jean-Claude nodded, almost a bow of acquiescence, before he stepped back through the other *avocats* to where Jill stood outside the grille.

"I'm sorry," he said. He looked as though he really meant it.

"It doesn't really matter," she said.

"But it does."

"Why?"

"Two reasons. First, the public minister can now have you testify. And your testimony can only hurt our case."

"What's the second reason?" asked Jill.

"I would have enjoyed having you at my side for the duration of the trial," said Jean-Claude.

Jill looked up and saw that Ral was looking at them, staring boldly. She tried to look at herself as Ral would see her, huddled close to Jean-Claude, their brief private conversation almost conspiratorial in the midst of the crowded courtroom. To Ral it must have appeared that she too was part of the conspiracy of authority, one more *gaje* determined not to let him say his piece.

She smiled back, but it was too late. The trial had begun.

"The accused was found . . . the accused has not denied . . . the accused refuses . . . Wanda Lanzer, a tourist from Amsterdam . . . assault . . . strangled . . ." The *acte d'accusation* droned on, a listing of facts without point or purpose. Jill's concentration faded in and out until she heard the flat voice of the *avocat général* read:

". . . on that very day, the accused told a woman he met in a café, a complete stranger, that he was searching for someone, for a woman . . ."

Jill expected the eyes of the courtroom to turn to her, but even Ral seemed oblivious to the deadly dull words. There was only a bored silence, punctuated with concert hall coughs and whispers.

The *avocat général* concluded in the same flat voice. ". . . the accused has steadfastly refused either to deny or admit to the acts and facts specified."

"Do you wish to make a statement at this time?" the president asked Ral.

Ral seemed surprised by the invitation to speak. He straightened up and scanned the courtroom, taking in his audience. His movements were slow and deliberate, an incredible contrast to the almost staccato pace of the procedural arguments. Jill had a premonition that something terrible was going to happen.

Ral stared at the president. "I'm a gypsy," he said.

The president and the *avocat général* simultaneously leaned forward from their perches far above Ral. The president spoke first:

"The accused will please confine his statement to the facts detailed in the *acte d'accusation!*"

Ral looked up, puzzled. "The court must understand that I am a Rom—"

"The accused—!" the president shouted, then stopped himself before he really began his speech. He looked down at Ral, again like a schoolmaster disciplining a naughty pupil. When he began again, there was a paternal quaver in his voice.

"The accused is trying the patience of this court. You have said that you are a gypsy. Very well. That is neither here nor there. The court is blind to questions of race or religion. But you must confine your statements to the questions and facts before the court, and particularly to the exposition of facts stated in the *acte d'accusation.*"

Jill bit her lip. No one, not even Jean-Claude, said a word in protest. Like the president of the court, Jean-Claude had his face buried in a stack of papers, as if he were catching up on his homework before he was called upon to recite.

The questioning of Ral began abruptly, without ceremony or warning.

"Did you know the woman Wanda Lanzer?" asked the president.

"Her name was Eva Ritter," said Ral.

The president looked down at his notes, thumbing through papers. When he spoke again, his voice was laced with exasperation. "Did you know the woman Wanda Lanzer who was also known as Eva Ritter?"

"Of course I knew her. It was impossible to be a gypsy and not know her."

The president fingered his gavel. "When and where did you meet her?"

Ral eased his tight grip on the rail of his box. This was the question he had been waiting for. For twenty years.

"In June 1940 I was arrested by the Criminal Police in Vienna and taken to the Lackenbach camp. I was one of four thousand gypsies in that camp. That's where I first saw her."

"What kind of camp was this?"

"It was a concentration camp, only run by the Criminal Police."

"Why were you arrested? For what crime?"

"There was no crime. I told you before: I'm a gypsy. The police arrested any gypsy who did not have a *Karte*. To them, we were all criminals. Our crime was to be gypsies."

From behind Jill someone shouted out: "They were right! It's where you belonged then and it's where you belong now."

She turned around and saw a fat, ruddy-faced man in a beret and a tight-fitting suit, shaking his fist. He seemed familiar, but she couldn't remember where she had ever seen him.

The president cautioned the man politely. "Could we please have no outbursts from the public?" Then he turned back to Ral.

"What did Wanda Lanzer do in that camp?"

"Her name was Eva Ritter," said Ral.

The president glared at Ral. "Go on."

"She interviewed the gypsies," said Ral. "She spoke a little Romany, our language. I didn't know then—"

"She was with the Criminal Police?"

"She told us that she wasn't. But she wore their uniform and lived in the barracks with the police. And she—"

The *avocat général* leaned out of his pulpit. "Monsieur le Président! The court has before it an affidavit from the office of the public prosecutor in Frankfurt am Main attesting to the victim's wartime service. The prosecutor carried out an extensive inquiry and concluded that her service in the Lackenbach camp was solely in the capacity of a social researcher. Indeed, it appears from the affidavit that the woman did all she could to aid the gypsies who were interned in the camp. Would it not be appropriate to introduce the affidavit into the proceedings at this time?"

The president turned to Jean-Claude, who was already at the grille, next to Jill.

"I have to object," Jean-Claude said to Jill.

"Why?"

"It's the only way to abort this line of questioning."

"Abort? Ral said more this morning than in the months in Les Baumettes. He admitted that he was in another camp."

"That's precisely the problem," said Jean-Claude. "If he keeps going, he'll build his own gibbet."

Jill grabbed Jean-Claude's sleeve. "It's not for you to decide," she said. "You can't play God. Let him tell his story."

"Does the Maître wish to object?" the president asked.

Jean-Claude looked at Ral, who was glaring at him. Then he turned to Jill again. "We have no objection," he said.

The *avocats* on both sides of the *prétoire* turned to stare at him and at Jill.

"Very well," said the president. He thumbed through the dossier of papers in front of him. "The affidavit of the public prosecutor in Frankfurt am Main will be accepted as evidence."

He turned back to Ral. "How did you come to know the woman Wanda Lanzer in the Lackenbach camp?"

"Her name was Eva Ritter." Ral saw the president's glance, and went on before the other man could respond. "All the gypsies knew her. She would call us into her office and ask questions. She asked so many questions that she knew more about us than we did."

"Why did she seek this information?"

Ral shrugged. "She was a *rye*. A Romany *rye*. A *gaje* who can't stay away from gypsies. She told some of the gypsies that in her soul she was a gypsy too, that her real name was Loli Tschai. She would sign that name on pictures that she gave us. She said that she loved the gypsies, that she was protecting us from the Germans."

"Then you agree with the conclusions of the document cited by the public minister—that Wanda Lanzer actually worked to help the gypsies in that camp."

Ral glanced at Jill before he answered. She remembered telling him about the transcript. It made her feel even more like part of the conspiracy.

"I don't know about any document," he said. "But I know what she did in that camp. She stopped the guards sometimes. Like when they would give the daughter of one clan to men of another. The gypsies liked her because she stopped the guards. When she came into the camp, the children would follow her around and shout her name. 'Loli! Loli!' they would shout. She liked that."

"Did the woman Wanda Lanzer ever harm you in that camp?"

Ral hesitated. "Harm me?" he repeated.

"Did she abuse you in any way?"

Ral hesitated again. "No."

Jean-Claude glanced from Ral to Jill, his expression puzzled.

"How long were you in the Lackenbach camp?" the president asked.

"Almost five months. Then I escaped."

"You escaped? You escaped from a concentration camp?" For the first time since the testimony had begun, the president seemed genuinely interested.

Ral described how easy it had been, how the guards had been so interested in the young gypsy girls they took to their barracks that they had little time to guard the perimeter or to watch the work parties that were sent out to cut trees or build roads.

"Do you mean that the young girls gave themselves, offered to . . . entertain the guards so you could escape?"

"Gave themselves?" Ral repeated the words incredulously. "Never! The guards took them, as you would pick a flower. And when they finished with those girls—"

"May it please the court!" The *avocat général's* voice was caustic. "Your Honor! Is it really germane to our inquiry to pursue these tawdry details?"

The president glared at him before he turned back to Ral.

"After you escaped from this Lackenbach camp, did you see the woman Wanda Lanzer again?"

Ral looked at the president as if he were mad. "See her? Did I see her again? I couldn't escape her. None of us could. Wherever we went, she was there. Wherever there were gypsies, she was there."

"Where did you next see her?"

"In Yugoslavia."

"When was that?"

"In 1941. I was looking for my mother and sister when the Germans came."

"Where in Yugoslavia did you see Wanda Lanzer?"

"It was at Zemun. In the gypsy camp."

"Was this a concentration camp?"

Ral scanned the courtroom before he spoke, taking his time, confident now that he could speak without fear of being cut off. Something had happened between him and the president of the court that turned the hostility into interest.

Jill followed every word, hung on Ral's responses. She tried to evaluate the testimony, the way she would evaluate the responses of a witness in a deposition, but she couldn't shake the awful premonition that had haunted her from the moment when Ral began to speak. His tale was coming too easily, like a wagon rolling downhill toward a cliff.

"Yes. It was a concentration camp."

"Why were you in that camp?"

"Because I'm a gypsy."

Jill expected an outburst, but the president was patient. "Could you explain please how you ended up in the camp?"

"I was with a band of Montenegrins. They were brave men, men who never surrendered to any enemy. They weren't afraid of the Germans either, even though the Germans were taking hostages then—fifty for every German soldier wounded and one hundred for every soldier killed. Mostly they took Jews and gypsies. They captured us and took us to the camp."

"You were captured as a hostage?"

"For the Germans, any gypsy was a hostage."

"What did they do with hostages?"

"They made the gypsies dig their own graves. Then they shot them. When that wasn't enough, they had a gas van, a big truck from Germany. They would fill it with gypsies and drive through the hills with gas from the engine going into the back of the truck. When the truck stopped, all the gypsies would be dead."

Jill suddenly felt chilled.

"And you saw Wanda Lanzer again in that camp?"

"She was there when we came. She interviewed us."

"Did she remember you?"

"Yes. She remembered me from Lackenbach."

"And did she have you punished because you had escaped from the other camp?"

Ral glared at the president. It took him a long time to answer, and when he did, the word exploded from his lips: "No!"

Jill shuddered. The cat-and-mouse game between the president of the court and Ral was going awry. It was as if Ral were avoiding the conflict, hiding the story from the president as he had hidden everything from her. She could sense the president's impatience from his tone.

"What happened between you and Wanda Lanzer in that camp?" the president asked. "Did she harm or abuse you?"

Ral twisted in his box, looking at the galleries, catching Jill's eyes. The expression in his own eyes was fierce. Or maybe desperate, thought Jill. She was afraid of whatever he was going to say.

"She selected some of the gypsies to be sent from Yugoslavia to another camp," said Ral. His voice was ominously flat. "She said we were to be protected from the fighting and the war, and especially from the Ustashi, the Croatian Fascists. They were crueler to the gypsies than even the Nazis. She said that those gypsies who did not belong in Yugoslavia, who were trapped there because of the fighting, would be sent to a new camp."

"I take it that you were fortunate enough to be sent to this new camp?"

"Fortunate?" Ral's face tightened. Jill could see his knuckles grow white on the railing of his box. "Your Honor, I was sent, but—"

The president, impatient now, waved his hand, cutting Ral off. "Answer the question, please. Did Wanda Lanzer select you to be sent away from the fighting?"

Stubbornly, Ral went on, standing up straight in the box as if to underscore his defiance. "Your Honor, there's more. It's not because I was sent away—"

The gavel came down. "The accused will remain silent except when answering the questions put to him. This courtroom is not to be used as a podium for speeches."

Ral waited until the president was finished. Then, softer this time, he said, "It's important that the court understand—"

"Silence! We have finished with the question. We have established that you were sent away from that camp by the intervention of Wanda Lanzer."

"I haven't finished."

The gavel came down twice, hard. "Silence!"

Ral shouted back. "Why must I be silent? Because I'm a gypsy?"

"The accused must hold his silence. This is not a brawling ground. This is the High Court of Assizes. You must show respect."

"Respect! High Court!" Ral spat the words. "It's the same here as everywhere. The *gaji* are afraid of what a gypsy will say. They don't want a gypsy to speak out. You only want the gypsy to be helpless, to beg in the streets."

The gavel pounded a quick staccato. "We will not tolerate this interruption. There will be a recess of ten minutes during which the accused will compose himself. Perhaps your distinguished counsel can explain to you why it is necessary to maintain the decorum and procedures of the courtroom. I assure you: it's for your own good, to assure the propriety of your trial."

Jill watched the courtroom explode into a hubbub.

Each group speculated and gossiped among itself. The judges were talking to one another as they trooped out. The *avocats* on the *prétoire* glanced around the courtroom, evaluating the audience, speculating in refined jargon about the judges and about the impossible brief that Jean-Claude Bernard had taken for himself this time. In the galleries, quips about the "uppity gypsy" were interspersed with comments of approval or criticism, comparing the revelations to other, more spectacular trials. And across the courtroom, in the section of the gallery that the gypsies had appropriated for themselves, Jill could see clusters of gypsies drawn up in circles, like at a tribal meeting, their coarse whispers in Romany impenetrable. They paid no attention to the rest of the courtroom, except to pull their circles tighter when they noticed eyes upon them.

The chatter in the courtroom was short-lived. Within minutes the guards had begun the painfully slow ritual of putting the handcuffs and manacles back on Ral. It was an unnecessary ceremony—there was no way he could have escaped from a room full of police—but the noisy ritual served its purpose, reminding everyone there that no matter what he might say on the stand, he was still the *malheureux*, the unfortunate one who stood accused before the Assizes.

Jill watched Ral disappear through the side door. Then Jean-Claude appeared at the grille, after extricating himself from a cluster of black-robed *avocats*.

"Well," he said. "Is that what you wanted to see?"

"Can we go talk to him?" she said. "If we could only explain to him, he could tell his story without antagonizing the president."

"Jill! The man is destroying his chances. I don't know what you're expecting him to say, but this testimony is disastrous. I can't in good conscience let him go on. Not after his utter refusal to confess the crime."

"It's his own history that he wants to tell. He knows he can't be heard except in the courtroom."

"Jill—if he goes on like this, he'll be condemned."

"Nothing he's said is incriminating."

"Maybe not by your standards," said Jean-Claude. "But if I were the public minister, I'd give anything to have that testimony for my case. I can't let it go on."

Jill reached through the grillework, holding Jean-Claude's arm. "Please, Jean-Claude. Help him! Help Ral tell his story. It's all he has."

"Why? Are you that anxious to see a performance in the courtroom? What is it that you have to see, the destruction of a man?"

"No! My God, no. It's not that at all. I just know he has something to say."

"A lady's intuition? Do you expect me to throw away a man's life for that? Jill, much of this testimony is damning. Without it, I could plead for mercy. I could cite suffering during the war, in concentration camps. I might stand a chance of a mitigated sentence. The worst he could expect would be Corsica, or maybe Les Baumettes. But with this ramble he's trying the patience of the court. And he's going nowhere except to the guillotine."

"I don't believe that," said Jill. "I don't believe that at all."

"What do you believe?" asked Jean-Claude.

"I believe Ral. I believe that he knows what he's doing, that he knows where his story is going. He's not a child, Jean-Claude. He knows what he's doing. And I believe him."

Jean-Claude stared at her, his expression frozen. She had never before seen him at a loss for words.

The recess of ten minutes stretched to thirty, and when the court reconvened, the crowd had mysteriously grown. There were dozens more gypsies, and dozens more colors and patterns in the skirts and *diclos* and bandannas. Jill noticed that it wasn't one group of gypsies, but many, each standing apart from the others as the gypsies themselves stood apart, separated from the *gaji* of the galleries by an empty aisle, a sort of no-man's-land. It was as though signs had been put up saying "Gypsy" and "Non-gypsy."

Jill kept her eyes on the gypsies as the president and the lay judges trooped to their places on the tribunal, their scarlet robes trailing. The gypsies watched curiously, but they seemed neither awed nor frightened. They followed the antics of the court the way a novice would watch the mysteries of a fortune teller, gawking at the magic symbols and rituals that might have seemed bizarre to the uninitiated.

The hum in the room quieted when Ral was brought to the door. He stood again for a moment, surveying the crowd, waiting until their eyes turned to his chains before he made his way across the courtroom. In his box Ral shook off the handcuffs and chains with easy defiance, holding his head up and staring back at the crowds, flashing his fiery eyes at the galleries behind the grille.

It wasn't until the president pounded the gavel for order that Jill caught Ral's gaze. His eyes fixed her with a steady, intense concentration, as if there were a private message in his stare. For a moment she felt as if she were all alone in the courtroom with him.

She turned in time to see Jean-Claude signal the president with a wave of his fingers.

"Maître Bernard?"

Jean-Claude got the attention of the *avocat général* with another invisible signal. A moment later the two men met in front of the tribunal. The courtroom could watch, but could not hear them confer with the president. When the huddle broke up, the president turned to Ral.

"I trust the accused has taken the opportunity of this recess to compose himself, and that we may expect no further outbursts."

Ral said nothing.

"Before the recess," the president went on, "you were telling the court about your stay in Yugoslavia, at the camp"—he looked down at his notes before continuing—"at Zemun. You described how the woman Wanda Lanzer had selected you to be sent away from that camp for your own protection. Your *avocat*, Maître Bernard, has assured the court that you wish to make only a short further statement about this matter."

Ral looked at Jean-Claude, his expression revealing nothing. Then he turned to Jill with the same flat, puzzled look. Finally he gripped the rail of his box and turned to the court, picking up his story as though the recess had never happened.

"What I wanted to tell the court is that when Eva Ritter chose me to leave Zemun, there were others she didn't choose. I can remember her words exactly: 'The selection procedures are only for German and Austrian gypsies of the first category' is what she said. I was chosen, my bride was not. She was Montenegrin, a wanderer. We had been married for only a day. I never even knew her as a wife."

Jill tried to imagine Ral with a woman. She knew that it had been twenty-five years before, that he had been a very young man, a boy really. But she couldn't imagine it.

Across the gallery she could hear whispers among the gypsies.

"What happened to this woman, your bride?" asked the president.

Ral stared at the president and spoke very calmly. "The Ustashi took her. Right there, on the ground, in front of me and the others, they shamed her."

"They shamed her?" repeated the president. "What does that mean?"

"They took her!" Ral was shouting now. "What do you say? They raped her. Right there on the ground, in front of everybody. I tried to kill them with my own hands, tried to tear the eyes from their faces. But I was dragged away."

The court was silent for a moment. Then the whispers started again in the gallery, and Jill realized that it was a woman paraphrasing the testimony into Romany. Some of the gypsy women began to keen, and the gypsy men shouted muffled phrases with the staccato intonation of curses.

Jill wished she too could shout. Everything was suddenly so clear.

"Where is your bride now?" asked the president.

Jill leaned forward. The question hadn't occurred to her.

"She's dead."

"What happened to her?"

"She was killed in the gas vans. Everyone who was left behind in that camp was killed."

"And you blame Wanda Lanzer for what happened to your bride?"

Ral's answer was in his stare, fixed on the playing-card figures on the tribunal. The courtroom hung on his silence.

Jill saw Jean-Claude looking at her, but neither of them was willing to speak, even to whisper.

It was the flat voice of the *avocat général* that broke the spell. "May it please the court . . ."

By the time the president turned to recognize him, the galleries had exploded into a hubbub of voices. The drama was more than any of them had expected.

Jean-Claude leaned close to Jill. "Is that the revelation you expected?"

"I don't know what I expected. It does change things, though, doesn't it?"

"Does it?"

"What do you mean? Can you imagine how he felt after that? After that woman was the one who separated him from his bride, and he had to watch them. . . ?"

"Jill!" Jean-Claude's tone was strange, as though his voice were trying to grasp her by the shoulders and shake her. Before he could go on, the president gaveled for order, staring at every corner of the courtroom until he had the silence he demanded. Then he nodded to the *avocat général*.

"Would it not be appropriate to ask whether the woman Wanda Lanzer had anything to do with the death of his bride?" asked the public minister.

"The point is well taken," said the president. He turned to Ral. "Did the woman Wanda Lanzer have anything to do with the death of your bride?"

Ral glared at the president and the other men and women on the tribunal as though they were madmen.

"Please answer the question," said the president. "Did she have anything to do with the death of your bride?"

"No!" shouted Ral. "How could she? She was with us. With the other gypsies."

"And where was that?"

"We were sent away on a train. They told us it was dangerous for us to stay in Yugoslavia. They said the new camp would be safe for us. She told us that the new camp would be a place where we could live as gypsies."

"Where was this new camp?"

"The train took a long time, almost a week, and most of us couldn't see where it was that they were taking us because we were in cars that were made for cattle. I never looked. All I could think about was my bride, and what they did to her. But some who were close to the doors described the country outside. We were all gypsies, so no matter where they took us, there was always someone in the train who knew that country, who had been there . . ."

Jill was amazed that the president didn't demand that Ral be more specific.

". . . We rode until we were beyond the battlefields, to where there were no more tanks or trucks, only endless fields. And when we saw that there were no more airplanes and tanks, we believed what they told us, that they were taking us away from the war. Finally we came to a little station, all freshly painted, with a little sign and a platform. Even the sign was new. It said 'Oswieçim.' "

"Oswieçim?" repeated the president. "Where is that?"

"In German it's called Auschwitz."

"The Auschwitz death camp?" said the president.

"Yes," said Ral. "Auschwitz-Birkenau. One was for work. The other was for death."

The courtroom began to hum again. Lackenbach and Zemun were strange places, stopping points on the journey of a single gypsy. But everyone had heard of Auschwitz. The very mention of it transformed the trial into something more than the story of a gypsy and an old woman.

"You were interned in Auschwitz?" said the president.

"Yes. In the gypsy camp."

"And the woman Wanda Lanzer was there as well?"

"She was called Eva Ritter. That was her name. She went on another train and she was there when we came. As soon as we got off the trains, she began again with her interviews and tables and charts. At Auschwitz there were twenty thousand gypsies for her to interview."

"Twenty thousand gypsies?" said the president. He was again absorbed in the testimony.

"Monsieur le Président!" The *avocat général* leaned over his pulpit, waiting for the president's nod. "The sworn affidavit and transcript from the Frankfurt prosecutor certifies that the woman Wanda Lanzer was exonerated from any culpability for what may have happened in the so-called death camp at Auschwitz. The document again cites her good works on behalf of the gypsies."

The president's glance seemed harsh, as if his prerogatives had been preempted. "We are aware of the document," he said.

Then he turned back to Ral. "You knew Wanda Lanzer at Auschwitz?"

"Of course. We all—"

"Were you aware of the good works she is alleged to have done?" The president glanced at the papers in front of him, then read excerpts of a document in a droning voice: " '. . . hospital . . . kindergarten . . . increased rations for the sick and the young . . . musical instruments . . .' "

Ral's face tightened in concentration. Then he exploded. "Hospital? Musical instruments? What can you know of what was there? They called it a hospital. Yes. And sometimes there were only three or four in a bed there, instead of six or seven. And there were sometimes straw mattresses instead of wooden *pritschen*. But there were so many who were sick that usually there were six or seven in a bed just like the other huts. And when there were too many who were sick, there would be a 'bad night.' That's what they would tell us in the morning, that there had been a 'bad night.' In the morning there would suddenly be many beds. And they would say that the bodies had to be burned for sanitary reasons. It was the same thing they told us whenever a new train of gypsies would arrive in the camp. A few gypsies would come to the camp, and they would tell us that they were on a train with five hundred other gypsies. 'What happened to the others?' we would ask the guards or the doctors. 'Typhus,' they told us. 'A bad night. The bodies had to be burned for sanitary reasons.' "

"Monsieur le Président!" The *avocat général* was shouting now, leaning down over his pulpit to be heard. "Surely it is beyond the purview of this trial to review the horrors of the German concentration camps."

The president raised his gavel. He didn't need to rap for order. "Monsieur l'Avocat Général!"

The public minister leaned out of his pulpit to speak: "May it please the court . . . . The question before this tribunal is not the events of twenty-five years ago in Poland or Yugoslavia or wherever, but the events of May 1966 in the village of Saintes-Maries-de-la-Mer. Unless the distinguished *avocat* for the defense proposes to introduce some extraordinarily novel variation of a defense based on justifiable homicide, it would appear that the interests of the accused are hardly served by the present testimony. And in any instance, whatever wrongs may have been visited upon the accused or his family in the various camps, it would appear—as the documents from the Frankfurt prosecutor attest—that it was not the woman Wanda Lanzer who bears the blame for his woes. Should we not redirect our testimony to the events of this year which are the proper subject of our inquiry?"

The president turned to Jean-Claude. "Maître Bernard?"

Ral glared at each of them in turn. When he started to speak, the president raised his gavel. "The accused will remain silent until recognized by the court," he said.

"You said that I could speak out in the open court."

"You will have your opportunity to speak."

"Why must I wait for the talk of these men? They know nothing of her. They know nothing of what she did, of what happened in those camps."

The president answered patiently, "You will have your opportunity to speak when the procedural matters before the court have been resolved."

Jean-Claude glanced at Jill. He didn't wait for her to say anything before he turned to the president.

"Monsieur le Président! This trial is not as simple as the public minister would have us believe."

Even Ral seemed intrigued by what Jean-Claude might say.

"The accused has cooperated with neither the police nor the *juge d'instruction.* He appears equally unwilling to cooperate with his own *avocat.* But we would argue that to follow the wise and necessary admonition of the court—to be unyielding in our search for the truth—we cannot exclude the present testimony. The accused has told us that he is a gypsy. We can see and hear that he is not like us, that he does not share many of our most basic values, that he questions even our respect for the law and the courts as the very backbone of civilized society. This disrespect and doubt on his part, we would argue, is precisely why we must hear him out—if only to prove to him that the very process and system of which he is so contemptuous in fact deserves his respect and trust."

Ral was listening carefully, the look in his eyes hovering between anger and curiosity as he followed the subtle direction of Jean-Claude's argument. Jill tried to imagine what it all seemed like to him, what he would make of the sophistry of the courtroom, the arguments that were spun like so many spiders' webs, trying to catch the unwary. She wasn't sure herself where Jean-Claude's arguments were going, and she was experienced in the courtroom. To Ral, she supposed, it was a wall of words that everyone was putting up in the way of the truth that he was so anxious to tell.

She saw Jean-Claude glance at her, as if to seek her opinion of the tack he was taking. Before she could respond, he went on with his speech, now from the center of the *prétoire.* The robes trailed easily behind him.

"The accused," he went on, "is made of the same clay as each of us. It is the shaping of that clay, the experiences that have molded this man, that we must understand. And I would respectfully suggest that if we are to understand the motives and events of that fateful day in May in the village of Saintes-Maries-de-la-Mer, we must look deep into the psyche of the accused, into the crucible of the experiences of those camps which have left indelible stigmata in the mind of this man, scars in his soul that can no more be ignored than a brand or a tattoo."

The president glanced at the *avocat général,* inviting a response.

"Almost thirty years back?" said the *avocat général.* "Why not three hundred years? Or three thousand? If we're to follow the logic of the distinguished *avocat* for the defense, should we not be tracing the anthropological origins of the first troops of gypsies who wandered to Europe from India or wherever?"

Like the referee at a tennis match, the president swung back to Jean-Claude, who was grinning in anticipation of the chance to return the last shot.

"May we remind the public minister," Jean-Claude said, "that it is not the gypsies as a people who are on trial in this courtroom. It is one man who stands accused before the Assizes. And his own experiences, the trail of events which have led him to this courtroom, appear to have begun in the Nazi concentration and extermination camps. If it is indeed the truth that we seek out in this trial, then we have no choice: We must hear his story."

"Is the *avocat* for the defense asking to examine the accused directly?" said the president.

"We are."

The president tilted his head back, as if he were consulting some higher wisdom. Jean-Claude's appeal had been bold, throwing down a gauntlet that was difficult for the court to refuse. Jill was amazed at the cleverness of the tactic, and not at all surprised when the president seemed to agree.

"Maître Bernard is persuasive," said the president. "We will permit the examination of the accused, but the testimony must focus on the accused's relationship with the woman Wanda Lanzer. We will not allow a general disquisition on the camps by the accused. You may begin."

Jean-Claude hinted a bow toward the tribunal, then strode to the center of the *prétoire*. Jill expected him to be smiling at his victory, but he seemed sad, as if he dreaded the prospect of questioning Ral. She had another strange sense of foreboding, her excitement and anticipation suddenly tempered by fear. She couldn't imagine Ral and Jean-Claude talking to each other.

"Ral! Could you describe the gypsy camp at Auschwitz for us?"

Ral stared for a long time at Jean-Claude, as if he were trying to decide if this man was in fact on his side. Then his puzzled expression gave way to a smile.

"The gypsy camp wasn't in Auschwitz," he said. "It was in Birkenau, the death camp. Our camp was plain wooden huts, with beds—*pritschen*, we called them—stacked up to the ceilings. Six or maybe eight gypsies slept on each bed. Before we came there, the huts were stables. But the horses weren't so crowded as we were."

"Then the camp was like huts in the photographs we've all seen of the death camps—the emaciated bodies on wooden planks, the pitiful rags, the drawn faces—"

"Monsieur le Président!" The *avocat général* wagged his finger in admonition. "The *avocat* for the defense is leading the accused in his testimony. Should the pleadings not be reserved for the appropriate moment in the trial?"

"Maître Bernard will please take note," the president said.

Ral glanced back and forth at the president and the *avocats*, answering Jean-Claude's smile with haughty contempt, daring them to go on.

"You were describing the camp at Auschwitz-Birkenau," Jean-Claude said. "Was it like the rest of the camp?"

"Our camp wasn't like the others," said Ral. "We didn't work. They let us grow our hair, let us wear our own clothes. We could live with our families. They said we weren't inmates like the others. We were internees. We were being protected from the war. Usually we had no roll calls. There was even a canteen where a gypsy with money could buy things. Some of the German gypsies were rich. There were even gypsies who had been in the army. They weren't allowed to wear uniforms, but they walked around the camp with their medals on."

"Did you have any other special privileges?"

Ral smiled, as if he had expected the question.

"They gave us musical instruments to play," said Ral. "Fiddles and guitars. On holidays the gypsies would play concerts for the visitors or for the SS officers. The gypsy girls would dance at the concerts, and the SS men would take some of them away, to their brothels. Then after maybe a month the girls would come back to the camp. Except that first they would go into the hospital. When they came out, they would be barren."

The courtroom hummed again. Revelations, horror stories of German atrocities, sex—these were what the audience and the press hoped for. It was for that that they were willing to endure the predictable routine of the trial. Even the *avocats* who had been intrigued because Jean-Claude Bernard had agreed to plead such an unpromising brief, now at least had the spectacle of direct examination of the accused. It hardly mattered that the testimony seemed unrelated to the crime.

"Do you mean that the girls were sterilized?"

"Sterilized? Yes, that's the word. They were made barren, so they could never have a child."

"How do you know that the girls were sterilized?"

"How do I know? My sister was in the camp. They made her their whore and took her to their hospital. Afterward she wouldn't speak. Not to me. Not even to my mother. She wouldn't eat. We got extra rations for her. My mother traded the jewels she had hidden for sugar and I stole bread and salami. We forced her to eat, but it didn't matter. Every day she grew thinner. She wanted to die. To be barren is the worst curse that can come to a gypsy woman. And to be a whore is the most terrible shame. We tried to tell her that it wasn't her fault, but she wouldn't hear. She only wanted to die because of her shame and that curse."

Jean-Claude waited for the hum in the courtroom to subside.

"Did this happen at Auschwitz?"

"Of course at Auschwitz. We were together there. My mother and my sister and I found each other there and we were together."

"Was your sister sent to a brothel and to be sterilized at Auschwitz?"

Ral stared at Jean-Claude, as though puzzled by the question. "No, but—"

Jean-Claude cut him off. "Did Eva Ritter have anything to do with your sister being selected for the brothel or for sterilization?"

Ral looked straight at Jean-Claude, avoiding the audience in the galleries. "When the SS officers watched the girls dance they would go crazy. The dancing would make them crazy."

"Ral! Did Eva Ritter have anything to do with your sister being selected for the brothel and for sterilization?"

Ral scanned the gallery again. His eyes fell on Jill's as he answered.

"What happened to my sister happened in another camp. At Ravensbruck. It was before she came to Auschwitz."

The *prétoire* buzzed with gossip. Jill was close enough to hear *avocats* whispering that Jean-Claude was making a fool of himself and a botch of the case.

"Is this line of testimony in the interest of the accused?" asked the president. It was as if he had heard the *avocats*.

Jean-Claude looked at Jill, then back at the president. "May we confer with our associate?" he asked.

The president nodded.

Jean-Claude came over to Jill, ignoring the eyes of the courtroom on them. "Still convinced that letting Ral tell his story is wise?"

Jill knew Jean-Claude's question was sincere. "I can't explain it as a lawyer," she said. "But I know it's right."

"And if it goes on like this? If the story leads even deeper into the quagmire that this all seems headed for?"

"It's not for us to decide."

"I have a duty to help my client, Jill, just as a doctor has a duty to help a patient. Can a doctor let a patient commit suicide?"

"That's playing God, Jean-Claude."

"No, it's trying to keep a man from harming himself. If what comes out of this testimony is the tale of revenge that I expect, it will be too late to do anything about it. He'll have condemned himself for premeditated murder."

Jean-Claude saw the eyes of the courtroom watching them. The *avocats* near them in the *prétoire*, and even some of the court-watchers in the gallery, could hear every word they said.

"Find out what she did, Jean-Claude."

"What makes you so sure she did something?"

"I don't know. I just have a feeling that's too strong to ignore."

"A feeling? Jill, I can't act on intuition. The law demands reason."

"Maître Bernard! Do you wish to continue the examination of the accused?" The president sounded more curious than impatient. It seemed to Jill that the entire courtroom was watching her and Jean-Claude.

"With the permission of the court," answered Jean-Claude, "we will continue."

The president seemed surprised. "You're certain, Maître Bernard, that you wish to continue this line of testimony?"

Jean-Claude answered without hesitation. "We realize that the testimony may appear unstructured. It may even be the case that as a counselor to the accused I would regret the testimony. But we believe it is in the interest of the truth."

"Very well," said the president.

The *avocat général* grinned as Jean-Claude turned to Ral.

"Ral," said Jean Claude, "you were telling us about the hospital in the gypsy camp. Was the hospital like other hospitals?"

"I was never in another hospital," said Ral. "We were gypsies. What did we know about hospitals? She—Eva Ritter—told us the hospital was for us, that it was a place where we would get medicine and rest. What did we know?"

"Could you describe the hospital?"

"At first it was two of the huts in our camp. The huts that had been stables. Each had a stove in the middle, made of brick. And an examining bench. There was a surgery in one. And a corner closed off with a curtain where they took the women."

"Were there doctors in the hospital?"

"There were French doctors, Polish doctors, Czech doctors. When they could, they would give medicine or bandages to a gypsy who was sick. Sometimes if you were sick they would give you a bed in the hospital, and you would have to share with only two or three people, instead of six or seven. Until the typhus. After that it was only bad nights, and taking the bodies away to burn in the morning."

"Ral—when they told you that those bodies were being burned for sanitary reasons, did you believe them?"

Ral seemed surprised by the question. He turned his gaze from the galleries to answer Jean-Claude directly.

"Of course we believed them. Why wouldn't we believe? We had never seen such a place. We knew nothing of war. We were like children. She told us that we would be protected, that it would be all right. She told us that we would be safe in the gypsy camp. And we could see that our camp was different. It was better than the rest of that place. If they would give us a hospital and let us wear our own clothes and have fiddles and guitars to play, could they really be so terrible? That's what we thought. That's what she told us. Why wouldn't we believe?"

"Ral, was Wanda Lanzer—Eva Ritter—in charge of the hospital?"

"In charge? No. She wasn't in charge. There was an SS doctor. We called him Uncle."

"Uncle?"

"The children named him that. Whenever he came into the camp, the children would follow him and gather around him. He gave them sweets, and they would shout his name. 'Onkel! Vater! Vaterchen!' they would shout. They loved him. He told them he loved them too, that he loved all gypsy children."

"What was his real name, this Uncle?"

"His name was Mengele. Josef Mengele."

The president, the lay judges, the *avocats* in the *prétoire*, even the *avocat général* in his pulpit—all stirred at the answer. Mengele was a name they knew, an infamous name. The reporters in the press gallery were suddenly awake, scribbling notes. The galleries chattered with comments.

Jean-Claude left the hubbub unpunctuated for as long as possible, until he saw the president start to raise his gavel for order. Then he turned again to Ral. The two men were absorbed in each other now, tied in the symbiotic relationship created by the testimony. Jill felt like a complete outsider, as though a machine she had set in motion had no further need of her.

"Did Eva Ritter work for Mengele?"

"They all worked for Mengele. Except he was only in the camp sometimes. She was always there. She was the one who would talk to us, tell us what we should do. She was the one we trusted."

"What did Mengele do in the gypsy camp?" Jean-Claude asked.

Ral was aware of the increased attention that the testimony had drawn. He hesitated before he answered, straightening up in the box and taking in his audience.

"He came almost every day. He told us that the gypsies were special to him, that we were his children. He liked to play with the little gypsy children. He would give them extra rations, sweets and milk and sugar. He would pick them up in his arms and carry them around the camp. The twins, especially. He liked all twins. He would let them ride on his shoulders, give them special sweets. And if one twin was ever sick, he would let both twins go to the hospital. It was for experiments, she told us. Experiments to end the war so we could all go home."

"She?"

"Eva Ritter. She told us that we should go to the experiments, because the sooner the war ended the sooner we would all be able to go home."

"What kind of experiments were these?"

"Everything in the hospital was an experiment. When they made the women barren, they said it was an experiment. When they had gypsies drink seawater, they said it was an experiment. With the twins, it was mostly experiments on the *noma*."

"*Noma?*" Jean-Claude turned around to see if anyone else recognized the strange term. "What is *noma*, Ral?"

"I don't know what it's called in French. We called it *noma*. The doctors said it was a water cancer. Many gypsies got it in the camp because the water was bad, and also because there wasn't much food. A man called Dr. Epstein did the experiments on the *noma*." Ral saw that he had his audience and went on.

"The *noma* would begin as a sore on the face, a little sore that wouldn't heal. Then it would grow and there would be terrible-smelling pus inside. It smelled so bad that no one could stand to be near the person. Mengele wouldn't play with the gypsy twins when they had *noma* like that. It would keep growing until there was a hole in the cheek. The doctors had medicine for it, but it didn't help. With the twins, if one had a *noma*, Mengele would put them both in the hospital, and Dr. Epstein would take the *noma* from one twin and give it to the other. Then they would get sweets and extra food, but no medicine."

"Did Mengele ever explain why they did this?"

"Explain? They said it was to end the war. And when the twins died— they always died—they told us that the bodies were burned for sanitary reasons."

"And you believed what they told you?"

Ral shrugged. "They told us we were helping to end the war. She said that when the war was over we would go home. Why wouldn't we believe her? They brought people to our camp, visitors. They would have the gypsy musicians play their fiddles and guitars. The girls would dance. Uncle would make a speech about the hospital. And she would make a speech about how they were protecting us, preserving our way of life until the war was over. And all along—"

"Monsieur le Président!" the *avocat général* shouted, loud enough to cut off Ral's testimony.

Jill looked up at the pulpit. The testimony had gone much further than she had expected. She wasn't sure whether it was Jean-Claude's persistence, the president's toleration, or the *avocat général*'s acquiescence that most surprised her.

The *avocat général* pounced as soon as he had a nod from the president.

"Was the woman Wanda Lanzer—Eva Ritter as you insist on calling her—responsible for any of the horrors, the experiments, you've described?"

Ral stared up at the pulpit without answering.

"It isn't necessary for the accused to answer," the *avocat général* went on, orating now, speaking directly to the tribunal. "We know that Wanda Lanzer was not implicated in those horrors, and we know from evidence that we can trust. Until today the accused has never even mentioned his alleged sojourn in the concentration camps—not to the police, not to the *juge d'instruction*, not even to his own *avocat*, if we're to believe the distinguished *avocat* for the defense. Can we not see the testimony for what it is—a gypsy stratagem to deflect this court from its proper subject, which is nothing other than the crime of May of this year in the village of Saintes-Maries-de-la-Mer, the brutal, vicious murder of the woman Wanda Lanzer by the accused?"

Ral shouted his answer.

"I never spoke out before because no one would listen. I know what happens to the words of a gypsy, how they're twisted and torn to pieces. I waited until I was in the open court so people could hear what she did."

The *avocat général* directed his reply to the court without so much as looking at Ral.

"Does it matter what she did—if indeed she had anything at all to do with the horrors of that camp? May we remind the court that it is not the woman Wanda Lanzer who stands accused in this courtroom? It is the man in that box who stands accused of the murder of Wanda Lanzer."

The president of the court held up his hands to stop the runaway proceedings. For a moment he seemed overwhelmed by the three-cornered trial.

Jean-Claude turned to Ral. When he spoke, his voice was unexpectedly sharp.

"What did Eva Ritter do?" he said. He stood close to Ral, just outside the box, his eyes squarely on Ral's. "Tell us what she did. Was she responsible for the experiments you've described? Was she responsible for the suffering and deaths of the twins or the others in those experiments?"

The questions froze the room like an unexpected flashbulb. Heads leaned forward. Not just the heads of those in the tribunal, but of the *avocats* in the *prétoire*, the audience in the gallery, even the *avocat général* in his pulpit. To Jill, Ral was like a patient on the slab in the center of the operating room. Everyone else was a physician poised with a scalpel.

The longer Ral hesitated before answering, the more hostile and threatening the silence seemed.

"Well?" said the president of the court. "Was Wanda Lanzer responsible for those experiments?"

"Responsible?" said Ral.

Jill felt suddenly cold. He was lost.

"Did Wanda Lanzer make people go to those experiments? Did she force people to submit to seawater or to the operations? Did she put the children in the hospital for operations with that cancer?"

"No!" said Ral. "No."

It took the courtroom a moment to grasp the simple answer. Then Jill could see the *avocat général* leaning back to gloat. In front of her, on the other side of the grille, the *avocats* hummed with questions and comments. "What was the Maître trying to do?" they asked one another in a dozen ways. The *avocats* right in front of her turned to glance at her. One shook his head in wonder.

Ral stared at the galleries. The gypsies on one side and the court followers on the other were absorbed in a hushed hubbub of speculation.

"Perhaps the *avocat* for the defense would prefer to terminate this line of questioning," said the president.

Jill waited for Jean-Claude to come over to her. She was ready to let him abandon the obviously fruitless testimony.

Instead Jean-Claude spun suddenly on Ral, pointing with an outstretched arm. His face was angry, the skin taut, the eyes and mouth hard. "What *did* she do?" he shouted to Ral. "Tell us!"

Ral looked first at Jean-Claude, then around the room. He seemed calm, frighteningly so, as if the jagged interruptions to his testimony had never happened. Jill was convinced that he had no grasp at all of what was happening, of how the trial was going. For the first time she felt sorry for him.

"It started after the Reichsführer came," said Ral.

"The Reichsführer?" repeated Jean-Claude. "Heinrich Himmler?"

"He came to our camp," Ral went on. "He was a little man, with tall boots and glasses and wire rims. Wherever he went, he was surrounded by men who would wipe off a chair before he sat down and reach for matches before he put a cigarette to his lips. He looked at everything from far away, like he was afraid he would be soiled by the camp."

"This man was Heinrich Himmler?" asked Jean-Claude. "He visited your camp?"

"For weeks before he came we had to get the camp ready. They brought us more guitars and fiddles from Canada—that was the part of the camp where they collected things from people when they got off the trains. They had us build a stage for the musicians and the dancers. They made us clean the hospital and the kindergarten. They brought us clothes to wear, coats and sweaters, and Greek blankets—thick woven blankets that came from the Greek Jews. We were a special camp, you see. They wanted the Reichsführer to see how special our camp was."

The president and the *avocat général* had seemed ready to interrupt, but as Ral's narrative went on, they became as engrossed as the rest of the courtroom. The president was following Ral's words with nods of his head. The *avocat général* looked to Jill as though he had decided that it didn't matter, that like everything else Ral had said so far, this new story would in the end prove incriminating.

"They had speeches and music and dancing when the Reichsführer came. There was a stage and a whole program of music. For a week she told the musicians from the different clans and families to prepare their music, and they rehearsed on the stage. Then when the Reichsführer came, they lined up chairs for him and Onkel and the others, and they listened to the music and watched the dancers. And she explained which music was from the Manush and which from Sinte gypsies and which from the Hungarian gypsies. Everyone was all clean and scrubbed. They set up big bathtubs outside and made everyone take special baths that would kill the lice. And we had new clothes from Canada to wear. But the whole time the Reichsführer looked at us through those little glasses like we were lepers.

"I think he saw right away what we had all forgotten. We were used to the camp by then. We didn't notice when people coughed from the TB. We didn't pay attention to the typhus or the *noma*. We didn't see the filth and the sores that the blankets and clothes didn't cover. We had been there so long, men and women thrown together in one big camp, that the gypsies had stopped trying to be clean. They had stopped respecting each other. When they served us food with the Reichsführer there, there were big pots of soup with meat in it, and bread and salami. I remember that we were all afraid of the food. We were afraid that there was some reason for the food and the blankets and clothes, so we waited. But the children just knew that there was food, and they ran for the pots and the bread. For me, it was the first time since I came there that I could see what had happened to us, to the gypsies. Those little ones weren't children anymore. They didn't know how to play. They would sit and stare at nothing for hours. And when they saw a scrap of food, they would fight for it like little animals. Children would steal food from their mothers and fathers. And mothers and fathers took food from the special rations that some of the children got. We were a broken people. The Reichsführer could see that.

"We heard Onkel and Eva Ritter tell the Reichsführer that he could meet some of the gypsies and ask questions about the camp, but he stood back, the way someone would stand back from the smell of a *noma*. He looked at us through those little glasses with the wire rims, and then he just got up and turned and walked away. All the men who had wiped off his chairs and held out the matches walked after him. After that, the camp was doomed."

"After that the camp was doomed?" repeated Jean-Claude. "What do you mean?"

"*Doomed!*" shouted Ral. "After that we were like the rest of the camp."

"You knew what was happening in the rest of the Auschwitz camp?"

Ral glared at Jean-Claude, answering in a flat, angry voice.

"The last barracks of the gypsy hospital was fifty meters from the siding where the trains arrived every day. We could see the platforms where Mengele and the other doctors selected which of the new arrivals went to Auschwitz to work and which went to Birkenau. Every afternoon and night we could see the red glow in the sky and smell the smoke from the bakery. Do I have to tell you what the bakery was? Do I have to tell you what they were burning in that hell? We were only dumb gypsies, but our eyes can still see. Our noses can still smell. We know the smell of death."

Ral looked around the courtroom. The audience was all his now. Jill had forgotten she was watching a trial. She was in a camp, surrounded by tall fences of barbed wire, guarded by dogs and soldiers, watching people slowly die of starvation and disease, waiting for something even more awful to happen. What Ral was telling wasn't a narrative of faraway, strange people. The story wasn't the dry horror of a book. It was real. She was more afraid than she had ever been in her life.

"You knew what happened in the rest of the camp and ignored it?" said Jean-Claude.

"What were we to do?" said Ral. "Our camp was different. They were prisoners. We were only internees. That's what she told us."

"What changed after the visit of the Reichsführer?" asked Jean-Claude. Jill was amazed at his control of the questions he posed. It was as if he knew what Ral would say.

"What changed?" Ral took in the room again before he answered. "We were sorted."

"Sorted?"

"Classified. Divided up. It took more than a year to do. The orders were that everyone had to fit a category. Pure gypsies, part gypsies, nomads, stationary gypsies, Germans, Hungarians, Sinte, Kalderash, Romanians, Greeks, Russians. There was a category for everyone."

"How was this classification done?"

Ral stared at Jean-Claude. His story had been with him for so long that he had forgotten that no one else knew.

"She did it! Eva Ritter. She sorted us like you sort horses at a fair. This one is good breeding stock, young and strong. This one here is only good for horsemeat, for the dogs. That's what she did with those interviews and charts she had."

Jill watched the whites of Ral's eyes, luminous and steady, his gaze unblinking. She was terrified of what was about to happen.

"And when the sorting was finished?" asked Jean-Claude. "What happened then?"

"It took more than a year to finish. They told her to hurry, but she was very careful. Every classification had to be just right. Then, when it was done, she told us that some of the young men were going on a train to Germany to work. She said that their families would join them later, that it was important for them to go first to get things ready."

"How many were selected to go?"

"All together a few dozen. Mostly Germans, musicians and performers."

"Were you on that train, Ral?"

Ral seemed surprised by Jean-Claude's question.

"Were you selected to go to Germany on that train?" Jean-Claude repeated.

"Yes, I was selected for the train. But I—"

"Monsieur le Président!" The *avocat général's* tone sounded exasperated, almost like a reprimand. He went on without a nod from the president. "Is the accused saying that once again the woman Wanda Lanzer saved his life?"

The courtroom started to buzz again. The *avocat général's* question had broken Ral's narrative in midstream.

Jean-Claude turned to Jill, as if she could explain what had happened.

"Saved my life?" Ral's voice was loud but controlled. His eyes roved the room, from the *avocat général* back to the tribunal, and then to his audience in the galleries. "You don't know what happened? You don't know what she did?"

He paused, as if he expected an answer to his questions. The courtroom was suddenly very quiet. A cough from the galleries stood out like applause between the movements of a symphony.

"No one knows," he said. "No one wants to know. No one wants to remember what happened to the gypsies."

He paused again, scanning the courtroom at leisure, taking in every eye, holding every gaze long enough to make the room his again before he returned to his testimony.

"For more than a year, while we were being sorted, nothing happened. Then one morning they came with trucks, to pick up the men who had been chosen to go to Germany. There was no warning. There wasn't even time to say good-bye. SS men came into the camp, with lists, and they got us. When they couldn't find some of the men, she told them where to find us."

"She?" Jean-Claude interrupted.

"Eva Ritter. She knew everyone, knew where to find anyone in the camp. The SS men didn't know us, but she did. So she found the men. It only took an hour or so, and it was so quick that when the trucks drove out of the camp, we could hear women and some of the old men shouting to the guards that they didn't believe we were going away to work. We had all heard of others going to Germany to work. Usually it meant digging up bombs in the cities. We never heard again about anyone who went.

"As we drove to the gates, men and women came out of all the barracks in the camp. They became very agitated. 'Where are they going?' the women shouted. 'When will the families go?' They began to follow the trucks, and the guards became nervous, because there were so many gypsies and so few guards. I think they were afraid that the gypsy men who knew how to use a grindstone had knives and other secret weapons in the camp.

"The trucks stopped outside the camp. We could still hear the shouts from inside, and we could see that the guards were fiddling with their guns, and shifting from leg to leg as they stood. She—Eva Ritter—came out to talk to us and then she talked to the SS captain who was in charge of the trucks. He said that our trucks would come around to the siding, and that the families would be able to come out to say good-bye to us there. He used a special speaking horn to tell everyone in the gypsy camp that they would be able to say good-bye, and then the shouting stopped.

"We were taken around to the train, at the siding, and they brought the families over. They gave the women packages of bread and salami to give to us. 'Wish them a good journey,' the guards shouted as the women ran up to the train. 'Tell them that you'll join them soon.' There weren't so many of us that we couldn't all get to the windows of the train, and I got to see my mother and sister. They came up to the window and held up their hands to touch my cheeks. Except that my sister, Keje, still wouldn't look at me.

" 'There's your brother, Ral,' my mother said to her. 'Wave good-bye to him.' She waved, but she wouldn't look at me. She was ashamed to look at a man, even her own brother. '*Bahtalo drom*,' my mother said to me. It means 'good road.' She always knew how to pretend that everything would be all right."

Jill could hear herself breathing. She had to fight tears when Ral said
'*Bahtalo drom.*'

"Then the train began to move. The men inside all cheered. They
shouted 'Loli! Loli!'—that was the name she had us call her—because she
had picked them to go on the train. Some of them began to eat the bread
and salami. It was like a picnic. The train was moving very slowly, because they had to switch it to a different track, and I went to the back of
the car to see better. And from the window in the back I could see trucks
coming to the gypsy camp. No one else paid any attention. Even the guards
paid no attention. Why would they? We were still inside the camp. So all
alone, in the back of the train, I watched while the trucks lined up outside
the fence. Only now, instead of two trucks, there were many of them.

"One of the bars on the window of the train was broken. And I knew it
was a sign, like seeing a red sun or a thundercloud. Only this sign was for
me, to tell me that I had to go back. I don't understand it, even to this day,
but as soon as I saw those trucks, I knew I had to get off the train. I knew I
had to watch. That I was to be the witness. No one was looking, so I
climbed through the window and jumped to the ground. I ran for the trees
that had been put up next to the railroad siding. They were there so that
people who arrived on the trains couldn't see into the camp. I hid in the
trees, standing in the mud. And I knew that as long as I lived I would remember what I saw there . . ."

No one in the courtroom said a word now. The audience in the galleries,
the president and lay judges on the tribunal, even the cynical *avocats* in the
prétoire, were caught up in the narrative. The *avocat général* tried to feign
a haughty indifference, but the hush and concentration of the courtoom
were inescapable. And yet, even though everyone else was listening to the
same narrative as she, Jill felt terribly alone, as if she were hidden in those
trees with Ral.

"Nothing happened for a long time," Ral went on, "until late in the afternoon. The trucks kept lining up, and *kapos* and SS men got out. Most of
the *kapos* looked like Ukrainians. They did the hard work in the camp. We
had seen them before, but never in the gypsy camp. Finally an SS officer
began shouting through a horn for everyone to line up for a roll call. He
said that they had to have a count so they could issue more special rations
like the bread and salami that the women had given us on the trains. The
gypsies stood there and listened to him, but when he finished they just
milled around. No one would line up.

"The SS officer kept shouting, telling the gypsies to hurry, that the special rations were waiting for them. And the *kapos* began pushing people
into lines. The gypsies made it very hard for them. As soon as they almost
had everyone in a line, the gypsies would begin to wander away. And they
were all talking, talking so loud that even from where I was, in the trees,
you could hear. It was so loud that no one could hear the shouts of the SS
officer.

"Then an old gypsy woman shouted out in Romany. Her voice was loud and shrill, and as soon as she shouted, everyone was quiet. 'These men are not life!' she shouted. 'They have no special rations.' Everyone turned to look at her, even the *kapos* and the SS men. She shouted again. 'These men aren't life. They're death!'

"All of the gypsies must have heard her, because the gypsy women began to shout and cry out in Romany. The shouting was very loud, and the *kapos* and guards became nervous. Usually they had a plan for everything, but when the women began to shout, the *kapos* and the SS men turned wild. They started to beat the old women and children with their clubs, pushing them down, trying to get them into lines."

Ral's hands were white on the railing of his box. His skin glowed like molten copper; his eyes were like flames. His speech and his movements were still calm and steady, but his face seemed close to madness, the face of a wild man.

"When they attacked those women and children, something happened that never happened before in the camp. The women and old men didn't go into a line when the *kapos* began to beat them, the way people always had. They didn't fall down and beg when the *kapos* raised their clubs. They didn't shout out for mercy. Right there where they stood, right in the middle of the open ground, those gypsies turned and fought back against the *kapos*. With their teeth and their feet and their fingers, they fought against the clubs and the whips. Old men raised their fists. Old women, so bent over they couldn't stand straight, with maybe only a few teeth left in their mouths, turned on the *kapos*, kicking them, biting them, tearing at their faces with crooked fingers. Even the children kicked and pounded at the legs of the *kapos* with their little fists. And the women screamed, shouting curses in Romany. They were so loud no one could hear the orders of the SS men.

"After the fight went on for a while, the *kapos* ran back to the fence of the camp. They lined up there while more trucks came, with more *kapos* and SS men. The officers shouted orders to them, and when they were ready they came across the camp with clubs and whips. The gypsies tried to fight back again, but there were too many *kapos*. They clubbed the gypsies down and dragged them away to the trucks. I could see them fill up one truck after another. I wanted to run into the camp, to bite and kick and tear at the faces of the *kapos*. I wanted to tear a whip from their hands and beat them with it. But between where I stood and the fence there was a belt of mud, plowed ground that was there to make it easy to see if someone tried to go over the fences. And outside the fence there were guards. I could hear them talk. One said that they never before had so much trouble in the camp, that no one had ever fought like those gypsies. At that moment I was proud to be a gypsy.

"It was almost dark when they got the gypsies into the trucks. Once they got most of them, it was easy to get the stragglers. They went into the huts and dragged out anyone who had hidden. It was then, when there were only a few gypsies left in the camp, that I saw my mother and sister. My mother had her arms around my sister, to protect her from the blows of the *kapos*. She tried to keep them from dragging her away. I think that she knew it would be hard for my sister if she was alone. For one moment I saw my mother look toward the trees, to where I was hiding. Even as the *kapos* beat her, she stared at the trees. I don't know what she saw. Maybe those trees reminded her of the old days, on the road. Or maybe—and I know you'll call this gypsy foolishness—maybe she knew I was there, that I was a witness.

"When the last gypsies were in the trucks, they closed up the backs and drove away. I listened for a long time, to the sounds of the engines. I thought I could hear the sounds of people, too, from inside. I waited there, in the trees, until night, until the sky was completely black. Then, long after the sun was gone, I could see streaks of red in the sky over the bakery and smell the smoke that blew across the camp from the chimneys. That red in the sky and the smell of that smoke is my last memory of my mother and my sister."

When Ral paused, the silence of the hushed courtroom lingered, like smoke. Jean-Claude waited, pacing the silence, before he asked, "Where was the woman Eva Ritter during all of this?"

"She was there," said Ral. "When the trucks drove away and the camp was finally quiet, I could hear music playing. It was from her office, one of the records she always played. A czardas, gypsy music. Only that night she was playing the Victrola very loud, loud enough to drown out the screams of women and children and old men. She played it loud so she wouldn't have to hear the cries of the gypsies she had chosen not to live."

It took a long time for the hypnotic silence of the courtroom to dissolve into murmurs. Everyone seemed to feel that it was wrong to talk, wrong even to react. And so they stood, watching and waiting, while Ral slowly turned in his box, staring in turn at the judges on the tribunal, the *avocats* in the *prétoire*, the crowd behind the grille. It wasn't until his eyes left each group that the stunned silence gave way to talk, and in French, in legal jargon, and in Romany, the crowds who had come to the Assizes expecting only ritual began to analyze the drama they had witnessed.

Ral's gaze ended on Jill, steady and unblinking. His eyes were dark and mysterious and wild. She felt chilled and very afraid. Never in her life had she wanted more to be in someone's arms.

The courtroom watched in silence as the chains were put on Ral. The ceremony seemed to take forever, and the clanging of the chains seemed louder than before. Only when the side door had closed behind Ral and the galleries began to empty into the streets did Jill see Jean-Claude standing at the grille of the *prétoire*, a few feet away from her.

"I have to clear up a few procedural matters here," he said. "I should be at my study in half an hour."

She was too anesthetized to answer with more than a nod.

Outside the courtroom, she watched the gypsies assemble around their cars and vans and caravans. The silence of the courtroom gave way to shouts when they came out into the late afternoon sunlight, and in moments the streets outside the courtroom were filled with a cacophony of Romany and French. The colors of the gypsy clothes seemed brighter too. It was as if they had all come alive outdoors. She had to walk through the crowds to get to Jean-Claude's office. She noticed that the gypsies pulled back from her and from anyone else who wasn't part of them. Their closeness to one another reminded her of the church at Saintes-Maries, except this time she envied them. They weren't alone.

Jean-Claude's office seemed even less pretentious than she remembered. Papers and books were scattered on his desk in a disarray that didn't seem to match the controlled neatness of the villa or Jean-Claude's own appearance. When he looked up from his table, he was wearing the half-glasses that she remembered from their brief session of negotiating.

He offered her a chair without getting up from his desk.

"That was wonderful, what you did in there," she said.

"Was it?"

"What do you mean? The court was fascinated. They never took their eyes off him. They hung on his words."

"Today was his day in court, Jill. That's what he wanted. Tomorrow the court turns to the case against him. I'm afraid that he'll pay for that story then."

"That story must count for something. How could anyone not be moved by that?"

"Of course they were moved. It was a very moving tale. But there was nothing in his story that I can build on. Nothing to plead. He was masterful in the telling, that much I'll give you. He watched his audience and gave them what they wanted. But the real question of the trial is still there: What do I plead? He's given me no answer to that."

"The court was affected; doesn't that count for something?"

"That's not a jury, Jill. Those nine judges have been sitting together for a whole session. It's impossible to predict what they'll do. If they've been merciful in the last few trials they may be inclined to be harsh now. If they've been tough for a while, they may turn soft. They have public opinion to watch: How will the public in Marseilles or Saintes-Maries react if a gypsy gets off too easy? And how threatening are all those gypsies in the back of the courtroom? Will they cause trouble if the sentence is too severe?"

Jill got up, walking over to the bookshelves that lined the walls of the little study. It was a mannered gesture, and she was self-conscious as she turned from the books to Jean-Claude.

"I don't think it was just one more story. Imagine that feeling of belonging, of being part of a people. And then seeing those people wiped out. Not just his mother and his sister, but everyone, the whole camp—all of the gypsies. His people. It's like he's homeless now."

"Is that his word or yours?" Jean-Claude asked. "Did he ever talk to you about being homeless?"

"I guess it's mine. I think I've told you everything we ever said to each other. When I first met him, I remember asking him if he was a gypsy. It seemed so exotic to me."

"What did he answer?"

"It's strange, now that I remember. He hesitated before he answered. It was as if he wasn't sure."

"Maybe he wasn't."

"How can you say that after that testimony today?"

"Jill—what I'm trying to tell you is that the testimony today doesn't matter. Picture the testimony tomorrow . . ."

Jean-Claude pointed at the chair where Jill had been sitting, and waited for her to sit down. He put his glasses on the desk and stood directly in front of her. His chin was up, his feet square on the floor. It was the mannered pose and bearing he had in the courtroom, and while the directness of his gaze felt intimate, she was frightened by the power of his manner.

"Were you in Saintes-Maries-de-la-Mer on the twenty-fifth of May of this year?" His voice projected in the ringing registers she remembered from the courtroom.

"Did you see the woman Wanda Lanzer there?

"Had you been searching for her?

"For how long had you searched for her?"

With each question, his voice sharpened. He leaned close to Jill, circling around her chair, then swooping, like a falcon spiraling for its prey.

"Twenty years you searched for her? All over Europe? Why?

"And when you saw her alone, on that forsaken road, what did you do? Tell us in your own words just what happened."

"Stop!" Jill put her arms up, then buried her face in her own hands.

"I'm sorry, Jill. But that's what's coming tomorrow."

Jean-Claude put his hand on Jill's shoulder, waiting until she looked up before he went around to his own chair.

"What kind of answers do you think we can expect from Ral? His testimony today was dramatic, but it was ultimately to no avail. I can't argue that he was brutalized by the woman. By his own testimony he wasn't. What's left?"

Jill looked away, avoiding the question.

"I'll grant you that the man is interesting. Fascinating, actually. Imagine! Twenty years devoted to a revenge that only he can understand! The public minister will probably say it's in the blood, that it's to be expected from a gypsy. But I don't think Ral is by any means an ordinary gypsy."

"What do you mean?"

"I'm not sure. I can't get a real measure of the man. It seems to me that this passionate pursuit of his, this search for revenge, has all but destroyed him. Imagine if by some miracle he were to be acquitted, if the charges were dropped. What life is left for him? The woman was a kind of solution for him. Pursuing her gave his life meaning. A focus."

"What's going to happen, Jean-Claude? If he's condemned, what will the sentence be?"

"I'd guess *travail à force perpétuel*, hard labor for life. A few months ago, when the newspapers first reported the crime, I wouldn't have been surprised by a call for the guillotine."

"Can you help him?"

"I'm not sure anything I might say or argue will matter now. Unless Ral denies the crime, or even admits the crime with some show of remorse, he's isolated himself in a limbo where no one can help him."

Jill pulled up her chair, throwing her head back to clear the hair from her face.

"The public minister's case against Ral—it's all circumstantial, isn't it? No witnesses, no direct evidence or testimony?"

"All circumstantial. But the testimony Ral gave today—that sad, moving story—is all the motive they need. Unless he denies the murder and comes up with an alibi, his story is tantamount to a confession. Except that they would be more inclined to mercy if he actually confessed the murder. The tragedy is worthy of Racine. The man sacrifices twenty years of his life to tell that story. And pays for that moment of revenge with the rest of his life."

"Hasn't he already paid the price? Isn't twenty years enough? Twenty years of nothing but following that woman? Why should he have to suffer more?"

"Jill, we're not rewriting a drama. We're defending a man on a charge of murder."

"It's more than that."

"Not to the court. If there's a higher justice, it may turn out that the woman is truly the guilty party. But the only question for this court is whether Ral murdered that woman in Saintes-Maries in May of this year."

"Do you think he did?"

"I don't know, Jill. I wish he would talk to me, or to you. I wish he would tell us enough to let me plead his case."

"And if he doesn't? If he insists on telling his own story, pleading his own case?"

"Then I have to decide whom I am to represent."

Jill looked up, quizzing with her eyes.

"It seems that I have three clients: Ral wants only to tell his story, to be heard. You want him exonerated. And my oath as an *avocat* and as an officer of the court is to search for the Truth. The three choices demand three different stratagems, all opposed to one another. I have to choose one."

Drained, unable to think rationally anymore, Jill stared at Jean-Claude, amazed that his face seemed to mirror the frustration and dread that she felt.

"What will you do?" she said.

"If I understood Ral—if either of us did—I could answer that question."

"It's too late for *if*, Jean-Claude."

Jean-Claude looked down at the crowded desk. The books and papers spread out all around him made it clear that he would be up most of the night pondering exactly that question.

"How do I decide?" he said. "In the end I suspect that a man has no real choice on a question like that. The decision is made for him."

"By circumstances?" she said.

"No," he answered with a sad smile. "By conscience."

Jill had planned to be in court early the second day, before the session opened at one o'clock. How French! she thought, to wait until after one to begin each day. Was it really because they didn't want a lunch break to interrupt the trial? Or were they wise enough to know that after the usual French lunch the court would be napping instead of listening? She remembered that on the day before, some of the lay judges had been nodding at the beginning of the testimony, before Ral's story unfolded.

She had the morning to herself. From her hotel, she walked up the Canebière, window-shopping in the elegant stores. Nothing really interested her; she couldn't force herself to go into a shop. She felt as if she were waiting for a train, passing time, trying to amuse herself. The sensation of being a spectator was loathsome.

She walked the length of the Canebière, then on to the Boulevard Longchamp. At the end was the Musée des Beaux-Arts. In all the time she had spent in Marseilles, she hadn't been to the museum a single time. Usually she was at the museums within days of coming to a city, if not with the directors and curators, then by herself, often with a special pass. It was pleasure, but it was also business, and for a long time she hadn't drawn lines between the two, hadn't in fact been able to distinguish one from the other.

And then Ral had come along. And Jean-Claude. And now the trial, and that cycle of obsession and helplessness that she still couldn't understand.

She wandered through the museum aimlessly. Nothing caught her eye except the huge Puvis de Chavannes murals on the staircase, glorious scenes of Marseilles as a Greek colony and as a port to the Orient. It made her think how at home Jean-Claude seemed. She had always thought that no one would ever *choose* to live anywhere except New York or Paris or London, or perhaps San Francisco. Whoever lived anywhere else did so because they had to, because they weren't part of the glorious whirl, the beautiful people, the in crowd, the free souls. It had been a ready assumption for her, for everyone she worked with, everyone she knew, it seemed. Until she had met Ral. And Jean-Claude.

For Ral, no place was home. And yet he had talked about belonging, about having a people. She tried to imagine being with him. She could picture him, see his eyes, his hair, the color of his skin. She could hear his voice, could imagine him walking along the beach or sitting in the café, silent, brooding, his eyes sad even as he smiled at her.

But try as she would, she couldn't picture herself with him. It was as if even the days they had spent talking in Saintes-Maries, or the hours in Les Baumettes, where she had spread her fingers on the wired-glass wall between them—were all only a dream.

And Jean-Claude, who was as sophisticated and elegant as any man she had ever met, was at home in a city that she would have dismissed as impossibly provincial, with its second-rate museum, its pretentions to status and grandeur. She remembered thinking that he must be a second-rate lawyer, too, but he wasn't. There was nothing second-rate about the man. He hadn't chosen Marseilles because he would be a big fish in a small pond there. She remembered him describing how he had left Paris to come back to Marseilles to practice, because it was home.

She wandered through the rooms, her mind a muddle. Three thousand miles away she had a desk full of work, clients waiting, lunch dates she had broken, meetings she would miss, negotiations pending, papers that were due. And here she was, wandering around a museum, killing time until the opening of the next session of the trial of a man she still hardly knew, a gypsy charged with murder. And for reasons she could hardly begin to understand, she knew that this was where she had to be.

The last room on the left was the Salle Daumier, a collection of thirty-six portraits, bronzes and lithographs. That's all I don't need, she thought, more satirical lithographs, like the hallway outside the partners' offices of every law firm in New York. But she wandered in, and somehow seeing the Daumiers in a museum was different: the satire was suddenly pungent and direct. Looking at the portraits made her uncomfortable. She found herself wanting to leave the room, wanting to escape the portraits.

Why? she asked herself. Was it because she saw herself in those statues and lithographs?

There wasn't a single portrait of a woman, not a single effort at satirizing Portia. But the stuffy, self-important, self-absorbed poses of those lawyers that Daumier captured so wickedly struck home. Was that what she had been, the way she had seen the world—looking down a raised nose at anyone who wasn't part of the safe, self-contained elite?

She thought of an argument she'd had with Hirschmann, when he had tried to suggest that the holocaust was more important to her than she let on. And she remembered those painful moments when her grandmother had tried to speak Yiddish, or when her grandfather had tried to tell her about her own past, the history that she had left behind.

When she looked at her watch, it was already past one o'clock. She went outside, looked for a cab, couldn't find one, and began walking. She was walking fast, but hardly running, and she knew that she couldn't even pretend she was hurrying. She was afraid of the courtroom, though not sure why. Was it Ral? What might happen to him? What they might do to the story he had told? She couldn't be sure, but she knew she was afraid.

The courtroom was crowded. It was already past two o'clock, and she found herself at the rear of the visitors' gallery, behind a crowd that filled the entire section from the grille back. The only empty area was the narrow aisle, punctuated by columns, which divided the gypsies from the other court spectators. She tried to work her way to the front of the courtroom, threading between the columns, winding part of the time to the gypsy side and part of the time to the other. Each time she got close to the gypsies, they would recoil, staring at her as they backed away. Across the invisible fence, a woman she recognized from the day before grinned broadly and tried to make room for her—as if to welcome her as a reinforcement to the *gaji* team.

In the reporters' gallery under the *avocat général's* pulpit, the pews were no longer empty. The men and women wore badges, and when she got close she could read the tags. Some were from the French press, from Paris and Lyon as well as the Marseilles papers. There was another reporter from *Der Spiegel* and a man in a slouchy gray suit who she guessed was a stringer for some American magazine or newspaper. Ral's story had been heard, she thought.

In the witness box a man with tinted glasses and thinning straight hair combed over a balding spot was reading from a prepared statement. Jill heard spurts of the medical jargon.

". . . delusions of grandeur and mission, a pattern of obfuscation of the tawdry and sordid reality of his life and deeds . . . not uncommon among the Romany, with their traditions of fakery and dissembly. . . . To the gypsy, faked papers and documents and false insurance claims for alleged medical accidents are accepted as the norm . . ."

An *avocat* on the *prétoire* saw Jill and whispered to Jean-Claude. He turned, saw her, and worked his way back to the grille.

"What happened to you?" he asked.

"It's not worth telling. What's happened here?"

Jean-Claude shook his head. "Terrible! The court was genuinely sympathetic when the session opened. I've rarely seen a president so sincere and interested in the questioning of the accused. Not a trace of hostility. It was remarkable."

Jill listened closely, anticipating.

"Unfortunately the memory that was so precise and convincing yesterday seemed to falter—no, fail!—today. Ral would answer no questions put to him about events since the war. The president warned him over and over that his silence was tantamount to a confession of culpability. It made no difference. Ral answered every question about Saintes-Maries with the same statement. 'I've told you about the murder that matters. I have no more to say.' He repeated that statement ad nauseam, enough to alienate the courtroom and lose every inch of ground that he gained yesterday."

Jean-Claude shook his head, tolling his incomprehension of his client.

"The tragedy of it, Jill, is that I still have nothing to build on. And now we've lost even the threads of sympathy for the accused that I might have been able to weave into a plea for mercy."

Jill listened, but her eyes were on Ral, in his box. He hadn't seen her yet. He was still listening to the droning testimony of the expert psychiatrist.

"Was there any other testimony before this?" she asked.

"The usual. The *commissaire* of police certified that there were no irregularities in the arrest or the detention procedures, that the forty-eight-hour limit on interrogation wasn't violated. His testimony is like a recording, and this time I think even a token protest on procedural grounds would have been foolish. This case is important enough to them that they won't risk it on a technicality. And frankly, I can't imagine that they would have prolonged the interrogation of a man who refused to say anything at all. He's strong-willed, your gypsy. Determined. I think he's willing to accept whatever sentence the court gives him as the price for telling his story."

As Jean-Claude spoke Ral turned and glimpsed Jill, huddled close to the lawyer through the grille. Ral's gaze was long and steady, his eyes almost mournful. He turned back to the witness in the box before Jill could even smile.

"What's left?" she asked Jean-Claude.

He shrugged, a tiny gesture. "The problem is that mounting any kind of a defense at this point means discrediting part of Ral's story. And if we start more than a perfunctory defense, the public minister will play rough. He'll almost certainly try to put you on the stand."

"Why are you so afraid of that?"

"Jill—you identified Ral at the Maison d'Arrêt. You spoke with him in Saintes-Maries."

"The commissioner said that I wouldn't have to testify."

"True. You could refuse. If you do, the public minister will argue that you're hiding something."

Jill stared hard at Jean-Claude. "I don't know what's right anymore," she said. "Do you?"

"I can try to tear up a little of the psychiatric testimony," he said. "But again I'm not sure what purpose would be served. There's no way to make rage or justifiable homicide a sustainable defense argument. And I don't know what else is left. I'm afraid Ral will sabotage any plea for mercy or mitigation of sentence. He seems to want to destroy himself."

The psychiatrist in the witness box put down the report he had been reading. "In conclusion," he droned, "the panel has found no evidence of mental disease or diminished cognizance. In our opinion the accused was sane at the time of the incident in question, and would be culpable under the law."

"Wish me luck," Jean-Claude said through the grille. Then he turned to the court.

"Monsieur le Président!"

"Maître Bernard!"

"May we question the witness directly?"

"Please."

Jean-Claude walked slowly toward the witness box, stopping directly in front of the witness and close to him, as if the conversation were to be solely between them.

"Professor Godechot! Are you familiar with the concept of obsession?"

"Of course."

"Could you define obsession for the court?"

The professor answered curtly, as if he resented the question. "An obsession is a mental compulsion based on a persistent or recurrent idea or concept. In general, it involves an urge toward some form of action. In the case at hand—"

Jean-Claude cut him off with a new question. "Is obsession a pathological condition?"

"It can be. In some instances pathological compulsions can be so severe that the condition can be relieved only by resort to electroshock or insulin therapy. There are occasional instances where it has been necessary to perform prefrontal surgery on the brain. But these are unusual manifestations. In general, the condition responds to psychiatric or drug therapy. In the present instance—"

"Thank you." Jean-Claude smiled as he cut the professor off again. His manner was so charming that only the witness could perceive the manipulation in the questioning.

"Now, Professor Godechot, in your report you indicated some familiarity with the Romany people and their customs. Are you familiar with the idea of vendetta?"

"Of course."

"Could you define vendetta for us?"

"It's a systematized form of revenge, a personalized remedy for a violation of accepted societal laws or mores. Primitive peoples who do not understand the concept of the social contract and the legal system resort to the vendetta as a substitute for true justice."

"In other words," said Jean-Claude, "when the legal system of society fails for certain peoples, they seek a measure of justice themselves?"

"The peoples we are discussing do not understand the legal system of society."

"Perhaps," said Jean-Claude. "But even if it has only failed them by being too obscure, it could be said to have failed, and thus to have driven them to the desperation of seeking their own justice."

The professor's answer was mumbled, a begrudging acquiescence. "You could state it that way."

Jill was fascinated by Jean-Claude's control of the testimony, although she had no idea where the questions were leading. She glanced at Ral and saw him following the testimony with intense, puzzled concentration.

"For what crimes would vendetta be used as a remedy?" asked Jean-Claude.

"Generally murder or rape."

"Could you explain for us exactly how the vendetta works?"

The professor smiled at the chance to expand. "It's quite simple. A man's brother is murdered. He seeks out the murderer to kill him. To the primitive mind, he has evened-up the wrong, as it were."

"But what if he cannot find the murderer? If his efforts to find the man, or woman, are frustrated? Is there an alternative?"

"You have to understand that the concepts underlying the vendetta are very primitive," said the professor. "The interpretation of what constitutes an appropriate remedy is usually quite literal. For example, in the case of a rape, the crime might be revenged with a comparable rape. The primitive mind construes something like 'You raped my daughter. Therefore I will harm you in exact proportion by raping your daughter.' The same revenge could be exacted with a murder as well. Hence, 'You murdered my brother. Therefore I will murder your brother.' And of course in such instances the vendetta goes on and on. But we aren't talking here of—"

"Is there another possibility?" asked Jean-Claude. "Could a vendetta involve abstract justice? I have in mind an instance cited in the testimony of the accused yesterday, when he described the practice of the German army in Yugoslavia of taking hostages—at random—in revenge for the wounding or killing of German soldiers. Could a vendetta involve a similarly abstract notion?"

Brilliant! thought Jill. But she still had no idea where the questioning could lead.

"No," said the professor. "What you suggest would be quite impossible among primitive peoples. It is an understood principle in primitive societies that the vendetta must be limited to accepted parameters: a brother for a brother, a daughter for a daughter, the killer for the killed. An exception, what you call abstract justice, would go beyond the tolerated limits of the society. It would either be punished or would set off a larger vendetta, which could be catastrophic. The concept of limit in the vendetta is necessary, in order for the vendetta to be self-policing."

"I see," said Jean-Claude. "The principle seems very logical. Are the Romany one of the primitive peoples governed by this principle?"

"The Romany are not a people, but many peoples. However, they have been found through research to conform to the principle of the self-limiting vendetta."

"Thank you, Professor. That is most enlightening. Now, I have one final question: Could a vendetta be the root of an obsession such as we discussed earlier? That is, could a vendetta, or the need to fulfill a vendetta, become an obsession to a man?"

Jill sensed that Jean-Claude was closing in, that his interrogation was about to pay off, until she saw the professor's mean smile.

"It could," said the professor, turning his smile to the court. "Anything could become an obsession. But the term *obsession* is simply not relevant here. We have already testified that the accused was sane, culpable, and fully cognizant, that he was in full control of his faculties. He was definitely not the victim of an uncontrollable obsession."

"Are you saying that he did not kill the woman Eva Ritter in a mad rage? That he was not the victim of uncontrollable anger brought on by the obsession to kill her?"

The courtroom began to hum again, that ominous low buzz of whispers that signaled intense interest. Jill stared, shaking her head, wondering why Jean-Claude would give up so easily, turning his whole line of questioning against himself. Was he working against Ral?

The professor straightened up in the witness box, taking in his audience, waiting for the courtroom to quiet before he spoke.

"It's not for me to say whether the accused killed the woman. But if he did, it was most certainly not in what you have called a 'mad rage.' And he was not a victim of uncontrollable anger or obsession."

"Thank you, Professor." Jean-Claude turned to the tribunal. "I have no further questions of the witness.

For a moment there was an ominous silence. The courtroom seemed not to know how to react, or what the testimony had meant. Before the *avocats* on the *prétoire* and the spectators in the galleries renewed their whispers, Ral jumped to his feet to shout out.

"What does the professor know? Has he ever lived with Romany? Does he speak our language? Does he even know of our *kris*, our courts? This justice of your court is not the only justice!"

The president raised his gavel, but before he could bring it down, Ral was already sitting, glaring at the court. The professor was worth no more attention.

And for her part, Jill couldn't sort out the testimony or the incredibly hostile glance that Ral threw at Jean-Claude as the *avocat* walked across the *prétoire* toward Jill. Until that testimony, Jean-Claude had seemed to be on Ral's side, encouraging the court to hear Ral's story, eliciting the story from the tangle of narrative and objections and procedural restraints. Now it seemed that they were on opposite sides of the case.

When Jean-Claude reached her, Ral was staring at them. It suddenly dawned on her that the struggle between those two men would be the real drama of the trial.

All afternoon witnesses paraded before the court.

"Your name and domicile?" the president would ask.

"I'm called Laszlo. I'm a musician; ordinarily I live in Paris."

"Is Laszlo your real name?"

"It's a stage name. My real name is Spadole."

"Have you ever seen the accused?"

"Yes."

"Could you tell us when and where?"

"In Saintes-Maries. I was there for the festival, in May."

"Did the accused tell you what he was doing there?"

"He was looking for someone. A woman. He showed me her picture."

"Is this the photograph he showed you?"

The testimony droned on through the afternoon. After the musician came the café keeper, then an affidavit from the concierge in Amsterdam was read into the record. The language of the affidavit was dry, scoured by the translation. As it was read, Jill remembered talking to the concierge, and the woman's dreamy recollections of Ral.

There were no revelations, no surprises, just tiny blocks that the public minister set one on another, clicking them in place as he slowly built the structure of his case. The portrait of the accused that emerged was of a cool-headed killer carefully and deliberately stalking his prey. By late afternoon the galleries, the *prétoire*, even the president of the court, seemed weary with the meaningless details. It was a ponderously slow second act.

"Has the public minister concluded the presentation of his case?" asked the president.

The *avocat général* turned slowly in his pulpit, until he faced the gallery. For a moment his eyes paused on Jean-Claude, and Jill saw a meanness in his glare that suggested that there was a rivalry, or at least a jealousy, that motivated the presentation of the case.

"We would like to call a further witness to confirm certain details in the *acte d'accusation*," he said. He waited until the eyes of the court followed his to the gallery. "Mademoiselle Jill Ashton!" he said finally.

Jean-Claude stepped forward.

"Monsieur le Président! Mademoiselle Ashton has been working with the defense in the preparation of our brief. We would argue that for her to testify would violate the privileged relationship of client and *avocat*."

The *avocat général* was ready, still smiling.

"Mademoiselle Ashton is not the *avocat* of record," he said. "Indeed, she has admitted that she is not an *avocat* before the bar in this or any other court of the French Republic. Nothing in the canons of ethics would preclude her testifying in this trial. In the instance, the questions to be posed relate only to events which occurred before the initiation of any quasi-professional relationship between Mademoiselle Ashton and the accused."

The president nodded. Then he smiled at Jill, twisting his head into a semblance of a bow.

"Sorry," said Jean-Claude.

"Will Mademoiselle Ashton please step forward to the witness box?" said the president.

A police officer opened the gate for her. As she walked the gauntlet of the *prétoire*, she knew that Ral would be watching her, but she couldn't see him until she passed the accused's box and made her way into the elevated witness box. His eyes admitted nothing. They held the same flat, brooding gaze that from the very beginning had alternately frightened and fascinated her.

"Would the witness state her name and domicile, please?"

The president was gentle and solicitous, complimenting her French, couching his questions in careful, guarded language.

"Could you tell us, please, Mademoiselle Ashton, were you in Saintes-Maries-de-la-Mer in May of this year?"

"I was."

"And when you were there, did you at any time see the accused?"

Jill remembered the dozens of times she had coached witnesses for depositions. Simple answers, she reminded herself. Don't give more than they ask for.

"I did."

"Did you speak with him?"

"We spoke briefly . . . as strangers."

"You had never met the accused before?"

"No. Never."

"Do you usually speak with strange men in an unfamiliar town?"

She pictured that first sight of Ral, imagined for an instant what it would be like to try explain how she had felt, what it had been like when Ral first looked at her. Explain? she thought. She couldn't understand herself what had happened.

"Sometimes." She saw Jean-Claude smile. He knew good testimony when he heard it.

"What did the accused say to you?"

"He offered me a cigarette."

"Is that all?"

"We talked about the festival. He told me a story about Sara."

The president looked puzzled, as if she had strayed from the script.

"Who is Sara?"

Jill remembered the story, and Ral's wry comment that a gypsy girl wouldn't have gone off like that. She glanced at Ral, wondering if he was remembering it at the same moment, but she couldn't catch his eyes.

Whatever he was thinking about, he seemed totally preoccupied, far away.

"There's a statue in the crypt of the church in Saintes-Maries, of a black Sara. It's the object of the pilgrimage for the gypsies. Ral . . . the accused told me a story about it."

"What else did he tell you?"

"Then?"

"Yes, then. In Saintes-Maries."

"We saw each other three times in Saintes-Maries." Jill kept her eyes on the court as she spoke.

"Where were the three meetings?"

"The first was at a café. Then we met outside the church. I had gone inside, with the crowds. It was very crowded and noisy. I was frightened, I ran out, and the accused was there."

"And the third time?"

"I went back the next day, to see the rest of the festival. We met again by chance."

She heard snickers at her answer, more from the *prétoire* than the galleries.

"Did the accused ever tell you why he was in Saintes-Maries?"

"Not really. No."

"Did he tell you he was looking for someone?"

She hesitated, then realized the effect her hesitation would have on the judges. "Yes."

"Did he say if the person he was looking for was a man or a woman?"

She remembered her jealousy of the woman. It all seemed very distant now. "I think he said it was a woman."

"Did he tell you *why* he was looking for her?"

"No. We only spoke for a few moments."

"Did the accused tell you anything else about himself or why he was in Saintes-Maries?"

She thought for a moment. It was hard to believe that she couldn't remember every word they had said. It had been so vivid, so much an obsession. Now the words seemed hazy, a dream more than a reality.

"He told me that he was a gypsy," she said. "We talked about what it was like to be a gypsy."

The president leaned forward. Jill couldn't tell whether he was again interested in Ral, or perhaps for some strange reason intrigued with her testimony.

"What did he say about his experiences as a gypsy?"

"He talked about the life on the road, the caravans, the annual route they followed."

"Did he mention the concentration camps or any other experiences from the war?"

"No."

"Did he mention the name of Wanda Lanzer or Eva Ritter?"

"No."

The president glanced at the *avocat général* and at Jean-Claude. Jill followed his eyes and saw Jean-Claude scribbling notes on a pad.

"The witness is excused," said the president.

As she walked back to the grille, she could feel the eyes of the courtroom following her steps. Except for the gypsies. She could sense them pulling back, turning their eyes away. She was just one more *gaje* to them.

Did Ral think the same? she wondered. His eyes told her nothing. She couldn't understand how it was possible for him to seem so distant and remote.

The *avocat général's* final witness was the medical examiner. He had a trimmed Vandyke beard and a monotone voice. His report was all forensic jargon, which under the boilerplate said little more than she had learned months before at the party. The language was so sterile that Jill hardly listened, until she noticed that Ral was fixed on every word of the testimony, leaning out of his box, not taking his eyes off the medical examiner for a moment.

"Was the victim sexually assaulted?" asked the president of the court.

"There was evidence of molestation. The clothes were disheveled and torn. The breasts were exposed when the body was found. We did not find evidence that a sexual act was completed."

"You mean the woman was *not* raped?"

"Rape may have been attempted and failed."

"From the traumae to the woman's body, could you tell anything about the assailant?"

"The extent of subdermal bruising indicated that she was strangled by someone of considerable strength in the arms and hands. An adult male, I would venture. Beyond that, there is no specific evidence."

As the examiner spoke the *avocat général* stepped down from his pulpit and walked toward an easel that had been set up on the edge of the *prétoire*. He was carrying a large manila folder under his arm. He waited until the medical examiner left the witness box to speak.

"Would it not be appropriate at this time, Monsieur le Président, to introduce the photographs taken of the victim in situ?"

"Here goes," said Jean-Claude. "This is what he's been waiting for."

Jill was puzzled for a moment, until she saw the *avocat général* posing on the *prétoire*, looking exactly like the Daumier statues at the museum.

"Yesterday we heard a sad and terrible tale in this courtroom . . ." The *avocat général* puffed his voice to high rhetoric. ". . . a story of oppression and torture and murder, of deeds so vile that our very souls rebel when we are reminded that these barbarities happened on our own continent, within our own lifetime. The horror of this story has perhaps made us forget that it is not Heinrich Himmler or Josef Mengele who is on trial here.

Nor is the woman Wanda Lanzer on trial. It is her murderer we are here to judge."

"Monsieur le Président!"

The president seemed to welcome Jean-Claude's objection. "Maître Bernard!"

"Unless we have already moved to our pleadings, would it not be appropriate for Monsieur l'Avocat Général to offer his evidence without preface or interpretation?"

The objection was perfectly timed, the arch tone deflating the *avocat général's* presentation and raising chuckles in the *prétoire.*

"The point is well taken," said the president. "Monsieur l'Avocat Général will please take note."

"The evidence will stand without interpretation," said the *avocat général.* He pulled large photographs out of his envelope and propped them up on the easel. His robe concealed them from all but the court.

"It was for this," he said, "that the accused stalked and plotted his way across Europe; for this that he lay in wait on a lonely road. What you see here, I would offer, equals in savagery and heinousness, in sheer vileness, anything that happened in any Nazi concentration camp." He stopped before the president cut him off, then backed away from the easel.

The courtroom let out a collective sigh. Even the staid *avocats* leaned forward to see. The photographs were large, easy to see. Under the garish light of a flashgun they showed a pallid gray body, the limbs askew, a gypsy skirt raised to the waist on one side. There were dark bruises on the neck of the corpse, and the eyes bulged from their sockets. The blouse was torn in front. It appeared that someone had draped the fabric to cover the breasts.

"We have no further evidence to offer," said the *avocat général.*

From behind her, Jill heard coarse whispers, then a shout.

"The guillotine!"

"Death to all the murdering gypsies!" answered another shout.

Across the gallery, she could see the gypsies pulling up into a tight circle. Their voices hummed, the words incomprehensible, the talk so intense it sounded like keening.

Then she turned to the accused's box, where Ral stood, motionless, staring at the photographs. There was no remorse on his face, no emotion at all. He seemed almost curious in the way he gazed at the photographs. Could he be that callous? wondered Jill. After all that had happened, could he be that unmoved? Through the din of the shouts from the gallery, the hum of the gypsies, the cries of the man behind her, through the whispers of the *avocats* on the *prétoire* and the banging of the gavel and the president's repeated calls for order, through it all, she stared at Ral, watching for the slightest expression on that mysterious face, the faintest emotion in those dark eyes.

The president's gavel pounded. "We must have order! The emotional level of this courtroom is not conducive to the administration of justice."

But the photographs had unleashed passions that until that moment had been kept in check. Now *gaji* and gypsy vented their fears in shouted epithets and threats. It was too late to stop them.

"Enough!" said the president. He rapped once more with the gavel. "We will recess until one o'clock tomorrow to hear the evidence presented by the defense. The police will please clear the room."

In the din, no one heard him. No one, it seemed, was interested in the evidence for the defense.

Police moved in to clear the gypsies from the gallery. From the doorway of the courtroom, Jill saw a group of gypsy women break away from the police and run toward the grille in the front of the gallery.

"Maître!" one woman shouted. "Monsieur! If we could speak to you . . ."

The woman's head was covered with a scarf and her body was stooped, like that of a begging crone. The women around her were whispering loudly in Romany.

Jean-Claude was almost out of the courtroom. He looked up, saw Jill behind the gypsy woman, and waved to her. It was too noisy to say anything.

"Maître!" the woman shouted again. She reached through the grille with a crooked hand. "It's very important. We must speak to you . . ."

Jean-Claude turned, but by then the police had come down to the grille. They recoiled from touching the gypsies, but took up positions before the grille, until the gypsy women turned for the door. Jill waited in the doorway, standing aside until the woman who had shouted at Jean-Claude came up to the door.

"Is there something you want to tell the Maître?" she asked the old woman.

The woman looked up at Jill. Her face was heavily wrinkled, the dark skin like worn leather. The other women gathered around her, turning toward Jill, until Jill was surrounded by dusky-skinned faces and brown arms and a swirl of brightly colored scarves. Huddled close to the skirt of one woman was a pretty girl, her eyes bright, her hair braided with gold coins. Her skirt and blouse were young and gay, but the cast of the girl's mouth and the steady gaze of her eyes made Jill wonder if she wasn't much older than the smooth skin and slim, childlike body suggested.

Jill felt hot and flushed. She remembered the church at Saintes-Maries. She tried looking down, at the bare feet on the pavement. She couldn't help noticing the filth that seemed to mar even the delicacy of the little girl's feet.

"I'll see the Maître later," Jill said. "Is there something you want to tell him?"

The old woman stared without answering. For a moment Jill wondered if she understood French, until she remembered that the woman had called out to Jean-Claude in French.

"I could take a message to him for you," said Jill.

The woman still stared, her face inches from Jill's. Then she threw her chin up.

"*You?*" she said. "You're no friend of the gypsy." She turned away sharply, taking the young girl under her arm as she walked through the door.

At the back of the courthouse a van was parked in the midst of the police cars. It was a Black Maria, a vehicle used to transport prisoners to and from the prison. Jill imagined Ral being led to the van, draped in chains, surrounded by police. Then she pictured him in the prison waiting room, the green fluorescent light bleaching his skin, draining the life from his face. She turned away.

What would she say to him? she wondered. If she could be alone with him, if there were no guards, no chains, no screens of wired glass, no hygiaphone. She thought of the beach, with the church behind them looming over the sea like a fortress, and the powerful white horses of the *gardiens* cavorting in the waves, and the trees rustled by the wind. There were no worries in the images she saw, no pressures, no demands. She was free, unfettered. How easy it would be, she told herself, how easy to feel and respond.

But try as she would, she couldn't imagine Ral's words to her. She could picture the luminous eyes and the coppery skin and the gaze that had once raised goosebumps on her skin. But when she tried to imagine him speaking to her, she saw only the old woman at the court, throwing her head back and turning away.

"*You?*" the old woman had said. "You're no friend of the gypsy."

The third day of the trial was Jean-Claude's. The eyes of the court were on him, and he was resplendent in his robes, dominating the *prétoire*. But from where Jill stood, at the edge of the gallery, she could see that his eyes were gray and ringed. His skin was sallow. He had been working all night.

Jill hadn't seen him since the close of the session the day before. She had planned to see him in his study, to discuss the tactics of his defense, but as she walked out of the Palais de Justice and down the boulevards, she found herself daydreaming and wandering. She drifted to the quays overlooking the old harbor. The last of the fishing boats were just coming in, and sailboats and speedboats dotted the water outside. She could hear gay voices from couples walking along the quay, mixed with the patois of the fishermen. Across from her was the Café New York. She had been there with Jean-Claude, eating *coquillages* and bouillabaisse, when he had agreed to take the case. She remembered the dinner, how graceful and easy life seemed for Jean-Claude. And then she thought of Ral, remembering chunks of the testimony he had given.

Behind her, she could see the cathedral, a huge mass of Byzantine stone. Women in bandannas were walking toward the main door, and she followed them until she was close enough to see that some kind of vesper service was going on inside. She thought about going in, but the idea repelled her. What would she do? Kneel in a pew and mumble prayers? Go to a confessional and tell a stranger tales about herself?

She remembered the day that Kennedy was shot, the empty feeling that she thought would be cured in a synagogue. The synagogue too had been Byzantine, a maze of imposing stone. She had walked into the hushed silence without thinking why she had come. A rabbi was in the pulpit, his voice soft and easy, his words expected clichés. She had been embarrassed, wondering what she would say when people the next day asked her the inevitable question: Where were you the night President Kennedy was killed? It was the kind of question and memory that would haunt, something you would always remember. And she would always have to answer that she had gone to a synagogue. She remembered thinking afterward about what she should have done instead, and finding no answer. Going to the synagogue had been instinctive, atavistic. And although the rabbi's words had been tired clichés, she still remembered a feeling of warmth in the stone building, a sense that she was not alone, that the people around her—not one of whom she knew—were somehow her people.

Her people? That was Ral's question: Who are your people? From the moment he asked, it had bothered her that she had no answer. Had those been her people, in that synagogue?

She called Jean-Claude from a pay phone.

"How's it going?" she asked.

"I'm trying to put together what I have," he said. "Some gypsies came to see me and I'm trying to sort out what they said. I've got a man from the Institute for Contemporary History, an expert on the camps, but I'm not sure how to use him. Whatever I do, it's a weak hand."

"I saw the gypsies," said Jill. "They were afraid of me. What did they tell you?"

"I'm still sorting it out, Jill. Still trying to put the pieces together."

"Want some help?" she asked.

He hesitated. "That's a lovely idea, Jill. But I think I have to grapple with this all alone for a while."

"I understand," she said. "I know you'll do what's right."

"Thanks, Jill. And good night."

She went back to the hotel, ate alone, and wondered.

The galleries were as filled on the third day as the day before. Even a day without revelations hadn't driven them away. The reporters were there too, although the prosecution witnesses had produced little real copy beyond the photographs of the dead woman that one Marseilles paper had run in its morning edition.

Ral came in, wearing the same suit, the same shirt buttoned at the neck, and the same ferocious, unyielding glare in his eyes. The sheer force of his anger seemed to prolong the ceremony of removing his manacles, and the rattle of the chains quieted every other sound in the room. As he shook off the last of the chains and held his hands up, Jill found herself fighting off the only question that mattered to the courtroom, refusing to ask herself whether he had killed the woman. It didn't really matter, she tried to tell herself. The question here was bigger.

But it did matter.

"Jean-Claude!" It took three tries to catch his attention.

"I'm glad you're on time today," he said. Up close, his eyes were deep gray. He seemed very tired.

"How's it look?" she asked.

He shook his head. "I don't remember ever working so much against a client. I don't enjoy deciding what's best for another man."

"Conscience?" she said.

The president's gavel rapped. "Will the defense present witnesses?" he asked. From his tone, it was a perfunctory question; he expected no surprises.

"We will," said Jean-Claude.

The *avocat général* leaned forward in his pulpit, as if the proceedings were suddenly of interest.

Jean-Claude's first witness was a short, slim man wearing gray-tinted glasses and a gray gabardine suit. He gave his name as Professor Émile Bloch, of the Institute of Contemporary History in Paris. Jean-Claude got permission to question the witness directly.

"Professor Bloch, what is your field of research?"

"I've studied the holocaust for twenty years. I have written three books and more than fifteen articles on the holocaust and the concentration camps. One of my books has been translated into nine languages."

Jill wasn't sure what to expect from the man.

Ral, too, she could see, didn't know what to expect. He stared at the professor, unblinking. Strangely, it didn't trouble Jill that Ral hadn't even looked at her yet.

Jean-Claude's opening question was a surprise to a courtroom expecting generalities.

"Professor Bloch, how do you determine whether an individual was ever in a specific concentration camp?"

"As an inmate?" asked the professor.

"An inmate or an internee."

The *avocat général* stood up in his pulpit. "Monsieur le Président! Does the court really question whether the accused was in these camps? This testimony seems totally irrelevant, even from the esteemed Maître Bernard."

"We are not suggesting that the accused was not in a camp," answered Jean-Claude. "The direction of our inquiry will become apparent in the following questions."

The president leaned over the edge of the tribunal. Some of the lay judges mimicked his gesture. It was obvious that they were all wondering how the famed Maître Bernard was going to weave a case out of flimsy thread.

"Proceed," said the president.

The professor took in his audience, swiveling in his seat to see the galleries behind him.

"Only scattered records have survived the war," he said. "It's very difficult to document that an individual was ever in a camp. Most of the lists we have are based either on the memories of survivors, or on the lists that the occupying powers made when they liberated camps. But of course those lists cover only a minuscule fraction of the total number of inmates. It is one of the most difficult aspects of our research, one of the reasons that the total number of individuals killed or incarcerated is always given in general terms—six million Jews, for example."

"Would a former inmate carry any identifying mark?"

"Generally, inmates and internees were tattooed on the underside of the left forearm."

"What information would be included in a tattoo?" asked Jean-Claude.

"An identification number and a code letter or letters. For example, a mentally deficient internee would have the letter B for *Blöde*, the German word for idiot."

"What letter would be on the tattoo for a gypsy?"

"The letter Z, for *Zigeuner*."

Jill saw Ral suddenly stiffen, his jaw and forehead tightening. His gaze was unblinking, his eyes fierce. The courtroom was hushed, except for the soft whisper of a gypsy woman translating the testimony into Romany.

"Was this practice followed with all internees?"

"That would depend on the specific camp."

"Was this practice followed at the Auschwitz camp?"

"At Auschwitz-Birkenau the practice was strictly observed, owing to the size of the facility and the number of inmates and internees."

Jean-Claude turned to the president of the court.

"May we ask the accused to expose his left forearm?"

Ral glared at Jean-Claude and the professor.

"Would the accused please remove his jacket and expose his left forearm?" said the president.

Ral looked down at his jacket, then thrust the arm out of his sleeve, holding it up and turning it slowly around. The forearm was powerfully muscled, the skin dark against the sleeve of his white shirt. There was no tattoo. The courtroom buzzed.

The president leaned forward, as if he were straining to see. "Could the accused explain to the court why he has no tattoo?"

Ral turned angrily to the witness box.

"I was there!" he shouted. "Two years I was there. Was the *gajo* professor there? There were others with no tattoos. The doctors had no tattoos."

"But you were not a doctor," said the president. "Why do you have no tattoo?"

Jill caught herself holding her breath in anticipation as Ral glared, silently, every eye in the courtroom on him.

"May we continue with the testimony?" said Jean-Claude. "It is our hope that the testimony of Professor Bloch will shed light on this question."

"Proceed."

"Professor Bloch!" Jean-Claude turned his back to Ral. "Were there exceptions to the tattoo requirement?"

"Yes. In special cases."

"And what could constitute a special case?"

"As the accused noted, many of the inmate-doctors were not tattooed. Some inmates who were employed as household servants or who were used for what we might call intimate purposes also were not tattooed."

"And who would have the authority to waive the tattoo requirement?"

"Higher officials in the camps could waive requirements at any time. The regulations were very precise, but the officials of the camps were only periodically accountable. They could therefore be quite arbitrary about granting or withholding special privileges."

Jean-Claude circled around the witness box, turning so he could see Ral.

"Professor Bloch! Who would have had the authority to issue exemptions from the tattoo requirement for a gypsy?"

"At Auschwitz, you mean?"

"Yes," said Jean-Claude. He smiled at the professor's precision.

"In the gypsy camp at Auschwitz I would think that an exemption would have to come from the office of the SS *Artz*, Dr. Mengele. He had a special interest in the gypsies and was ultimately responsible for the camp."

"And for whom would Dr. Mengele grant exceptions?"

"I believe that many of the physicians who assisted him in his so-called experiments were exempted."

"He would have been the only one in the gypsy camp who could exempt an internee from the tattoo requirement?"

"I know of no one else who had that authority."

Jill saw Ral's fingers tighten on the rail of his own box. There was an ominous pause in the testimony.

Finally Ral burst out. "It wasn't Onkel. He had nothing to do with it. It was her. Eva Ritter. She was the one."

The courtroom gasped, like one person. "The woman?" someone said.

The president raised his gavel. He didn't need to bang it. The room was pin silent.

"May we question the accused directly?" said Jean-Claude.

The *avocat général* leaped. "The *avocat* for the defense wishes to examine his own client during the testimony by witnesses and experts? Is the court ready to permit such a stratagem?"

"Given the direction of what we have heard," said the president, "it would hardly seem a stratagem. Any additional testimony that can sort out the relationship between the accused and the woman Wanda Lanzer/Eva Ritter would be welcome." He nodded to Jean-Claude.

"Ral—" Jean-Claude wasted neither words nor gestures, turning his back on Professor Bloch to face Ral directly. "Why did Eva Ritter exempt you from a tattoo at Auschwitz?"

"Why?" Ral shook his head, as if he could shake the question away. His hands were tight on the railing of the box, his eyes luminous as he stared at the tribunal. "I have no tattoo because she told them to give me no tattoo."

"We know that, Ral. We're asking *why* she exempted you. Why did she grant you this special privilege?"

"Because. . . ." Ral's face tightened in anger. "Because she could do anything she wanted. Whatever she told them to do they did."

"And she told them—the administrators or guards or whomever—to give you no tattoo at Auschwitz?"

"Yes. She told them. She was the one."

"Why, Ral? Why you? Why did she treat you differently? Why did she exempt you?"

"Because. . . ." Ral gripped the railing of his box tightly. His body began to shake. When he answered, it was a shout.

"Because I helped her!"

The only sound in the courtroom was the whispering of a gypsy woman in the middle of the galleries. Jill listened for her own breath.

The whispers and buzzes began slowly, welling up from every corner until the courtroom was a whirl of gossip.

"He what?"

"He helped her?"

"Did he just say . . . ?"

The president rapped his gavel, admonishing the galleries and the *prétoire* to silence with his glare. Ral stood shaking, watching as fingers and voices pointed at him. Jill felt numb, as if what she was watching were somehow unreal.

Jean-Claude waited until the courtroom was totally quiet before he went on. He never took his eyes off Ral for an instant.

"You helped her?" he said. "Do you mean you were her assistant?"

"*Yes!* I curse the day I ever met that woman, but I helped her."

The buzzes and whispers started again from every corner of the room.

Jill tried to stave off her own thoughts, tried to concentrate on the reactions in the courtroom, watching as every group dealt in its own way with the impossible revelation. The gypsies were the last to react, and she could see the reactions rippling out from the old woman who translated the

French testimony into Romany. The president banged with his gavel, but it wasn't until Jean-Claude turned to Ral with another question that the courtroom quieted.

"How did that happen, Ral? How did you become her assistant?" It amazed Jill how Jean-Claude was able to temper his tone, making the sinister question sound innocent.

Ral answered softly. He wasn't shouting, and his hands didn't grip the rail of the box with the tension that had frightened her before. There was a deadly calm to his voice.

"It took a long time," he said. "The day after our train came there, she had me brought to her office. It was a little room, with only one window, right at the edge of the gypsy camp. It was in a barracks, one of the huts that they made into a hospital. When they came to get me to go there, I didn't want to go. I didn't want anything to do with her. But in that camp, when guards came for you there was no choice. Two SS guards came, and when I went into her little office she told them to wait outside. She said she remembered me from Lackenbach, that she remembered that I could read and write. She said that I could help her, become her assistant."

"And you agreed?"

"No! I told her that I would never help her, that I cursed the day I ever met her. I told her that I hated her."

Ral was shouting, but the president of the court let it pass. Jean-Claude held up his palm, and Ral read the signal.

"She called me to her office every day. And when they made the work assignments, like to Canada, where they sorted things, I didn't have to work. When the others went off to work, I would be left alone. And then I would have to go to her office and she would tell me that if I would help her, she would be able to help all of the gypsies. And every day I just sat there. I wouldn't even talk to her. The first day I shouted at her. After that I wouldn't even talk to her.

"Then one day she told me that she had saved me. That I was a fool if I didn't understand that. And that if I would only help her, she would help all the gypsies, save all of them. It made me so angry when she said that that I told her about Elena, my wife, how they had shamed her in front of me and everyone. When I told her that, she cried. She said that she didn't know that the girl was really my wife, that there was nothing she could do, that there were regulations. She said that she hated them, hated the SS and the regulations. That all she wanted was to help the gypsies, to protect them. She said it had been hard even to get the Austrian and German gypsies out of Yugoslavia, because of the Ustashi and the regulations.

"She had a sofa in that little office, and whenever she had me come, she would have me sit next to her, and she would play records of gypsy music. She would touch me, my cheeks, my arms, my hands, my hair. She would talk of the gypsy temperament—that was the word she used—temperament. She said that deep inside her own soul she was a gypsy too. She told me to call her Loli Tschai. And she said that together we could save the gypsies."

"Did you believe her? Is that why you became her assistant?"

"Of course I didn't believe her. How could I believe a *gaje* who had done what she did to my wife?"

"But you did become her assistant, Ral. Why?"

The *avocat général* rapped gently on the railing of his pulpit, attracting the attention of the president.

"Monsieur le Président! Must we continue this tedious testimony? Is there reason to suppose that anything the accused might say will illuminate the murky questions before the court?"

The president didn't even turn to the *avocat général* to answer. It was clear that he, like everyone else in the courtroom, wanted to hear Ral's story.

"The accused will please answer the question."

But Ral had no answer. He stared at Jean-Claude and said nothing.

"Was it because she brought your sister and mother to the camp, Ral? Is that why you became her assistant?"

"No."

"But she did bring them, didn't she?"

"Yes. She found that they were in the Ravensbruck camp, and she had them brought to Auschwitz so we could be together. But that was later."

"Was it because she got you extra food and privileges? Because she made sure that you didn't get the work assignments?"

"No. I wanted to have work assignments. I wanted to have the same assignments as everyone else."

"Ral—"

Jean-Claude hesitated, and Jill felt herself trembling in anticipation. There was a subtle change in Jean-Claude's style, perceptible only if you were used to watching a skilled lawyer in the courtroom. He was moving to the offensive, ready to elicit the testimony he wanted and that he alone in the courtroom seemed to expect. And he was going to get it by whatever means he needed.

"Ral—this is a difficult question, perhaps, but the court needs your answer: Were you her lover?"

Ral stared at Jean-Claude before he answered: "Lover? You think that I would do that for a *gaje?* You think I would be a whoreman to get a special privilege? You understand nothing."

"You're right, Ral. I understand nothing of what you have told me. I don't understand how you could have become her assistant." This time the word *assistant* sounded sinister.

Ral hesitated, taking in the eyes all around him before he answered in a flat, dull voice.

"It wasn't like other camps there. When you came there, you stopped being a person. They told us we were special, that we weren't like the other inmates. But we were like bears on a chain. If they told us to dance, we would dance. If they thought it would be funny, they would beat a gypsy. If a guard wanted a gypsy woman, he would take her. What could she do? What could anyone do?"

Jill couldn't watch Ral testify. She could only listen, hearing the words in a haze of horror. Part of her wanted to reach out to Jean-Claude and beg him to stop the testimony. And another part of her wanted to hear it all, wanted to know exactly what happened, exactly what made this man. It mattered desperately. She didn't know why.

". . . That camp was the most terrible place there ever was. Everything was gray. The sky was gray, the mud was gray, our clothes were gray, the food was gray. Our skin and our hair was gray. It was a gray world. There was no life there. But in her office it was different. In her office there would be music, and she would talk softly, and there were shelves with books. She would talk about the different clans and families, about the lives of the gypsies. She knew more about the gypsies than any gypsy did. She had read all of those books, hundreds of books. She had pictures of cities and paintings and statues, statues I had seen in museums. And outside that room it was only gray."

Ral looked down, at his feet, then up, at the court. "How can you know what that was like? No one can know what that was like."

Jean-Claude was following every word Ral said. Jill thought she could see him smiling as he listened, which seemed an odd response. But then she tried to understand her own response, and couldn't.

"What did you do when you helped her?" asked Jean-Claude.

"What? She would interview the gypsies, ask who their mothers and fathers and aunts and uncles were, and sometimes their grandfathers and grandmothers. She wanted to know where they came from, the names of clans and *kumpania* and families. What did they do before the war? Where did they wander? If they took a tour each year, where did they go? She would ask about their clothes and the tools that the men used, even the music that they played. Before long, she knew them all, every family and clan. She knew who was Kalderash and who was Sinte. She knew every clan. Most gypsies didn't know their own families as well as she did."

"And what did you do, Ral? What did you do when you were helping her?"

"I watched. And listened. She gave me books about the gypsies to read."

"And?"

"And what?" said Ral.

"Ral, what did you do after that, after you had watched and listened, after you had read the books she gave you?"

"I . . . I asked questions. She spoke a little Romany, but she couldn't understand the gypsies very well, so I would ask questions for her. I would ask questions in Romany and explain the answers to her."

"What kind of questions did you ask?"

"The same as she asked. 'Who is your mother? Who is your father? Where do you come from? What do you do?' Questions like that. I helped her ask those questions. I didn't know then. I didn't know why she asked those questions."

Jill watched the courtroom hang on Ral's testimony. Every answer from Ral seemed to raise an obvious question. And yet Jean-Claude didn't seem eager to plunge to the heart of that question.

"What did she do with the answers to those questions, Ral?"

"She made charts. And tables. There were little boxes, with lines between them. It was like a tree, with arrows pointing up and down. Sometimes the arrows would point both ways, when there were marriages between clans."

"Did you help her with the charts?"

Ral looked up at the gypsies in the galleries before he answered.

"I thought I was helping the gypsies. She taught me how to make the charts and tables, showed me how to write out the names and when to make boxes and arrows. She explained about the clans and the relationships. I thought I was helping the gypsies. I trusted her. We all trusted her."

"Ral!" Jean-Claude had to wait for Ral to turn from the galleries back to him. "Ral—what did she do with those charts and tables?"

Ral's eyes flared, glowing like white-hot metal as he stared at Jean-Claude. The testimony was now a private, wrenching moment between the two men.

"What did she do?" Ral's voice modulated from a shout to a whisper. "I didn't know then. I didn't know until it was all over."

"Until what was all over, Ral?"

Ral looked up at Jean-Claude. His eyes were ineffably sad. "I didn't know."

Jean-Claude turned to the president. A silent message passed between the men, an understanding.

Then, after a moment, Jean-Claude asked again. "What did she do with the charts that you helped her make?"

"That was how she decided," said Ral, his voice flat and emotionless. "That was how she decided which gypsies would go on the train and which would stay in the camp to die."

"Ral—" Jean-Claude waited for total silence in the courtroom. "Before, you told us how you and some of the other men were selected for the train that left Auschwitz. Who were the other men?"

"They were Sinte, German gypsies. Musicians and performers. The Germans liked gypsy music. They liked the dancing. So they decided that the Sinte were true Germans, that they could be part of the New Germany. They would be musicians and performers for the circus."

"Were you a musician?"

"No."

"A performer?"

"No."

"What clan are you from, Ral? Are your people Sinte?"

"No. We're Lovari. We're horse traders. My father bred horses, and his father, and his father's father. Lovari are born on horses." The sentence came out a mechanical phrase.

"Were any other Lovari chosen for the train, Ral?"

Ral looked up, as though he would answer, then stopped. He closed his eyes and his head began to sway. He looked around the courtroom, this time avoiding the galleries.

"The others were all Sinte," he said. "They had been chosen from the charts and told to go on the train. Then she called me to her office. She made the guards wait outside, and she had me sit on the sofa. There was gypsy music playing on her Victrola, a czardas. She took my hands in hers, she touched my cheeks and my hair. She told me I should always help the gypsies, that we had a duty to help them. Then she . . ."

Jean-Claude waited, then prodded gently. "She . . . ?"

"She kissed me. And walked with me to the train. It wasn't until that night that I understood what she had done. I trusted her. We all trusted her. And she betrayed us."

"What had she done?" Jean-Claude asked.

"She . . ." Ral's voice, still the flat, emotionless monotone, broke as he spoke. "She chose who would live and who would die. We trusted her, we called her a gypsy name, talked to her as if she were Romany. When she walked through the camp, women and children would touch her skirt. They would make presents for her. And then she chose them to die. She saved my mother and sister. And then she chose them to die."

"And you blame her for that?"

"Yes, I blame her. She's the one who decided."

"Ral, what about those in the camp who abused and killed gypsies, people like Mengele, or the doctors who did experiments, or the guards and *kapos*. Don't they deserve the blame?"

"We knew they were bad. But she was different. We trusted her. We loved her. And then she betrayed us. For that, she deserved to die."

"Thank you," said Jean-Claude.

In the hubbub of comments and exclamations that reverberated through the courtroom, Jill saw the *avocat général* grinning. That grin, as much as any analysis she could muster from her exhausted and confused mind, was enough to tell her that Ral's testimony had hardly been a triumph for the defense.

What was Jean-Claude doing? she asked herself. Would it have been better if he had done nothing at all? She wondered if the incriminating testimony was her fault. Was it all because *she* wanted to hear Ral's story?

She tried to get Jean-Claude's attention, but she was too late. He announced that he had another witness to call.

"You have no other witness scheduled," said the president.

"We ask the indulgence of the court," said Jean-Claude. "As a result of the testimony given here yesterday, a witness has come forward to offer new evidence."

"A witness has come forward. . . ?" The president sounded incredulous.

Jean-Claude was ready: "Yesterday evening, after the session closed, a witness came to us, offering new testimony relating to the events at hand. If we are to seek the truth, we have no choice but to hear the testimony."

"Monsieur le Président!"

The *avocat général* stood with a deliberate, bored expression, blowing out through unpursed lips. It was a peculiarly French gesture, fraught with deep sarcasm. "But of course . . ." he seemed to be saying. "What else can one expect?"

"Is it really in the interest of the court to dwell on these events of twenty-five years ago which have nothing to do with the case at hand?" he asked.

"The witness will offer evidence on the events of last May in Saintes-Maries-de-la-Mer," said Jean-Claude.

"A surprise witness?" the *avocat général* cocked his head in disbelief, then turned his eyes to Jill. "We would have thought better of our distinguished colleague. Perhaps there has been too much American influence in our proceedings. Is our trial to be like one of those American television serials in which a convenient witness suddenly appears at the telling moment, thereby reversing months of careful investigation and research? Is this to be our way of justice?"

"Monsieur le Président!" Jean-Claude's voice was like a bell, drawing the attention of the entire courtroom. "It is not our intention to fault the prosecution brief or to surprise the court. But would it be wise to reject a witness to the events in question solely because the testimony has not been offered until this late hour?"

"There were no witnesses to what happened in Saintes-Maries," said the *avocat général*. "The only witness was the accused. The investigation was thorough and exhaustive. No objection has been filed on procedural grounds. Can it conceivably be in the interest of the court to permit these theatrics?"

The president finally waved both lawyers silent. He looked to his colleagues, turning to his left and then his right before he spoke.

"We agree with the public minister," he said. "Surprise tactics and stratagems do not belong in our system of justice. This is the High Court of Assizes, a tribunal of the French Republic! What would happen, we ask, if the public minister were allowed at the last moment to introduce evidence which was not included in the prosecution brief? Would the *avocat* for the defense be willing to allow such surprises to the public minister? Of course not! And can we then allow to the defense what we would deny the prosecution?"

He paused, turning to Jean-Claude. The courtroom followed his eyes.

"However," the president went on, "the court respects Maître Bernard's distinguished career before the bar and as an officer of this court. Indeed, it is only our respect for the Maître and our trust that he will abide strictly by his oath to the court that prompts us to allow the testimony of the witness."

"The surprise witness will testify?" said the *avocat général*. "It is most unusual."

"This trial is most unusual," answered the president.

"Jean-Claude!" Jill's whisper was loud enough to attract attention in the *prétoire* and the gallery.

He turned, long enough to look at her with a strange half-smile before he went to the tribunal to talk with the president. Then, as Jean-Claude came back, a police officer walked through the *prétoire* to a gate in the grille, and into the gypsy side of the gallery.

"A gypsy?" Jill heard someone say from behind her.

"He's mad," said an *avocat* on the *prétoire*. "The Maître can't believe that the court will accept the testimony of a gypsy witness."

Gypsies surrounded the police officer, shouting among themselves in Romany. When he finally emerged from the gallery, he was escorting a young girl, her thick black hair braided with gold coins.

Jill recognized her immediately. She seemed tinier and younger than she had the day before as she walked across the courtroom, through the ranks of *avocats*. She accepted a helping hand as she climbed up into the witness chair.

Once in the chair, she turned to the president of the court with a broad smile and sparkling eyes. He smiled back.

"We will question the witness," he said to the court. His tone was grandfatherly. "Could you tell us your name?"

"Kevja," she answered in a tiny voice.

"You'll have to speak a little louder, Kevja. This is a big room. Now, what is your whole name?"

"Kevja Sintelle."

"And how old are you, Kevja?"

"Eleven."

"Can you tell us where you live?"

"We're Romany people. We travel, from Spain to Italy. Right now we live in the Camargue. And sometimes here, in Marseilles."

"You have no permanent address, no place where you can get mail and go to school?"

"We get mail. It comes to the post office. When I go to ask, I ask for *poste restante*. I go to school in the winter, when we're camped."

The president grinned again. "I can see that you must go to school, Kevja. You speak French very well."

"Thank you." Her smile melted the president into a grin. Jill glanced around: from the smiles on all sides, it appeared that the little girl had charmed most of the courtroom.

"Now, Kevja, there is something you must understand. Here, in the courtroom, you must tell the truth to every question you are asked. If you don't know the answer to a question, that's all right. Just tell us you don't know. Do you understand?"

"Yes. I understand."

"Monsieur le Président!"

It was Jean-Claude. He walked up to the tribunal to confer with the president, then came back to the front of the witness box.

"Maître Bernard will examine the witness directly," said the president. From his tone, it was clear that he would not welcome a challenge to his ruling.

Jean-Claude's smile to the girl was very gentle.

"Kevja, could you tell us please, were you here, in this courtroom, yesterday?"

"Yes."

"Where in the courtroom were you?"

"Over there, behind the fences. With the people."

"And did you see the photographs that were on the easel yesterday?"

She made a face of disgust. "Yes."

"Do you remember those photographs?"

"Yes. They were horrible."

"Did you recognize the woman in the photographs?"

"Yes."

"Had you seen her before?"

"Yes."

"Where did you see her?"

"I saw that lady near Saintes-Maries. On the road that led out to the campsites. It was during the festival."

"Are you sure that it was the same woman?"

"Yes, I'm sure. Not many gaji ever come out on the road. They all stay in the town to watch the procession and the horses. I remembered her from the road."

Jean-Claude smiled, very reassuringly. "What was she doing on the road?"

"She was taking pictures. And writing in a little book."

"What was she taking pictures of?"

Kevja smiled. "Me, I think."

There was a titter from the audience, and she waited for the courtroom to quiet before she went on.

"I was gathering reeds, for baskets. I had my skirts—" She stopped, looked up toward the gallery. "My skirts were tied up so I could walk in the water. And that woman was taking my picture. I remember because I ran into the bushes to hide. I was ashamed. You see, now that I'm a woman I know it's not right to have my skirts up."

The laughter in the courtroom ranged from polite chuckles to belly laughs. Ral stared at the girl, without even a hint of a smile.

"Was anyone with the woman?" asked Jean-Claude.

"Not just then. A man came later."

"Do you remember the man?"

"Yes."

"Was he on foot, walking?"

"No, in a car. A truck, really. An old black 2cv."

"Could you identify the man if you saw him again?"

"Identify? You mean would I know him?"

"Yes, that's what *identify* means. But you must be sure."

"I'd be sure."

"Is he in this room now, Kevja? Please be very careful before you answer."

The girl sat up, propping her arms on the railing of the witness box as she looked around the room. Her concentration was exaggerated as she paused on one man or another before moving on. She stared at Ral for a long time, then turned to the grille that separated the galleries. People behind Jill started to move away.

Finally the girl pointed. "Over there," she said. "The man is over there. The fat man with almost no hair."

Behind Jill, people were scuffling, getting out of the way. Across the gallery, gypsies were pointing and shouting.

"What do you want with me?" a man shouted. "You trust the word of a gypsy over that of a Frenchman? The child is lying. I never had anything to do with the woman, with any of that lying filth."

Jill looked closely at the man. He seemed familiar, someone she had seen on the street perhaps. He was fat, with a comical mustache, and a shiny, ill-fitting suit. In his hands he clutched a beret. She pictured the beret on his round head. Then she remembered: The first day she drove through the Camargue, when the gypsy children surrounded her car—he was the man who showed up and frightened the children away.

"Are you sure that's the man you saw?" Jean-Claude asked.

"Yes. That's the man." She pointed, and her thin arm with a filigree gold bracelet on the wrist singled out the fat man with the silly mustache and the beret.

"You believe that little animal?" shouted the man. "She's lying. They all lie and cheat. It's all they know."

"You will please remain silent in this courtroom unless questions are addressed to you," said the president of the court. Then he turned to Kevja. "Are you quite sure that is the man you saw on the road with the woman?"

"Yes."

The president turned back to the gallery, to the man with the mustache. "What is your name, please?"

"Who?" said the man.

"You. What is your name?"

The man squirmed, aware that the eyes of the courtroom were on him. "Borel," he said. "Louis Borel."

"You may continue," the president said to Jean-Claude.

"Kevja," said Jean-Claude, "had you ever seen that man before you saw him on the road that day?"

"Yes. Many times."

"Where did you see him?"

"He lives near here. He comes to our camps. He follows the women around and says dirty things to them."

The *avocat général* stood.

"Monsieur le Président! This testimony is quite outrageous. That man in the gallery is not on trial here. He is a bystander to our proceedings. It is highly inappropriate that he be slandered in this room by a so-called witness, whose credentials can hardly be verified."

The president turned to Jean-Claude. "Maître Bernard will please take care that the testimony elicited from the witness does not exceed the bounds of propriety." It was a perfunctory reprimand. Jean-Claude still had the court.

Jill glanced over at Ral. He seemed very alone.

"Kevja—" Jean-Claude stood in front of the girl again, his smile warm and comforting. "Tell us what happened after the man drove up."

"Well—" The girl looked up at the gallery, as if for a cue, before she went on. "First he drove along, right behind her, behind the woman in the photographs. He talked to her through the window, shouting things to her. I think maybe he thought she was a gypsy, because she wore a skirt like a gypsy woman and a *diclo* in her hair. But of course she wasn't a gypsy. What gypsy would be taking pictures like that?

"She started to walk faster, and he drove right along with her. Then she turned and walked back the other way, and he turned the truck around and followed her, shouting to her. Then he stopped the truck and got out and ran after her. He caught up to her and put his hand out to her, but she pushed him away. Then she was shouting too, and he pulled her to the side of the road, the other side of the road, in the reeds. I heard the woman yell, and then she yelled again. And then I didn't hear anything else. I waited a long time, hiding in the trees, until the man drove away in his truck. Then I ran home."

"You didn't go over to see what happened to the woman?"

"No. I was afraid."

"Kevja—did you see that man over there, in the box, on the road that night?" Jean-Claude pointed to Ral.

The girl looked at Ral. The expression on his face was strange, contemptuous.

"No," she said. "Not on the road. I saw him in the village, at the festival. He asked questions of everyone. But no one knew him."

"Kevja—has anyone ever asked you questions about the woman?"

"You mean like a *gajo* policeman?"

"Yes. Did a policeman or anyone else ever ask you if you had seen the woman?"

"No. Why would they ask me? I'm only a gypsy girl. The police don't ask us when they want to know something."

"Did you tell anyone else about what you had seen?"

"No."

"Why not?"

The girl's shrug was worldly-wise, a surprisingly mature gesture for such a little girl. "What happens between *gaji* is none of my business," she said. "It was the time of the festival. There was much to do."

"You didn't know the police were looking for information about the murder of the woman?"

The girl shrugged again. "The police are always looking for information. We know our place. We know to stay out of *gajo* business."

Jean-Claude grinned. "And why did you come now? Why did you come yesterday to find me and tell me what you had seen?"

"Because of the photographs. I saw them and I remembered the woman. And when I told my mother, she said I should tell you."

"One last question, Kevja. Why have you been coming here, to the trial, every day?"

The girl looked up to the gallery again before answering. "My mother brings me every day. She says that I should hear what the gypsy man is saying."

"Thank you, Kevja."

Jill watched Ral, expecting to see in his eyes the same relief, the same lifting of dread anxiety that she felt. But Ral just stared at the girl, neither hostile nor sympathetic, as though what she had said had nothing at all to do with him. Maybe he doesn't understand, she thought. Maybe he doesn't realize that Jean-Claude just saved his life. She tried to catch Jean-Claude's attention as he turned away from the girl.

"Does the public minister have questions for the witness?" asked the president.

"Not at this time," came the quick response from the pulpit. "We'll not waste the time of the court with questions for the alleged witness."

Jean-Claude turned to look up at the *avocat général,* apparently surprised by the answer. Then he came up to the grille while the girl was escorted back to the gallery. Jill reached out for his arm.

"That was fantastic," she said. "How did you . . . ?"

"Was it?" he asked.

"What do you mean, Jean-Claude? That girl's testimony clears Ral."

"If they believe her. She's a gypsy."

"So? Ral's a gypsy too," said Jill. "You believe her, don't you?"

"I don't know what to believe anymore. I just know that unless Ral denies killing the woman, that girl's testimony won't mean a thing. It's up to him. He has to decide whether the future matters more to him than the past."

Jill looked hard at Jean-Claude. "You really care," she said. "It matters to you. You're not just here from some sense of obligation. Why is it so important?"

He grinned. His teeth were white and even. "We all like to win."

"Will the *avocat* for the defense be presenting additional evidence?" asked the president.

Jean-Claude nodded. "We would like to call Monsieur Borel, the man identified by the last witness."

The *avocat général* objected. "If we were to require testimony from every man named by a gypsy girl who so opportunely came forward, we would delay the deliberations of this court for weeks. Are we to remain prey to such distractions?"

Jean-Claude answered without hesitation, as if he were ready for the objection. "The credibility of the last witness has not been impeached. According to her testimony, Monsieur Borel was on that road in Saintes-Maries in the presence of the murdered woman, on the night of the murder. Perhaps he can shed some light on exactly what happened there."

"Gypsy lover!" someone shouted from behind Jill.

She turned, thinking for a moment that the epithet was intended for her. It was a man in the gallery behind her, and when he had the attention of the courtroom, he shouted, "Gypsy lovers! Apologists! Let them steal your stock and filth your land and chase your women!"

The president rapped for order. "Monsieur Borel will please come forward to the witness box."

A police guard met him at the gate in the grille. Jill caught his glance, but it wasn't clear if he too remembered that chance meeting on the Camargue.

"Your name, please?" asked the president.

"You know my name. Why do you ask again? I've done nothing." Borel's voice was gruff, more accustomed to shouting than speaking.

"We must ask each witness to identify himself for the records."

"Witness? I didn't witness anything."

"Monsieur! You are being very difficult. Please give your name."

"Borel. Louis Borel."

"Where do you live, Monsieur Borel?"

"I live in Albaron, in the Camargue. I pay my taxes and go to church and farm my land. Not like that trash with no addresses that wander around causing trouble."

"Monsieur Borel! Would you please answer the questions put to you without adding comments? Tell us, please, were you here in the courtroom yesterday?"

"Yes."

"Did you see the photographs that were displayed on the easel over there?"

"Yes."

"Had you ever seen that woman before?"

"No."

"Are you sure?"

"Of course I'm sure. You don't have to ask me twice."

A gypsy woman called out from the gallery, "Pig! Tell them what you say to the women! Tell them the dirty things you've done!"

The president gaveled. "Silence in the courtroom! If there is a single further outburst I shall have the courtroom cleared."

Then he turned back to Borel. "Have you ever visited the gypsy encampments in the Camargue?"

"Visit? Of course not."

"But you know of these encampments?"

"A decent person can't avoid them."

"Monsieur Borel—have you ever seen the girl who testified in that box earlier today?"

"The girl? How do I know? They all look the same to me."

"Pig!" shouted a gypsy from the gallery.

The president banged once, loudly. "Silence in the gallery. This is the High Court of Assizes!"

Then, to Borel, he said, "Have you ever seen the accused before?"

Borel glanced at Ral, who was staring at him.

"How do I know? He looks like the rest of them to me. I never pay attention. How do I know if I've seen one or not?"

The president looked up at Jean-Claude. His shrug was almost an apology.

"May we question the witness directly?" asked Jean-Claude.

The *avocat général* leaned forward. When the eyes of the president came up to his, he apparently changed his mind.

"Proceed," the president said to Jean-Claude.

Jean-Claude stood in front of Borel, turning his back on the gypsies in the gallery, as if to demonstrate where his own sympathies lay.

"Monsieur Borel—you said before that it's impossible to avoid the gypsy camps. Why is that?"

Borel shrugged, twisting his beret in his fingers. "They're by the road. All over. You drive by, you see them."

"Which camp are you speaking of?"

"I don't know the name. They're all the same to me."

"Where is the camp that you see?"

"On the road to Saintes-Maries. They're all over that road with their filthy trash and their naked kids. Like dogs, they are. You see them all the time."

"Where did you say that you live, Monsieur Borel?"

"Albaron."

"Albaron," repeated Jean-Claude. "That's between Arles and Aigues-Mortes, isn't it?"

"Yes."

"Why do you go to Saintes-Maries, Monsieur Borel?"

Borel squirmed in his chair, looking up at the tribunal, then back at the gallery. "I don't remember why I drove there. Maybe I was just out for a drive. Is there a law now that a man can't go out for a drive?"

"Do you go to Saintes-Maries to sell crops or stock?"

"No. There's no market in Saintes-Maries."

"Do you buy feed or fertilizer?"

"No."

"Do you hunt in the zoological park?"

Borel forced a laugh. "Of course not. I told you before. I was just out for a drive."

"And that's the road you pick when you're 'just out for a drive,' even during the gypsy festival in May?"

"What do I know about their festival? There's no law against taking a ride, is there?"

"No, Monsieur Borel, there isn't. When you go for those drives to Saintes-Maries, what kind of car do you drive?"

Borel squirmed again and mopped his head with the beret. "It's like all the cars down in the Camargue—old and beat up."

"What model is it?"

"Like almost every car around here, a 2cv."

"What color is your car?"

"What color? The same as all of them. Black."

"And the style?"

"Style?" repeated Borel.

"Is it a sedan?"

"No."

"Well, what style is it?"

"I told you, it's like all the cars down here. It's a kind of small truck."

"Thank you," said Jean-Claude. "We've finished with the witness."

"Lying pig! Filthy liar!"

The president answered the shouts from the gallery with his gavel.

"Does Monsieur l'Avocat Général wish to question the witness?" he asked.

"We have no questions for this witness."

"Does the *avocat* for the defense wish to call any further witnesses?"

"We do not," said Jean-Claude.

Jill sighed, looking forward to a recess for the day and a chance to think. She waited for Jean-Claude's eyes to catch her own.

"In that case," began the president, "the court—"

"Monsieur le Président!" the *avocat général* caught the president in midsentence, wrecking the opening of his speech.

"With the permission of the court, we would like to recall the gypsy girl to the stand for questions."

"You have no objections?" the president said to Jean-Claude.

"Of course not."

But Jill could see from Jean-Claude's face that he was worried.

The girl smiled broadly as she was escorted back to the witness box. She seemed to enjoy her moments on the stage.

"Kevja, can you read and write?" asked the *avocat général*. He was smiling.

"A little."

"Do you go to church?"

"For the festival, yes."

"Do you understand what it means when someone says that you must tell the truth?"

"It means to tell what really is," she said.

"Excellent."

The girl grinned, pleased with herself.

The *avocat général* blew out from unpursed lips again. The gesture seemed ominous to Jill.

"Kevja, you said before that you only go to school in the winter. Is that right?"

"Yes. In the spring and summer we're traveling, on the road."

"Do you have a school-leaving certificate?"

"Of course."

"May we see it?"

"My mother has it," said the girl. She pointed to the gallery.

"Your mother is here?"

The paper was passed forward and brought first to the president, then to the *avocat général*. While he read through the document, the courtroom buzzed with whispers.

"Is this your certificate?" he asked the girl.

She glanced very quickly. "Yes. That's mine."

"How old did you tell the court you were?"

"Eleven."

"In what year were you born?"

"1955."

"Can you tell the court why on your school-leaving certificate your birth year is given as 1951, which would make you fifteen years old?"

The girl looked straight at the *avocat général,* not embarrassed, apparently not even aware of any contradiction.

"Because," she answered, "I wouldn't get a school-leaving certificate if I was only eleven. So my mother went with me and we told them that I was fifteen. Otherwise I would have to go to school all the time and I wouldn't be able to help my mother with baskets." She shrugged. It was all quite obvious to her.

"Thank you," said the *avocat général.*

The girl seemed relieved to be off the stand. Jill watched her walk back to the gallery and the safety of the clustered gypsies. None of them, it seemed, saw the contradiction.

Jill fought the thought: Maybe they *all* lie when they need to. For the first time, she avoided Ral's eyes.

"We will recess until tomorrow for the pleadings," said the president of the court.

Jill watched the faces in the courtroom as the president gaveled the session to a close. The mood had changed. Even the gypsies had lost their ebullience. The day before, they had been laughing as they left, telling stories, enjoying their defiance of the police who tried to herd them through the doors. Now they were somber and quiet, avoiding the glances of the hostile *gaji* in the galleries.

Among the *avocats* on the *prétoire,* too, the mood was different. The discussions a day before had been betting propositions, speculations about what Maître Bernard would do with his impossible case. Now the betting had shifted to the court. What would they do? It was clear that the president liked Jean-Claude. It was also clear that Jean-Claude's case would be tenuous at best, a filament of speculation and conjecture and possibility. How would he convince the court that there was enough doubt to drop the charges—especially when his client gave no hint of cooperation, of even being willing to deny the crime? One *avocat* put it succinctly: "Jean-Claude might convince the court, but he'll never convince the gypsy!"

Jill listened to the voices, watching Jean-Claude talk with the president at the tribunal, watching the guards go through their now-practiced ritual with Ral, while Ral stared in defiance at the crowds who trooped out. She had a sudden thought that no matter what happened in the trial, no matter what Jean-Claude and the *avocat général* said in their final pleadings, Ral would lose. *Lose.* The word stuck in her mind. How often had she gone into a trial or a negotiation, or even a relationship, determined to win no matter what the cost. She had seen herself as a winner. Losing was impossible, unacceptable.

But Ral wanted to lose. He wanted to tell that story so much that he was willing to be condemned. The story of what happened to those gypsies, that forgotten or maybe unknown episode of history—twenty-five years ago—was more important than his own life.

Twenty-five years ago? She was eight, not even as old as Kevja. She was living with her grandparents because her father was off in the army. She remembered the old war stories he used to tell, usually with her uncles, and how they had been ridiculed away with the same persistence as the stories that her grandparents had told. Everything that belonged to the past had been ridiculed away, cut off. For the Ashtons there was no past. They were people without a history.

There was one tiny window in Ral's detention cell, a rectangle set just under the ceiling in the west wall. It was so high that no one had ever bothered to clear away the cobwebs and grime. On the outside there was a heavy wire screen which, together with the grime, made the window so opaque that the light was too diffuse to make shadows. He had watched the window every afternoon since the trial began, waiting until the sun was low enough to shine through. Then he would stand on the bed and hold his hands up in the orange beams of light, trying to make shadows on the wall. All week the weather had been clear, with few clouds. But inside the cell the light was still too diffuse to make shadows. And without sharp, clear shadows, he didn't trust the light.

The trial was that way, he thought. He remembered when he had read the newspapers after the trial of that German Eichmann, how the reporters had written down every word the man said, how the witnesses had told every detail of what happened to the Jews in the camps. He hadn't seen the newspapers yet for his trial, but there were only two reporters there the first day, and they hadn't been writing notes. Nothing he had said mattered to them. Gypsies weren't Jews. No one would ever believe a gypsy.

There had been moments, like the first day of the trial, when it seemed that maybe the Maître understood, that somehow the man had grasped what Ral had to say and why, that he had understood that there were things the gypsies had to hear, things that had to be told.

The Maître had helped him then, had let him tell his story, let him tell what she had done, what had happened to the gypsies. And the gypsies in the galleries had listened. He had seen them, watched them listen to every word. Even though he spoke in French, instead of Romany, they had listened and understood and believed him. And they would go home and tell their children. And the children would tell their children. For as long as those families lived, they would sit around the fire or the stove and tell what they had heard, tell what happened to the gypsies. They would tell other gypsies too, and the gypsies would remember the past that they had forgotten. They would be a people again; they would learn what happens to a gypsy who trusts the *gaji*.

But then he remembered how the Maître had turned on him. The tattoo, the rest. Why? What did it matter to the Maître? To any of them? And the girl with her story. The man Borel. Why? Ral had waited twenty years, given twenty years, just to tell what had to be told. Why would the Maître bring the girl and that man to destroy everything?

He heard the metal door jingle.

"You awake?" came the voice of the guard.

"Yes, I'm awake." A visitor? he thought. Perhaps Jill. What would he say to her?

"Open the slot. It's your dinner."

"I don't want any dinner."

"If I were you, gypsy man, I'd eat it. From what I hear, you aren't getting too many more."

"I don't want your filthy *gajo* food."

"Suit yourself."

He heard the cart roll down the aisle to the next cell.

There wouldn't be any visitors. Jill would be with the Maître. And who else would visit him? The gypsies? He was alone, as he had always been, as he had to be.

After three days of scarlet and gilt and robes and rituals, Jill thought herself immune to the impact of the courtroom and its ceremonies. She had been in the Palais de Justice long enough that the calculated architecture of the room, the deliberate separation of tribunal, *prétoire*, and gallery that mirrored the ranking of judges, *avocats*, and *la foule*—the crowd—seemed expected rather than exotic. Sheer repetition had rubbed the horror off the ceremony of the chains, to which Ral was submitted each day. The rituals had so numbed everyone, including the actors on the stage, that the elegant poses of mannered defiance had given way to slouches of indifference, even occasional boredom.

Yet when the president stood up from his throne on the tribunal, Jill couldn't fight down a chill of awe, a sense of witnessing once again the sheer magic of a trial. The president was taller than she remembered from the day before, his features leaner and more angular. He seemed almost stark, like a character playing Death in a film.

Jean-Claude was engrossed in thought, and she noticed that none of the other *avocats* had spoken to him. Was it superstition? she wondered. His solitude made her think of an actor, alone with his thoughts before he mounts the stage.

Jean-Claude finally looked at her and smiled.

She said, in English, "Break a leg."

He looked puzzled. "I don't understand, Jill."

She laughed, remembering when he had talked about the spider on her ceiling. "It's an expression actors say to one another before they go out on the stage. It means 'good luck.' "

His grin made her remember how very charming he was.

Ral's entrance was different that day. He wore the same suit, and the chains jangled as they always had, but after a quick glance toward the gallery, Ral searched out Jean-Claude and stared at him, not taking his eyes away until he had been led to his box and his chains were removed. Then Ral glanced at Jill, and she realized that both men were looking at her. It made her intensely uncomfortable.

"Is Monsieur l'Avocat Général prepared to plead?" asked the president.

"This trial has been delayed long enough by theatrics and stratagems," said the *avocat général*. His voice was dry, pretending boredom. "We are prepared to plead."

"Is Monsieur l'Avocat *pour la défense* prepared to plead?"

"We are," said Jean-Claude.

"Then—" The president addressed the courtroom as if he were ordering the executioner to drop the trap on the gibbet. *"La parole est à Monsieur l'Avocat Général!"*

The *avocat général* lifted his shoulders, redraping his robes. The gesture made Jill think of the Daumier prints, and the satires in Flaubert's *Boulevard et Pécuchet*. She waited for the man to blow through his lips.

"Why are you here?" he asked the court. His voice was a dull octave lower than it had been before, with a hollow, artificial projection. His arm swept toward the tribunal in a grand gesture. Every word that followed was so mannered, dripping in so much rhetoric, that Jill found it hard to concentrate.

"Should it be necessary to pose such a question? From the testimony— the tales of maltreatment and perfidy, the horrors which occurred twenty-five years ago—the accused would have you believe that you are here to judge the crimes of war that he has chronicled . . ."

He summarized his case, dwelling heavily on the testimony of the Frankfurt inquiry to portray Wanda Lanzer as a gentle old woman, almost saintly, the victim of a brutal, premeditated murder. The summation was flat, an emotionless recitation of evidence, and his gestures seemed stilted, slightly off in timing. He would turn suddenly to point an accusing finger at Ral, but the accusation of the finger would be out of synch with what he was saying, an instant too early or too late.

"What do you know of the accused?" the *avocat général* asked suddenly. "He has told you that he is a gypsy. He is proud of his race! Fine, we say. We accept the differences of the gypsies. We accept the differences of all peoples. We are Frenchmen, sons and daughters of the Great Revolution, of the Declaration of the Rights of Man. Hundreds of years of culture and civilization have taught us that the laws of ordered society can serve people of all colors and persuasions and races, whether in the cities of France or the jungles of Africa or the deserts of Asia. Are we suddenly now to discover that the laws which have sufficed in Algeria, in Indochina, in Guiana, cannot function in our own *département*? Are we to accept that these laws which have served us so well are not sufficient for these people, the gypsies?"

Jill kept listening for the kernel of his argument, for the point he was try-ing to make. The longer she listened, the more it seemed that he didn't have a point. He was reciting a perfunctory statement, filling in the blanks in a canned plea.

He tried to preempt any reference to the vendetta, and to anticipate the arguments Jean-Claude might make: "Ours is a society which cannot toler-ate blood revenge, which maintains, as it must, that revenge is an act which threatens the very existence of civilized society. The vendetta is sim-ply inimical to the preservation of the rule of law as we know it.

"What, then, are we left with? You have the facts uncovered in the ex-haustive police investigation: facts that show the man tracked and pursued this woman Wanda Lanzer across Europe, tracked her to her quiet retire-ment in a modest boardinghouse in Amsterdam. From the concierge he found that she was in Saintes-Maries-de-la-Mer for her holiday. He fol-lowed her there, asked questions about her, showed her picture to whoever would look at it. Even to a passerby, an attractive woman he happened to meet, he could not help telling of his search. How overwhelming, how fa-natical, his drive to find this woman must have been if he would reveal it even to a passerby.

"And finally, on that lonely road, in the fading light of early evening, he found Wanda Lanzer. And on that very evening, the evening when she was strangled by the strong fingers of a man, the police discovered the ac-cused, standing over the body. Just standing, like a hunter proud of the trophy he has shot. The evidence is circumstantial, the *avocat* for the de-fense will argue. But from that moment right up to this very instant, the accused has never denied his guilt. Not once has he said that he did not commit that brutal, merciless murder of a helpless old woman.

"And although the accused has never denied his culpability, the dis-tinguished *avocat* for the defense and his American assistant present a defense. In the very nick of time, like the cavalry soldiers who gallop up to relieve the besieged fort in American Westerns, he brings you a wit-ness to say that the accused was not the one to attack and kill Wanda Lanzer. A gypsy girl, eleven years old if we are to believe her testimony, fifteen years old if we believe her school-leaving certificate and the lies she readily told to get it. Did she appear during the police investigation, when public notices were posted requesting information, when the in-vestigators left no road untrod and no door unopened in their inquiries? *No!* Perhaps it is because she and her people cannot read. They pay no attention to notices, or for that matter, to laws. Our society, it appears, is not theirs.

"There are so many things about the gypsies and their strange world that we must learn in this courtroom. The frailty of truth, it appears, is one such thing. But truth, as we know it, is an absolute, like the law itself. It is one of those foundations that we require for a civilized society. Just as we require that all men be subject to the full judgment of that law."

Jill watched Ral, marveling at his total detachment from the man in scarlet who was begging the court to condemn him. Ral watched as though the trial were a curiosity, an intriguing drama at which he was only a spectator. And Jill, who had felt so awkward as a spectator, felt now that it was her own life that was being decided. She hardly listened to the words of the *avocat général*, yet dreaded when they would end, afraid of what Jean-Claude might say, of what his plea could do to Ral.

". . . After exhaustive inquiry, the psychiatrists have concluded that there is no diminished responsibility, no mental disease, no legal insanity. This is not a madman! This is a man of will and determination, a man capable of tracking a woman for more than twenty years, of uncovering the solace and anonymity of her life as a pensioner, of stalking and murdering her in cold blood. That is the crime you are here to judge—nothing more, and nothing less.

"What will be just? you must ask. The guillotine? An eye for an eye? This is what the accused sought. His loved ones were taken from him, and he struck back, not at those who hurt him, those who brought pain and death to his loved ones—but at a woman whose only crime was to befriend him, to try to assuage the lot of the gypsies in those camps, a woman who took this man, fortunate among his people in being able to read and write, and allowed him to help his own people.

"And what did he do by way of gratitude? He struck out in cold revenge, exacting his own penalty for the crimes allegedly done to him. An eye for an eye! For the republic to do the same, to call for his life as he demanded hers, would be to perpetuate that chain of revenge. That we shall not do. We call instead for *travail à force perpétuel*—strenuous, diligent labor for life! We do so for the sake of the accused, in the hope that in the experience of hard labor that can only partially atone for his crime, he can at least find the realization of what it is to be a productive member of society. You can do nothing more just or more kind for this man."

The *avocat général* stood after he had finished, posed as though he expected spontaneous applause from the courtroom. But there was no applause, only silence, punctuated by a single shout of "Death to the gypsy!" from the gallery behind Jill.

The courtroom was disappointed. After the revelations of the last days, they expected drama, or at least elegance and style and refinement in the plea. Instead the *avocat général* had dismissed everything that went before as irrelevant. He had given a boilerplate plea, staying away from controversial arguments and questions. It was all he needed, he seemed to be saying.

Why have a trial at all? thought Jill.

She anticipated a break after the plea and waited for the guards to appear with Ral's chains. But the president turned directly to Jean-Claude.

"Is the *avocat* for the defense prepared to plead?"

"We are." The president leaned forward, and Jill saw that the lay judges at his sides copied the gesture. All over the courtroom, eyes turned to Jean-Claude with the same questions: Why had the Maître taken this impossible brief? What could he possibly argue in view of the fragmentary evidence and absolute intractability of his client? She saw the journalists stir from their half-naps, the *avocats* jockey for position, the crowd jostle one another for a spot near the grille. This was the moment of the drama they had come to see. Amidst the excitement of anticipation, Ral stood alone, unnoticed, as the president intoned his words:

"La parole est à Monsieur l'Avocat pour la Défense!"

Jean-Claude took the floor without a formal gesture, his manner more relaxed than in the earlier days of the trial. The robes seemed part of him, and his casual stride across the *prétoire* made the stage appear to shrink.

"What a strange tragedy we see played out on our stage!" he said. His tone was conversational, surprisingly informal. "We're accustomed to the stage of Aeschylus, a stage with only two characters, and our trial presents us with three—a drama with all the subtlety and conflict of Sophocles. At times we strain our beliefs and expectations sorting out who is arguing which position. The *avocat* for the defense appears to elicit testimony supporting the public minister's case. The accused seems to argue for his own condemnation. The press and the crowd watch in amazement, looking to us to sort out this tragedy, forgetting that we seek not drama, but the Truth. No one can envy us. This is no easy task."

A few short sentences, and everything had changed in the courtroom. The *avocat général* had spoken *at* the tribunal. "You must decide," he told them. "You must uphold! You must condemn!" But for Jean-Claude it was all first person plural: ". . . *our* stage . . . no one can envy *us* . . ." He presented himself as a loyal officer of the court, serving no goal but the truth. And while it was all a rhetorical ploy, it worked. The court was rapt in its attention and anticipation. Even Ral had dropped his guard, watching Jean-Claude with genuine interest, as though he were about to tell an intriguing story about a man Ral hardly knew.

"The public minister's case seems simple," Jean-Claude went on. "The accused had a motive, which he willingly, clearly, forcefully articulated. He admits that he searched Europe looking for the woman he knew as Eva Ritter, that he tracked her all the way to her quiet retirement in Amsterdam, and from there to the gypsy festival in Saintes-Maries. He told everyone—strangers, café keepers, even a passerby—that he was looking for the woman. He carried her photograph, showed it to anyone who would look. And then he was found by the police standing over the body, staring at her as though he were helpless, like a man paralyzed by the reality of what he has done."

Jean-Claude shrugged. "What more do we need? He had a motive; we know he searched for her; he was found standing over the body. QED. He must have murdered her. What could be simpler? What explanation could be more elegant in its economy, could offer more clarity amidst the tangled testimony we've heard?"

Jean-Claude paused, letting his own summary of the *avocat général's* case sink in. It had been more concise, and more convincing, than anything the public minister had said. Jill saw Ral smile.

"How simple and elegant it would be if only the accused would confess to the crime! How tidy matters would be! But he refuses. And in our efforts to understand his refusal, we find other evidence, other testimony, which leaves matters far less tidy than we would wish. It appears that the truth is not so simple after all.

"We have a witness whose testimony in this courtroom seems to mar, perhaps to destroy, the elegant simplicity of the public minister's case. We must decide what to do with her testimony, whether to believe her and ruin our simple solution, or to reject her testimony. That too is not an easy choice.

"The witness is only eleven years old, a gypsy girl. She looks, dresses, speaks, lives a life different from the world we know. We cannot deny those differences. The public minister assures us that as Frenchmen we have no prejudices, that our laws and our faith in the basic rights of man will deny understanding and compassion to no one, even to a gypsy."

Jean-Claude spun around, animated now, hurling his words. "Would that it were so! In fact, a wall of superstition and fear and misunderstanding separates us from these people, the gypsies. *Gypsy!* What images the word conjures! How many of us have crossed the street to avoid a gypsy beggar? How many times have we told our children that if they were bad, the gypsies would get them? How often have we used the word *gyp* to refer to a swindle or scam? How often have we assumed, believed, that these people are filthy, that they *do* steal children and anything else they can appropriate? Even our laws reflect those beliefs. Think of the sign '*Nomades Interdits'!* Or the *carnet anthropologique* which gypsies, and gypsies alone, must carry in France, a book which requires a fingerprint and a chest measurement as marks of identification. These are not harmless laws and idle thoughts. These are the bedrocks of a prejudice that colors our perceptions and tempers our judgments."

Jean-Claude didn't look for his audience. He didn't have to. He had them, even Ral. And while Jill could separate the rhetoric from the substance, she felt herself swept along by the flow of words.

"The gypsies are different. They have chosen to be different, to ignore, even defy, the most basic values of a Frenchman. The gypsy has no fixed family, no church, no regular address, no job. He stands outside that network of café and church and market and work that defines a Frenchman. The gypsy's a misfit, a man who doesn't subscribe to our belief in the importance of labor, or our faith in the law, or our trust of the state and its instruments. Look at the girl who testified: Did she believe in the laws, the schools, the sanctity of the bureaucracy?

"No! The gypsies are different, different enough that we have set them aside in our society. The Germans called them asocials, and on the basis of that classification they built a network of laws and camps, badges, classifications, tattooes, and ultimately mass extermination for the gypsies. That is where stereotyping and prejudice can ultimately lead. But as the public minister has reminded us, this is not Nazi Germany. It is the French Republic.

"What are we to make of our witness, the young gypsy girl? Can we believe her? The public minister has already caught her in a lie. When she wanted to leave school to work, she lied about her age. To us this is a serious matter: supplying false information under oath on an official form is perjury. But we must remember that the gypsies live without the formalities of birth certificates and passports and identity cards. They make no point of remembering exact ages. A number on a piece of paper is meaningless in such a world. What is not meaningless is the requirement that this girl stay in school when she wanted, perhaps needed, to work. So she lied, with a cause. Can we really argue that some purpose would have been served for her to have followed the letter of the law?

"She lied with a reason before. So we ask, why would the girl lie now? To protect this man who stands accused? Is it because he's one of their own? Because they're a clannish people who will do anything to protect their own? If that were the case, why would they have sent a little girl to testify? Why not send a respected elder of the clan, perhaps one of the gypsies already known to the police as a reliable informer. Such a witness would be much less likely to challenge our credulity. It would have been simple to arrange, but no other gypsy has come forward to identify him. No other gypsy admits to having seen him. For a people so accustomed to dissembly, it would have been easy to have invented a story, to have produced multiple witnesses. The public minister has assured us that gypsies will lie whenever it suits their purposes. But they didn't set out to protect him, and for good reason."

Jill saw Jean-Claude turn toward Ral. The glance lasted only an instant before Jean-Claude turned back to the tribunal, but it was long enough to bring back a sense of foreboding that Jill dreaded. Ral's hands were tight on the railing of his box.

"The accused is of the Lovari clan of gypsies, horse traders from Hungary. The girl and her family are Manush, native French gypsies. There is no love between the two clans. Look up in the gallery, how the gypsies stand in clans, as distrustful of one another as they are of the non-gypsies around them. It is our imagination that suggests that any gypsy will automatically come to the rescue of another.

"Why didn't the girl come forward earlier? we ask. Why did she wait until the last moment? Is it not a citizen's duty to come forward? The answer is the other side of that prejudice we have already examined: Where there is hatred, there is fear! She saw something between *gaji*, non-gypsies. At the time it seemed none of her business. Like most gypsies, she's afraid of the police. And why wouldn't she be. What would the reaction of the police be, other than to round up the usual suspects, who would all turn out to be gypsies? That girl, perhaps all of the gypsies, is as afraid of us as we are of them.

"And yet, questions remain . . ."

Jean-Claude paused, taking in the courtroom. His gaze caught Jill's but he didn't smile. His eyes were hooded, almost apologetic. And like the glance at Ral, the look was too quick to break the momentum of his plea.

"The accused tracked this woman Wanda Lanzer across Europe for twenty years, devoted his life to the pursuit. Why? If it was not to murder her, to exact some revenge, a vendetta of blood, why did he follow her? Why did he squander twenty years of his life walking from town to town, showing his photograph, asking questions? This single-minded, fanatic compulsion surely borders on obsession. He has given us ample reason why he would hate the woman. He blames her, indirectly, for the deaths of his bride, his mother, his sister—all the women in his life. Was he not out to exact from her the blood price for those he had loved? Was there not a compulsion, a code perhaps, that demanded revenge?

"Our expert witnesses have assured us that in strict terms, this was not a vendetta. The proper revenge for what happened would have been directed against those who actually harmed his bride and his mother and his sister. And there were guards in those camps, recognizable men, probably known among the underground of gypsy survivors of the camps. They would have been no more difficult to find than this woman, who through false names and stealth all but disappeared for over twenty years. But it seems that the accused never gave a thought to pursuing those guards, that he never sought out the men who raped and killed his bride, or the men who dragged his mother and his sister, the only family he had, to those gas chambers. Instead he devoted his life to searching for this woman, this quiet, kindly woman whose constant reappearance in camp after camp haunted him as a living nightmare.

"For twenty years he sought her. Twenty years! Yet there has been no evidence or testimony that he ever carried a weapon. No weapon was found on him when he was arrested. No weapon was used in the murder. Think of it! He tracked this woman for twenty years and he was unarmed when he finally found her. Why?"

When Jean-Claude paused, Jill could hear a woman in the gallery translating or paraphrasing his plea into Romany. The gasps of exclamation from the gypsies came a moment too late, a syncopated rhythm to the plea. When she glanced over, the gallery seemed sparse compared to earlier in the trial.

"The reason the accused carried no weapon is that he did not search out that woman to kill her. He sought her for reasons we can only understand by going back to where his own testimony began, to the story of the holocaust itself. Not the familiar holocaust we know from books and movies and monuments, but a secret holocaust, shrouded in mystery and silence because its victims were a people who do not write their history for all to read.

"From the very beginning the gypsy holocaust was different. The others in the camp were inmates, prisoners; the gypsies were internees, detainees. They were being held for their own protection, they were told. And they believed what the Germans told them, what the woman Eva Ritter told them. 'Naive!' we say. But what did gypsies know of such camps? What experience did they have? And they were treated differently. Others in the camp worked; they did not. Others wore prison uniforms; they did not. Others had their heads shaved; they did not. Others were separated from their families; they were not. And because they were treated differently, they were convinced that their fate would not be the fate of the others, that they would not become those wisps of red smoke that blew back upon the camp with the indescribable smell of death.

"But the accused was even more different. From non-gypsies he had learned to read and write. That skill made him unique among the gypsies. And because of that talent, that special status, he was selected to work for the woman Eva Ritter. He became her assistant, helping her to interview other gypsies, helping her compile the information gleaned from those interviews into a vast classification system. It was he who translated the Romany of the other gypsies, the secret language that is so important to the identity of the gypsies, giving her access to the world that would otherwise remain closed to her.

"How would other gypsies react to this man? What would they think of a man who chose to work with the *gajo*? Would he continue to be part of, to be welcome in, their clannish world, a world that holds the total distrust of the *gajo* as one of its most basic tenets? Would this man who traveled so easily in the world of the *gajo* be able to go back to the gypsies?

"Look at the accused! He's an attractive man, with dark eyes, wavy black hair, a mysterious, undefinable quality to his gaze. To us, he's a gypsy. The cheekbones and eyes and coloring call up those reserves of stereotyping that we have all learned from earliest childhood. But what is this man to the gypsies. Does he belong to a clan? A tribe? When the war ended, did he seek out his own people, his own clan of Lovari from Hungary? Did he find another clan that would welcome him, take him in? Was he welcome among the gypsies of Germany or Austria or France or anywhere else that he wandered? When he came to the village of Saintes-Maries, the mecca of gypsy life, was he welcome?

"The answer is *no!* This man is not like other gypsies. They wander the roads in search of a special kind of freedom, a life without the burdens of responsibility that bind the rest of us. They have a society of their own, their private rites and rituals, shrouded in secrecy and myth, a world apart. But this man, the accused, doesn't belong to that world. He wandered not for freedom, but for an obsession, to find the woman Eva Ritter. Why? Why did he give up the prime of his life to pursue her? What did he want from her? What could she give him? Revenge? Money? Fame? Glory? Why did he need to find her?"

When Jean-Claude eased up on the relentless questions for an instant, Jill glanced at Ral. He looked like a madman. His jaw was clamped; the whites of his eyes glowed; his body trembled so that it seemed that only the strong grip of his fingers on the rails of the box kept him anchored there. It took Jill a moment to parse the overwhelming emotion, to realize that she had never in her life seen more anger in the face of a human being. She couldn't bear to look at him.

"Eva Ritter couldn't give money or glory or fame to the accused. And revenge on her would satisfy neither the strict law of the vendetta nor his own hurt. We have heard from the accused himself that Eva Ritter was powerless to intervene in what happened, that the Germans had relegated her to being little more than a scientist-clerk, carrying on her classifications while she did her best to ameliorate the lot of the gypsies. There was really only one thing that Eva Ritter could give to the accused, and that was what she had once taken from him: his identity as a gypsy. She had once pronounced him the purest of the gypsies, pure enough to be saved when others were condemned to the gas chambers and furnaces. She did it because he helped her, worked for her. Work! The word is important. The other gypsies in the camp didn't have to work. The aphorism etched into the gates of the camp, *Arbeit Macht Frei*, 'Work Leads to Freedom,' was meaningless to the gypsies. Yet for the accused it was true. And the price of that freedom was great: he lost his people and his identity. He had strayed into the halfway ground, between *gajo* and gypsy, accepted by neither, everywhere a stranger and a foreigner, an outsider, condemned by his past to be a man without a people. And so he became a wandering gypsy man, no longer a gypsy.

"We know now why the accused carried no weapon, why he had no gun or knife. He had no plan of what he would do if or when he found Eva Ritter. All he knew was that he had to confront her, the expert on gypsies, the woman who had the power to decide who was a gypsy and who was not. She had made of him a prisoner, and only she could set him free. And so he pursued her, for twenty years, walking the lonely roads of Europe. And by the time he caught up with her, by the time his long search was over, it was too late. She was already dead, herself a victim of the ubiquitous hatred and fear of gypsies. And there the police found him, staring at the body, paralyzed by the realization that his search had been for nothing. Twenty years, half his life, for nothing!"

The courtroom began to stir with buzzes from the *avocats* and exclamations from the gallery. Jean-Claude cut them off. The pace was still his.

"And yet one question remains. If the accused did not kill Eva Ritter, why does he seem to insist on his own guilt? The paltry circumstantial evidence against him would collapse in an instant if only he would deny the crime. The court has given him ample opportunity to offer an alibi. He has had months to offer a simple denial. Yet he answers every query about the crime with the same adamant silence. Why? If he did not murder her, as I have argued, why will he not deny the murder?"

Jean-Claude paused long enough to glance at Ral, then at Jill. He looked burdened by what he was about to say.

"The answer to those questions," he went on, "is in this courtroom." He pointed to the gallery, waiting for his last sentence to be translated into Romany. "The accused is being judged not only by monsieurs and mesdames on the tribunal, but by another court. And to that court in the gallery, that court of gypsies from whom he has been estranged these many years, he cannot deny the crime, because to deny that he sought simple revenge for the shaming of his bride and the deaths of his mother and sister would deny that he was a gypsy, that he had the primitive impulses and obsessions of the vendetta that a gypsy ought to hold against those who have hurt him as this man was hurt. To prove he is a gypsy, he must accept guilt for a crime he did not commit, for with Eva Ritter dead, only the gypsies themselves can offer him the identity he has sought for so long.

"It's a sad and wrenching story, the tale of this man and his search. Were he other than a gypsy, he might have written his story. It might have been received with acclaim. The Prix Goncourt, perhaps. Fame throughout France, the world. But the gypsies would never have heard or read his words. To reach them, the people who were once his people, he has resorted to the strange gesture, incomprehensible to us, of accepting blame for a crime he did not commit. Call what he has done what you will—madness, obsession, compulsion, fanaticism—it is not a crime against the *Code Pénal Française*. This man is not a killer. He is a lost soul, condemned to wander in search of a people he long ago lost. He deserves not our condemnation, but our pity." Jean-Claude stared for a moment at each member of the tribunal, a crystalline smile just under the surface of his somber expression. He knew, without a signal from any of them, how they would react to his plea.

Jill expected the room to burst into applause, but there was only a prolonged silence. She watched the eyes of the *avocats* and the judges turn to Ral, as if they expected something of him. He answered with a stone-cold stare. It was as though the rage of only a few minutes before had calcified, the lava turning to rock.

Up in the gallery, even the gypsies were quiet, watching Ral and the court with a strange detachment, as though the events on the other side of the grillework no longer concerned them.

Finally, when the silence of the courtroom was oppressive, like humid still air, the president spoke out.

"The accused shows yet another instance of poor judgment," he said. "It is traditional to say '*Merci, Maître*' when your *avocat* has been so forceful and articulate on your behalf." Ral glanced at the president as though his words had been completely incomprehensible, then turned back to Jean-Claude. His glare was unyielding, filled with anger and hatred.

"We will have a brief recess before hearing the final statement, if any, of the accused," said the president. He made no effort to conceal the anger in his voice.

Jean-Claude took a long time to work his way through the *prétoire*, shaking hands and nodding in acknowledgment of the accolades from all sides.

"I'm sorry," said Jill when they were close enough to talk.

"Sorry?"

"Ral should have said something. I'm not sure he understands what you've done for him."

"I don't expect gratitude," said Jean-Claude. "What I did was blunt and cruel. Every man is entitled to some degree of privacy, and I stripped his away. No man with a measure of pride and self-respect would thank another man for doing that."

Jill reached for his arm. "What you did out there was amazing. It was like a surgeon giving life back to a man."

Jean-Claude shook his head. "In the end it's still Ral's future. The choice is his."

Jill found herself staring at Jean-Claude, not sure what she wanted to say. He had done so much more than she expected, more than she thought anyone could do. She had always been impressed by talent, but it wasn't Jean-Claude's virtuoso skills on the *prétoire* that had moved her; it was his total grasp of Ral's life, his ability to piece together the scraps of information and *understand* the man. To understand another man as Jean-Claude understood Ral, a man had to know himself, had to be comfortable with his own identity.

Jill's face clouded. "Do you think he's going to throw it all away? You've given it all to him, Jean-Claude. He had the chance to be heard in the courtroom, and now he's got a chance at a real life. He can't be too stubborn to see that."

"He's still a gypsy, Jill."

Both of them looked up at the sound of chains. The guards flanked Ral at the doorway, and Jill saw Ral's head crane, looking toward the galleries. Then he turned and saw her and Jean-Claude. His eyes were dark, his face expressionless, his body tense. Jill couldn't decide whether he was a lion, ready to roar his dominion over the court, or a bull, waiting for the sword.

· · ·

"We have heard the pleas of the public minister and the *avocat* for the defense," said the president. He was standing, but his tone had shifted from the grandiose to the paternal quaver he had used when he first questioned Ral. "Does the accused wish to make a final statement?"

Ral's eyes slowly scanned the room, pausing first on the gallery, then passing over the *avocats* to glare at Jean-Claude and Jill. She couldn't tell whether he was smiling. Her palms turned sweaty as her fingernails dug into the flesh.

"I will speak!" said Ral. He rubbed his wrists, reminding everyone that it was he who wore the chains each day. When he spoke, it was to the president.

"You said before that I am supposed to thank the Maître for his great speech. I'm only an ignorant gypsy, and I'm supposed to thank him because his speech explained everything. He made of my life a neat package, like one carries home from a store. After his words everything is understood. There are no more questions. It's as a *gajo* would want it, yes or no, this or that."

He paused, pacing the silence, gathering eyes, waiting until the silence in the courtroom was excruciating. Then he suddenly spun, pointing to the gallery.

"Look! Until now, that gallery was filled with gypsies, gypsies from all over Europe. Why? Because they wanted to hear the truth about the crimes against their people. They wanted to know how their brothers and sisters and fathers and mothers and cousins and aunts and uncles were betrayed. They listened, and they told others to come. They understood what I told them. They believed. They learned the history of our people that isn't written in *gajo* books or taught in *gajo* schools. Now they're gone."

Jill counted heads in the gallery. There were only a few dozen gypsies left, not the hundreds who had been there before the recess.

"Why have they gone? I'll tell you. The gypsies in the gallery listened to the Maître, and he told them that I was only a man of words. For the gypsy, there have already been too many words.

"You talk here of the laws and the *Code Pénal*, the crimes that must be judged, the punishments that must be given. But *gajo* laws are not the only laws. There are laws that don't need to be written, laws that men know in their hearts. Do you need to write down a law of honor? Do you need to write down a punishment for betrayal? Does it take so many books and professors to tell what is right for a person who betrays a whole people? A gypsy is not so ignorant that he doesn't know with his heart what is right for such a person.'

He turned slowly, once more, his gaze steady. The anger and hatred were gone from his eyes. There was no emotion at all in his gaze.

"No," he said, in a quiet voice. "The Maître is wrong. He spoke with his fine words of the prejudice against the gypsies, but it is he who has this prejudice, for he does not understand that a gypsy does not think as he does. Any gypsy would know by the laws of men—not the laws in your books and codes, but the laws that men must truly live by—that I had to find that woman Eva Ritter and see in her eyes the hurt that I once saw in the eyes of those women and children and old men. I did not give twenty years of my life searching for that woman for words. I did what I had to do. Nothing else would have been justice."

He turned to the tribunal. The president's eyebrows went up, as if he expected more. But there was no more. Ral was finished.

Murmured questions from every corner of the courtroom broke the silence like raindrops on a still pond. Question followed question until the surface of the pond was roiled and broken. Whether in the elegant jargon of the *avocats* or the argot of the crowd or the verbal shorthand of the reporters or the incomprehensible buzz of the gypsies, they were the same questions.

"What did he mean?"

"Gypsy fool!"

". . . either a martyr or an idiot . . ."

"Why would he say that? He was off free!"

Jill heard the questions, but she never took her eyes off Ral. She could hear herself breathing, found herself listening for a sob or a quaver, an emotion beyond control. There was none. She felt only loss and sadness.

Suddenly, as suddenly as it had been made, the connection had broken. The current that had once flowed between them had stopped. All that was left was the sparking of the broken wire. She wanted to say something, but there was nothing to say, nothing to tell him. He knew. She couldn't even cry.

The colors of the room seemed very strong—the red of the robes on the tribunal, the gilt of the moldings, the white of the police uniforms, the black of Ral's suit. The buzz of questions she heard from every side was unbearable.

When she ran from the room, Jean-Claude followed her.

They stood close to each other on the steps of the Palais de Justice, watching the crowd from within merge with the waiting crowd outside. The judges had stayed out only the fifteen minutes required by custom and courtesy before returning with their decision and sentence. Ral's had been the final surprise.

Avocats, some still in their robes, came over to Jean-Claude with words of praise and regret. Then the *avocat général*, a plain-looking man without his robes, came over, offering his hand to Jean-Claude. He deliberately ignored Jill.

"What else could you expect?" he said. "The fool wanted his own rules. They all do these days. What good did it do him? He'll still spend the rest of his days at hard labor."

Jean-Claude shrugged.

"It could have been the guillotine," the *avocat général* went on. "The man flouted the law, wasted our time, wasted the court's time. If he'd confessed at the start, without all the speechmaking and storytelling, he might have ended up with less than *travail perpétuel*. But the fool wanted his day in court. What a waste!"

"Waste?" Jill said angrily. She pointed to the crowds in the streets— hundreds of animated gypsies, milling in expectation as they stood vigil. "Was it a waste for them?"

A police car appeared, turning the corner from the side of the building. Groups of gypsies broke away and ran after the car, shouting and waving their arms. Within minutes the streets were blocked as the crowd surrounded the car. People jostled and shoved one another, reaching out to touch the car. Small children were held up on shoulders so they could get a glimpse through the rear window.

"Ral?" said Jill.

"He's a hero now," said Jean-Claude.

She started to answer, then felt a quiver deep inside, a final spark. She held Jean-Claude's arm close to her and looked away, letting the emotion subside.

As they watched, gendarmes appeared in two more cars. It took them half an hour to disperse the crowd enough for the car with Ral to drive away. Then, all around the steps of the Palais de Justice, the gypsies began piling into their cars and trucks and vans and old schoolbuses. Eight, ten, even more would climb into each car. Slowly, the cars set off down the streets, swaying on their overloaded springs like caravans on a rocky road.

Epilogue

Los Angeles, 1968

Sidney Millman had frowned when Jill said she was taking a couple of days off.

"You aren't going job hunting, are you?" he had asked over lunch. "What would we ever do without Wonder Woman?"

She had laughed. "No, I'll be back. There's just something I have to do."

"Another guy?"

She shook her head, grinning.

"Whew! I really thought we were going to lose you over that last one. I never saw anything get to you like that before. Then that last week in France and you were all of a sudden a changed woman. What the hell happened to you over there anyway? You haven't been the same since you got back."

"Good or bad?" she said.

"Are you kidding? It's like you found religion or something. That Bernard must be one amazing man."

"He is," said Jill.

"Are you . . . ?" Millman stopped when he saw Jill's smile.

"It's not what you think," she said. "Let's just say I saw some real lawyering, and learned a little bit about what home is."

"Lawyering? I thought you and he—"

Her smile turned to a laugh. She was feeling good about herself and the world. Millman shrugged, then laughed himself.

"I guess I'll never understand," he said.

She had the cab at LA International take her directly to Hillside Cemetery. Instinctively, she started to tell the taxi driver to wait for her, as if she had a dozen meetings on her calendar; then she caught herself, paid him, and left her bag with the caretaker while she wandered over the grassy slopes. Most of the stones were alike, flat slabs set into the earth, not in rows, but in a pattern that had been calculated to give each stone a measure of privacy. She wandered for half an hour, reading names and dates off the stones, trying to imagine the lives that went with the names. Finally she asked the caretaker, who looked up the name in a directory and sent her up a slope on the other side of the mausoleum, toward a row of trees that looked out of place against the brown hills.

She had never seen the stone before. There was supposed to be a ceremony a year after the funeral, but she was long gone to New York by then, and she suspected that it had never happened. She could imagine her mother ordering the stone on the phone, the salesman expecting a vulnerable survivor, caught by surprise when the answer to his pitch was something like "Where they're going it doesn't really matter, does it?"

The slab was pale granite, with an inset bronze plaque. Both names, her grandmother's and her grandfather's, were written on the same plaque. Names and dates, nothing else. She pictured their faces, and dozens of gestures and mannerisms—her grandmother echoing every word with a dance of her fingers, her grandfather mixing Yiddish and English when he tried to tell a story. When she tried to remember the stories, there was only a blank. All she could think of were the times when she had been embarrassed by the Yiddish, by the faraway tales.

She was sorry that she hadn't brought flowers with her, until she saw a vase of plastic flowers on another stone. The phony plastic seemed cruel, worse than the barrenness of an empty gravestone. The granite and bronze were emotionless, but at least there was a grave, a connection with the past, a place for memories and regrets. She remembered Ral in the courtroom, describing the last memory of his family—a wisp of smoke, a red glow in the evening sky. She had felt so alone listening to him, imagining what it was like to lose everyone, to lose who you were.

The gravestone next to her grandparents' was smaller, the engraved letters hardly large enough to read. It had been brushed clean, and along the edge there was a row of tiny pebbles. She suddenly remembered a story Ral had told her, about wandering to Prague with his friend Yitzak, going to the old Jewish cemetery together to leave a message for the Golem and a pebble on the grave. She couldn't remember why they had left a pebble, wasn't sure Ral had even explained it. But a pebble, a stone, seemed so right. Foundations were built of stone. . . .

It took her a long time on her knees in the grass to find a pebble, and when she put the stone on the plain granite, it looked strange, all alone. She tried moving it around, and thought of getting another, as if she could build a whole pile of pebbles in an instant. No, she decided, just one. For a long while she sat in the grass next to the stone, feeling the sun on her face and the breeze on her arms as she brushed away the newly mown grass clippings.

ABOUT THE AUTHOR

Ronald Florence has authored novels and narrative histories. He holds a Ph.D. in European history from Harvard University; has taught at Harvard, Sarah Lawrence College, and the State University of New York; and was the first director of the New York Council for the Humanities. He now lives with his wife and son on the Connecticut shore, where he sails and bakes bread when he is not writing.